I HAVE CALLED
YOU BY NAME

I HAVE CALLED YOU BY NAME

Tell of My Kingdom's Glory
Book Two

Sonya Contreras

Bull Head Press

Scripture taken from the NEW AMERICAN STANDARD BIBLE®, Copyright ©1960, 1962, 1963, 1968, 1971, 1972, 1973, 1975, 1977, 1995 by the Lockman Foundation. Used by permission.

I Have Called You by Name is a work of fiction. Although retelling the Scriptures' events as closely as possible, the real people, events, establishments, and locales are used fictitiously. All other elements of the novel are drawn from the author's imagination.

Published by Bull Head Press
Squaw Valley, California
Paperback ISBN: 978-0-9907237-2-1
eBook ISBN: 978-0-9907237-3-8

Library of Congress Control Number: 20016934326

Cover Design by Kirk DouPonce of DogEared Design
Content edited by Rachel Contreras
Copy edited by Titania Porter
Formatting by Joseph Contreras, Jr.
Typeface: Felix Titling, Bell MT, and Constantia

Printed in the United States of America.

UNTIL MY NAME IS KNOWN

Book One

The series *Tell of My Kingdom's Glory* began with Book One *Until My Name Is Known*, where God brings all to see Him. Pharaoh is god, worshiped by his people. Israel's God challenges Pharaoh. His power touches all. They must change. Some don't concede: They suffer. Others yield: They find freedom. *Until My Name Is Known* brings all to see the one true God.

The series continues with Book Two, *I Have Called You by Name*. The Israelites are not ready to be God's People. They wish to reach their Promised Land, but God has other plans for them. They find God seeking them. Some do not want His restrictions. He is jealous and demands their obedience. Others find safety in those boundaries. All must depend upon this God to reach their Land.

Dear Reader,

My purpose in writing I Have Called You by Name is to present the faithfulness and holiness of God. He seeks His people to be conformed to His pleasure.

They must recognize Him as supreme, holy, and the only source for their needs.

Their journey, found in Exodus, Numbers, and Deuteronomy, is hard, made harder when the lessons are not learned. The consequences seem severe, because we do not understand God's holiness.

If you are reading this book for adventure, you have come to the wrong book. This book chronicles a people who lived a mundane, dreary life of desert, sand, and sameness. But if you read this book because you want to see God in that sameness, then you have come to the right book.

Readers want strong, independent, controlling characters. That attitude keeps us from knowing God. When we see God, we realize our own weakness, nakedness, need. No one likes that shame. But that is where God brings us.

Today's readers desire entertainment with a happy ending. This portion of Scripture is not happy; thousands died on that wilderness journey. But know their God, Who is real and lives today. He still gives hope. He still seeks His people to be conformed to His pleasure.

Come with me to know the God Who has called you by name.

Sonya Contreras

To Warren Pettit, my high school science teacher,
who knew God, and awakened a thirst in me
to want to know Him, too.

They will tell of the glory of Your kingdom...
so that all men may know
of Your mighty acts.
Psalm 145:11–12

... For you have found favor in My sight and
I have known you by name.
Exodus 33:17

CHAPTER 1

Sinai Desert 2450 B.C.

M oses followed the cloud that led the people from Egypt. From the Reed Sea, they had moved into the Desert of Shur. The desert's dry wind sucked moisture from his skin, leaving it as withered as an over-dried raisin.

Moses licked his lips, tasting the salt of his dried sweat. He willed his feet painfully forward. Were they even attached to his body? He leaned on his staff. The tool that so often aided his sheep, back in his shepherd days, he now used to hold himself upright.

He looked at the people. The initial excitement of escape from Egypt and going to their own land had dissolved in the desert's heat. Now they trudged behind the cloud, like ants mindlessly following the next one in line.

They had found no water for three days.

He tightened his cloak around him, rubbing at his forehead with its sleeve. He could not sweat, but chills sent spasms through his body. After shivering, he threw his hood off in frustration at being hot again. His heat varied like the wind, only no wind brought relief.

He tried to focus on the cloud. He rubbed his arm across his face, seeing double. He blinked, but his dry eyes would not focus.

Was it a paradox that the Lord led by a cloud that held no water for His people?

Would they die in the desert before reaching the Land promised to them?

His steps faltered, jarring his thoughts from doubt. He glanced at the cloud again. The Lord was faithful. He would give His people water.

A scream sliced through his mind's fuzziness. In the back of the wagon rolling beside him, a woman had thrown off her blanket. "Give mercy!" She then fell back lifeless.

The wagon stopped.

Moses's eyes met Nathan's, who drove the wagon. Moses could read the fear in his face.

Nathan had been one of the slaves. The desert had equalized the needs of all men, leader and slave alike. Nathan shook his head. His voice cracked, "Her thirst makes her see dreams."

Moses turned his gaze next toward Ellis, sitting beside Nathan on the wagon seat. He remembered Ellis as the slave who had spit in his face after Pharaoh had refused to provide any more straw for the slaves who made his bricks. What would this hardship do to him?

Ellis was watching his wife Dinah and their son, lying lifeless in the wagon bed. He shook his head, muttering, "Where is the Lord?"

Nathan hung his head. He held his head in his hands. When he spoke, his answer was quiet, muted by his thirst, "The Lord has not changed. If He knew of our suffering under the hands of Pharaoh, He knows our suffering under the heat of the desert. I don't know what the Lord wants." He raised his head to look again at Moses. "Ask Him. I have been."

Moses nodded. No other words were needed. The Lord's people were getting to know Him.

The horse's increased gait jolted Reut from her stupor. Her head hurt from moving, but she sat up anyway, for she smelled something besides dust.

Beside her, her sister threw off the blanket that shaded them and crawled forward to the wagon seat.

Adlai, her *abba*, braced her with his arm. "Tamara, don't fall!" He pulled back the reins.

The horse strained against the bit.

Ahead Reut saw a *wadi*. Would it be another empty water channel? She struggled to stand, bracing against a pile of bedding, squinting ahead at the reflection of the sun off water. Water!

Abba stopped the wagon closer, then set the brake. Before he could stumble to the ground, Tamara scrambled from the wagon, and ran.

Reut watched her small form squeeze around people. She shook her head. Tamara always pushed her way into the midst of things. Why didn't she take a vessel to bring water for *Ima*? Reut looked back at the blanket, unmoving over her mother. Did she still breathe?

Tamara reached the water. Stumbling into it, she drank. She jerked away from the water, spitting, "Marmar. Bitter."

Others crowded behind Tamara.

Reut could no longer see her. When she next caught a glimpse, all she saw was her little sister's hair floating on the water. "Abba, she's not coming up!"

Abba ran through the wall of people toward the water. To Reut, watching, his progress was slow.

Tamara's head came to the surface for a moment. She clawed at the air.

Breathe... Reut watched unable to take a breath herself.

No one else noticed.

Why wouldn't someone help her? Everyone was at the water. No one seemed to notice.

Reut wove in and out and around the wall of people until she reached the water's edge. But where she had last seen Tamara, she saw only waves and more people. Was she too late?

"Reut. Here." Abba called.

She glanced along the waters' edge.

Someone held Tamara.

She was alive!

Reut hurried through the crowd. "Oh, Seth. You got her!"

Seth nodded, holding Tamara.

Abba stroked Tamara's hair from her face.

Tamara clung to Seth's neck. "I couldn't breathe. People kept pushing me deeper."

Seth licked his lips, then grimaced. "They push like cattle."

Reut leaned against her father's shoulder and looked at Tamara. "They didn't even notice you were drowning."

Seth gestured to the cattle on the far side of the water, tasting once, only to turn away. "Look, the animals won't drink it!"

Tamara laid her head on Seth's shoulder as they walked to their wagon. She wiped her mouth. "I'm thirstier."

Seth placed Tamara beside his aunt.

Covering Tamara with a blanket, Abba patted her arm; then turned to face Seth. "Words cannot tell my gratitude. If I lost her..." His voice broke and he swallowed.

Seth interrupted. "Glad I was there."

Reut straightened the blanket over Tamara. "She needs someone to protect her."

Abba brushed his face with his cloak's sleeve. He shook his head, lowering his voice. "How do I protect my family from the dangers of the desert when I can't even provide them water?"

They pushed against Moses like wolves surrounding for the kill. "Give us water! Do you want us dead?"

Moses braced himself with his staff to keep from falling.

One man stumbled to the front of the throng. He held up a small, limp bundle. "My baby died." His voice rasped with the thirst that plagued them all, but there was menace in his tone. "My wife couldn't feed him. What are you going to do about it?" The challenge was hurled at their leader for all to hear, and silence hung over the waiting crowd.

Moses looked at the motionless bundle in the man's arms. He could not form tears to weep.

A chant rose. "You caused our death."

Some shoved and pushed him.

Moses backed up.

Others picked up stones. "You led us here to die."

Moses licked his lips, forgetting that they bled. His tongue scraped his skin as if it was a dry mortar. Words would not settle their hearts. Only a miracle would calm this mob. He turned from the crowd and hiked up the mountain, leaning on his staff. When he had reached a summit, he looked back at the people.

Their chant could still be heard.

He knelt before the cloud. "This people will kill me if they don't have water soon. We depend upon Your mercy. Give what we need. We are Your people."

He raised his head to look at the cloud. What more did God want him to do? As he stood, he stumbled. He grabbed an acacia tree to stand.

"Take that branch."

Moses paused. Was that the Lord's voice, or his own dizziness speaking to him? He looked at the branch in his hand. He obeyed and broke the branch.

As he descended, dragging the branch, the people stopped chanting and grew quiet.

He stood before them. "The Lord has heard your plea. He has granted your request." He lifted the branch over his head and threw it into the water.

The people stepped back as it splashed into the center of the pool.

Moses rubbed his hands down his cloak to free himself of the branch's dirt. He bent to drink, gulping the sweetness, quenching his thirst. He splashed water over his face and arms, wiping his face with his sleeve. Bracing himself with his staff, he stood. He motioned to those still holding stones. "Drink."

One man knelt, brought a handful of water to his lips and licked. Then he dropped to his knees and immersed his head in the water.

Others fell before the water and drank.

Moses watched. "My God, You have satisfied Your people. We are at Your mercy."

Nathan drank, wishing to never leave the water. It filled the longing of his body. Its coolness soothed the cuts and soreness on his lips and mouth. His knotted insides relaxed. Water washed away the tingling of his legs where he had lost sensation. He submerged his head and arms, letting the water drip down his back and wet his tunic. The heat of the past three days fell from his body as the coolness of the water covered him. His flesh expanded, absorbing the moisture like a hungry man taking in food.

Wiping his mouth with the back of his hand, he looked around him. He could see better. His head no longer felt detached. He was whole again.

He watched the people splash, sing and dance in the water. They praised the gods that brought them there. Some bowed, giving homage to the water.

He submerged his head once more before filling his jars. He was torn, wanting to linger at the water, but remembering Salome and his own children lying back at the wagon. He stood, watching the people crowding into the water. He filled the jars and raised them to his shoulders.

Ellis joined Nathan. "The water so easily becomes a god." He looked at the people. "How quickly they forget the Nile, where the Lord showed that He was God over the water."

Nathan thought of Salome, shouting out her dreams because she had no water. He paused to grip a jar better. "We worship what we see. We must seek the God Who cannot be seen. I could not praise God when He withheld the water and Salome dreamed.

Now it is easy to praise."

Ellis lifted his own jars to his shoulders. "Why did He wait?"

Nathan pushed his way against the crowds. "Don't we depend upon Him more when we have nothing else?"

Hannah shifted the water vessel on her shoulder as she moved through the crowd.

Amos, her brother, could not have kept his balance on his wooden leg with this jostling crowd, so it was good he stayed behind. Didn't she struggle with two good legs? She stumbled, falling to her knees. She grabbed for the jar. It rolled out of her reach.

Someone stepped on her hand.

No one allowed her to stand.

Another tripped over her.

Someone stepped on her foot.

"Make room." A man forced people from her. "Give me your hand."

She looked up and saw Phinehas. In Egypt, she had helped him treat those afflicted by the plagues.

He grabbed her hand and lifted her to her feet.

Placing weight on her foot, she winced, stumbled, and fell into his arms. She felt her cheeks grow hot.

He caught her, supporting her.

He fought against the flow of people.

No one allowed them to move.

They were pushed together. "This is not working." Phinehas lifted her in his arms and carried her.

Hannah clung to his neck for balance.

Finding a break in the people, he asked, "Where's your wagon?"

She pointed. "But I can walk now."

"I'll look at your foot before I decide that."

"People kept falling on me..." She stopped when she felt his gaze on her. Her hair had fallen around her face. She closed her eyes self-consciously, then opened them again to find him still looking at her. She could feel her face flush.

As they reached her wagon, Amos hopped towards them on his wooden leg. "What happened?"

"I fell."

Phinehas placed her on the wagon bed. "The people trampled her."

Amos peered over his shoulder, color rising in his face. "I should have gone for the water."

Hannah shook her head. "No one could move in that mob."

Phinehas reached for her foot. "Men act like animals."

She tucked it under her tunic.

He looked at her face. "I must see your foot."

Hannah hesitated before extending her foot.

He removed her sandal and watched her face.

Hannah pointed as she sensed his eyes on her. "My foot is here."

"Yes, but I watch your face to know your pain." He took the other foot and stretched it out.

She retrieved it. "It's only this foot."

His eyes twinkled as she looked into them. "You doubt my doctoring skills? I compare it to the other."

"I wonder at how long you study my foot." Hannah retrieved her good foot from his hand.

Phinehas nodded. "I'll wrap it to prevent further twisting."

Amos hovered over him. "I have canvas to rip into strips. Would that do?"

Phinehas examined the material and nodded. "You must stay off it. Keep it up to prevent swelling."

She nodded.

He tapped her wrapped foot. "I'll return with water." He grabbed one of their water vessels and turned to leave.

Hannah grabbed his arm. "Wait!"

Phinehas searched her face.

Hannah dropped her hand. She could feel the heat rise in her face again. How forward he must think her! "Please, don't get water, now."

"You are thirsty?"

"Yes, but no water is worth getting hurt."

Phinehas smiled. He had started this journey because of Hannah. He cared not for the Land that they were promised. Now he would have a reason to visit. "I'll shove through any crowd to bring you water."

"No!" She was surprised by the force of her voice.

Phinehas gentled his voice. "I won't act like an animal to do it."

"Will that stop others from acting like one?"

He shrugged and smiled. "I'll return."

Moses and Aaron stood before the congregation after all drank their fill. The water had brought healing.

Moses sighed.

Aaron looked at Moses. "What?"

"It's good to see the people satisfied."

"Why the sigh?"

"The people know nothing of freedom and its responsibility. As slaves, they were told what to do their entire lives."

Aaron shrugged. "They come to us when things go wrong, just like they went to Pharaoh. How do you teach responsibility?"

Moses watched the people, raising their tents. "They must have rules and structure. Total freedom without boundaries will bring mob rule."

Aaron shook his head. "They would have stoned us today."

"It's not rules for its own sake." Moses hesitated. "Rules without reason are tyranny."

Aaron leaned on his rod as he watched the people. "How do we teach that reason?"

"We don't."

Aaron lifted his eyebrows.

"We tell them the Lord's Words. Sometimes, He doesn't give the reason. Sometimes, we obey, then understand." He shrugged. "Maybe."

Moses raised his voice to speak to the people. "Listen to the voice of the Lord your God and do what is right in His eyes, then you will not have any of Egypt's diseases." Moses met Aaron's glance. The reason behind the rules.

The cloud had not moved since the water had been given. Reut heard the Words of the Lord but thought more of what she needed, not what God wanted. She scrubbed a tunic beside her mother at the water's edge. Feeling around her neck for the gold *menat* of *Taurt*, a goddess who protected infants and pregnant women, Reut covered the necklace with her hand. She may not be pregnant, but at thirteen and ready to marry, she felt the goddess's hand protecting her. Did she not heal quickly from thirst by Taurt's hand?

Carmel, Reut's mother, rubbed a stone across a soiled spot. She turned to her sister-in-law Salome. "You're feeling better?" she asked.

Salome glanced at the children playing by the water. "Yes. Nathan said I was quite out of my head during the last day without water."

Carmel looked over the twelve springs. "It's hard to remember thirst, sitting by these pools."

Salome laughed. "The shade from the palm trees helps, too. Etania counted seventy of them."

Carmel watched the children skipping rocks in the water. "They do keep you busy."

Dinah wrung water from a cloak. "Before we depended upon Pharaoh to supply our needs; now we depend on God for everything. Ellis reminded me that 'everything' is more important as we travel."

Reut threw the stone she used to scrub. "Why do you depend upon this God? He doesn't feed us!" Reut could feel her ima's eyes on her, but she would not apologize for her rudeness. "Egypt's gods never made their people go without water or food."

Salome spread her wet blanket on the hot sand to dry. "God leads us to our Land flowing with milk and honey."

Reut glared at her aunt. She wanted to shout, "Where's the honey now?" But she bit her lip instead.

Dinah sat in the sand. "How long before we reach the Land?"

Carmel still watched her daughter. "Perhaps our God brings us to know Him before He brings us to the Land."

Reut spit out, "Why would I want to know Him? He gives thirst and hunger."

Salome responded, "Hardships make us look to Him. His peace holds us through them."

Reut studied Salome's face. Did she want to look to Him?

Phinehas strolled over to Amos's wagon, looking for Hannah. He had cared for Hannah's ankle every day.

Hannah's father, Hakeen met him. "*Shalom.*"

Phinehas nodded. "Be at peace."

Hannah did not rest in her normal place.

Phinehas continued to look for her.

Hakeen pointed to a pallet under the shade of his canvas. "Drink? We must talk."

Phinehas settled on the pallet. After drinking, he cleared his throat and rubbed the back of his neck.

"You like Hannah, yes?"

Phinehas breathed deeply. He had been practicing for this discussion. "Very much. I ask your permission to marry her. I could provide well for her."

Phinehas studied Hakeen's expression. He could read nothing. What else could he add? Surely, being a doctor was enough; after all, Hakeen was only a lowly stone carver. Phinehas gulped the cold drink, swallowing the lump in his throat. He waited.

"Is that all?"

Phinehas veiled his anger but spoke directly. "What more would you like to know?"

Hakeen prompted him. "You are the grandson of Aaron, yes?"

Phinehas nodded with confidence. Apparently Hakeen wanted his lineage, his tribe. "Aaron is my grandfather; Eleazar is my abba who married one of the daughters of Putiel." That should validate him.

Hakeen shook his head. "You lack one thing."

Phinehas could feel the heat rising in his face. How could Hakeen say that he lacked anything? His station was better than Hakeen's could ever be! Had he not treated the elite of Egypt?

"You lack the peace of knowing the Lord."

Phinehas shook his head. Was Hakeen jesting? How could God have anything to do with his marriage? He stared, unable to speak.

Hakeen continued, "Hannah accepts the Lord's control over her life. When her mother died, she grieved but accepted the Lord's choice to take her mother from her. When Amos lost his leg, she praised the Lord for saving his life. Her countenance shows the peace of submission—which you admire. She will not be given to you if you do not know the Lord."

Phinehas could not hold his words back any longer. "What difference would it make, knowing her God?"

Hakeen paused at the interruption. "If you tell her to do something contrary to what the Lord desires, she'll be torn in half— for she would want to please you, but her love for the Lord would call her in another direction. You would destroy her."

Could he believe what he was hearing? Could a God demand such control that a wife could not obey her husband? "I saw this God in the plagues of Egypt. I saw His power in the Reed Sea. I know of Him. I see His control." He stopped short of saying that this God controlled him, for he would not lie. His knowledge of God was enough.

Hakeen nodded.

Phinehas was encouraged. "So when can we arrange the wedding?"

Hakeen stopped nodding. His face grew stern. "Knowing of the Lord is not knowing Him. When you know Him, you will not need to convince me of His presence in your life. I will look on your countenance, and I will know. Until that time, do not come near my daughter."

Phinehas glared into Hakeen's granite eyes. Hakeen would not be a man to cross.

Memories of Hannah's hair curling around her face floated into his mind. He would not let her go. Phinehas stood.

Hakeen stopped him. "Do not attempt possession of my daughter until you have the Lord possessing you." He extended his arm.

Phinehas looked at the outstretched hand. He wanted Hannah now. Awkwardly he met Hakeen's hand.

Hakeen shook it heartily. "When you meet the Lord, we will talk." He smiled.

Phinehas nodded. What had he just agreed to? What would knowing this God do to his life?

Esmail watched his sheep graze as the sun set over the western mountains. The darkness would soon spread the evening coolness. His flocks had flourished in Egypt's pastures of Goshen, where they had lived since his ancestor Joseph called his brothers from their own land. Goshen produced content, healthy flocks. Esmail knew all the best water and grazing spots in Goshen. At night, they had corralled the sheep for protection.

Now in this desert, nothing but his watchfulness protected his flock from lions, jackals, and cheetahs.

With nighttime approaching, Magal, his brother, approached. He detested sheep. He thrived with people.

Esmail shook his head. He understood only the quietness of his flocks.

Magal sauntered towards Esmail. "Here's dinner. Where do I watch tonight?"

Esmail took the offered meal. "The hills to the north hold the animals at bay. That is where we watch. Bring the mothers with young close, and have your rod at hand."

Magal nodded, glancing toward the hills. The instructions never changed. "Think we'll see any action?"

Esmail responded as usual. "Preparation is the best safety."

Magal shrugged. He turned and studied the cloud that led them. "It will soon turn to fire."

Esmail glanced at the cloud of this God Who led them. Knowing Him did not bring Esmail comfort. "Didn't He kill all Egypt's livestock?"

Magal shifted his rod and shrugged. "Ours weren't touched."

Esmail squatted to eat his meal. "I lost ten lambs and seven ewes when we had no water."

Magal looked at the flock. "Looks fine now."

"The ewes were my best mothers, giving twins every time. Without water, they could not nurse." Who was this God Who could give water if He chose, but waited until his flock suffered loss? If this God were present, Esmail would demand payment. No one took from his flock without retribution.

Magal looked again towards the campsite

"Do you look for someone?"

Magal startled at the question. "No, not at all."

Esmail could tell that he was lying, but before he could question further, a lamb bleated beside him. He laid down his meal and drew the lamb to himself with his staff. He did not want his scent on the lamb. He rubbed a dead lamb's fleece over its face, securing the fleece under its belly. He then united it with a ewe that had lost its lamb. The ewe smelled her dead lamb and accepted the orphan. It nursed.

Magal watched him work. "Looks like they'll make it."

Esmail motioned toward camp with his meat back in his hand. "Hear about when we'll reach this land?"

Magal shook his head. "We just follow the cloud."

Esmail wiped his mouth. "What will it be like?"

Magal shrugged. "They say our ancestors had herds that made them rich." He sauntered toward the hills to begin his watch.

Esmail finished his meal and tossed the bone to his dog at his feet. The death of his lambs had not been in vain. Their food supply had been replenished. But Esmail would remember the loss of his flock for a long time.

Who was this God Who waited to give water?

CHAPTER 2

The fire cloud led them from Elim to the Desert of Sin. Reut glanced at the now stationary fire cloud. She was more than ready to stop. She could not wait to escape Tamara's endless chatter. The moon had risen. The light was enough. She grabbed one of the water vessels from the wagon. "Ima, I'll get the water!" She ran the first few steps to make sure that she could not hear if her mother called her.

Women had already gathered when she arrived. She dipped her jar into the shallow water, trying not to stir the mud. The water felt like tepid, used bath water. How could she drink this?

The woman beside her wiped her hand across her forehead. She braced her bosom as she squatted. She seemed ready to give birth. "I'm weary of moving. How long do you think this journey will take?"

Another woman had lifted her vessel to her shoulder, but turned back at a chance to linger in conversation. She did not seem eager to leave. She put her filled vessel at her feet and sat. "How long have we been moving?"

A small woman in a worn tunic rinsed her vessel before filling it. "Aren't we half-way through the second month?"

The one, who lingered, moaned, "Only the second month? Feels like we've lived here all our lives."

Another woman walked into the water until her tunic was wet above her knees. She dipped her vessel and smelled the water before filling it all the way. Standing up straight, she tossed her head. "My husband's a merchant. He says this is the only land available."

The woman behind Reut still had not left. She moaned again. "I can't live here all my life! I haven't eaten in days."

One woman stopped filling her vessel and sighed. "What I would give for some of Egypt's fish!"

The merchant's wife added, "Just give me a running stream, instead of this brown hole fit for cattle."

The woman, who still did not leave, whined, "Aren't you tired of eating weeds?"

The woman with child mumbled, "If I chew another piece of bark..."

Reut laughed, for she too had eaten weeds only to spit them out. Oh, for the glory of Egypt. How she regretted not staying. Surely Egypt would soon rebuild. They had power. Anything would be better than seeing this brown desert, feeling the grit under her skin, and hearing crying babies and whiny children, and now smelling this stagnant water.

The woman sitting behind her asked, "Do you remember what food tastes like? When did we last eat?"

The merchant's wife held her stomach. "My insides no longer growl."

Reut watched the woman behind her. She seemed to enjoy stirring up discontent. "What would you eat, if you could?"

The woman with child looked wistful. "A juicy, ripe melon, right off the vine."

The merchant's wife spoke without hesitation, "A crunchy cucumber."

Other women arrived. They added their wishes. "I miss the onions and garlic on everything."

"Remember the lamb we ate for Passover?"

The woman who led the complaints moaned. "If only we had died in Egypt where we ate meat and had plenty!"

The merchant's wife nodded. "The Lord brought us here to die slowly of starvation."

The woman with child dropped her vessel back in the water with a splash. "This desert gives nothing!"

The instigator grabbed her vessel and finally rose to leave. "This God can't bring us to our Land. We'll die and not even be buried here in this deathbed. The birds will pick our bones clean."

The merchant's wife stamped her foot. "What does Moses know of this desert? Why does he lead us?"

Reut stood to leave. Such conversations only added to her confusion. Besides, her vessel was filled. She lifted it to her shoulder. From the corner of her eye, she saw a flame break from the fire cloud.

No one else seemed to notice.

She cleared her throat, pointing to the streak of fire falling through the sky toward them. She could not speak.

The air crackled with power.

The flame fell upon those who complained.

Reut felt the jolt of power through the ground. It curled her toes and numbed her legs. She sank to her knees, unable to remain standing.

Screams slashed the night.

The fire's brightness blinded her. Reut blinked without seeing. When she could focus again in the darkness, she looked for the others.

The clothes of those who had complained were charred but recognizable. Their bodies lay face down, streaked as if lightning had traveled through them. The body of the merchant's wife floated on the water.

After such screams of agony, the silence was charged.

Reut's legs shook beneath her. Her insides churned. She gulped trying to breathe. She could not scream. Leaving her water vessel, she fled.

What kind of a God did they follow?

How could she escape from Him?

At last, she stood, panting in front of Moses where he was putting up his campsite. She held her chest, trying to still her trembling and catch her breath. "Fire consumed the women!"

Moses dropped his tent stake. "Have mercy on us! Forgive whatever we have done against You."

She stared at him. Who was he talking to? They had done nothing wrong.

Maessai fingered the bag of gems in his pocket. It was the blood money he had been paid to kill Moses in Egypt. How ironic that he still had it, and Moses still alive. He chuckled. The death plague had killed the vizier before Maessai had fulfilled his duty. Never had he received such easy payment.

Before the plagues, he had traveled, taking from others. Young girls were the easiest target. Found at wells in lonely places, they made easy wealth and good pleasure. He supplied Egyptians with fresh slaves. He was paid well, using the girls until he sold them. A prosperous arrangement.

But now, that would not be. He had watched Egypt's wealth

poured into the Hebrews' hands as they left. He had followed the wealth to see what was available for the taking.

Desert life was not to his liking. Traveling with these people did nothing for his comfort. They followed Moses as if he was some god, demanding he get them water and food instead of finding it themselves. And this Promised Land? He knew what lay ahead. He had traded with merchants who told of the strong people who lived there. Maessai shook his head. These Hebrews would not be so excited to get to their Land, if they knew what waited for them.

He returned to his tent after caring for his horses. His wife had done nothing to prepare the campsite. The tent was not pitched. No fire was started. Where was she? She always dawdled. And he was thirsty.

He stormed into his neighbor's campsite. "Where's my wife?"

Hakeen swallowed before responding. "An alarm has spread about some women getting water." He stopped and could not continue.

Maessai grabbed Hakeen's cloak and shook him. "What happened?"

Hakeen swallowed. "The fire of the Lord killed them."

Maessai released his grasp and ran. As he neared the water, he slowed his steps. No one was there. If his wife was one of those dead, who would get his water?

The moon had risen for the night. The fire cloud cast red, yellow, and orange reflections over the ripples of the dark water. The light showed several mounds by the water's edge. Maessai recognized his wife's cloak partly submerged in the water. Squatting, he lifted her body from the water. He dragged her out and turned her over in the sand. He could only stare at her blackened face and garments charred to her skin. What power had done this?

Maessai sensed someone behind him. He glanced back.

Moses stooped, resting his hand on Maessai's shoulder.

Maessai shook Moses's hand off and stood. He spat a scarcely veiled threat, "I know of this Land you go to. These Hebrews, if they are not killed in this wilderness, will be massacred by those in this Promised Land."

Moses stood as well, slowly, leaning on his staff. His answer was quiet and sure. "The Lord prepares His people for His Land."

Maessai clenched his hands. "You may have convinced these slaves that they need you, but I don't. I bow to no man."

"Nor should you."

Maessai stepped back.

"Bow to God Who controls you."

Maessai vowed. "I bow to no God!"

They called the place "*Taberah*," for the fire of the Lord burned among them. The people had settled for night by the time Moses finished putting up his tent by the light of the moon and the fire cloud. He glanced once at the fire cloud before closing his tent flap. He had appeared to the people confident of this God Whom they followed. And he was. Yet how was he to feed these people and keep them from complaining? He had watched husbands bury their wives and mothers weep over their young, because the food was not there. Blame was etched on the faces that glanced his way. What was he to do?

Inside his tent, he fell on his knees before the Lord. "Why are You so hard on me? This burden is too much. Should I slaughter an entire flock or catch fish by the sea? If I have found favor in Your sight, kill me now, so that I won't have to see my own wretchedness."

The Lord answered, "Am I limited? I will rain bread from heaven. The people will gather enough for each day."

The cloud stayed at the waters for several days. The days allowed Esmail's flocks to rest. His does and ewes needed water to supply milk for their young. But that did not concern Esmail now. His brow winkled in anger as he muttered to himself. He searched for tracks. Retracing his steps, he found no evidence of wild animals. He suspected two-legged thieves instead. Magal had watched closest to the campsite. Could he trust his brother?

Magal swaggered towards him for the night's watch.

Esmail spit out his words. "We lost five sheep and their lambs last night."

Magal acted as if he had not heard. "Should I take the same place tonight?"

Esmail drew a deep breath, trying to remain calm. "They were taken where you watched."

Magal curled his lip. "You think I'd steal your sheep? I hardly love them enough to watch for the night, let alone take them for the day."

"Tonight," Esmail commanded, "I'll watch by the campsite."

The people had no food, and hunger motivated wrongdoing. His flock would not last if all his breeding ewes were stolen.

This Land, where they were going, could not be worth losing all his flock.

Rich flocks at this new Land, indeed. He shook his head in disbelief.

Michael walked beyond the camp, away from the lights of the cook fires and the noise of people. Sound traveled well, but they were quieting for the night. The people had mourned the women's loss. Moses told the people of God's mercy that did not consume all who complained. The people returned to the time of the desert where all is the same.

Michael stretched his arms toward the sky. He could feel the freedom from Egypt's bondage. He breathed deeply as the cool evening air settled over him. He had not worn his cloak, and his arms tingled as the desert air penetrated his light tunic.

Nathan had told him of this God Who desired to be his Friend. Michael had watched Nathan respond with praise to this God, even after being beaten for not making his quota of bricks with his ten-man crew. Michael was part of Nathan's ten-man crew. The beating was not justified. No team could do the impossible. Michael had gone for the doctor, in spite of the danger of being a slave in the Egyptian streets. He was loyal to Nathan and to this God Who had done mighty miracles to set their people free. Michael had found this God to be his Deliverer. Now Michael sought Him to be his Friend. This God was worthy to be praised.

Michael gazed at the stars. The ebony blanket covered all that he could see. The stars dotted its expanse with pin-pricks of light, giving a glimpse of this Friend's eternity.

God had promised a nation to Abraham, as many as the stars in number.

God's people even now were as many as the stars in number. God did what He promised.

Now He led them, not only to freedom, but to their own Land, where no one would tell them what to do but God Himself.

Michael smelled deeply of the night air, as if he could already smell the new Land. He longed to touch the Land that would be a gift from this Friend. What would it be like to walk on Land that was his own? He could do whatever he wanted with the Land. His heart swelled with the gift. His eyes teared.

"I should slit your worthless throat!"

Michael, wary and alert, unsheathed his knife. He moved toward the voice, hurrying around the boulders concealing a flock of sheep.

Sheep mingled in the foreground, stirred by the violent voice.

One man straddled another on the ground, holding a knife to his throat.

Michael approached them from behind. He searched the surroundings for others. "What's going on here?"

A dog growled by the prone man's head.

The man on the ground squinted to see him.

The man on top did not lessen the pressure of his knife. "I'm missing more sheep every night. I found some tied in his wagon over there." He jerked his head, not moving his eyes from the man's face.

The prone man swallowed, a bead of blood formed on his neck. "My children go hungry."

Michael squatted by the head of the man. "Children stumble, falling from weakness. Women bury their young, for they cannot make milk on nothing."

Esmail lifted his knife slightly. "I cannot give to all who hunger."

Michael looked into the shepherd's face. "Nor do you want his blood on your hands. We will bring this matter before Moses tonight. He will judge. I will witness and return to tell you of his decision. Will that do?"

Esmail hesitated. "My anger may be gone, but my loss is not."

Michael took the knife from the shepherd. He extended his hand to help Esmail stand. "I am Michael from the tribe of Judah."

"Esmail from the tribe of Manasseh."

The third man stood beside them. "Simon from the tribe of Manasseh."

Michael turned toward the campsite with Simon. "I will bring justice from the Lord's hand."

As they walked to camp, Michael looked to the stars again. The Friend of Abraham knew they needed food. Hadn't he asked Him? If he had family, would he steal rather than see his little ones die of hunger? This situation required justice, but also mercy.

He found Moses with Adlai. "Moses, I must speak with you."

"Yes?"

Michael motioned to Simon, standing behind him in the shadows of the fire. "In private."

Moses pushed himself off the ground. He bowed to Adlai. "Shalom."

He led them to his own tent. "I meet you with pleasure."

Simon lowered his head. "Perhaps you should withdraw any pleasure until after you hear what I've done."

Moses embraced him. "If the Lord talks with me, I can talk with you, regardless of what you've done." Moses motioned to the cushions around his tent.

Michael settled beside him and recounted the night's events.

After listening, Moses tapped his staff as he thought. He turned to Simon. "What do you have to say?"

"My little ones hunger. I watch them fade before my eyes. I steal out of pain for my family. I am guilty. If I could restore the sheep, I would."

Moses stroked his beard and nodded. "You will work for Esmail until your debt is paid."

Simon grabbed Moses's arm and hugged him. "Your mercy has saved me."

Moses embraced him. "My mercy is nothing compared with the Lord's. Make peace with Him."

Reut had watched as Michael approached their campfire. She sighed when he left. She could feel her ima studying her.

Carmel took one of the empty water vessels. "Come with me, Reut."

Reut sighed, but took one of the vessels and followed her ima, the cloud of fire giving a glow to show their way.

"Reut, you've lived with Egyptians and watched their ways."

Reut readjusted the vessel on her shoulder.

Carmel licked her lips. "Egyptians show their power, not only through their army, but by their manners. You have seen Egyptian women as leaders. They rule their homes and control their men."

Reut nodded, as if she agreed. Reut had watched Amunet control her husband, the general of the army, by gentle ways. Was that so wrong?

"Our people speak with humility. Women do not look at men

directly, nor speak to them. That is not our way." Carmel paused.

Reut tried to listen but could not concentrate. Michael's face came to her mind. What would it be like to speak to him?

"Allow the man to lead, even in greeting." They filled their vessels. Carmel dried her hands on her tunic.

They walked back to the camp.

Reut glanced at her ima. She hesitated long enough to make her mother think that she still listened. Was she finished? "Ima, how did you know that Abba would be kind?"

Carmel slowed her steps. "Your abba desired our people to know God. I had seen Egypt's gods. They brought uncertainty. I wanted to know this Friend of Abraham that your father knew."

Reut looked at the stars. "How did knowing this God make him kind?"

Carmel shifted the water vessel to the ground. "The closer you get to God, the kinder you become."

"God wasn't kind in killing Amunet's baby and husband."

Carmel sighed. "He warned them. They ignored His warning."

"He destroyed Egypt. That's kindness?"

Carmel lifted the filled vessel to her shoulder. "Egypt had turned from Him and would not recognize Him as supreme. Our God's kindness rescued us from Egypt's bondage."

"So it's right to destroy one people to help your own?"

"Pharaoh fought against God. He had many chances to repent."

"What about those women at the water? Their screams haunt me in my sleep. All they wanted was something to eat."

"Reut, I can't explain why God does things. He made us, so He makes the rules. But I do know that God makes us look to Him, doesn't He?"

Reut shook her head. She lowered her vessel to the ground. "I don't want to know this God."

Carmel softened her tone. "Even when He will give you what is best?"

Reut lifted her vessel to her shoulder. "He makes us hungry when He has the power to give us food? That's His best? I don't want it."

Esmail had watched Michael and Simon leave. He was not familiar with people's ways. He understood sheep. Now in the dawn of the new day, Esmail paced. His sheep grazed contentedly, but he could not rest. Why had he trusted them? How could he be such a fool? He'd had the thief by his neck!

He glanced toward the camp again and distinguished two figures coming. He sighed in relief. Would this God bring justice?

Magal returned from his watch to the fireside. He drank from his waterskin. "Who's that?"

Esmail ignored him.

When they arrived, Simon stepped forward. He rubbed his hands down his tunic. "If it pleases you, and you're willing, I will work for you until the loss is restored."

Esmail scrutinized the man. "Do you know sheep?"

Simon's expression faltered. "I know nothing of sheep." He looked him in the eye. "But I am willing to learn. I'll guard so you can sleep. I won't allow anyone to take them."

"Even your family?" Esmail interrupted.

Simon dropped to his knees, bowing his head to the ground. "Especially my family. Please, grant me mercy."

Magal coughed. "Sounds like I could be free of these stupid beasts."

Esmail looked at Magal before nodding. "If you prove trustworthy." He extended his hand to Simon to seal the contract.

Simon stood, extending his. "When should I begin?"

"Tonight. You will train with me several nights before you begin your own night duty. Be forewarned; I know my sheep, and they know me. If any are missing, I will know. My knife is by my side."

"I know that all too well." Simon smiled but swallowed when he glanced at Esmail. "I will remember it nightly."

"I will tell Moses of your contract." Michael started to leave, then turned back. "The Lord has done justly."

The people gathered around Moses, demanding to be heard. Their food had been gone for weeks. Their insides had stopped rumbling and knotting. They felt empty and faint. Children stumbled. Families lost babies. No mother could make milk without food. Since the fire had burned the women days ago, the people simmered over this God Who would not help them.

Moses searched their faces. He noticed red-rimmed eyes from those mourning family. His heart softened to their need. Then he saw Maessai near the back of the assembly. Moses set his jaw against their rebellion. He raised his staff to quiet them. It was the Lord's time to give. "You grumble not against me, but against the Lord. He has heard.

"The Lord will give you meat in the evening and all the bread you want in the morning. You will know that He is your God.

"Gather what you need, but only what you need. Do not leave any for the next day. On the sixth day, prepare twice as much as you gather on the other days."

Moses looked beyond their campsites toward the desert where the cloud stayed. What was that glow, blinding his eyes? He walked toward it.

The sun shone through the cloud, but the brightness came not from the sun. The cloud shone with its own brightness, in colors that sparkled like gems and precious stones. Its intensity increased rather than diminished farther from the cloud, as if it would cover the earth. How could anything contain the glory from a God Who made the world with His spoken Word?

The people fell to their knees in wonder and worship.

At the crossing of the Reed Sea, one short month ago, they had praised the Lord. They had sung, but their hearts had not been changed.

Today, they glimpsed their God's glory.

It blinded them.

It seemed to look inside them, reading their thoughts, motives, intents.

They dropped their heads to the ground in submission, shame, and repentance. They worshiped.

The colors retreated back into the cloud as if passing through a door. The door slammed shut. The colors were gone. The glory vanished from view.

The people felt the radiance leave them. They blinked and raised their heads. All that remained was the cloud. Had they dreamed such wonder?

Were they changed?

No one broke the silence as they left Moses and Aaron to return to their tents. Their hunger was forgotten. How could they face such a God? Would they remember, or once His light left, would the darkness again penetrate their hearts?

Reut heard Moses speak of the Lord sending bread and meat. She licked her lips and rubbed her stomach as she anticipated eating again. But as Moses spoke of their need to worship, her mind wandered.

She longed for Egypt where the walls kept the heat away. The meals, although nothing like what Amunet ate, had satisfied her.

She heard the congregation gasp. Around her, people fell to the ground, their faces prone. She alone stood. Clutching her blue cloak more firmly around her, Reut faced the desert.

No longer brown and barren, it glowed with a radiance greater than the sun. Its brightness consumed the desert. Its jeweled colors reached toward her, warming her skin, but exposing her uncleanness.

She fell before the light, blinking, unable to raise her head to look again.

She remembered Moses's words. "He heard your grumbling against Him."

Reut clutched the dirt. If only she could dig a hole to hide her unworthiness. Who was she to question this God's best?

Maessai also stood with the assembly, but cared not for what Moses said. He fingered the gems in his pocket and considered how he would find someone to make his dinner and get his water.

He missed his wife. She had done what he liked, most of the time. Early in their marriage, she had spoken against his acquiring women and bringing them home. She told about her God and what He thought of Maessai's actions.

Maessai had quickly cured her of speaking against him. The first time, she could not leave her bed for seven days.

He did not blame this God for burning her—she did complain too much. Maessai only wished that he had found someone else to make his meals before this God took her. He missed her cooking. She did that well.

Maessai watched for a replacement. Hakeen's daughter had visited his wife when they first left Egypt. She was pliable, young, teachable, and beautiful. When he asked Hakeen for his daughter, Maessai had dumped his gems in his hand, transferring them from hand to hand.

Hakeen had not given the gems a glance. He refused.

Maessai laughed now. There were other ways to get what he wanted, without parting with his gems.

Moses was still talking, but no matter. He would neither respect nor obey the words of Moses.

He was deep in thought when the people fell to the ground. He did not. But as he looked, he saw a maiden in a deep blue cloak, standing far in the front. She hesitated, then dropped to her knees, but not before Maessai had found the solution to his need.

Then he looked to where the people had.

The desert flamed with a white fire that changed to glow like his gems.

He stared, unable to look away. Protecting his eyes with his arm, he felt the radiance pierce him. This God had known of his plan in Egypt to kill Aaron and Moses. He took his hand out of his pocket as if the gems were hot. God also knew of his plans now.

How could this God know? The vizier had paid him in secret.

He backed away from the congregation, but the light continued to penetrate. If he hid, this blazing fire would find him.

He knelt, not in repentance nor submission, but in acknowledgment of this God's superior strength.

Later, he would run from this camp, but he would take one maiden with him. He would not face this God again.

In the evening, Moses walked through camp, speaking to the people, feeling their shame. Moses stopped at Nathan and Salome's tent. He remembered Etania from collecting berries in Egypt. He placed his hand on her head. "Are you ready to eat meat?"

She nodded, fidgeting. "What kind?"

Moses squatted beside her. "I can request, but God decides. What kind would you like?"

"We won't have fish, will we?"

He stroked her hair away from her face. "You don't like fish?"

Etania shook her head. "After the frogs died in Egypt, my abba smelled of rotten fish. I don't like fish anymore."

Moses laughed. "The Lord will not give us fish. But I'll ask to make sure." He stood to embrace Nathan who had entered.

"My daughter doesn't hesitate to ask God what she wants." Nathan squeezed her shoulder.

Moses nodded. "Your daughter can teach us much."

As the evening coolness began to creep through the campsite, Adlai gathered his cloak tighter around his waist. He walked away from the campsite toward the mountains. He had listened to Moses's words of promised food. He wanted to believe. Watching his family struggle, the hunger in their eyes, his wife being too weak to rise from sleep, Tamara's lack of chatter and movement, Reut's angry glares, all told him of the pain that they held inside. He could no longer watch them struggle to exist. He wanted to believe that food was coming.

The wind had risen, wafting the smell of the sea over the mountains. The faint fishy-salt smell reminded him of the Nile. He shook his head. How could he smell fish? As he walked toward the mountains with the wind blowing in his face, he knew the smell was not his imagination. And the smell did not tempt him to long for Egypt's fish; it reassured him that God would supply his family's need.

He remembered that time in Egypt when he sat on his wagon seat, ready to bring Joseph's bones from the pyramid. There had been that wiggling doubt, yet his faith in his God overrode his fear. He did what he had to do. Now the same doubt tried to worm its way inside. He sniffed again, and nodded. All would be well.

The wind increased—an unusual thing for the evening. He turned back reluctantly to his tent, glad that the walk had calmed his heart. By the time he reached his tent, the wind felt like a sand storm was coming. The camp seemed deserted. Others had already found refuge in their tents. He entered his, tying the flap securely.

The wind lifted their tent; then allowed it to settle again, as if it sighed under the wind's power.

He met Carmel's glance across the tent and smiled. Her eyes turned toward Reut. He looked too.

Reut sat huddled under a blanket.

The wind had been hot. Adlai went to Reut and placed his arm around her. "What's wrong?"

She shivered. "Do you remember when the wind came in Egypt? It brought lice, flies, locust..."

Adlai squeezed her and moved the blanket to look into her face. "This wind brings good."

Reut raised her face to meet his. "How can you tell?"

Adlai sniffed. "Smell that?"

Reut gave a tentative sniff. Her face took on a look of pleasure.

Adlai laughed. "That smell tells me that God will provide."

Reut smelled again, then laughed. "Maybe He will."

Adlai looked across the tent at Carmel.

She nodded and smiled.

They listened to the wind and waited.

Suddenly the wind died down. It seemed as if it signaled something. But what? Adlai stepped from his tent, his eyes searching the horizon beyond camp. He shook his head several times to make sure he was seeing right. He turned back to those in the tent. "May God be praised!"

Carmel stepped from the tent behind him. She grabbed his hand as they watched.

Quail, visible only by the light of the fire cloud, flew two *cubits* above the ground. As the wind stopped, they landed exhausted on the sand.

Adlai squeezed her hand. "God brought meat for His people."

Reut and Tamara stepped outside the tent to stand beside them.

Tamara's eyes twinkled. "It's like a table spread before us, calling us to eat."

Adlai hugged Reut's shoulder.

People all around them ventured from their tents. With a scream of victory, they pushed, shoved, and fought to reach the quail first.

Adlai shook his head. He wanted his family fed. They hungered like everyone else, but couldn't they acknowledge God Who gave to them?

Adlai's praise caught in his throat. His hollow insides turned into knots as he saw the greed. How could God be pleased?

He cringed. The people were like hyenas, fighting over a kill. Would they frighten away the birds?

He watched without breathing. When the people reached the quail, the birds hunched, still, and unmoving.

Adlai breathed a sigh of relief. "May God be praised! We did not hinder Your blessings by our greed."

The people grabbed the quail, broke their necks, ripped off their feathers, and sunk their teeth into their raw flesh. They gnawed at the raw carcasses like animals.

Suddenly, the Lord struck the people with a plague.

Men dropped dead, their mouths full. Others, not even noticing those fallen around them, gathered for their own feast.

Adlai shook his head. "Kibroth-hattaavah, death by greed."

The people ate. But were their hearts full? They desired temporary relief for a need that would last forever.

How long would the Lord's patience be tested? This people saw their need, but not Him Who provided for their need.

Was it just this afternoon that God had shown them His glory? Darkness had rushed into their hearts faster than the sun could set!

Nathan settled on the cushions after taking a final bite. "That was good."

Ellis added, "So easy to catch. They sat for us to take."

Nathan laughed. "If we had to trap them, you know we'd all be hungry, except Michael." He pointed a bone at Michael. Most had no knowledge of hunting nor skill in the ways of the wild. He shook his head. "Did you see the people eat the birds, without cooking them?"

Michael nodded. "They were consumed with their want."

Nathan threw a bone in the embers and watched it sizzle as the flames leapt up. "Do you blame them? I would have been the first to feed my family, if I could've moved faster."

Ellis caught Japhet as he ran by him. He tickled him with his beard and squeezed him. "Yes, but you would have taken a moment to thank God first."

Japhet giggled and squealed to be let loose.

Ellis let him go. "When I thought about freedom, I didn't expect this."

Michael drank from the dipper at the tent's door. He moved the dipper closer to their circle, so they all could share. "What did you expect?"

Ellis looked at the mountains. "I skipped over the journey. I just saw the Land and what we would do."

Michael shook his head. "What are we ready to do?"

Nathan looked at Salome where she sat with the women. "Is God preparing us for the Land, or is He preparing us to be His people?"

Ellis stretched out his legs. "How does He prepare us to be His people?"

Nathan shrugged. "It was easy in Egypt. I was beaten."

Ellis interrupted. "It was easy? I was angry for you."

Nathan stared into the embers. "I could deal with my own suffering. I saw God. Now, I see my family suffer... I have trouble accepting that from the hand of God."

Michael caught Nathan's glance. "Doesn't He own them, too?"

Nathan watched Salome across the tent.

She caught his glance and smiled, but it did not reach her eyes. She had not recovered from the lack of water. Without food, she had lost much flesh.

Nathan tore his eyes from Salome and looked back at Michael. "I sometimes wish that He didn't."

Maessai watched the campsite as families and clans enjoyed the quail. He lounged against his cushions. His hunger was quenched after eating six raw quail.

But watching the maidens that evening as they went for their evening water, he felt a different kind of hunger.

He sharpened his dagger as he waited by the water's edge.

The maiden with the blue cloak came for water.

He stopped sharpening his dagger.

She did not want to be here. He read it in her face. She was angry with this God.

He would save her from the desert and take her from this people who depended upon their God to supply everything, and this God Who looked into his very soul.

CHAPTER 3

The fire cloud moved and settled at Hazeroth.

Moses rose early in the morning. He enjoyed the quietness before the people's needs were brought before him. He hiked partway up the mountain to overlook the campsite. Their canvas coverings provided shade for the hottest part of the day, warmth for the coolness of evening and night. In the last days of their stay in Egypt, many had been showered with Egypt's riches, canvases, garments, even sandals. The people were not in need. All found some form of shelter under the scorching sun.

God's people spread out as far as he could see to the south, their tents rippling over the rock-strewn terrain like waves of the sea. God had promised to Abraham descendants as many as the sand of the land. Moses smiled. God did keep His Word.

He squinted to see the land beyond their camp. The scattered grasslands held the animals where herdsmen guarded their flocks with care. They were mere dots to his eyes as he focused. Only by their vast numbers clustered together could he tell they were there.

He looked again at the land between the camp site and the animals. Scattered over the sand and shale, Moses saw the white flakes provided by the Lord.

He laughed. God had not only delivered His people from the suffering of Egypt, but also provided for their every need.

He nodded. God would lead them to their final destination. He could hardly wait!

The women began gathering the flakes for their morning meal. Seeing them touched the longing in his heart to have his own wife, Zipporah, at his side.

How was Zipporah? He could see the stubborn set to her jaw when she would not relent. She had looked that way when he had requested Gershom, their first-born, to be circumcised. He might as well have asked her to give up breathing!

But when an angel had demanded either their obedience or death, Zipporah had circumcised both boys.

Moses was relieved that battle was over. Fighting with Zipporah reminded him of trying to break a donkey to ride. Only the donkey would eventually give in. He shook his head. He did miss her.

If the Lord could change Pharaoh's heart, at least long enough for His people to flee Egypt, could He prepare Zipporah for living with His people?

Moses had been gone for over a year and a half now. Gershom would be six years old and Eliezer almost three. Would Eliezer even know him? Would Zipporah be ready to live with his people?

He shook his head and focused his thoughts on the people. Many had assimilated the Egyptian culture, including its superstitions and empty worship practices.

Now, God must separate His people unto Himself.

Most remembered the miracle of the water, but they had already forgotten God's glory that pierced their hearts.

Remembering the glory reminded him of God's original call to this mission. The Lord had called him from that burning bush that didn't burn. He still trembled at the memory. But God did not wish to destroy him, but to use him. God had called him to lead His people out of Egypt to their Promised Land. He could not wait to finish the mission!

Before the sun's rays had turned from their pinkish hue to the brightness of yellow, Dinah and Salome rose. With their young still sleeping, they slipped out of camp together with baskets to gather the food given by God.

Salome looked over the sand. "It's like the dust of an angel!"

Dinah licked a piece. "It tastes sweet."

Salome was pleased. "Between the quail in the evening, and this dew-dripped, honey-coated wafer, we won't need anything."

Dinah stifled a giggle as they filled their baskets.

"What are you thinking?" Salome paused in her gathering.

Dinah whispered, "Do you think if we ask the Lord, that He could give our husbands something to do? Ellis is always underfoot. If he volunteers to do one more thing, I'll run away. Do you know what he did yesterday?"

Salome shook her head.

"He hauled water for me. I almost asked if the women laughed at him for doing my work. Traveling doesn't keep him busy enough. In the evenings, he has too much energy. I love him, but..."

Salome laughed. "A man needs work. They've worked hard in Egypt. Now, they're idle."

Dinah joined her laughter. "Let's pray that God gives them something soon."

Etania met Salome at the tent flap as the women returned to the camp. "Ima. What's in the basket?"

Salome gave her a piece. Jabin came running to join them. "Me, too."

Salome laughed. "There's plenty. They cover the ground like dew on a wheat field ready to harvest."

Nathan came behind her and hugged her. "Let's go see!" He scooped up Jabin in his arms and grabbed Salome's hand.

When they reached the camp's edge, Etania's eyes grew big. "It's like a festival, and we'll never stop eating!" She twirled and sang, "We won't be hungry anymore!" Grabbing Jabin's hands, she ran in circles, scraping up handfuls and stuffing it into her mouth. "It melts in my mouth! Jabin, get some!"

She stopped dancing and chewing. She dropped her hands. Her eyes became big. "Ima, this won't make me sick like the radishes, will it?"

Salome laughed, remembering the radishes in Egypt that Etania had eaten until she was sick. "No, this is from the Friend of Abraham. It soothes the belly and fills the empty cracks with substance."

Etania jumped and circled around her abba.

Nathan squeezed Salome's hand. "Will it help you?"

Salome nodded toward the field of food. "We will eat, and feel better."

Etania caught Nathan's hand. "Will we eat this with our milk and honey in the new Land?"

Nathan squeezed her. "We won't need this when we have milk and honey to eat."

Etania squealed and wiggled free. She started dancing again. "Our Friend sends food from heaven!"

Reut rose early. She rubbed her arm where Tamara had kicked her during the night.

Tamara tossed all night. She moved like the ripples of the Nile—constantly. Didn't her body ever need to rest?

After putting on her blue cloak, Reut left to gather the food. Others already were gathering. She examined one of the wafers. They would eat this? She held it between her teeth. Surprised by the sweetness, she allowed it to sit on her tongue and melt. She was startled by the taste of honey. What would this God do next?

She fingered the amulet around her neck. On that last morning in Egypt, Amunet had ripped it off her own neck and given it to her, along with her blue cloak. In Egypt, Reut has seen the power of this God. His power was destructive. His control had changed her life. How could this sweetness could come from the same God?

As she mused, she retrieved the sweet wafers from the ground. She glanced toward the pastures where their people kept their flocks.

Michael and another man were returning to camp. It was the same man from the other night when Michael had come to speak to Moses. She stopped gathering wafers and stood staring.

Michael walked toward her. "Your father is well?"

Reut lowered her eyes. Why had she stared? She could not stop thinking of his visit last night. How could she make him visit again and stay longer? She spoke quickly. "Yes, he invites you to his meal tonight."

Michael glanced at her basket. "You gather for a feast."

Reut looked at her overflowing basket. She had enough wafers for three days for her family. Heat rushed to her face. She could not allow him to think that this was all for her. "My sister, she eats a lot."

Michael nodded, looking into her eyes. "I'd be honored to join your family for a meal."

Was that twinkle in his eyes because he was laughing at her? She pulled her cloak's hood further over her face. He was laughing at her. Why had she made a complete fool of herself? She had been so forward! Her mother had just told her that she should not look directly into a man's eyes. Reut coughed. "I plan for your visit."

Her cheeks heated anew. And she had invited him to dinner.

She could not ignore the Egyptians' way of taking what they wanted. Their ways worked. They controlled the world. Until this God had interfered.

Michael still stood before her. "What time?"

She raised her eyes to meet his. The twinkle was still there. She swallowed. "When the sun begins to set and the cloud turns to fire." She dropped her eyes and fidgeted with her basket.

He smiled and nodded. "Until then."

She turned and fled toward camp. How would she tell her ima what she had done? She gulped, feeling her face burn. How would she tell her abba?

Hannah heard the baby stirring in the tent beside theirs. She stretched and prepared to bring the water needed for the day.

She still favored her ankle, but the coolness of the morning kept the swelling down until she could elevate it.

She reached the edge of the campsite before she looked out. It was like a table set before her! She would hurry to bring the water so she could gather the wafers. They would not have to fill their hollow insides with water. They would be full from the food of God.

She reached the water's edge and rinsed the vessel out before filling it again.

Her thoughts drifted to the family she would like to have. Most girls her age had married, but her abba still saw her as his little girl. Did he even realize that she had left her childhood and longed for motherhood?

Her ima had died seven years ago. Hannah missed her, especially at times like these. She would have encouraged Abba to find someone for her.

Hannah had visited Maessai's wife, before she died, hoping to prepare for marriage. Mostly she had just ended up listening to her complaints. Hannah felt uncomfortable in Maessai's presence. She had left depressed by the visit and too discouraged to go again.

She missed Phinehas's attention. In Egypt, she had helped him with those afflicted by the plagues. He made her feel special, but he did not follow the Lord.

She had stopped filling the vessel and caught herself staring toward the mountains. This would not do. Shaking her head, she stood to return to her tent.

Nearby women's voices rose in the quiet air. "She acts above us, even though her father's just a sculptor."

Hannah hesitated and stood listening. Were they talking about her?

"She's past the age to marry. Not even the slave men want her."

"Yet she flirts with the son of Eleazar."

"Isn't he Aaron's grandson?"

"As if she would be good enough for one from his station."

"He doesn't want her. He only plays with her."

"He visited her tent daily while she pretended to limp. How could he be so deceived by her act?"

"I told my husband to move our tent far from hers. I don't need her kind influencing my children."

Hannah's eyes brimmed with tears. She lifted her tunic and ran to her tent, ignoring the pain in her ankle and splashing water from the jar as she went.

She hurriedly gathered enough manna for the day and returned. Back in the tent, she breathed deeply, trying to calm herself as she prepared the flatbread, stepping gingerly now on her injured ankle.

"Shalom, my daughter." Hakeen kissed her head.

"Be at peace, Abba."

"Looks like you had a rough night?"

"Why so?" Hannah tried to look away.

Hakeen turned her face toward his and studied it. "Your limp is far worse today."

She lowered her eyes, but the tears still pooled. "I hurried from gathering your meal."

"Because...?"

"I wanted to make your breakfast." She raised her head and tried to smile. Why did the tears still gather behind her eyes?

"Because...?" Hakeen asked again as he wiped her tears with his thumb.

"Oh, Abba, why does no man want me?"

"Ah." He brought her to his chest and patted her back. "My daughter has become a maiden, in thought, as well as body."

He paused. "I have waited for this day with fear and concern." He sat down on the cushions and patted the one beside him.

"This is a job for your ima. She would know what to say. I cannot tell you the mind of a woman. That is one of the great mysteries God keeps to Himself." He cupped her face in his calloused hand. "Were the old women talking?"

She nodded. "They say not even a slave would want me."

"They speak of what they don't know. They are jealous of your beauty. You've attracted the attention of several men."

Hannah thought of Phinehas. "And you said?"

"You are my only daughter..." Hakeen's voice broke.

Hannah looked into his eyes to see tears.

He stroked her cheek gently. "I want you to have what your ima and I had—a love that stood the test of time."

So what did that mean? Who had asked? Hannah held her breath, waiting for his explanation.

He smiled sadly. "Two cannot travel the same path unless they are agreed. If you both love God, you can walk hand-in-hand through life's troubles. But if you desire to please God, and your husband doesn't..."

She prodded him when he didn't finish. "What, Abba?"

"Who would you serve if your husband asked you to do something that would displease God?"

"I can't imagine that..."

"Your ima knew Maessai's wife before she married. She encouraged her to trust in God's care. Then Maessai came..."

Hannah nodded. On many nights she had covered her ears with her cloak, trying not to hear the slaps that Maessai gave his wife. She had not been able to follow her God and her husband's wishes. She had lived unhappily.

"Maessai has requested your hand in marriage."

Hannah gasped. Surely her father would not consent!

He shook his head. "My daughter, I won't allow it. But I fear he will not take no for an answer. Avoid him. He is evil. God has shown me who should have you. I simply wait for the right time. Can you trust me?" He lifted her chin so that her eyes could meet his.

"Yes." Did she dare ask him who he had in mind?

Hakeen nodded, kissing her forehead. "You are precious to me, my daughter. God will reward your patience. He will prepare the man for Himself first; then he will be truly yours to have." He patted her hand. "Was I an adequate substitute for your ima's words?"

Hannah smiled. "Yes. There is something that has bothered me, Abba..."

"You seem bothered by many things lately." He chuckled. "I'm sitting, so I might as well hear it."

She paused, embarrassed now that the conversation was hers to direct. "Abba, why do you not remarry?"

He laughed at her question.

"You have several women's attention," Hannah hurried to explain. "The one who brought the extra quail over last night, and the one who offered to sew your cloak."

Hakeen's face flushed. "Oh daughter, I am content with good memories of your ima and what God has given. My time is better spent in prayer for your future than planning mine."

"But Abba, you have many more years to live. Don't you feel alone?"

"Alone—with God? My Hannah." He shook his head. "Part of me is missing without your ima, but that is what God does when He makes man and wife. They become one. When death parted us, I became half a man. God is willing to use that. No other woman should only have half my heart."

Adlai approached Moses' tent, surprised to find him alone. "No one needs you?"

Moses smiled. "What may I do for you?"

"I've come to ask your permission to teach the men to read. They must know not only the history of our people but also what God tells you."

"That might minimize instructing them when they come for disputes." Moses paused. "Good. The men have too much idle time. I will leave you to organize it."

Adlai nodded, pleased.

Moses stood to leave.

"I sense a change in the people."

Moses turned back. "In what way?"

"A shift in their worship from many gods to one god."

"That is good."

"But," Adlai looked Moses in the eye, "the one god is you."

Moses' face showed his surprise. "I am no god."

"The people want a god they can see and control. If the people know more of their history, of the Lord's Hand guiding them, they may see Him for Who He is."

"Then begin!"

"But," Adlai studied Moses. "When a great leader disobeys, he falls farther."

"I cannot dwell on what could happen. I'm too busy. I focus on the Lord. But your words are good counsel."

Adlai rested his hand on Moses's shoulder. "I only caution."

Moses remained silent for a moment, his brow furrowed. "Your teaching the men to read excites me. I will announce the news. The scrolls where I recorded Abraham, Isaac and Jacob's stories passed down by generations, told to me by my mother in my younger years in Pharaoh's palace, are available for your use." He paused before adding, "This other matter I must give to the Lord."

Adlai moved from the tent of meeting to water his horse. He waited by the pool as it drank. In Egypt, he had watched God honor Joseph's request that he be buried with his own people, even though that request was fulfilled more than four hundred years later. Adlai knew his people needed to know this God better. Learning to read their history would help. How would He make that happen?

He scraped a burr out of his horse's hoof. He dropped the hoof and checked another leg.

Michael's voice interrupted his thoughts. "Shalom."

Adlai patted the flank of his horse and dusted his hand. "Be at peace."

Michael hesitated. "Your daughter told me of your invitation to eat with you this evening. I accept."

Adlai coughed, "My daughter told you that I had spoken?" He caught himself at the lack of politeness. "Was this Tamara?"

Michael shook his head. "The older one. She gathered for quite a banquet."

Adlai nodded, hoping the surprise did not show on his face. "I look forward to your presence."

Adlai pondered as he made his way to his tent. He must ask Carmel about her. How could he understand the mind of a girl turning woman? Those matters were better left for his wife and the Lord.

The sun's rays rose as the day progressed, and the white flakes melted like fat in a jar, leaving only the hot sand. What if that was their only chance for food until they reached the Promised Land?

Miriam patted her basket of wafers that she had kept aside, enough for a few days. She would not go hungry, even if everyone else did. Nor would she share her surplus. She was tired of her insides feeling knotted and hollow. She felt dependent and weak whenever her head spun and the ground rose to meet her.

She ground her manna flakes into a fine powder, adding water until it was just the right consistency to flatten into cakes. She heated a few flat cakes on a hot stone over her embers; then folded it with leftover quail pieces. She sat against her cushions to enjoy her meal.

Biting into the bread, she savored the sweet, filling meal. She would leave some for Moses. He would forget to eat, if she did not make him. What a perfect excuse to ask him what the people were doing! These former slaves did not know how to function as civilized people. She must instruct them. Moses needed help with all these people. Hadn't she led the singing when they had crossed the Reed Sea? She could still feel the pleasure when everyone joined with her as they sang in praise. She wanted to unite these people.

She turned from finishing her meal to see the basket overflowing with manna. She had heard Moses's instructions about gathering the manna for only one day, but she knew better. He was just her little brother. What did a man know of planning for a household? She would not hunger again. And he would thank her when tomorrow came and she offered her extra to fill in for his lack. But, oh, she was tired of this desert. She was weary of this God who waited until she grew faint before giving what she needed.

CHAPTER 4

Ellis took Japhet's hand as they climbed the boulders outside camp. He squatted, watching Japhet throw stones over the edge of the rock. His son would grow to be a free man. He would not have his energy drained by the whips of an Egyptian foreman. He would not have to labor until the sun set, returning before the sun rose the next morning for another day of forced work.

Ellis had worked with Nathan and Michael pouring bricks that had built temples and palaces for Pharaoh. He remembered the seeding and harvest. Their people had built Egypt to be world-renowned for its great feats. He had once glimpsed the pyramids, and the number of slaves required to move those massive room-sized boulders into place.

Ellis had felt the rhythm of the work, of something bigger than himself, of the teamwork. He rebelled against the control, but the work itself gave him a feeling of accomplishment. Now with freedom, he experienced a loss. The camaraderie of accomplishing something great was gone. Instead he felt listless, and a need for something more.

He grabbed Japhet, who had started to slip over the edge. He took his son's hand and began their walk back towards the tent. The walk was only reminding him that he owned nothing. His cloak, the tent, food: all gifts from God. Ellis appreciated what God had done. But what had he earned?

Japhet was tiring, so he bent down and carried him. Shouldn't freedom feel better? He had moved from serving Pharaoh, to what?

How would he provide for his family when they reached the Land? He had no skills. How could support his family?

The Lord provided water, meat, and bread, but could He give man a dream and a drive to live?

Japhet squirmed in his arms. "Abba, I wanna walk wit' you."

Ellis smiled and put him down again, holding his hand tighter. When they reached the bottom of the hill, he allowed Japhet to toddle freely.

Japhet ran to the water and knelt for a drink. He stood again, his tunic dripping.

Ellis followed and stooped to bring a handful to his lips. The sun was setting, and the crimson colors reflected off the water as the women had started to come for their evening water.

Across the water, a man watched the women, sharpening his dagger.

Ellis caught Japhet's hand protectively. "Let's bring Ima some water."

"Me, too."

"Yes, my son. You may help." Ellis wondered if that was how God was, taking one step at a time, holding his hand. That seemed enough for Japhet. "Make it be enough for me, too."

Aaron worked beside Mack in the stuffy, hot canvas tent. He could hear the laughter and squeals of the children scampering outside. "It's good to hear the children happy."

"Yes." Mack ground herbs with his stone and pestle; then poured the powder into a vessel of oil for a tonic. He and Aaron had worked together as servant and master in Egypt. Aaron had given him his freedom when they had left, and now Mack helped when Aaron needed him. During the days Mack mingled with the people and helped with basic doctoring needs. "The people ask what this new food is from God. What would you call it?"

Aaron shrugged. "Manna."

Mack laughed. Manna meant food. "Then manna it is. What is in it that makes one satisfied, and yet it's sweet to the lips?"

Aaron shook his head. "It's like nothing Egypt ever had. It's bread from heaven."

They settled into quietness, each working at some herb.

After some time, Mack spoke again. "What do you think will become of the slaves?"

"What do you mean? They're free."

"They know nothing but to do what they are told. In Egypt, they looked to Pharaoh for all that they needed. He provided their job, food, shelter. Now they look to Moses. To some, he is like a god. He is their deliverer, their provider."

Aaron laughed. "My brother is not a god."

Mack persisted. "Listen to what they say. They don't praise God. They praise Moses for giving them food. He's a visible form of the God that he serves. He mediates for them. Remember the glory in the desert?"

Aaron stopped mixing tonics as he considered Mack's words. "The people already forget that, don't they?"

Mack shook his head. "No, they remember their littleness and don't like it. They remember their need. No one likes vulnerability."

Aaron stared out the tent's flap. "So they blame Moses. And they do not change."

"Exactly," Mack agreed. "Some are steeped in Egypt's ways. If Egyptians couldn't understand something, they invented a new god to explain it. The uncertainties of life were then controlled, and they could find peace."

"But most of our people didn't mingle with the Egyptians. They were taught from childhood that there was only one God, the God of Abraham."

Mack nodded. "Yes, but they have learned from the glory in the desert that it is better to keep their distance from God."

Aaron considered Mack's words as he put the tonic in his basket. "So Moses takes their needs to God instead." He looked at Mack. "Do you think that Moses knows about this?"

"No. He's too busy judging the people."

Aaron opened the tent's flap to allow in a breeze.

A group of women returned with baskets of clean clothes. He heard fragments of their conversation as they passed.

"We finally have enough. We have Moses to thank."

Aaron saw the truth of Mack's words. But he was the elder son, entitled to receive the blessing and the honor. Instead, his brother's name was spoken by the people, not his. Why should he always have to follow in the footsteps of his little brother?

When Moses had his burning bush experience, Aaron had been tempted to envy him. God spoke to Moses. Why didn't He speak to him?

Since leaving Egypt, Moses had come to lead the people. Why didn't Moses allow him to judge the people? Moses had no time to do anything. Aaron could judge the people as well as Moses. In many ways, he knew the people better. Hadn't he shared in their suffering, while Moses escaped to the desert for forty years? Aaron began to see things differently, and it was not to his liking.

After watering his horse for the evening, Nathan hesitated before entering his tent.

Etania was waiting for him and grabbed his hand. "Look, Abba, I made flatbread all by myself."

Nathan held her hand.

She placed uneven flatbread in his hand.

You made this?"

Her head bobbed, as her hair shook.

"Good." He looked back the way he had come and shook his head. "Put it back where we sit. I'll eat it there."

Salome stood from the embers where she heated the bread. She wiped her floured hands on her tunic; then walked to stand beside him. She glanced in the direction he was watching. "What's wrong?"

He tried to smile, but he didn't look directly at her. "Nothing."

She hesitated, not speaking until he looked at her. "The children waited for you."

He massaged the back of his neck and glanced back outside. He finally looked at her and forced a smile. "Let's eat."

Etania scrambled to sit as close as she could to Nathan. Jabin squeezed on his other side.

His prayer was short and direct.

Etania placed her lopsided flatbread by Nathan's hand. "You didn't pray long. Is that because we now have food?"

Nathan tussled her hair and tried to smile. "No. Couldn't wait to taste your flatbread."

She smiled. "I made it just for you."

"Then I'll enjoy it." He did not add anything to the chatter of the children. He caught Salome's glance a couple times through the meal, but he ignored her unspoken questions.

Once the meal was completed and the children played outside the tent, Salome leaned against Nathan on the pallet. "What's wrong?"

Nathan sighed. "I overheard men fighting over an ox. One claimed it was his, but the other three beat him. Poverty didn't make people act like this. Lack of boundaries did. They beat him over an ox, Salome."

Salome rubbed his shoulder. "The people grow restless."

"What if that ox was mine? What would I have done?"

"Moses—"

"What can Moses do? He can't be everywhere. And he certainly can't control a mob. The people tried to stone him when we had no water."

Salome glanced at the children. Jabin was poking Etania.

Etania squealed. "That hurts! Don't, Jabin."

"In Egypt, we were too busy to fight." Salome glanced at Nathan. When he did not reprimand Jabin, she shook her head. "Jabin, stop."

Jabin continued to pester Etania.

Salome's voice grew stern, "Jabin!"

He stood before her, his eyes repentant.

Salome leaned on Nathan's knee, getting his attention. "Find something for this son of yours to do. Without it, he finds all the mischief that is to be found."

Nathan swung Jabin onto his shoulders. "That's it!" He bent to give Salome a kiss.

"What's that for?" Salome asked.

"You have solved our people's problem. I must speak to Adlai."

Tamara fluttered around all morning. "What else can we do with manna? How much sweeter is it than honey, do you think?"

Reut sighed. "Is anyone even answering your questions, Tamara?"

"Why are you so distracted? All you've done is watch the tent opening and sigh."

"All you've done is chatter about nothing."

Tamara huffed. "I don't think food is nothing."

Carmel interceded. "Tamara, why don't you help Salome with the children?"

Once Tamara left, Carmel turned to Reut. "He will be here soon enough."

Reut dropped the knife she was using to slice quail. She tried to answer innocently. "Who?"

Carmel sighed. "Your abba told me of your invitation this morning. Tell me about this man."

Reut fidgeted with her eyes downcast. "He worked with Uncle Nathan while they were slaves. He spoke to me."

Carmel's eyes widened. "Why did he speak to you?"

Reut shrugged, then sighed. "I invited him to eat with us... I told him Father desired it."

Carmel sighed, frustration on her face. "You spoke to a man in public? Reut, those Egyptian ways hold you strongly."

Reut glanced at her ima. She was watching the roof of the tent. "What do you see up there?"

"I am counting the flies on the ceiling, so I don't say something I will regret."

Reut looked at the flies. "Does it work?"

Carmel shook her head. "The man you seek loves the Lord. If you are not interested in obeying God, then he will not be interested in you. He remains a slave to His Master."

"Why would he choose to remain..." Reut cut her words short as the tent flap opened and Adlai entered with Michael, Ellis and Nathan.

"...but let's eat and discuss it," Adlai finished as they entered. The men settled on the cushions.

Michael nodded in Reut's direction.

She could feel heat rise to her face. She did not meet his eyes.

Adlai continued their conversation. "I want to teach reading and writing, so the men would know our history."

Ellis's face shone with excitement. "I could read what God has done for our people."

Nathan leaned toward Adlai. "How did you teach in Egypt?"

"I read from the scrolls what the Lord had done to Abraham, Isaac, and Jacob. Then we discussed it."

"Isn't that what Moses does when he tells us God's Words?" Nathan asked.

Adlai nodded. "But reading would put in front of every man the Words of God to see for himself."

Nathan pointed his finger at the scrolls in the corner of the tent. "Could we organize the people in groups, by tribes and families? Those from your class in Egypt could teach the beginnings. The groups would be big at first, to get the basics. But as some learned faster, they could be separated to help those who struggled, until all men could read."

Michael sighed, a look of pleasure on his face.

Nathan sat back. He gestured to Michael. "You've been quiet; what do you think?"

Michael took a few minutes to answer. "I cannot wait to hold the Word of God in my heart where it cannot be forgotten. Knowing our history will help, but we need protection. There are those who do not want to obey Moses. Their grumblings could inflame an uprising in these tight quarters. There are disputes that don't make it to Moses before someone is hurt."

Nathan squeezed Jabin's shoulder as he sat beside him. "My son finds mischief if he doesn't have something constructive to do. We're like that. What can we do?"

"A man watches me when I get water. He makes me feel unsafe," Reut blurted. She cringed, wishing she could sink into the floor, regretting her hasty words.

"I've seen him," Ellis agreed. "I get the water for Dinah because of him."

Adlai redirected the discussion. "How safe are our people from dangers among us? What are your thoughts?"

Nathan was thoughtful. "Moses can't be everywhere."

Michael nodded. "Even if he was, how could he stand against an angry mob throwing stones?"

"I want to protect my family," Nathan said.

Michael asked, "What about when we reach the Land? Won't we have to claim it?"

Ellis leaned forward. "Some men were soldiers in Egypt. Couldn't they train us for battle?"

"Swords aren't lacking," Michael agreed. "Many gathered the armor and swords from the soldiers around the Reed Sea."

Adlai looked around the circle of men. "If we trained for battle, the men would not be idle."

Ellis's voice rose in excitement. "We would have a purpose."

Adlai considered all that had been said. "Writing and reading can be taught during times of rest. All would come to know the Lord from the pages of history. Today's training would lead us into tomorrow's victories. Let's pray, requesting the Lord's direction."

As the men prayed, Reut slipped away to clean the bowls from the evening meal. She had many wafers left. She covered them with a cloth and tucked them under the canvas flap of their wagon. She would deal with the extras later.

She felt elated that she had spoken her mind in front of the men, for she had been uneasy ever since setting up camp here. At the water, a man watched her. He did not say anything, only sharpened his dagger with vehemence. She did not feel safe.

After seeing what God had done to Egypt, she had no desire to ask Him for protection. But she would feel better with a few more men who knew how to wield a sword.

It was late by the sign of the stars. Adlai could not believe how quickly they had organized the men for training. Moses had been enthusiastic. Former Hebrew soldiers were willing to train the men. Joshua would help with drills. The cloud of fire hovered over them as they planned, as if the Lord approved. Adlai walked to his tent, whistling.

Reut's words had led them to this plan. He had been surprised by her discernment. True, her skills may not be equal to Carmel's, but she was just a little girl. He sighed. Carmel had reminded him, that afternoon, that she was a young woman, growing up too fast.

He must ask her about this danger that she felt by the water. What could he do to protect her?

CHAPTER 5

Miriam began to fan the embers of her fire into flames. For fuel she added bits of animal dung gathered from the flocks outside of camp. She would have Moses's flatbread made before he had risen. She smiled to herself. Moses needed her. Without her, he would forget to eat.

The fire was ready. She retrieved the basket of manna wafers that she had saved from yesterday. Removing the linen covering, her stomach rolled at a stench like rotting meat. The manna had turned into a slimy mass, crawling with worms. She gagged and held the basket away from her.

Hurrying outside the camp, Miriam looked for a spot to bury the entire mess, making sure no one saw her. She could only hope some desert animal would not uncover her secret.

How had Moses known they should not save any manna for the next day? Could he really hear the Words of God?

It was no longer like it had been as they were growing up. She was the elder sister, respected, admired, and appreciated. She had saved Moses's life by watching him in the basket in the Nile; then reunited their mother with Moses by suggesting to the princess that she knew of a certain Hebrew nursemaid who could care for the infant.

When Moses became an important man in the palace, he forgot about her. He had helped Aaron get an apprenticeship as a doctor, but she was ignored. Couldn't he have arranged a wealthy Hebrew to marry her? When Moses had fled Egypt, she remained stranded in her lowly state of life.

When they had crossed the Reed Sea, she had led the worship and praise. She liked the way it made her feel. How could she use Moses's position to influence the people? The women respected her. They listened to what she said. She felt important. Could she make Moses follow her counsel to increase her influence?

Reut woke early. Tamara had asked to go with her to gather manna this morning. She glanced at her sister, sprawled over the pallet that they shared. Tamara had again kicked her all night.

As she retrieved the bowl of wafers saved from last night, Reut was pleased with herself. She would not have the tedious work of gathering manna this morning, thanks to her foresight. She would make the bread before anyone else awoke.

She lifted the linen covering from the bowl. She tried to quiet her gags as the awful stench rose to her nose and she saw the writhing white worms. She sputtered and coughed as she ran from the tent to throw away the rotten manna and clean the bowl before Tamara woke and informed the entire campsite that she had disobeyed the Lord's command.

Grabbing her cloak, she hurried to the pool before anyone else wakened. She slipped, dumping the contents down her tunic and cloak. She knelt by the water to scrub her clothes. Everyone would know that she had disobeyed. She felt like the light from God's glory was shining on her for everyone to see. How could she ever hide from that light?

She heard a soft step right behind her. "Tamara, don't you dare tell anybody!"

A man answered her. "Don't worry, I won't."

Reut turned, startled.

The man, who had watched her at the water, stood behind her. His eyes held a look of desire.

She screamed.

His rough hand snaked out and covered her mouth.

Her scream came out like a muted yelp. Would anyone hear? She bit his hand, tasting his uncleanness. She spit, but his hand held fast.

He grabbed her, lifting her off the ground. His touch made her feel unclean, like the maggots down at her feet.

Reut did not think, she only responded, fighting, kicking and pelting him with her fists. No one would control her.

He cursed, tightening his hold. Tossing her to the ground, he held her arms behind her back. He jammed his knee into her back, smashing her face into the sand. He fumbled with his belt, using it to tie her arms together.

The coarse hemp cut into her skin. A memory of a slave in Egypt who had run away came to Reut's mind. She had watched the slave submit after a beating that left him motionless. Ropes around his arms had only insured his submission. Reut had the ropes, but she had not submitted. She could not.

She turned her head to scream, but could only spit sand before he jammed a filthy cloth into her mouth. It smelled of dung, smoke, and animals. She gagged. Her insides rolled. She closed her eyes, concentrating on breathing deeply through her nose. She had to think. She must be calm.

He lifted her to her feet and held her tightly against his body, hissing in her ear. His hot breath smelled of old food. His clothes reeked of unwashed man's smell. "You have seen the last of your people. You are mine."

She swallowed, gulping air around the rag. Who was this man? Was he of their people? Where would he take her? She could not let him take her away. She stomped on his foot.

Cursing, he jumped, loosening his hold on her waist.

She struggled free, only to stumble, and fall at his feet.

Having recovered from his shock, he laughed. "A girl with fight! I like that." He picked her up, half carrying, half dragging her away from camp.

She took her last look at the campsite. Her bowl lay abandoned in the sand. Would she ever return?

No one was awake this early. She had not even heard the baby crying in the tent beside theirs, a regular sign that the day had started. When would someone know she was gone?

The man paused at the boulders on the other side of the water.

She fought his grip.

He slapped her face. "Enough!"

She bit her tongue, tasting blood. She faced him. How dare this man touch her! She was never a slave to be treated with contempt. She would not be treated like one now. She glared at him.

His eyes crinkled in an unaccustomed smile. "You will soon submit. They all do." He raised his hand over her face.

She flinched.

He laughed. He touched her face with his rough hand, as if he were touching a fine vessel of wine to appraise its value.

Reut cringed. Could hands feel evil? She recoiled, backing against the boulder behind her. She wanted to crumble in a heap, anything to get away from his touch.

But she refused to look away. She would not allow him to see her fear. She could not let him win. She clenched her fists, willing her insides not to shake.

He nodded and smiled. His eyes spoke evil.

Reut blinked, no longer able to stare at him. She could read his evil. She felt unclean. She closed her eyes, cowering away from his soft caress.

He smacked her again. "Look at me."

Startled, she opened her eyes.

He leaned his face into hers. His lips brushed against hers, in spite of the rag still wedged in her mouth.

She shivered. Could her legs keep her standing? She wanted to wipe her lips, to smack him, to run. She was wedged against the boulder and his body. She could not move.

The image of the slave came to mind again. She had watched him struggle until he could not breathe. She was still breathing. She must fight. She thrust back her shoulders.

He whispered, "You are mine."

A noise from the campsite made him turn.

She dared not move her face from his, but her mind raced to what she could do.

He lifted her over his shoulders and carried her like a sack of wheat away from camp.

With her head upside down, she thumped against his back as he twisted around boulders. She felt like a leaf tossed by a sandstorm. How could she fight now?

Her amulet fell from her neck and bounced against her eyes. Could any god protect her now? Was she beyond the Lord's reach?

Reut's mouth hurt where he had smacked her. She swallowed. She tasted the stench of the rag.

Fighting panic, she focused on something else. Michael came to her mind. His eyes twinkled when he spoke. He enjoyed life. When she had watched him talk with the men at the meal, he had caught her staring and returned her look with a smile. His smile was contagious. She had felt her face grow hot. She had lowered her eyes, but smiled.

Her hair caught in a bush, jarring her from her thoughts. This man had only touched her face, but she felt defiled. She would not let him touch her again. She must escape.

The man continued to walk, not even pausing to yank her hair loose from the bush. He weaved between boulders, heading toward the cliffs where she would never be found.

She must fight. She wiggled and squirmed.

He dropped her, maintaining his hold. He leered at her.

She lowered her eyes.

He grabbed her chin, forcing her to look at him. His long crooked nose touched hers. He hissed, "You are mine."

She swallowed, closing her eyes.

He removed the rag, sticking his fingers far into her mouth.

She spit in his face.

He jerked; then laughed. "A wild cat, eh? Not the Egyptian snob I thought you were." He pressed his lips against hers.

She backed away, but he wrapped his arms around her waist, holding her tight, as if he owned her. She recoiled, shivering. Her body stiffened. She held her breath, still smelling his uncleanness. She closed her eyes. How could she escape?

If he would loosen his hold for just a moment... She fought her repulsion, relaxing in his arms.

He pushed against her body. His grip lessened.

She needed more space.... She tilted her head and stood on her toes to meet his lips.

He covered her lips with his. He held her against him.

She fought her disgust, relaxing, leaning into him. He would not control her. She had enough room, now. She had to be quick. She snapped her leg upward and made contact.

He grunted, sucking in air. He hunched over. "You *daughter of Lot!*"

Reut fled from his weakened grasp. She ran clumsily, as her hands were tied behind her.

She almost smiled. At least her submission would not be easy for him. *Lot's* daughters had deceived their father after escaping destruction from Sodom. They coerced him to drink so they could have incest to carry on his line. Reut had to escape this man's evil.

She heard him gaining on her. She ran faster, tripping over a boulder. She stumbled, yet kept on her feet.

He grabbed her, jamming the rag into her mouth. He smacked her. When her face was turned from him, he backhanded it. "Look at me! I am saving you from this people."

She would not allow him to see her fear. She looked into his, her hatred for him obvious. She tried not to flinch. She breathed through the rag, catching her breath.

He smiled, but showed no pleasure. "That's better." He breathed into her face. "You will be all mine, tonight. But for now, you will disappear. You have made it easy for me."

Reut bit her lip. She had run away from camp instead of closer to it!

He smacked her in the face again. "You are ready to go, yes?"

Reut nodded. She had been so close to escape. She tried to keep tears from pooling in her eyes. She stumbled as he dragged her across more boulders and granite pathways.

A few more feet revealed a hole chiseled by flood rains of many seasons. The hole was not visible unless you were nearly on top of it.

He tied her feet with a cord from his cloak's pocket. Picking her up, he dropped her into the hole. He pushed her, forcing her to fit through the tight hole. "Wait for my return tonight." He laughed. "You have seen the last of this people."

Reut cringed as something slithered over her hand. She shrieked, but no sound came through the rag. The hole grew dark. Startled, she looked up.

He had covered the opening with a boulder. No light entered.

Fear froze her heart. What animals shared this hole with her? She screamed, without hearing any sound. It was like being closed in a jar with no sound, no air, no moisture. Was this what it was like to be buried alive?

Closing her eyes, she forced herself to slow her breathing and tried to think. What should she do? Working her tongue near the front of her mouth, she pushed on the rag. It would not move.

She must concentrate. She scraped her face on the wall. Chunks of dirt crumbled and fell. She bruised her lips, but the rag did not budge. If she would not submit to this man, why would she resign herself to this rag being stuck in her mouth! She banged her head on the wall in defeat. Tears of frustration filled her eyes and she could not even wipe them away.

If only she had obeyed. Tamara would have gone with her. She wouldn't have gone to the water by herself.

Thinking of water made her realize how thirsty she was. The rag sucked away her moisture. Her tongue felt like a board covered in sand. And she had to surrender to a rag jammed in her mouth!

How long could she resist this man? She was already weary.

Who could help her?

Her abba's stories came to mind. He had told of Abraham going to Egypt. He feared the pharaoh would kill him for his wife. He told his wife to lie about being his. The king took her.

The Friend of Abraham protected Abraham's wife. The king did not touch her, but returned her to Abraham. Abraham's God had protected her.

She sat forward, looking at the opening, even though it was darker than a moonless night with no stars. She saw a glimmer of hope. If this God could help Abraham's wife, maybe He was a God Who gave good. Could she believe Him before she saw His goodness? Or did she have to see before she could believe?

What about her disobedience with the manna? The darkness of the hole reminded her of how she felt after seeing His glory in the desert. He had seen her wickedness, and it did not please Him. How could she hope to please such a God?

Hope died within her. She was not worthy of this God's help. She could only hope that tonight would not come. She wasn't sure that was enough hope.

Michael woke early, a troubling heaviness in his spirit, prompting him to leave his tent and walk.

Last night he had felt invigorated. They had discussed how to organize the people to read and to fight.

Why then this urge, this morning, to flee to the desert? He had felt these promptings before when he needed to tell the Lord his frustrations. But today, he had none.

He left the tents behind, watching his feet and his horizon. It would not do to startle a snake and be left paralyzed or dead by its bite.

As he walked, he thought of Adlai's daughter. She was a bold one, speaking to him privately, then speaking her mind in the midst of men. When she had retold her account of the man at the water to her father and the men, her dark eyes had flashed, first with fear of the man watching her, and then with anger that anyone would think of controlling her. Her eyes spoke, leaving a message on his heart.

He looked across the water pool, catching a sudden movement on the other side. A man dragged a bundle behind a boulder. His heart thudded as he recognized the blue cloak of Adlai's daughter.

Michael ran, watching the ground as he would while hunting. He noticed the vessel at the water's edge. He smelled the spilled manna with maggots. He noticed the footprints by the vessel, even as he hurried by them. The man had approached from behind. The girl had struggled. He looked again at the boulders. They had left.

Drawing his dagger, he ran after them. He should see them. He had not been far behind them.

This man knew his way, for the path twisted and turned several times between boulders and around cliffs. Michael halted and listened. No tracks were made here, as the path continued over boulders. He smelled again the odor at the water. He looked for signs, but found nothing. He had not been far behind them. He should see them. Yet they had vanished.

He stooped, studying the ground. He understood waiting. While hunting, he had learned patience to wait the right moment to kill his meal. It did not help to hurry. But that was for hunger. Hunger could wait. This was not just a meal that he would miss if he did not find the tracks. He did not want to consider what would happen to the girl, if he did not find her.

He could see her dark, flashing eyes, studying him from the dark corner yesterday at dinner. He could not dismiss the beating of his own heart toward the girl with the bold spirit that captured his thoughts.

The sun rose and shed its light. The sun would cook the surface of the sand soon. His thirst went unnoticed. He paced, finally settling against one of the boulders, thinking. Leaning his head back, he listened. Where could they have gone?

He concentrated. He felt no stirring to continue his search.

A lizard scurried across the sand after an insect.

A falcon perched high on the cliffs, overlooking his position.

He settled back and waited.

The boulders offered no sound.

Did the sand and sky swallow her?

Anger filled him. Could the women not be safe with their own people?

Tamara woke, feeling the pallet for Reut. It was empty. She had not waited for her, again! Tamara's lips puckered into a pout. She left the tent, grabbing her cloak. Her sandals made no sound as she left the tents, heading to the water where she knew Reut would be.

Something lay abandoned at the water's edge as she approached. Picking it up, she smelled the odor and felt the squirming mass of the maggot-covered manna. She flung it away from her.

The vessel looked familiar. Lifting her tunic to avoid the maggots, she turned the vessel over with her foot. Her mother's signature was etched on the bottom. Why would Reut leave their dish? And where was Reut anyway? Tamara scanned the desert.

Fear grabbed her.

She shivered. Something must be wrong. Grabbing the vessel, she ran to their tent. "Abba!"

Adlai opened the tent flap. "Tamara, hush! You'll wake the camp."

She pushed the vessel into his hands. "Reut is gone! I found this at the water."

Adlai turned it over in his hands. He traced the emblem with his fingertip. "You looked around camp?"

Carmel approached behind him. "She wouldn't leave our vessel and wander the desert. She goes to gather water in the morning and then comes home."

Adlai put on his sandals and grabbed his cloak. "Tamara, have Nathan meet me at the water."

Carmel met Adlai's eyes. "Where could she be?"

As Adlai ran, his mind whirled. When they had gone without water, he had been helpless to provide for his family. His wife had been close to death. When Tamara had almost drowned, he had watched, again helpless.

Was it just last night that Reut had spoken of her fears of the man? Why hadn't he cautioned her about going to the water alone?

If it had been Tamara missing, it would be different. He would have searched everyone's tents for her new friend.

But Reut was quiet, responsible, and...Adlai shuddered. Mature. Carmel had told him that she was growing up. His little girl was growing into a woman.

Adlai reached the water and studied the mess of manna.

Nathan startled Adlai, touching his shoulder. "What is it?"

Adlai nodded to Ellis who joined them. "Reut is missing. Tamara found our vessel by the water." He handed their vessel to Nathan.

He pointed to the footprints in the sand by the water's edge. "She was here. Someone came behind her." Following the story past the waterhole, they lost it in the dry sand.

Adlai paced beside Reut's footprints. His head felt numb. Why hadn't he asked Reut about that man last night? What kind of father was he, that he couldn't even protect his own daughter?

Women started coming for water.

Ellis said, "The camp's waking up. We should tell Moses."

Adlai stared without hearing. How could people continue like nothing happened? His daughter was missing! Adlai ran towards the women. "Don't come to the water alone! It's unsafe."

The women backed away from him, gathering their water and hurrying back to camp. They looked over their shoulder at him before entering the campsite again.

Nathan squeezed Adlai's shoulder. "Stop, Adlai. You're frightening the women."

Ellis hissed for Nathan's attention, nodding at a man coming from the boulders on the other side of the water. "That's the man that she spoke about. I'll follow him."

Nathan directed Adlai to his tent.

Adlai paced within his tent. His expression hindered any comfort. What could he do?

Nathan hugged Carmel. "Shalom."

Carmel clung to her brother. "Peace seems far away." She gulped, "I keep hoping she's just lost.

Nathan squeezed her. "We'll tell Moses. The cloud doesn't move. That gives us time."

Adlai stopped pacing. He was poised, ready to strike like a serpent. "Time? For what? For some man to work his evil on my daughter?"

Carmel gasped.

"Don't look at me like you haven't thought it, Carmel. That's what's happening. And I sit and do nothing!"

Carmel's shoulders slumped. "What can you do?"

Tamara spoke, looking at her father for approval. "I could check the neighboring tents to see if any have seen her."

Adlai shouted. "No!" He never shouted. What was wrong with him? He gentled his voice, but spoke with force. "Tamara, you will not leave this tent."

Carmel soothed. "She wants to do something..."

Adlai held Tamara's gaze. "I have already lost one daughter. I cannot lose another."

Nathan interceded. "Tamara, think of who may have seen her. I'll find some men who can search." He turned to Adlai. "If the man returned alone, she is hidden somewhere. If he is not with her, she is safe for now."

Adlai could only nod, but not believe.

Moses found Maessai packing. "Going somewhere?"

Maessai grunted. "Aren't we always going somewhere? Do you want to stay here?"

Moses nodded. "We will soon be settled in our Land."

Maessai laughed. "Our Land? Our Land is owned by some of the cruelest warriors that are known. You bring these people to their death, either by this desert without water or by the Land that you promise."

Moses looked at the cloud. It always calmed his words. "We search for Adlai's daughter. She is missing."

Maessai grunted. "In this desert? Good luck."

Moses laid his hand on Maessai's pack. "You know where she is."

Maessai stopped packing. Then he shrugged. "What is one maiden among so many?"

"She is special to Adlai and to God."

"God did not think my wife was special, when He smote her with His fire."

Moses tightened his grip on the pack. "Do you hold God's actions against your own and find them equal?"

Maessai lifted the pack to his shoulder and moved outside his tent. "I care not for this God nor for His actions, as long as He leaves what belongs to me alone."

Moses followed him outside the tent. He tapped his staff on the ground. "There's a problem...What you think is yours is God's. And He will fight you for it until He wins."

Maessai challenged Moses with his eyes. "Then there will be a fight, won't there?"

Adlai paced as he looked at the sun. It was rising quickly. Time did not stop.

The men had gathered at the water's edge. Nathan informed them, "We last saw her prints here. She may be hidden in the boulders and cliffs."

Moses stepped forward. "I questioned the man that we suspect. He admits to nothing."

Nathan nodded. "Ellis watches him. He packs like he's leaving, so we don't have much time. Separate into groups. Yell when you find anything. Anything else?" Nathan looked around the group for any other comments.

Moses stepped forward. "Let's request God's help."

Adlai sighed. Another delay. Every minute she was gone meant she was still in danger.

Nathan squeezed Adlai's shoulder as Moses prayed.

Adlai could feel his muscles relax under Nathan's hand. But it did nothing for his fears.

After Moses finished, Adlai was the first to leave. He would search those hills until he found her.

Nathan quickened his stride to walk with him.

They had walked most of the morning. Their pace had been frantic at first, pushed by the fears of Adlai's mind. Their pace finally slowed, not because his fears were gone, but because his body could not keep up with his fears.

Nathan paused long enough to catch his breath. "Your family leans on your faith."

Adlai shook his head. "Where is He now?"

Nathan looked the way they had come. They were in the midst of boulders that had many crevices. They searched each one. He looked back to the cloud that led them. "This is not the brother-in-law who taught me to know God. The Evil One questions your faith and causes doubts of your God."

Adlai breathed deeply and looked at the cliff in front of them. "Reut was taken from me when just a child. Now she is taken again."

Nathan nodded. "Seems like yesterday when she was a baby."

Adlai looked back at Nathan. "Carmel reminded me that she is ready to marry."

"Marry?"

Adlai searched a depression in the hill. It was big enough for a small animal's den. They moved toward another. "I've missed my daughter's life."

Nathan slipped on some loose gravel and caught himself. "Time goes too fast."

Adlai looked at the sun's progress in the sky. He sighed. "I fear I'm too late."

Nathan paused to look at the sun's position. He shook his head. "You once told me God's time was perfect. Remember Joseph's bones? Joseph's request was fulfilled because you believed God's Words. His bones now lie in Moses's wagon because of your faith."

Adlai shrugged. "It was easy to believe when it was a dead man's bones. This is my daughter." He felt Nathan's scrutiny, as if he tested his next words.

"Abraham had to sacrifice his son." Nathan reached another cave.

Adlai followed, his thoughts on Abraham's test. Abraham did not kill his son. God had stopped him. But he had to be willing to sacrifice his son to prove his love for God. Could he do that with his daughter?

Nathan peered into the cave, then continued toward another.

Adlai caught up with him. "I just want my little girl safe with me."

Nathan nodded. "Who owns your little girl?"

Adlai pressed his lips together. He shook his head. He could feel the tears burning the inside of his eyes. He did not want someone else to have his girl, not even God.

Adlai felt empty. He had fought in his mind all morning over what he should or should not have done to protect not only Reut, but Tamara, and his wife. His thoughts whirled around but did not find answers. He saw God reaching for his little girl, but he held her tightly. His hands clasped tightly around her. God had shaken His head and begun to turn away. "No!" Adlai leaned against the cliff, hiding his face in his arm. If God turned His back on him, what hope did he have? If God did not protect, how could they be safe? He must let go. Could he allow God to do what He wanted with Reut?

Adlai and Nathan returned for news. Adlai's mind was numb. He did not feel the hot sun on his back as it moved through the sky. When he entered their tent, his one look at Carmel's tear-streaked face confirmed there was no good news. He choked down a few bites of flatbread, but they only made his insides turn and his head ache.

Carmel startled him by touching his arm.

He hugged her. "What could I have done to protect her?"

Carmel shook her head.

"I didn't protect her when she was five years old."

Carmel squeezed him and leaned back to look into his face. Adlai had met her when she was a servant of Amunet's. In order to marry, they had promised their first girl as servant when she became of age. "She had to fulfill my *mohar*. Without it, we could not marry."

"I felt as if I became a slave that day."

Carmel nodded. "We both cried."

"Her loss was almost like death."

Carmel looked at the embers that had grown cold. "But God delivered all His people from Pharaoh. She was set free."

Adlai tried to smile. "It was almost as if I had been the slave set free.

Carmel did smile. "Our family was united again."

"But when you almost died without water..." He choked on his words.

Carmel held him tighter. "But God provided."

He still did not look at her. "And Tamara almost died in that pool of bitter water. I couldn't even save her from drowning." Who was he even deceiving to think that he could protect anyone?

Carmel's words were like soothing oil poured over his aching heart. "God still protects. He holds our girls in His arms."

He looked through the tent opening.

Carmel followed his glance. "While you searched, I could either ask God why or give God praise. I had to trust Him or I would fall apart. I know He protects our Reut."

Adlai studied Carmel's face. She had calmness and peace. Adlai's voice cracked, "I should have protected her!"

Carmel shook her head. "Against the entire world? Adlai, that is for God to do."

Adlai picked up the dipper to drink, but then threw it down again. "She's my little girl!"

Carmel's voice was gentle and firm, "She's God's girl. You've told me that. That's how we could give her to Amunet to serve in Egypt. That's how we can wait for her to look to Him." Carmel sighed. "Maybe this will lead her to look to Him."

Adlai shrugged. "I'm not sure I'm even looking to Him."

Carmel nodded. "Sometimes I feel like I'm sinking. The sand sifts under me. The wind blows through me. A whirlwind rushes around me. I question God. I doubt Him. I blame Him." Her eyes had filled with tears.

Adlai stepped toward her and rubbed her back. That's where he was: questioning, doubting, blaming.

Carmel swallowed. "But, I see the future darkly. He's already there with the answers. I know there is rock under me. The sand may sift, but the rock stays firm. And I know He has our Reut."

Adlai wiped away her tears. It sounded so simple. Yet so hard.

Carmel rested her head on his shoulder. "Let God be God."

Reut had fallen asleep out of exhaustion. When she woke, she shook her head to remind herself where she was. She bumped it against the wall. The memories were not just a nightmare.

She leaned back. What time was it? Would he come soon? She shifted where she sat, unable to feel her arms. Even her legs tingled from lack of movement. She rubbed her face against her shoulder trying to wipe his feeling from her face. She sighed.

She sighed? She did it again, breathing deeply. Where was the rag? How had it fallen out of her mouth? She had tried everything to remove it. Had this God done it? Could He care enough to do that for her?

She started to thank Him, but stopped. She felt heat flush her face. She strained against the rope on her arms. He was the reason she was here. If He didn't give so many rules to follow, she wouldn't be scrubbing maggots from their jar!

She stopped. No, she was to blame. She did not follow His rules.

She threw her head back and screamed, "Lord, You win. I'll obey." Screaming reminded her of her thirst. She licked her dry lips, tasting the rags odors. She shuddered, wiping her lips against her cloak. That only got sand in her mouth, so she licked her lips again. She tried to spit, but could not make any moisture.

The hole felt cool. Was evening coming? When would he come? She panicked. Would she never see her family again?

She closed her eyes and saw his eyes, peering at her like she was just a piece of...she shook her head, bumping it against the side of the wall. Maybe he wouldn't return, and she would just die in this hole. Wouldn't that be better than if he did return? She screamed in anguish. "Don't come for me!"

What would her family do? Tamara. Even her chattering and non-stop movement would not annoy her now. Her ima. Calm, reassuring, wanting her to be the proper lady, even in the midst of sand and tents. Beneath her reassurance, Reut could see her tears. Her abba. She gasped at his image. His face was ragged. He looked haggard, beyond his years. His hair had turned grey. His face old. He would never stop his search for her. My abba! Her head sagged against her knees. She would never see her family. She felt no hope.

After losing the trail, he had felt compelled to stay here, but he did not know why. The sun had made Michael drowsy. He had dozed.

He woke with a start. What had wakened him? He leaned on the rock beside him, listening. A muted noise came from under it. Now that he looked at the rock, it seemed out of place. His heart skipped a beat. He heard a noise again. He lifted the rock, exposing a hole. Peering into the blackness, he saw a figure huddled at the bottom. "Daughter of Adlai, is that you?"

"Lord, is that You?"

Michael laughed. His relief flowed from him. She was safe! "It's just me, Michael. Are you able to stand?"

"I can't feel my arms and legs. They're tied."

"I'll lift you." Michael reached into the pit and grabbed her arms. He lifted her out of the hole and held her close to him, steadying her. He studied her. She still lived. Her face was covered with dirt and scratches. "You are well?"

She nodded, keeping her head down. Her hair fell around her face. Her shoulders slumped.

Her quietness alarmed Michael. This was not the girl who had spoken her mind last night. What had that man done to her? Michael cut the ties on her arms and feet. He rubbed them, bringing movement to them. "Wait until the tingling stops before you stand."

She leaned against him as she sat, her head down.

Michael looked anxiously into her face. "Can you feel your feet now?"

She nodded and leaned on him to stand. He held her as she stood, watching protectively.

Reut grabbed his cloak with both hands and hid her face against him. "He said that he would come back for me, that I would never see my family, that I was his."

Michael looked at her dark, tangled hair. He felt her small frame against his. "The Lord wouldn't let you go."

It was as if the dam had broken loose and her tongue was set free. "I was just cleaning out Ima's vessel. I didn't encourage him. I didn't see him. He grabbed me and carried me away from my family." She fell against him, shaking.

He held her, patting her back. He felt helpless to take away her pain. Her face lay hidden in the folds of his cloak. Anger toward this man seethed in his blood. What man could do this to her?

She pulled away from his chest. Her tears made a trail on her face. She wiped her face, streaking it with dirt.

Michael offered the front of his cloak.

She gave a choked laugh. Embarrassed, but taking his cloak, she wiped her face. "I've left a mess." She wiped at his cloak with her soiled hand.

He squeezed her hand in his. "Nothing that can't be washed." He ran his finger over her cheek. "You are hurt."

She winced. "He didn't like it when I spit at him."

Michael laughed. "Nor would I, my fighter. Where else did he hurt you?" He searched her eyes.

She rubbed her hands over her lips and shook her head.

He nodded. He swallowed the anger that boiled for this man who would touch her. "Are your legs strong enough? I must return you to your family. They must fear for you."

Stepping back, she nodded.

He held her waist as they walked toward camp.

When they reached the water pool, no one was there. The heat of the sun had driven all to take their rest.

They drank.

She splashed water over her face and scrubbed. She submerged her arms, rubbing sand over them. Her voice broke. "I can't wash away his touch."

Michael watched her. "Only by replacing his touch with the Lord's healing can that be done."

She stopped scrubbing. "How would He heal me?"

Michael skipped a stone as he looked across the pond. "When I tell Him my thoughts, my heart's thoughts, He changes what is inside of me to be pleasing to Him."

She tilted her head as she considered. "Why would you want to please Him?"

"He is worthy."

She shook her head. "But my good is worthless. So how could I please Him?"

Michael smiled. "He takes it and makes it pleasing. We just submit to His wishes."

She shook her head. "I don't submit very well."

"You called me 'Lord.' That's submitting."

She blushed. "Yes, I did, didn't I?" She lowered her head. "He only desires my service."

"He doesn't want service until He has you."

She stared at the trail they had just walked. "I fear to serve a God Who controls so much. I cannot control Him."

He laughed. "No, you can't. But do you control anything?"

She stared at her reflection. She pushed back her hair from her face. She wiped her hands over her face. "I'm a mess." She glanced at Michael. "But if He could control this man, why would He allow him to hurt me?"

Michael pushed his own hair away from his forehead. "Would you look to Him without hardship?"

She started to answer, then shook her head.

"He seeks you to know Him. Maybe your attention is hard to get."

Reut rubbed her arms. "What kind of caring God is that?"

"A God Who wants you so much that He would fight all evil to draw you to Himself."

"I don't understand this God."

Michael laughed. "Would He be God if you could?"

She pushed herself to stand and walked away from him, ending their conversation.

He stood, wiping his wet hands on his cloak. Had he said too much?

She paused on the path, waiting for him. She no longer needed his support.

His hands felt empty at his sides. Before reaching her tent, Michael stopped. "Daughter of Adlai, what is your name, if I may be so bold as to ask?"

She smiled. "You are not bold. You saved me. My name is Reut."

"Reut," Michael repeated. It rolled off his tongue like music. "The Lord saved you; I'm just His instrument. But I would help again if I knew how."

Moses pondered what the Lord, the good and perfect Judge, would decree. Moses knew what the man could have done, but Reut had been spared. His crime was only stealing her. Yet no woman would feel safe with him in camp.

Moses called him to his tent, with Aaron, Adlai, Michael, and Nathan as witnesses. "Maessai, your sin has caused great sorrow in the camp and in the household of Adlai. What payment do you think worthy of the shame you have caused?"

Maessai glared at Moses.

Moses sighed. The people had no written law to dictate punishment. Women were possessions. If a girl was raped, the offender must marry her. After all, the offspring would be his. But in this case, the offense had only been kidnapping, not abuse. Still, marriage would hinder further theft. Moses studied Maessai. He remembered him from the water pool when the women were burned. This man would bow his knee to no one. Nor would he treat the girl with kindness. Moses glanced at the cloud again. This was one part of his job he did not like. "Do you wish to marry Adlai's daughter?"

Maessai did not speak.

Michael interrupted, "I don't—"

Adlai shook his head.

Michael stopped. He pursed his lips and clenched his fists.

Moses cleared his throat and started again. "Maessai, you give me no choice. I fine you before this court of witnesses ten pieces of silver for the damage to Adlai's daughter. Also, you must leave the camp by tomorrow morning at sunrise. You are not welcome at any campfire of our people."

Maessai reached into the folds of his cloak and drew out the bag of gems given by the vizier. Dumping its contents into his hand, he picked out the required payment and threw it at Adlai's feet. "She was mine without payment."

"She didn't belong to you." Michael stepped forward again.

"Egypt's plagues are too good for you," Maessai spat as he stalked out.

Moses breathed deeply and looked at Adlai. "Will that be satisfactory?"

Adlai did not answer, but closed his eyes.

Michael interjected, "He holds hate in his eyes and evil in his heart. Will she be safe until he leaves?"

Moses sighed. "We cannot remove evil from the nation. We can only encourage him to choose good. The Lord must give this people a heart to obey Him."

Adlai clenched his fists. "His offense merits the punishment, but my revenge desires more. I never wished so much evil on a man before."

Moses nodded. "Take it before the Lord, and leave it there."

Maessai stalked from camp to load his donkeys. His possessions lay packed, ready. He would leave the camp without the girl tonight.

Ever since he had found her, he knew she was the one for him. Catching her by herself had been too easy. She had practically walked into his hands. The fact that she had disobeyed Moses's words proved that she did not belong here.

He smacked his donkey on the back, startling it. She had slipped through his fingers, but not for long. He would watch for the right moment. Since he had paid for her, in a hefty sum of silver, she was as good as his.

He could still hear his mother's words, growing up. "Maessai, you're the most tenacious child. You get what you want."

Well, how else could he get anything? Everything had been given to his oldest brother. Maessai laughed bitterly. The death angel had taken care of that obstacle.

His second brother was good at begging for things. He followed anyone who had something to give. He had stayed behind to beg from the Egyptians, who had nothing to give him.

That left Maessai to get what he wanted. He liked it that way. He depended on no one. And no one, not even Moses, would hinder him from having the maiden with the blue cloak.

As he walked from Moses' tent, Adlai tried not to think of what justice he would give to Maessai. The pieces of silver clinked in his cloak's pocket, reminding him of his failure to protect his family. He wanted to throw them as far away from him as he could.

Michael joined him, interrupting his thoughts. "Was the judgment to your liking?"

Adlai sighed. "We have no law to judge by. Cain killed Abel and he went free with a mark on his head. Shouldn't I be pleased that my daughter lives? I won't tell you what my heart cries for."

Michael fingered his dagger in its sheath. "I could tell you what justice I would give. The buzzards would not find a single piece of him!"

Adlai placed his hand on Michael's shoulder. "I don't understand God's justice. Much is missing for us to form a nation."

Michael nodded. "Much would be missing from Maessai if I

would execute justice."

Adlai sighed again, weariness filling his heart. "How do I protect my family? If I had, Reut would not have been taken."

Michael shook his head. ""You cannot be everywhere. You cannot stop all evil. That is for God to do."

Adlai shrugged. "Carmel said the same thing."

Michael looked at the cloud. "Why do we prepare our people for battle?"

"To fight for our Land, to protect our own..."

"That's what you do for your family. You teach them to recognize the evil for what it is, to avoid the evil when possible, but also to fight the evil when necessary. You want to stop all evil. That is for God to do. If He does not, we are truly a hopeless people."

They walked for a time without speaking.

Adlai rattled the silver in his pocket. "Please, take these." He held them out for Michael to take.

Michael shook his head. "I didn't save Reut for a reward."

Adlai motioned toward the cloud. "Take it. Not for your service, although I'm indebted to you, but as a help to me. I don't want it as a reminder. I will see that man's face before me in my sleep!"

Michael stopped walking and studied Adlai. Slowly, he took the offered silver. "It will help me buy horses."

"Horses?"

"To raise in the new Land. And so I can chase a man like him if he should ever touch your daughter again."

Adlai studied the man in front of him. "You will do well."

Michael cleared his throat. "Speaking of doing well... May I request your permission?"

"For what?"

"To visit your daughter."

Adlai silently thanked Carmel for preparing him. "Horses and Reut..." He laughed and nodded. "You will indeed do well."

Michael could not conceal his smile. "Perhaps we can both keep her safe."

Adlai added, "Or remind her of the One Who can."

Miriam stepped from the dark corner of the tent after Moses had judged Maessai and the men had gone. "Moses?"

Moses turned towards her, startled. "Miriam, I didn't realize you were here."

She brushed her hair from her face. "Moses, is that enough of a punishment for that man? He doesn't look repentant."

Moses sighed. "Miriam, I ask God for direction. He leads His people. Ask your question of Him."

Miriam huffed. "Do you really hear God's Words? Or do you just manipulate us to think that you do?"

Moses opened his mouth to say something, then shut it again. Finally he spoke. "Miriam, when I am judging the people, you do not belong in this tent. Is that understood?"

"I was only suggesting..."

"Not in this tent."

"I was cleaning your things."

Moses waited.

She nodded and left, but couldn't resist turning back on her way out. "You are not the leader that you think you are, my little brother."

CHAPTER 6

Zipporah brushed the flour off her hands as she looked out her doorway for Gershom and their flocks. Out of habit, she also looked to see if Moses was coming. How many times had she watched, hoping to see his return? She had heard of the Lord's deliverance of His people from Egypt. Moses's God had freed His people.... But they were not her people. She was Moabite. She wanted nothing to do with the Hebrews.

She wiped a stray hair away from her face before kneading the dough again. As she worked, she relived the last days spent with Moses. They had traveled towards Egypt in response to God's call. Moses had spoken of circumcising their two boys. She had refused. The issue had kept them distant.

One night, the Angel of the Lord had threatened Gershom's death. Moses had sat motionless while she circumcised their sons. The next morning Moses had sent them home, continuing on to Egypt alone. He was consumed with his God's mission.

Traveling merchants had brought news of plagues—water to blood, locusts, darkness. Finally the great exodus had happened.

Zipporah received no more news. No one left Egypt anymore. The country was like a skeleton picked clean in the sand.

Wasn't Moses finished with this people yet? They were free now, weren't they?

Zipporah shook her head. She knew Moses would not leave them. He would hold their hand as they meandered through every sand pile in the desert. She sighed.

But really, that was why she loved him and missed him. She wanted to hold his hand and have him walk through the struggles of sheep and goat care with her. She rolled the dough into a cake of bread. Thinking of Moses made her miss him more.

She tapped the bread one more time before standing to look for Gershom again. This time she could see him in the lower pasture, watering the sheep.

Gershom pushed the ewes with lambs toward the water, watching as they drank. He used his rod to guide them with all his six-year-old experience.

Zipporah wiped her hands down her tunic. Gershom was growing up too fast. He followed his father's footsteps. Would this God take her sons, too? He had already taken her husband

When would Moses send for her?

As a doctor, Phinehas had never treated battle wounds. In Egypt, he had treated the wealthy. They could pay him well, enabling him to live a comfortable life. He had found the lifestyle to his liking.

When a messenger came through the camp announcing the soldier training, Phinehas ignored him. Egypt commissioned slaves as soldiers. He was no slave to be sent out to fight.

He drifted to the outskirts of camp to watch.

He approached Moses. "Shalom."

Moses nodded. "Be at peace. Why are you not with our tribe?"

Phinehas glanced at his tribe where they drilled under their banner. Their bodies glistened with sweat.

He shrugged. "In Egypt, only the slaves were soldiers."

Moses glanced at Phinehas, his face amused. "I was a soldier."

Phinehas coughed. "Sorry, Uncle. I forgot. But being the General of the Army does not make you one of the lowly soldiers."

Moses raised his staff and nodded to Joshua who stood beside him.

Joshua yelled a command. The soldiers switched groups and began another drill.

Moses turned to Phinehas. "You will find one day that something you value must be protected. I hope that you will be ready."

Phinehas shrugged. He could protect what he valued. He squared his shoulders and walked away.

Returning to his campsite, he was drawn to look at the cloud. He shook himself. He could not forget the glory of this God. God made him feel inadequate, needy, unworthy.

Hakeen had told him he must know God in order to have Hannah, but he would not search for a God Who made him grovel on the ground and hide. This God was so much bigger. Would He take revenge on him if he didn't bow to Him?

Phinehas turned from the cloud and entered his tent. Could anyone really turn his back on a God Who owned so much glory?

But he wouldn't waste time thinking about that. He must focus on one thing—one battle—that of winning Hannah. Nothing would stop him from getting her.

The people gathered manna, for that was what they called it. Moses reminded them that in two days they would worship. It would be the Sabbath, the day God rested after He created His world. He had established a pattern since the beginning of time to give His people rest. The Israelites had not been permitted this rest in Egypt, but now they were free to remember it. God's cloud would not move, so that they would have the time to remember the Lord and honor Him.

Moses raised his hands to quiet the people and to call attention to his words. "Tomorrow, collect enough wafers for two days, so you will not have to work on the Sabbath."

Moses lifted a jar with an *omer* of manna to show the people. "I place this jar before the Lord's Testimony to remind future generations of the Lord's provisions when we had nothing."

When the Sabbath Day came, Moses rose early to hike a hill outside the campsite. He could watch the camp awaken for the day. He would prepare his heart to worship.

As he prayed, women came searching the ground. Such brash disobedience kindled his anger. This was the Sabbath! He caught sight of a figure coming from his tribe. Was that Miriam? Could she not obey his words?

Moses returned to the campsite. Instead of calmness from being in the Lord's presence, his heart was clouded in anger. He marched into Miriam's tent.

She stopped searching her vessels. "Moses, you startled me."

"Shalom. You didn't come to my campsite yet with the morning meal. I wondered if you were feeling well?"

Miriam's cheeks flushed. "No, I'm not."

"Where's the manna from yesterday, Miriam? I'll find someone to prepare it for you, so that you can rest."

She shook her head and bit her lip. "I couldn't eat a bite."

Moses persisted. "I could use some food."

Miriam dropped her shoulders. "I have none."

Moses took her by the shoulders. "Miriam, the Lord's Law applies to you. You must obey, like everyone else."

Miriam looked at him, her eyes blazing. "Why are you the only one who hears the Lord's voice? Can't He speak to others?"

Moses dropped his hold on her shoulders. "Are you listening to His Words?"

"I don't see that we should stop eating just because it's the Sabbath. We've gone four hundred years, working all the time. Now we must stop, and not even eat?"

Moses worked to keep his voice low. "We don't eat, Miriam, because you disobeyed. Next day before Sabbath, I suggest that you gather enough for two days."

Miriam entered Aaron's tent. She waited in the dark corner until Aaron finished speaking with someone who needed medical help. She tired of watching all these people, busy with their families. Without her own family to care for, she had time to see how things should be done. If Aaron led, she could help lead the people to their Land. She stepped forward. "Shalom."

Aaron nodded. "You do not find enough to do?"

Miriam shrugged. She fingered Aaron's cloak collar. "Don't you wonder why the people look to Moses, when you were the spokesman in Egypt?"

Aaron covered her hand with his own. "We lead together."

Miriam shook her head. "No, there can be only one leader. The people look to Moses, when they should look to you as the elder brother."

"Does it matter who leads, as long as our people reach the Promised Land?"

Miriam turned away from him and lowered her voice. "Will we make it to the Promised Land if Moses leads too harshly?"

Aaron sat on the cushions spread around his cook fire. "Why do you say he judges too harshly?"

Miriam sat beside him and patted his leg. "You lead the people with compassion. You understand the people."

Aaron laughed. "Moses doesn't soften his judgement, that's true."

"He's forgotten his family, in his pride of leading."

Aaron nodded. "He is busy."

Miriam shook her head. "He rules as if he were God." She studied Aaron's face by a sideways glance.

His forehead was creased, and his hands were clenched.

She smiled inwardly. He would think about her words. She could direct the people, if she could get Aaron more involved. He could be controlled.

Once the Sabbath ended, the cloud of the Lord moved. Israel entered the wilderness of Sin and camped at Rephidim. The cloud had stopped. The people began to prepare their campsites.

Nathan looked at the cloud and sighed. One day sifted into another. He rubbed his eyes. The sand burned them with its brightness. He pulled his tunic away from his body. Sweat had already evaporated, leaving a coating of grit. When would they reach their land? He looked at Salome.

She caught his eye and smiled. She needed to rest.

He grabbed their water vessels. "I'll return. You stay here."

She nodded.

Nathan hurried to the group gathered around Moses.

Already the people had picked up stones. "We need water. Why did we stop where there's no water?"

Nathan put down his vessel. His anticipation of bringing water to Salome was choked by the dryness of the sand at his feet. He looked again at the cloud. May God be pleased to give water.

Moses searched the crowd. "Instead of petitioning the Lord for your needs, you demand. How slowly you learn the Lord's ways!"

Nathan tried to swallow, his dry throat constricted.

Around Nathan, people threw stones. When he had watched the men beat the owner of the ox, he could do nothing. This time he was able to interfere, waving his arms. "Stop!" His yell spurred them to more anger.

They hurled stones at Moses as he walked from them. "We should've stayed in Egypt. We had all the water we needed. We thirst. You give nothing."

Nathan caught one man's arm before he could throw. "Think what you are doing!"

The man shoved him and threw his stone.

Moses walked away from the people up a hill and knelt, facing the cloud.

The people attempted to hit him with their stones, but he was too high up. They continued to chant. "Give us water!"

Nathan watched. How could Moses ignore the people? Could he hear the Lord's voice over this yelling? Nathan rubbed his eyes. The dust they had stirred by their rocks reminded him of his thirst. He licked his lips. They felt like the bottom of his feet, dry and hard.

Moses rose from his knees with the help of his staff. He walked to the boulder on the ledge of the hill where he prayed. Raising his arms over his head, he struck the rock with his staff.

Lightning fell from the cloud to the rock.

Cracking echoed around the cliff sides where they stood.

Nathan bowed his head to avoid the brightness of the light. He covered his head with his arms as rock pieces flew through the air.

The people stopped their chanting.

Nathan could hear dripping. He raised his head to watch the rock. The dripping increased to a stream of water pouring from the rock's center, falling over the side, pooling at his feet. As the water covered his feet and spread towards all the people, he raised his arms in worship. "May God be praised!"

The people dropped their rocks, fell to their knees in the water, and drank.

Nathan filled his vessel and pushed his way through the people to where Salome sat in the shade of their wagon. "The Lord has provided again."

Salome gulped the water from the dipper. "He is to be praised."

Adlai approached Moses at the tent of meeting. "Shalom."

Moses finished writing on the scroll in front of him. He laid down the quill and placed the lid on the ink. "Be at peace."

"What do you write?" Adlai leaned forward to read.

"I am recording the rock of Massah and Meribah" (where the Lord's people quarreled and tested Him by asking, "Is the Lord here?" And yet the Lord gave water.) Moses wiped his hands on a linen rag and gestured to a cushion beside him. "But that is not what you came to discuss. How's your family?"

"Fine."

Moses pressed. "Your daughter?"

"Reut remains bound by her fear."

"And you, my friend. How do you fare with the turmoil

within?"

Adlai sighed. "I came not to speak of this."

"Yes?"

"The men do well with the training, but do you have a leader? You are far too busy..."

"And too old." Moses laughed. "I know of no man better than Joshua. He leads the men with army training. The men follow him. When he isn't leading the drills, he searches to know the Lord at the door of the meeting tent."

Adlai nodded. "He will do well."

"I'll instate him in front of the assembly next Sabbath during worship."

"This training unites our people for the Lord's purposes and prepares us for our Land."

Moses drank from the dipper at his side. "He protects His people."

Adlai swallowed.

Moses leaned forward to study Adlai's face. "You have learned that you cannot protect your own. Have you not?"

Adlai looked at his hands. "My protection is as nothing."

"It is when we find we are not enough, that we find that our God is enough."

Adlai's voice cracked as he spoke. "I struggle to remember that."

Moses squeezed Adlai's shoulder. "The Lord teaches hard lessons in the desert, does He not?"

Joshua stood before the congregation on the following Sabbath.

Moses appointed him General of the Army. Aaron blessed him and poured oil over his head, anointing him for the Lord's service.

The people's cheers echoed over the desert.

Joshua bowed, accepting the position. He looked over the faces of the people, seeking his abba.

His father stood at the front of his tribe, his arms crossed, his face glowing with pride.

Joshua rocked on his toes and could not help but smile back. Caleb stood beside his abba. Caleb, his best friend, could not have been prouder had he been the one chosen. Joshua nodded; his smile broadened. He wiped the oil from his face with his sleeve. He looked over the people and saw the cloud. His eyes focused. The Lord had blessed. The Lord would lead. Joshua would follow

Him anywhere.

He looked back to the people. Their number like the sand beneath his feet. He could not expect to protect all these people in his own strength.

He continued to study the faces of the people. He saw frowns and scowls on some. Some would always be displeased with Moses's decisions. May he do what God wanted in spite of what the people desired.

After the ceremony, Joshua remained beside Moses.

Moses rested his hand on his shoulder. "Do you feel the weight of protecting the people on your shoulders?"

"It is not I who protects; only God. I just obey."

Moses laughed. "You have been listening to my words. You do well."

Joshua smiled. "I have a good teacher."

Aaron stood behind Moses, listening to him speak to Joshua. He pursed his lips together tightly to keep from speaking. Moses had not asked him who he thought should lead the army. Of course, Joshua was the assumed leader. Aaron had been surprised that morning, after the sacrifices, when Moses called Joshua to the front of the people and dedicated him to the Lord for leading the men. What had happened to the two of them leading the people? In Egypt, Aaron was the spokesman, interceding for the people's needs, petitioning for their suffering.

He remembered Moses's story about the bush that flamed but didn't burn. He had wanted that same reassurance that he would be the people's leader. God had not given him any sign. He only saw it through his brother's words.

Now he heard his brother's words echoed by Joshua. They stirred inside him a burning that he did not like. Why didn't Joshua look to him as leader? Had all the people stopped respecting him, just because his younger brother had returned?

He looked back at the altar where he had sacrificed. The ashes still smoked. He could smell the meat that they had offered to God. He clenched his hands at his sides. He led the people in worship. That was all. Was that enough?

Hannah remembered Reut from Egypt, when she had treated Amunet's boils. Her acquaintance had grown recently by washing clothes with her. She decided to visit her. "I've brought tea for you to try."

Reut looked at the withered plant with sticky little green leaves on thin twigs and grimaced. "Only if you do."

Hannah picked up a sprig and held it to Reut's nose. "You can't say the little yellow flowers don't look lovely!" They both laughed.

Reut refilled a clay pot with water and pushed it closer to the embers, adding dung to start a flame. "So what will this great little drink do for me?" She collected two clay vessels for drinking and placed them outside the ring of ashes.

"Calm you."

"Maybe we should let Tamara drink an *ephah*."

Hannah crushed the herb in the bottom of each drinking vessel. "If it calms Tamara, then the sun would stop shining. It's *N'heyda*. Aaron showed it to me. But I didn't come to talk of plants. Amos finished the canvas sheeting you requested."

Reut's eyes lit up. "How should I give it to Michael?"

Hannah hesitated. "It'll be a nice gift. He sleeps under the stars."

"You don't think that he will like it?"

"It'll make a nice gift for what he has done. Only..." Hannah lowered her eyes.

"Only what?"

Hannah looked into Reut's face. "He doesn't want you to stay in this tent, hiding in fear. You won't even wash your clothes with us anymore. I know you were frightened, but—"

Reut's face reddened. "That man is still alive. I still feel the evil of his touch."

Hannah poured the hot water and handed Reut's vessel to her, smelling her own. "Ah, that smells good." She cradled her vessel in her hands. "I lost my ima when I was only seven. I clung to my abba, fearing he would die, too.

"Everything became another fear... that Amos would die...that if I ate what my ima did, I would die.

"Fear consumed my life.

"I didn't hear my abba's reassurances. Fear doesn't listen to reason."

Reut sat forward on the pallet. "How did you lose your fear?"

Hannah sipped her tea. "My nightmares kept my abba awake. In desperation, he brought stones home from his work."

"Stones?" Reut laughed. "How did that help?"

"Whenever I was afraid, my abba told me to count them. With each stone I must tell myself that the Lord loved me."

Reut's eyes shone. "That worked? How?"

Hannah laughed. "Every day, my abba brought home more. Before long, I could have built a wall from the pile."

"Where can I get some stones?"

Hannah stopped smiling. "Reut, it wasn't the stones. They only represented my abba's presence. As a little girl, my abba's love and presence helped me know God's love. My doubts were replaced with confidence in God's love for me.

"When Amos lost his leg, I could be thankful—not that he lost his leg, but that he had his life. I don't fight life's hardships when I know the Lord controls them. Nothing catches Him by surprise. He has made things good.

"Yes, evil is in this world. We suffer from evil. The man that hurt you is still around. But the Lord is good. He controls even the evil. He was in charge even when the man took you. You dishonor Him by living in fear when He has given you life."

Reut sipped her cooling tea.

"When you hold onto the hurt, you don't heal, Reut. When you dwell on the hurt, that's all you have. It eats at you until you are nothing. When you focus on the Lord, He gives life. Why hurt, when you can live?"

Walking through camp as the men practiced maneuvers, Phinehas overheard the women.

One woman watched him, with open disgust on her face. "What kind of man is he, who would not protect his own?"

Another stood and shook her head. "No man at all."

Phinehas shrugged. He cared not what others thought; he would not do a slave's task.

He called at his grandfather's tent.

No one answered.

Moses called from his tent. "Phinehas, Aaron trains with the men."

"My grandfather?" Phinehas laughed as he reached Moses's tent. "But he is how old?"

"Eighty-four now. And what does age have to do with anything?" Moses asked, his eyes twinkling. "The men need a mission, as do you, Phinehas. What's yours?"

Phinehas answered honestly, surprising himself. "In Egypt, it was position..."

Moses pressed. "And now?"

"I have none. Well..." He looked away.

"Your eyes tell me it's a girl you desire. Am I right?"

Phinehas nodded. "But her father won't have me. My doctor skills are not enough."

Moses gestured to the water vessel. "Drink." Pausing, briefly, he continued. "You've been rejected, but your doctor skills have nothing to do with it."

"I cannot make him happy." Phinehas threw down the dipper. "What am I to do?"

"Don't take her by force."

Phinehas stared at Moses. Had he read his mind?

Moses laughed. "You're no different than any other man in love. It consumes you. You can think of nothing but her hair, her soft face, her gentle ways."

Phinehas raised his eyebrows.

"I miss my wife. I haven't died yet."

Phinehas shook his head. "And you better not until we reach our Land."

"Who's the maiden?"

"Hakeen's daughter, Hannah, who helped Grandfather in Egypt."

Moses nodded. "I know her well. She will not make you happy, if you do not love the Lord."

Phinehas paced by the fire. "What does loving this God have to do with marrying Hannah?"

"If you married a slave girl, but she desired only to please her master, how would you feel?"

"But I accept Hannah for her low station in life. She has no master now."

Moses shook his head. "But she does. She serves the Lord."

"I don't see statues. Uncle Moses, you speak as if we still live in Egypt."

Moses looked at his vessel as he shook its contents. "And you speak as if you have no respect."

"Sorry."

Moses drank. "Your passion runs hot. But you love her very little, if you do not know what she values."

"Oh, but you are wrong."

Moses coughed and raised his eyebrows. "If you did, you would know her Master. You would not jump up and down like a little child speaking of love when you do not know what she cares about."

Phinehas started to speak, then shut his lips. He gulped the rest of his water, dipped more water, and swallowed another vessel before speaking again. "How do I learn to care about this Master?"

Moses laughed. "You are motivated, are you?"

"More than you can imagine."

"If you wish to serve God, you think of what is best for Him. You ask, 'Would this please Him?' Your life becomes a service to Him. He is pleased. He becomes your Friend. He fills the longing of your heart."

Phinehas shook his head in disgust. "He's not a woman to please a man."

"You'll find there's more to life than just a man with a woman." Moses paused and smiled. "But that is good, too."

CHAPTER 7

A malek looked over his lands, green from the recent rains. He breathed deeply of the fresh air, cleaned of the dust from the dry season. This time of year new lambs and kids would enlarge his herds. They would fatten well on the pastures made by the rains. His shepherds had taken his flocks to the low lands, west of his home, to take advantage of the rains' gifts. His lands extended as far west as he wanted to claim, although who would claim the sands of the desert with its heat and harsh life? Most of the time he kept to the foothills, where there was enough water to support his wealth until lambing. He rubbed his hands in pleasure. Yes, this year would bring plenty.

Amalek's servants reported to him, "The people who escaped Egypt consume our pastures. How will we feed our flocks?"

Amalek listened. He had heard from merchants many moons ago of the destruction that these people caused in Egypt. Now they came to his land. If Egypt could not control these people and their God, what was he to do?

His clan numbered many thousands of fighting men. He controlled the land east of the Moabites over to the land of the Philistines to the west and as far south as the Red Sea. He pastured his flocks high in the hills during the dry seasons, but in the rainy seasons his flocks spread into the valleys, including Rephidim, where these Hebrews now grazed their flocks.

He tapped on his bearded chin in contemplation. How difficult would it be to conquer slaves? He would protect his water and lands, and expand his possessions from Egypt's wealth.

Another servant entered. "Master, a man has come from the Hebrews' camp." He bowed and backed out of the tent, allowing another man to enter.

The man removed his hood as he entered. He ran his fingers through his unkempt hair. He appeared to assess everyone in the tent. His hand tapped the sword by his side. His eyes rested on Amalek, and he smiled. His cloak smelled of camp smoke. "I come from the camp of the Hebrews. I have news."

Amalek gestured for the man to sit. "Drink?"

The man took his time sipping the wine offered. He belched in appreciation of the drink. Leaning back against the cushions, he finally looked at Amalek. "The Hebrews are using your water. I will help you."

Amalek studied the man before him. "Why?"

"You're a mighty tribe that fights for what is yours. While you fight for what is yours, I will claim what is mine."

"How do I know you don't lead us into a trap?"

He laughed. "How do I know you won't kill me for what I share with you?" He pointed to Amalek. "We are two of the same blood, you and I. You fight for what is yours. So do I."

Amalek did not trust this man, but liked his thinking. "What do you want?"

He laughed again bitterly. "You are seeking control of your land; I only want a girl that was stolen from me."

Amalek watched the man before him, considering. "So we create a diversion and you obtain a girl. That is all? No bounty, no spoil, no flocks?"

The man drank again. "I have enough."

Amalek settled against his cushions and drank from his vessel. He stretched out his legs. "Tell me about these people who destroyed Egypt and took all her wealth."

"They are slaves turned free. They know nothing of fighting. They can't take care of themselves." He waved his hand dismissively. "You will conquer them easily."

Amalek pointed to the man's sword. "Egyptian, isn't it?"

He removed the sword from his sheath and slid his finger along the blade. "Pulled it off an Egyptian soldier on the shores of the Reed Sea. He wouldn't need it again." He met Amalek's glance.

"I heard....Something about Egypt's entire army, chariots— everything destroyed by this God. You were there?"

"Yes. Saw the entire army washed away by the sea."

"An entire army destroyed by a wave and a God?" Amalek shook his head and emptied his cup. "Were you there when Egypt was destroyed?"

"Their God didn't destroy the land where the Hebrews lived. I saw what happened to the Egyptians. Do not worry. You only protect what is yours. You're just letting them know to stay off your land. Their God can direct them somewhere else."

"How does this God lead them?"

"They follow a cloud during the day."

"A cloud in the desert? Have you seen this thing? Only during the rainy season can I hope to see anything in the sky."

"Oh, I've seen the cloud. The people move when it moves and stop when it stops. They are a people who cannot think on their own. During the night, they follow a fire."

Amalek stood, spilling his drink. "Fire! Does it burn my grasses before these people trample them?"

The man laughed. "It stays in the sky and burns without fuel. It lights their path when they travel at night."

"This is another feat of their God?"

"These people depend totally upon Him."

"Why do you travel with them?"

He hesitated, then shrugged. "I'm a merchant seeking my fortune. Right now, my fortune involves one girl who is mine."

Amalek nodded. He understood this man's greed, for one thing. His own interest lay in his land. He would protect it at all costs. No people, no matter how powerful their God, would starve his flocks while he watched. He would fight and win.

The women took advantage of the quiet in the camp to wash clothes. The shade cast from the mountainside made it easier to stay cooler in the afternoon heat.

Reut looked at her cloak in the water and sighed. She had scrubbed and pounded it with a stone. She couldn't see any soil marks, nor smell the moldy manna, but she continued to scrub, as if the memories could be scrubbed away.

Hannah joined her. "Let me help you wring out the water." She grabbed one end, twisting it, and helped Reut spread it in the hot sand to dry. "What a beautiful color!"

Reut offered, "Want it?"

Hannah studied Reut. She nodded, accepting the cloak. "You're making progress—and not just on your laundry."

Tamara entertained some of the small children nearby as their mothers washed. "Etania, catch!" She tossed a linen rag tied in a ball.

Jabin clapped his hands. "Throw to me!" As he scrambled to

catch it, he fell in the shallow water, drenching his tunic.

Tamara grabbed him, kneeling in front of him. "Stay out of the water, Jabin! It scares me."

Reut paused in her pounding. Did Tamara still live in fear from her near-drowning? She studied Tamara with new concern. Did all their people fear? Would their Land put an end to their fears?

Tamara stepped from the water. Tamara, trying to distract the children from the water, stepped away from it and called to Etania. "Throw it to me." She caught the ball and turned to toss it to Japhet when she noticed the dust. She pointed to the hills. "What's that whirl of dust? See how the wind whips it around the mountain. Is that the men?"

Reut stood. "That's not where the men are training."

"See that reflection off the sun?" Tamara stood on tip-toes. "They're soldiers!"

Carmel gathered their laundry, dumping washed and un-washed together into baskets. "Tamara, run to the men training! Tell no one except Moses. Hurry! Reut, help Dinah and Salome with the children."

Reut wiped her hands down her tunic, staring at the swirling dust. Why did any danger bring back the smell of that man's breath against her face?

After Moses announced the coming of the soldiers, Adlai returned to his tent. His heart beat rapidly. He tried to calm his breathing. The last time he should have been protecting his family, Reut had been taken. If he couldn't protect his family from one lone man, how could he protect his family against an army?

He looked at his wife and daughters. He had never fought. He had missed many of the training sessions while teaching the men to read. He felt so unprepared.

He paced inside their tent, trying to focus long enough to gather what he needed for battle.

Carmel stood before him and rubbed his arms. "Adlai, it's not your battle. Don't be discouraged by the approaching army. The Lord fights for us. He didn't bring us here to die: not by hunger, not by thirst, and not by an army of mere men. The Lord has prepared us for what we need to do today."

Magal returned from the disrupted training session eager for battle. His brother Esmail could never understand his need for adventure. Esmail was content with sheep. But Magal needed action, danger, thrill. Watching sheep sleep on a hillside was not his idea of a pleasant night.

The army drills had strengthened and toned his flesh so that he could wield the sword and defend his position without hesitation. He had practiced with his friends even when the army did not train. They would form a unified front that could not be broken.

He retrieved the armor taken from a soldier at the Reed Sea. This was armor not from a foot-soldier but from an officer. He put his arms through the straps of the breastplate and pulled the straps snug. It fit like it was meant for him. He sat down to attach the arm and knee guards. He stood, sliding his hand over the shiny metal. Nothing could slice through this metal. He bent to pick up his shield. The armor made his balance different. It was heavy, like he was carrying all their belongings on his chest. He must remember to lean backward. Lifting his sword, he swung it a few times to feel the weight of its hilt. He smiled. He was ready. He stepped out of his tent.

He heard a gasp and turned to see his sister staring at him.

"Magal, you're a real soldier!"

He thrust his shoulders back farther.

Pelia rubbed his breastplate. "You will fight?"

"The first to go."

She jumped to throw her arms around his neck. "You'll be careful?"

Magal shifted to balance his weight. He laughed. "I'll be in battle, Pelia. Not watching sheep."

"Does this mean we are close to our Land?"

Magal shrugged. "We are seeing other people, finally. I wonder how much fighting we must do before the Land will be ours?"

Pelia stepped out of his embrace and studied his face. "I hadn't thought about that."

Magal chuckled. "You didn't expect the Land to be rich without someone living there, did you?"

She looked down. "I didn't think..."

Magal softened his tone. "Our people are ready for the Land. We have practiced; the army is ready to be tested."

"Can't it be tested without fighting?"

Magal laughed. "Can the thread that you spin so fine and thin hold the weight of all your belongings?"

"Only if that thread is woven tightly with other threads."

Magal lifted her chin and looked into her face. "That, my little sister, is what our army has been training to do. Now, we will see if our threads will stand the test of another army."

Pelia sighed. "But you will come back?"

He squeezed her cheek, like he did when she was just a little girl. "With victory."

That evening, Joshua and his father hiked the mountain to watch the army's dust cloud, as it settled for the night. "They are a great people who come to fight us."

Nun continued to look at the desert. The sun's rays reflected through the dust onto the sand and pastures in colors of red and orange. "You must be sure of the outcome, or your men will magnify your indecision.

Joshua nodded. "Our men have formed a bond that will bring a unified front tomorrow."

His father leaned on his staff. "The Lord has given the men purpose. They are trained well. Tomorrow they will know what to do. The Lord will provide."

Joshua's voice broke. "But am I trained to do this?"

Nun smiled. "You have sat at the feet of Moses and learned of his wisdom?"

"You know I have, Abba."

"You have watched as he directed the men in the drills?"

"Yes. I know the men are ready. But am I ready?"

"Do you think God would give you something that you cannot handle?"

Joshua looked over the dust now settled. "What words of wisdom would you give me, Abba?"

Nun looked back the way they had come. "Do you remember crossing the Reed Sea?"

Joshua nodded.

"Could you walk across on the dry river bed?"

Joshua nodded again, "But..."

Nun pointed to the cloud as it was starting to turn to fire "God does not ask us to walk where He does not lead. He is still before you.

"The battle is the Lord's. I do not know Him except for what He has done with this people in the last months. But if He can take a people bound by slavery and free them while destroying the very nation that holds them captive, then He is a God I will follow.

"He gives us water and food from a desert that shows no life. This God I will trust.

"Do what He tells you. The results will be His. Take no glory. This God deserves it all."

Joshua glanced over the Hebrew campsite. "So many people to protect. How can I lead them?"

Nun shook his head. "You do not lead them." He nodded to the cloud already showing its fire. "When you think that you lead this people, you are already defeated. Do not look at what you are. Look to Whose you are. Show your men how to follow Him."

The fire turned to a cloud for another day. The sun rose over the sand, the Israelites, and Amalek with his army. The women gathered the manna, preparing a hasty morning meal.

Nathan dipped his flat bread into the broth from the night before. "Finish your meal, son."

Jabin gobbled his food.

Nathan glanced at Salome over Jabin's head, and then focused on Jabin. "You won't be going with me today."

Jabin chewed slower. "But you'll fight?"

"Yes. But not practice. You will protect Ima while I'm gone."

Jabin swallowed his mouthful. He looked doubtful. "Protect Ima?"

Nathan nodded. "If Ima is not protected, the baby that grows within her will not be strong and able to fight."

Etania rubbed against his arm. "I'll take care of Ima and the baby today, Abba."

Jabin took a swallow from the dipper kept in the middle of their circle of food. Drops ran down his chin before he wiped his mouth with his hand. "Me, too."

Nathan rose and put on his leg and arm guards. He attached his waterskin to his belt. His actions were slow, deliberate. His thoughts were not on the battle, but on Salome. She looked pale this morning.

Etania and Jabin hovered around him.

Looking into their big eyes, he laughed. "The Lord goes before us." He ruffled Jabin's hair. "Bring me my sword."

Jabin lifted it with both hands and wobbled as he handed it to him. "When will I go with you?"

Etania laughed. "When you can carry your own sword without staggering."

Nathan wrapped its sheath around his waist with ease, adjusting it, so it lay within reach of his hand. "The Lord prepares us for battle. When it's your turn, you will know."

Jabin watched, his eyes shining.

Salome grabbed his tunic and leaned her head on his chest. Her voice was muffled. "You'll be careful?"

Nathan squeezed her tightly. "It's the Lord's fight. I must go." As he felt her shoulders rise and fall, he hugged her tighter. He whispered, "I will come back, even if I must crawl."

She let go of his tunic and looked into his face. She stroked his beard. "Do not crawl; your knees will bleed."

Nathan laughed, gently wiping her tears with his thumb. "My shin guards will keep my skin on my knees."

She gasped and rubbed where their baby grew.

Nathan placed his hand over hers. "You will be fine. Dinah will be close?" At her nod, he squeezed her hand as it rested on her bosom. "Stay in camp. You have enough water for the day?" To assure himself, he looked at the vessels he had filled that morning.

Salome breathed deeply; rubbing her bosom. "You have water?"

He tugged at his waterskin tied to his waist. "I will fill it at the water pool before we go."

"Be sure to drink, all day."

He nodded. Fighting in this heat would require more water than when they practiced.

He studied her face, memorizing each feature. She was biting her lip to keep from crying. She wouldn't beg him to stay. It was hard to leave her. "A fighting pack of hyenas could not keep me from returning to your side when day is done." He hugged her.

She squeezed tightly.

He felt as if she gained strength for the coming day from him.

Jabin pulled at his tunic. "Hug me, too."

He broke from her embrace and knelt to give Etania and Jabin hugs. Burying his head in their hair, he whispered, "I love you."

He stood once more and kissed Salome on the lips, then in her hair. "I love you. I will return." He turned quickly, before he could see her tears, and stepped out of the tent.

Ellis waited outside.

They started off without speaking.

Nathan's thoughts were absorbed on how pale Salome had looked. He glanced back once, before the tent was out of sight.

They stood by the tent door, watching.

Etania and Jabin jumped, waved and screamed. "Shalom, Abba!"

Nathan raised his arm in a final wave before setting his face toward battle.

Ellis and Nathan reached the water pool.

The morning's coolness made it easy for him to forget the coming heat of midday. Nathan drank deeply of the water, then rinsed his waterskin, and filled it. Splashing water over his face, he allowed the cold drops to awaken his thoughts for the coming battle. He wiped his face.

Other soldiers were preparing around them. The air seemed charged with anticipation, with excitement, with uncertainty.

Ellis grabbed Nathan's arm. "Do you sense victory in your blood?"

Nathan shrugged. "Something's in my blood."

Ellis adjusted his waterskin around his waist. "We fight, not as slaves for another country, but for our God. He gives me confidence!"

Nathan nodded, but his mind remained on Salome and how pale she had looked when he left.

After watching the men prepare for battle, Phinehas returned to his tent to prepare bandages. He was deciding which tonics would be needed when Aaron stepped inside his tent.

"Phinehas, you're not ready for battle?"

"To fight beside slaves?"

Aaron pressed his hands to his temples. "What does being a slave have to do with whether or not you fight?"

"They don't think like we do, Grandfather."

"The Lord limits their choices in this desert because they're not ready for all of life's choices. They must see Him as the God for their needs. Just like you.

"Because you weren't with them in training, and now in battle, you will feel nothing when victory comes. You will be an outsider, unable to truly praise God. You must live among them, not just by them. They will be united as a people under the Lord, but you will remain distant."

Phinehas shook his head.

Aaron was not finished talking. "Your angel of mercy knows great suffering."

Phinehas stilled his hand on the tonic that he was mixing.

"Because she was greatly wounded, Hannah suffers with her patients. You suffer very little. These people can teach you much on how to suffer, yet still hope. Their hope has come. The Lord has answered."

Phinehas moved his tonics around in his basket. "I have no need to suffer."

Aaron shook his head. "I fear for you, if you continue this attitude of arrogance. Their suffering should unite you to their needs, not make you judge over them. You must fight with them, protecting what they value."

Phinehas sighed. "They have nothing that I value."

"Someday you will fight for what you value. I hope it's not too late.

"Get a sword and do battle. I don't just mean with outsiders, but with your arrogance. If you don't, the Lord will. His wounds will make you look to Him." Aaron squeezed Phinehas's shoulder. "You were meant for something great—not above this people, but with them."

Phinehas watched Aaron walk away. He threw the bandages that he had been wrapping into a basket. They seemed little. So did his skill and position before a God Who demanded more of him.

Moses stood before the men in the valley, outside the camp. He glanced at Aaron and smiled. Aaron looked confident of victory, or maybe relieved that he did not fight. Joshua stood on Moses's other side. He appeared excited, not the childish excitement of adventure, but the anticipation of what God would do with His people. Moses nodded. His confidence was placed well. Moses lifted his staff to silence the shuffling and nervous commotion. "Shalom." This battle would test the men and prove Who they served. Shalom seemed a wrong word to tell the soldiers, since they were going into battle. Yet, Moses could feel a settling in the soldiers as he spoke it. They would have no peace, if they could not defend their right to be here.

He paused and spoke again. "Shalom." The men had settled down to listen. "The Lord's peace goes with you into this battle. He is the One Who leads. He fights with you. He fights for you. He brings you home tonight. He not only brings you home, but brings you home victorious!"

The men raised their hands and shouted as one, "Amen!"

Moses pointed to the hillside behind him. "Aaron, Hur, and I will stand between you and our God. We will intercede on your behalf. God will hear and answer. You will win."

Another shout rippled through the soldiers.

Moses stepped back and motioned for Aaron. Aaron raised his arms and waited until the silence was all that could be heard. "The Lord bless you and keep you. The Lord make His face shine on you, and be gracious to you. The Lord lift up His countenance on you, and give you peace." Aaron bowed to the men and stepped back.

Next Joshua stepped forward. He was dressed like an officer, with breastplate, arm and leg guards, and sword. He swallowed as he looked over the men he would lead. He looked at the cloud, a habit that he had learned by following Moses. "We did not seek this battle. But the cloud leads us forward, so we must go. This enemy does not fight against us, but against our God. We fight for the Lord, so that all men may know of His mighty acts. His acts are mighty. His power is great. Because we fight for Him, we will conquer. God has trained us. God will enable us."

Joshua paused. He pointed to the cloud that hung in the sky, waiting for them to follow into battle. It had already changed from fire to cloud as the sun crept over the mountain. "Men, for whom do we fight?"

They lifted their deep voices together in a shout of victory, "God."

Joshua repeated, "For whom do we fight?"

Again they answered. "God!"

Joshua pointed toward the camp of Amalek. "Let's go!"

Joshua strode out from camp at a fast pace. They marched toward Amalek and his men. The men fell in line behind each tribe's leader.

Moses watched Amalek approach the people of God. Amalek's army was vast. The battle would be hard. He could hear their distant trumpet call as it roused them to march.

Moses watched their own men march into battle; then he turned to hike the mountain with Aaron and Hur by his side.

The men had never proven themselves in battle. Today they would. Moses remembered when he had been general of the Egyptian army. That fluttering in his gut, anticipating hand-to-hand battle. That rush of power. That tinge of doubt in his ability. That thirst to conquer. He looked again at the cloud. God had made men with a passion to protect their own. He had trained them. God would work.

Moses was quiet as he hiked. He almost missed going with the men. He used his staff as he stepped around a boulder. He must remember his age. Not that it slowed him down, but his role was different now. He must intercede for the people, not help fight for the people. By the time he reached the top, the armies had met each other and had attacked.

The battle raged.

The Hebrews not only held their own, but pushed toward victory.

Moses raised his staff and petitioned God.

The sun rose higher in the sky. The heat reflected off the sand. The men fought.

Moses grew faint, and lowered his staff.

Aaron wiped his brow. "The men grow weary. Our men are retreating."

Hur rolled a boulder closer. "Moses, sit. Aaron and I will help keep your staff toward God for His favor."

Moses looked at the battle. The fighting had moved closer to camp. He raised his staff in his shaky arms. He would never be able to wield a sword in battle, if he could not hold a staff in prayer. He focused on his prayer. He kept his arms lifted, asking the Lord for His victory.

The battle turned; the men renewed their efforts.

Moses, Aaron, and Hur interceded. When they grew weary and lowered the staff, their men suffered.

An invisible thread linked the soldiers' success with Moses raising his staff toward heaven and crying to God for help.

And the people were protected.

Hannah returned to her tent from hauling water. She had filled as many vessels as she could find, in anticipation of cleaning wounds. Her brother sat silent in the dark tent corner.

She watched his stony face as she arranged her water supply. "You're upset that you can't join the battle?"

Amos grunted.

"What makes men want to fight, anyway?"

Amos shrugged. "We protect our own."

Hannah nodded but did not understand. She lifted her basket. "You could help me look for ghagha." She would use the plant for healing wounds.

When he turned from her, she sighed. "I'll look outside camp, away from the battle."

He only mumbled in response.

She hurried as she left camp, appreciating the coolness of the morning air. She adjusted her hood, glad for its warmth over her face. Wearing Reut's blue cloak reminded her to pray for her.

She found the plant amongst some boulders close to the water pool. The recent rains had been enough for the seed to germinate and the plant to reach maturity before the sun dried it again. She gathered carefully, making sure not to pick the trampled ones.

A shadow fell over hers. Glad Amos had thought better of his moodiness and come to help her, she said without turning, "You finally came."

"Yes, I've come."

She gasped.

It was not Amos.

She turned to face Maessai.

He grabbed her arm and twisted her against his body. He pushed a wad of cloth into her mouth, silencing her screams.

His breath was hot against her ear. "I have waited for you, too."

Phinehas strapped his sword to his side. He did not need to know how to fight. He was still angry about his grandfather's words. Why did he need to suffer? He was a good doctor. Hadn't the highest-ranking Egyptians sought his help?

He glanced up at Moses, just a speck on the hill. He could dimly see his grandfather and Hur helping Moses raise the staff.

The morning passed slowly. He should haul more water for cleaning wounds. He missed the comforts of Egypt, where he could demand a servant to bring water. Now, he grabbed his vessel himself and walked to the water.

As he approached, he saw a young woman among the boulders,

struggling with a man.

Was that Hannah? Dropping his jar and drawing his sword, he ran to her. Moses's words came to mind, "You will find one day that something you value must be protected. I hope that you will be ready." He grabbed the shoulder of the man. "Let her go."

Maessai pushed him away, even as he held her tighter. "She's mine. This is none of your affair."

Taking advantage of Maessai's distraction, Hannah stomped on Maessai's inner foot.

Maessai relaxed his hold.

She tore free of his grip and ran, stopping at a distance to watch the men. She spit the rag from her mouth, and wiped her lips.

Maessai drew his sword, raising it to strike.

Phinehas regained his footing, raising his sword to parry Maessai's sword. He acted from reflex, not skill. His sword was heavier, more awkward to maneuver, than he had thought. He swung his sword, with thoughts of protecting what he valued.

Maessai stepped toward Phinehas, lowering his sword to gut level. His eyes showed annoyance, as if he smacked at a fly.

Phinehas stepped back, lifting Maessai's sword away with his own. How he wished now that he had trained with the men for battle! His skill, strength, and weight were no match for this man before him. He glanced at Hannah to reassure himself that she was safe.

Maessai's sword came down faster than he could move.

Hannah watched, unable to tear her eyes from the scene. Phinehas held his sword awkwardly, without experience, whereas a sword belonged in Maessai's hand. He maneuvered it like it was part of him. The weight did not slow him. He played with Phinehas, pushing him from the campsite with his maneuvers.

Would he push Phinehas against the boulders and kill him? How could she distract him?

Maessai raised his arm to strike.

She screamed.

Phinehas raised his sword with both hands to defend himself. His foot slipped on loose shale, his sword wavering.

Maessai struck.

Phinehas's sword clattered to the ground, rattling against the shale. He ducked his head in time, but the sword caught his arm, slicing through his cloak and into his flesh.

Hannah gasped as blood poured from his arm. She heard a shout but could not look away.

Maessai raised his arm to strike again, this time without any hindrance. The smile on his face reflected his victory.

Phinehas backed against a boulder. His foot kicked his sword. His eyes were fixed on Maessai's face.

Hannah could not move. She felt like she was wedged against the boulder. She did not breathe. But she had to watch.

When a hand touched her, she jumped and screamed. "Amos." She placed her hand on her chest and breathed deeply. She pointed, frantically blurting out, "Help him. He tried to take me."

Amos listened no further. He broke a dead branch from one of the nearby acacia trees. Then wielding his branch toward the fighting pair, he drew back his arms for a sweeping blow.

Hannah screamed. "Not him!"

But he was already swinging.

The branch hit both Phinehas and Maessai's heads broadside. Taking most of the impact, Phinehas slumped in a heap. Maessai shook his head, glancing at Amos in stunned surprise. He lowered his sword.

Amos regained his balance and leaned on the branch, surveying his opponents.

Hannah rushed to Phinehas's side. "Amos, how could you?"

Amos stared at Phinehas' bleeding head and neck. "You said that he tried to take you..."

Maessai shook his head and looked back at Hannah. "You are not her..." He backed away from camp with his sword raised in readiness.

Hannah fell to her knees, raising Phinehas's head to her lap. She stroked his hair away from his forehead and studied the gash. "Phinehas, you saved me, again."

The sun set. The battle ended. The Lord had once more protected the Hebrews from disaster. Joshua watched the beaten army retreat toward the hills. The day had been hot. Drinks few. He licked his dry lips. He must remind the men to drink. The battle had been long. His sword weighed heavily upon him now. He massaged his shoulder as he fingered the hilt of his sword. His back felt the weight.

How could he have prepared the men better? No army drill could show a man the sights, smells, and sounds of war. He wiped his forehead. With the setting sun, the coolness came quickly. His sweat had dried, coated by the dust and blood of fighting. The coolness chilled him.

Could he wipe away the memory of all the men that he had struck down in combat? Some seemed just boys, but able to lift their own sword to strike. A man had come from nowhere, his sword raised to kill, charging Caleb by his side. Joshua had barely enough time to smite him. His sword rang true.

The man's surprise changed to unbelief that he had been mortally wounded.

Joshua had saved Caleb's life.

Caleb turned from striking down his opponent to nod to Joshua before moving to another.

When Joshua removed his sword, the smell of the gut wound lingered in the air, churning his own insides. No amount of training prepared anyone for the smell of war. He stepped away from the smell, but not before losing his flatbread from the morning.

Sounds of battle filled the air: clanking of swords, moaning from wounded. Their cries would haunt his dreams that night. He could not grant their requests for a quick death, since more men kept coming at them.

They had been tested today. The men had proved ready.

The enemy army had retreated. Israel had prevailed. Joshua turned from the battlefield, calling the men to leave. He walked over bodies that would look no more to the next day. Tomorrow, they would return to bury them. He drank from his waterskin, finishing its contents. The warm water reminded him of his thirst. He grabbed a waterskin from a dead body and drank.

He called for order, and the men marched toward camp. Joshua thrust back his shoulders, forgetting his weariness from the battle. The campsite was a welcome sight. They had protected their own. Their people were safe. He did not stop his men at the water, but dismissed them at the edge of the campsite. He squinted through the lowering sun. The camp seemed deserted. Where were the women to welcome them? Why didn't they cheer the men as they entered camp? No one noticed him.

With his thoughts on Moses and the people, he found them,

sacrificing to God. Why had he not remembered his Abba's caution of the day before—to give all glory to the Lord, where it belonged?

Joshua glanced at the fire cloud that lit the sky and illuminated their praise.

Their victory came, not from Moses, nor from himself, but from the Lord alone. The glory belonged to God alone. He fell on his knees in worship and thanksgiving.

Ellis paused at his tent's doorway, calming his racing heart, the momentum of the battle still bumping through him. His eyes grew accustomed to the darkness of the tent where no candle burned.

Dinah lay with Japhet curled beside her, her arm over their son. Ellis watched them for a moment before lying down beside her.

She turned to hug him. "You're safe."

"Dinah, freedom is sweet. Today we fought, not for Egypt's wealth, nor Pharaoh's whims, but for our right to be here. I cannot tell you that I did not fear, especially as we approached their great numbers. My heart was in my throat, and I thought only of returning to your side. Joshua shouted before we reached the approaching army. "Fight for the Lord." I looked to the mountain where I could see Moses, Aaron, and Hur standing as a speck on the top. Then I looked to the cloud that hovered by our side. But when I looked to where I knew your tent sat, I took courage. My fear settled. The Lord was with us.

"Nathan and Michael fought by my side. We proved a strong line that kept advancing. When I grew weak, the sun was hot, Nathan encouraged me to keep up the fight. Sweat hindered my sight at times. I'd swing my sword without seeing." Ellis shook his head. "In Egypt, I could have killed overseers in my anger. This was different. I had no anger, just a quiet strength, like a peace. How could I have peace in the midst of battle, Dinah?"

Dinah pushed his hair from his eyes as she held his head between her hands. "Salome has told me that peace only comes from God."

Ellis squeezed her against his breast and laughed. "The peace of God...in the midst of battle. Only our God could give that. But it didn't hinder my quest for victory. I thought of you, and I knew we must have victory. I would have done anything to return to you."

Dinah pulled away from him. "You're not hurt?"

He lay his head against her hair. "Not a sword touched me."

"Hungry?" Dinah started to rise.

"Stay by my side. I am famished, but I will hold you first. The Lord has filled me with contentment. Sometimes I get anxious about what I should do in the new Land. But then the Lord reminds me that He gives us water, and bread. And now He shows me victory in battle. He will prepare me for whatever He wants me to do in the new Land."

When Michael returned from the battle, he drank first from the water falling down the mountain. The rains had come, replenishing dry wadis and filling crevices in the mountains, where water would stay for the season.

He looked over the pastures that had grown quickly from seeds that matured before the sun could bake them. The grass would put flesh on the horses that he had acquired by trade with his people. He could not wait to see how the new Land would make his horses' coats shine!

He washed himself, submerging his head and scrubbing his arms of the battle's dirt and blood. Savoring the refreshment, he stepped away from the boulders to look over the campsite, as it was prepared for the night.

The cloud of fire blazed brightly. It never failed to amaze Michael. It burned with no smoke, no ashes, only a light that continued to shine.

He drank again before heading toward Adlai's tent. Adlai had been giving him extra help with reading. Still, the letters jumped around in the sand, and he could not connect them to make the words. Studying letters in the sand taxed him more than fighting a battle all day.

But tonight he would not try to read, only assure himself of Reut's safety.

Why could he be strong and fearsome during battle, yet wilt, unable to speak, in the presence of one woman? As he approached Adlai's tent, his insides turned to the consistency of mud for making bricks. Could he ask Reut if she was ready to marry? She still feared too much. He would wait. But waiting was harder than trying to read the signs of a freshly drawn word on the sand.

The stars had long begun to twinkle, and the fire cloud had lit the sky before Moses returned to his tent after sacrificing. The day had started long before the sun had risen, and he looked forward to rest.

Miriam waited for him inside his tent. "Why did you stay on the mountain during the battle? Couldn't you lead the people back with glory?"

"God deserves the glory."

"But you could have at least done something better than sitting there with your arms in the air. How can anyone praise that?"

Moses spread out his pallet. "Miriam, I do not seek the people's praise. I just obey God."

"But you could have received glory from the victory..."

"Today has been a full day, Miriam. I wish to sleep."

CHAPTER 8

After Moses had finished judging the peoples' disagreements for the day, he walked to Hakeen's tent to see Phinehas. The sun was low on the horizon. He had not eaten. "How is he?"

Hannah bathed Phinehas's head with cool cloths and applied herbs to his wounds. "He falls in and out of sleeping. His wounds flare red with heat."

Moses chewed on his lip. Phinehas wasn't even in the battle. Phinehas had fought and been wounded among his own people!

Moses looked through the tent's opening toward the cloud. He wanted the cloud's reassuring presence, but all he could see was the next campsite. He wished for wisdom to know how to lead this people. How could he make them look to God? Moses felt this was the bigger battle...the people must know God. They must see Him. No fighting, with sword or shield, would win this battle.

Hakeen drew Moses aside. "What can be done?"

Moses shrugged in frustration. "Maessai can't be found."

Hakeen lowered his voice, as he looked at Hannah, "Maessai thought Hannah was Reut."

Moses studied Hannah's face. "You are sure?"

Hakeen nodded. "He said so. She wore Reut's cloak."

Moses nodded.

Hakeen shrugged. "The story that Hannah is doctoring the doctor spreads. They tell it with laughter, but concern... Without some form of government, are the people safe?"

Moses tapped his staff. "The Lord will make it so. Shalom."

As Moses walked through the pathways between tents he considered how the Lord could make it so. The Lord knew what the people needed. In the meantime, Moses must do the next thing. He took a deep breath. He did not wish to bring any more fear to this family, but he must warn Adlai.

Moses met Adlai under the awnings of his tent. "Shalom."

Adlai stood. "Be at peace."

Moses sat, pointing to the scrolls by the cushions. "How does the teaching go?"

"The people are hungry to know their God. They thirst to read His Words for themselves."

Moses nodded. "They must make it their own."

Adlai offered him a vessel. "Heard your grand-nephew received quite a wound."

Moses swirled the water in his vessel. "He wasn't even in battle." He drank its contents. "Maessai was behind the wound."

Adlai's hand stilled. "Maessai?"

"He attempted to abduct Hakeen's daughter."

Adlai glanced at the tent door. "In camp?"

Moses nodded, lowering his voice, "But he came for yours."

Adlai's hands shook as he held his vessel. "You are sure?"

Moses grabbed his shoulder. "God is your shield and protector. He alone will carry this burden."

Adlai looked only at his drink.

Moses stood, nearly bumping into Reut as he did so. Moses studied her expression. She had heard.

She held the menat at her neck.

Moses shook his head. "That won't protect you."

She dropped her hold and grabbed a handful of her tunic. "I can't trust a God Who does evil."

"So you trust a god who can do nothing?"

She turned away.

Adlai still stared blankly into his vessel.

Moses squeezed Adlai's shoulder. "The Lord is your shield and your protector."

Biding them shalom, Moses left with heavy steps. God's people had a long way to go before they only saw Him.

Moses slowed his steps as he neared his tent. He had no sanctuary where he could be relieved of the heartache of the people. He turned away toward the desert, where he could be reminded of the Lord's peace and of Zipporah.

But not before Miriam called him. "Moses!"

He sighed. He could not ignore her; he would get no peace now.

"The family that you judged a few days ago...don't you think your judgment was harsh?"

Moses breathed deeply. "I listen to the Lord's Words. If they are harsh, He makes them so."

Miriam huffed. "But they are friends. They should really be treated—"

"Without justice?" Moses squeezed his staff and then loosened his grasp before he answered. "Do I tell you how to make flat bread?"

Miriam studied Moses for a moment. "But they are Levites, of our own clan."

Moses pursed his lips. "Do not tell me how to lead."

Miriam walked away but turned back. "I didn't cook your flat bread, but I'm sure that your God will tell you how."

Moses watched her leave. How was he to lead these people when he could not even control his own sister? How could any heart be made to see God, when they would not even look?

Zipporah hurried down the path to the sheep corral. "Father!" She hugged him. "What news do you bring?"

Jethro hugged her. "News has reached me that Moses leads his people across the desert. They're in Midian. I'll take you to him."

Zipporah stepped out of his embrace. Moses had told her that he would come for her after he left Egypt. But he had not. Why not? She missed Moses, but she also feared what his presence would bring. Before he left, Moses had stood against her. His mission for this God caused them to argue. Had Moses forgotten her? Had his God made him forget about her? She was afraid to see Moses. She shook her head. "What if he doesn't want me?"

"You question your place with your husband? Be ready to go."

Zipporah looked at the hills without seeing them, blinking back her tears. "When?"

"As soon as you are able."

Zipporah looked at their sheep. They could not travel when so many ewes were with young. They would need one more cycle of the moon before all of the lambs were born and they could travel. "Who will care for our flocks?"

Jethro rested his hand on the fence post. He tapped his fingers. "We'll leave them for your sister and her husband. They need land for their growing family."

Zipporah faced her house and all that she held dear. "But where will I live?"

Jethro squeezed her shoulders and softened his tone. "Moses leads his people to their Land. Their Land will be your Land."

"But this is my land. My inheritance. My house. You won't take that away from me, will you?"

Jethro hugged her. "Zipporah, you have nothing here."

She bit her lower lip to keep it from quivering. She had lived here her entire life. Moses had changed; she could feel it. He only thought of his God. He did not remember her. Why else did he not call for her to come to him?

He patted her back. "You belong to Moses. You go where he is."

Zipporah felt tears pooling. "You suggested that I stay while he went to Egypt."

"Your safety was my concern. Going to Egypt with Pharaoh in power could have brought you into slavery. Moses's people are free from Pharaoh's power. Now you can return to be with your husband. This land is not an excuse for you to hide from your responsibility."

Zipporah could no longer hold back her tears. "But they are not my people. This God demands all of him."

Jethro patted her back. "This God deserves all of him. Moses is your husband. You are his wife. He needs you."

Zipporah looked into his face. His jawline was set. His eyes firm. She would not tell him that with this God, Moses did not even know she existed. With this God, Moses had no need for her. Jethro had made his decision, and she would not be able to change his mind. She hunched her shoulders. "I cannot compete with this God."

Jethro whispered into her hair. "Nor should you try."

Moses yawned as he listened to a dispute. Days melted into days. He lived at the tent of meeting, hearing the people's disputes and telling them how to make them right. The people were many, their needs great. He took a drink from the vessel in front of him. This person's needs were important. He must concentrate.

Joshua whispered to him. "A stranger wishes to speak with you."

Moses rolled his neck to loosen the tightness. He had judged the people since early morning. Now the sun sat low in the sky. Moses nodded his approval.

Joshua led a messenger before Moses.

Before the messenger could speak, Moses threw his arms

around his neck. "Jaden, what news do you bring of my family?"

Jaden returned the embrace. "I come on behalf of Jethro. He brings your family. They wait outside the camp."

Moses grabbed his staff and followed Jaden. He ran, bowing before Jethro. "You honor our camp."

"You are well?" Jethro asked.

"The Lord has blessed."

After greeting his father-in-law and his brother-in-law, Hobab, Moses turned to Zipporah. He stared at her, but could not speak. All the words he had wanted to share with her these past seasons stuck in his throat. He swallowed the lump, but could not speak.

Zipporah grabbed his tunic, and pulled herself to him. She rested her head under his chin.

Moses squeezed her tightly, as if he could get back the lost time with one embrace. He did not want to let go. "I've missed you."

She buried her face on his shoulder.

He touched her hood, her hair, her face. He held her face between his hands, looking as if he could memorize every feature. He saw new lines that hadn't been there when he left. It had been so long. Why hadn't he sent for her? The weight of all the people's problems seemed lightened by her presence.

Moses heard a shuffling behind him. He turned in time to catch Gershom, as the boy flew into his arms.

"Father!"

Moses felt tears tickling the inside of his eyes. Watching other families with their young children could never take the place of holding his own. He wrapped his arms around the boy and squeezed. His voice broke. "Gershom, my son."

Moses saw another boy running to him. Kneeling down, still holding Gershom in one arm, Moses extended his other arm toward the little one. His words caught in his throat. "Eliezer, do you even know me?"

Gershom answered. "I told him your stories about your peacemaking with all the shepherds."

Moses laughed and looked over Gershom's head at Zipporah's arched eyebrows. "How much do you remember of my peacemaking?"

Gershom thrust out his chest. "Shepherds wanted to fill our wells that we dug. You approached them, five against one, and made peace. Mother says you make the world listen and do as you say."

Moses glanced at Zipporah as he lowered his sons to the ground.

Zipporah added, "Didn't Pharaoh obey your voice?"

"The Lord caused Pharaoh to listen. He proclaimed His Name in all the earth."

"Indeed, He did." Jethro stepped toward them. "Merchants fleeing Egypt told of His wonders. But as the seasons passed, we heard less. Merchants had already left, and none were returning to Egypt. Now we have come to hear what God has done since Egypt."

"And you shall." Moses stood with Eliezer still in his arm and Gershom's hand in his. Zipporah walked beside him. He could not remove the smile from his face.

A meal was prepared, and news was shared. During the meal, Moses recounted all the Lord's miracles in Egypt.

Jethro shifted on his cushions. "What has happened since then?"

Moses sighed. "His people learn slowly. When water was needed, He gave. When food was gone, He provided manna and quail."

"What's manna?" Gershom asked.

Moses massaged Gershom's shoulder. "The Lord rains food from heaven every morning."

Aaron had joined them for the meal. He nodded to Gershom's hand. "What does it taste like?"

Gershom closed his eyes and took a bite of the flat bread in his hand. "I can taste honey. Did you mix it with honey?" He opened his eyes expectantly.

Aaron shook his head.

"The Lord knows just what His people need. The women gather it every morning." Moses patted Zipporah on the leg as she sat behind him. "At first, many gathered extra for the morrow, against the Lord's command. I was angry when I smelled the foul odor throughout camp."

Gershom wriggled into Moses's lap. "What happened to it?"

Eliezer snuggled beside him.

Moses wrapped his arms around both of them. "Worms ate it."

Gershom's eyes widened. He bounced on his lap. "Wish I could've seen it!"

Eliezer added. "Me, too!"

Zipporah leaned against Moses and shook her head. "Ah, boys!"

Aaron laughed. "We had quail for a month. They dropped from the sky and fell in our laps. The meat was filling and good, but the people grew tired of it."

Gershom's mouth fell open. "They dropped without a sling-shot?"

Moses nodded. "They covered the ground." Moses stretched out his legs and leaned back against Zipporah. He teased. "We didn't need a slingshot with Pharaoh's swords at our side."

Gershom's eyes shone with excitement. "Father, do you have the king's sword?"

Moses laughed. "When the Lord delivered us at the Reed Sea, Pharaoh's army was destroyed. We retrieved swords, shields, and breastplates from the beach. Enough to supply our entire army. But no, son. I do not."

He drank from his vessel. "The cloud leads us every day. I did not tell you of the fire that protects during the night."

Gershom asked, "Fire! What about the pastures?"

Moses squeezed him. Gershom had grown so much in the time he was away. He thought of the dangers for his flocks. That was good. He nodded his head, smiling. "This fire stays in the sky, burning without fuel or ash. It reminds us of the Lord's presence."

Gershom interrupted, "Will we see this great wonder?"

Moses motioned toward the tent opening. "Every night when the sun goes down."

Gershom's eyes sparkled. He jumped to look outside. After glancing outside, he returned to Moses's side. "Do you grow tired of the wonders that you see?"

Moses grabbed another flatbread and took a bite. "When we first started our journey, the Lord showed the people His glory." Moses paused. "We could not look at Him. All fell in worship. But so quickly they forget His glory, for want of their empty bellies and parched lips."

Aaron added, "But the Lord leads us step by step to recognize He is our God, and we are His people."

Moses hugged Gershom. "It is little steps. Yes."

Jethro's eyes twinkled. "Any step in the right direction, is...a step in the right direction. As I recall, a certain shepherd did not enjoy slow-learning sheep. The Lord knew what He was doing when He sent you into the desert for a time."

Moses laughed. "Sheep are easier to teach."

Jethro corrected, "The Lord wasn't teaching sheep then. He was training a leader to listen to his flock. The Lord called you for this job. He will help you to finish it. The Lord is greater than all other gods." Jethro stood. "Let's sacrifice to this One and only God."

Moses called the elders to sacrifice. The fire burned late that night, in praise to the God Who delivers, provides for, and protects His people.

As the worship and feasting continued, Zipporah showed Naima, her mother, and Keshet, Hobab's wife, where they could settle for the night. The Levites' tents surrounded the tent of meeting close to the outside of camp. Zipporah's family could live on the outskirts of the campsite, still under the protection of the people. As she cleaned the dishes, using sand outside their tent, Zipporah asked Naima, "Did you see how the people stared at us when we entered camp?"

Naima nodded. "We are a dark-skinned people."

Zipporah shuddered. "They look at us like we're diseased."

Naima turned one of the vessels upside down by the side of the tent door. "They're curious. Especially when their leader welcomes us as honored guests."

"Did you hear their whispers, Mother?" Zipporah lowered her voice. "They say they must guard their things. Do they think we'd steal from them?" She shuddered. She had not even met any of these people, but already she felt threatened. How could she protect her sons from people who judged without knowledge?

Naima stacked the few vessels by the tent flap for morning. "Allow them time to know you." She placed her hand on Zipporah's. "Moses has changed this year. God has become real to him. His time is not his own. He will be busy with the people. You must help him."

Zipporah nodded. She looked outside the tent where she could see the glow from the fire cloud. Fire was something that had always brought warmth to her. But this time she shivered. Everything was so different from home. The people lived crowded together. When people walked by her tent, they looked in her doorway. She felt watched. Even the flatbread was different, sweeter than the bread she made at home.

She missed hearing the herds of sheep and goats settle for the evening of quietness and grazing. Where were the people's flocks?

She especially felt the loss of Moses. His embrace when he had seen her reminded her of the security she felt in his arms. She could not mistake his intensity when he first saw her. But did he need her? She almost snorted. He had this people. And they certainly expected his time. What could she do to help with that?

Miriam watched from her tent's door as Moses entertained his guests. Moses respected them greatly. Who were they? She could not hear, except the high-pitched voices of the little ones. She shuddered. They were so loud and uncivilized. Did they not know to keep their children quiet while the adults talked during the meal? When would they leave? That woman...she held some kind of power over Moses. He had spoken to her many times during the night, even in the presence of the other men. Then that older man...he led the sacrifices! That was a job for the Levites. How could the sacrifice be acceptable? She yawned as she waited. She could not sleep until she found answers. She called from the doorway of Aaron's tent as soon as he blew out his candle.

Aaron laughed. "Come in, Miriam. I should have known you'd be here."

She settled beside him on his pallet. "Don't delay. Tell me. Who are they?"

"Moses's family."

"People from the desert? How could Moses corrupt himself with them? Which one did he marry? Not the darkest of them!"

Aaron covered himself and settled against the cushion behind him. "She's a nice girl. Moses has two sons."

Miriam almost yelled, but stopped herself, "Those on his lap were his? Those are babies. What was Moses thinking?"

"They've been separated over a year. Allow them time before you control them."

Miriam glared at Aaron through the darkness. She shifted off his pallet as he settled more comfortably under the blanket. "She needs help adjusting to our ways. I won't have her living like some desert dweller."

Aaron put his arms behind his head as he stretched. "Aren't we all desert dwellers?"

She hissed through closed lips. "Those people steal. I must hide my things, before they take them."

"You now have two nephews that you can cuddle and hold."

Miriam huffed. "Maybe that's one way to keep them out of my things."

Aaron turned from her and adjusted the blanket over his shoulder. "It's late. I'm tired."

"How can you sleep, when thieves lie in the tent beside yours?"

Aaron responded wearily, "Give her time to adjust."

Miriam was leaving, but she turned back, "What a perfect reason for me to visit tomorrow."

Aaron faced her again. "You will push Moses too far if you meddle. Moses is not the young child that you manipulated in your youth. But you do have a point. Why a dark-skinned woman?"

Morning came and Zipporah rose early. She had fallen asleep the night before waiting for Moses to finish sacrificing. She yawned now. The predawn light didn't filter through her tent. She touched Moses's place beside her. Empty. What must he do so early in the morning? They hadn't even talked in private yet.

Moses had mentioned gathering manna. With her basket, she left their tent.

Naima was building a fire at her tent. "Shall we go see this wonder on the sand?"

Zipporah pulled her hood over her hair in the morning's chillness.

They hurried outside of camp. Zipporah stared at the sparkling wonder. These white flakes on the ground must be gathered for a meal?

A woman came beside them. "Shalom. You must be Moses's family."

At Zipporah's nod, she continued, "News travels fast in crowded tents. I'm Carmel, Adlai's wife. This is my daughter, Tamara. Did you sleep well?"

Zipporah watched as Carmel gathered the wafers. She stayed close to her as she filled her basket.

Carmel lowered her voice, gathering close to Zipporah. "The women must not be alone outside the camp. There have been some..." Carmel swallowed, choosing her words before continuing, "some abductions. My other daughter was one of them—" She found words to continue. "It's safer in numbers."

Zipporah listened. "You are not safe with your own people?"

"The man has been sent from camp, but rules and order we don't have."

Zipporah glanced at Tamara. She lowered her voice, "How do you live with such fear?"

Carmel tried to smile. "We do what we must. We leave the rest with the Lord. After all, He controls it all anyway, doesn't He?"

Zipporah studied Carmel's face between gathering the manna. The lines in Carmel's face showed that it was not always easy to allow Him control. "Are my boys safe?"

Carmel paused to put her handful in her basket. "How old are they?"

"Gershom is six and Eliezer is two."

Carmel looked more closely at Zipporah. "Only little ones. I assumed that Moses would have a much older family."

Zipporah felt the scrutiny and hid her face deeper in her cloak's hood. She wandered closer to other women gathering.

One woman whispered, "Who is she who steals our food?"

The other woman openly stared at Zipporah. "Foreigners, taking our children's food!"

Zipporah's cheeks burned as she stood by Naima. "I'm finished."

Carmel glanced into her basket. "You'll have plenty. Don't save any for the morrow. One of my vessels was ruined, and I had to burn the cloth because of its stench!"

She included Naima. "You'll enjoy meeting my sister-in-law and her little ones. They await their third child. She has a girl that is six and a boy three. We meet after the heat of the day. Join us."

Zipporah hesitated. What was expected of Moses's wife?

"Don't tell me now. I'll check after the heat of the day." Carmel added. "What people are you?"

Naima shifted her basket. "We are Midianites."

Carmel nodded. "Not many came to Egypt."

Naima stood. "We are a desert people who live contented lives. Our tribe is from the son of Abraham."

Carmel asked in surprise, "Keturah's offspring?"

Zipporah's eyebrows arched. They knew of Abraham's second wife? "Yes."

"Then we are cousins!" Carmel hugged both of them.

Zipporah swallowed. "What are your people like?"

"Most are slaves turned free. God prepares us to own land after having nothing." Carmel walked beside them. When they reached Zipporah's tent, she asked, "I didn't get your name."

"Zipporah."

"Like the desert flower. I've seen it, now that we've become desert travelers." Carmel laughed. "And yours?"

"Naima."

"It'll be good to have your wisdom about the land we are traveling in." Carmel added. "I'll come after we rest, if you wish to join us."

Zipporah heaved a sigh. She wasn't accustomed to being with people. When merchants came, her father did the talking. She grew up with only her sisters and her brothers' wives. Maybe she would stay in her tent.

Gershom came running toward her. Eliezer toddled behind him. Obviously, hiding in a tent with two active boys would not work.

Maybe she needed someone like Carmel to help her understand these people's ways.

Zipporah ground the manna flakes into powder for their first meal of the day. Naima formed the powder into flat bread to heat on stones over the coals.

Zipporah already missed the cheese from her flocks of goats and the herbs that she gathered in the rainy season. How could she have forgotten to bring some herbs from home? She had rushed to be with Moses.

Shaking her head, she fingered the wooden ring in her cloak pocket. Moses had carved it and presented it to her on their wedding day.

His words still warmed her heart. "All the gold and silver of Egypt could not compare to my love for you." He had held her hand, putting it on her finger. When it fell off because it was too big, they both had laughed. He had retrieved it from the dirt and placed it in her hand. His gaze was intense, his words precious. "Just like the ring that I carve is too big for your finger, so my love for you is more than you need."

Heat rose in her face. She closed her fingers over the gift, treasuring the words in her heart. Holding it, especially these past seasons when he had been absent, reminded Zipporah of his love. She squeezed the ring. The edges of the wood had softened over the years of handling. She had wished for his presence for so long. Now that she was here, she still didn't see him. When would she see Moses? Had he changed?

Miriam had watched for her chance. She looked both ways before stepping into Moses's tent at midmorning.

"Who are you?" A voice came from the darkened corner.

Miriam jumped at the voice. She had expected no one to be there, but she would not defend her presence. She faced the voice, but could not see her. "I'm Moses's sister, Miriam. I take care of Moses's every day chores while he judges."

"Thank you. That won't be needed anymore."

Miriam could not ignore the tone of dismissal. Her eyes had adjusted to the darkness. She surveyed the clean floor, the folded goats' skins from last night's sleep, the bundles from their arrival the previous day. She noticed the flatcakes ready to be heated. The figure in the corner was nursing a child. She huffed and left.

By mid-morning, Zipporah allowed the flames of the fire to burn down to embers. Her family had eaten, but still Moses had not come. When a breeze fluttered the tent flap, she looked up expectantly. No one. She sighed. Where was Moses? Would she see him at all today? After Carmel's warning, she hesitated to leave her own tent. Was Miriam's entrance without a greeting part of their culture? Should she expect people to wander into her tent without warning?

Her thoughts were interrupted when someone grabbed her by the waist. Remembering Carmel's daughter, she could only imagine someone taking her. She screamed.

The chuckle in her ear calmed her.

"Moses, you scared me."

"Can't I hold my wife, without her thinking a shepherd is taking her away?"

She turned to face him, her head fitting snuggly under his chin. "A shepherd took me away, but then disappeared and did not return. Besides, Carmel told me of one who took her daughter. I fear to leave my tent."

Moses raised her chin so he could see her eyes. "There's danger. Carmel did well to warn you. Don't go outside the camp without someone. Keep the boys close. But this isn't what I wished to discuss with my wife after not seeing her for so long." He drew her against him. "Rested from your travels?"

She smelled the fire smoke on his cloak from the sacrifices of the night before. She used to smell the goats and sheep that he herded. This new smell only reminded her that her role had changed. Moses was no longer just hers. He was this people's leader. Sheep could be eaten when they became obstinate. What could you do with people when they grumbled?

She settled against him.

A cough behind her interrupted their embrace. "Moses. I hate to intrude, but my ox is missing. I don't wish to blame anyone wrongly, but Itamar wanted to buy it. I wouldn't sell. Now my ox is missing, and Itamar has fresh beef."

Moses moved from Zipporah to stand beside the man. "Where's Itamar now?"

"He refuses to speak with me."

Moses led the man from his tent.

Zipporah watched them leave. She had been forgotten. Must she share her husband with all the people?

After the evening meal was finished, Jethro settled on his cushions. "What do you do all day, Moses? I haven't seen you since yesterday."

"The people bring their disputes to me."

Jethro drank from his vessel. "You are a leader, a good leader, but this will wear you out."

"What should I do? The people seek justice."

Jethro looked around the circle of family. "You cannot do this alone. Select men who fear the Lord, trustworthy men of honor who will not seek dishonest gain. Place them as leaders over hundreds, and fifties. Let them judge the people. If they lack wisdom for a case, allow them to present it to the leader above them. If they cannot decide, let them bring it to you."

Moses stretched. Touching Zipporah's knee, he smiled at her, then turned back to her father. "Your wisdom is sound."

Jethro shrugged. "Otherwise, you will grow weary of this people before you reach your Land. Their disputes will affect the way you lead them."

"I'm honored to learn from your wisdom and spare this people a grumpy shepherd." He turned to Aaron, "You know the men. Who would you recommend?"

Aaron paused for a moment. "As slaves, some were foremen, heads of their teams. We should look among them for men who understand God's truth."

Moses nodded. "Let's do it."

Nathan found Salome resting when he returned with the vessel of water. The coolness of the evening had started to settle around him, and he pulled his cloak tighter. He pushed his hood off to better see their pallet in the darkened corner of the tent. He studied Salome's face. She looked so frail. How could he lessen the journey's hardship on her? The baby seemed to drain her of all her energy. Yet she looked so calm and peaceful.

Salome opened her eyes and smiled. "What was the noise about?"

Nathan knelt beside her. The dirt was packed from their long encampment, and it dug into his skin. He brushed her hair from her forehead. "Two elders in camp, filled with the Spirit of God, spoke of the Land of Promise."

She sat and stroked a lock of hair from his forehead. Her eyes shone with excitement. "What did they say?"

"They spoke of trees rich with fruit, grape vines producing plenty, green pastures, water flowing..." Salome could eat and have what she needed. Nathan smiled. "You could get fat on the Land."

Salome laughed. "You speak as if I'm a cow."

Nathan laughed. "You need to gain some weight."

Salome grabbed his hand and squeezed it. "You worry too much over me. Each child requires the mother to rest. You were too busy in Egypt to notice with the other two. Now, you see what it takes to grow a child."

Nathan squeezed her hand. He saw every day how much rest she had to take. He brought water, because the weight seemed such a strain on her. "The journey drains you."

Salome shook her head. "You forget the Lord's provision. You emphasize the hard times. The Lord is good. Remember Egypt when you were beaten?"

Nathan nodded, he instinctively reaching to scratch his back where the scars still itched when he sweated.

Salome stroked his beard. "I had to give your suffering over to God, every day, or I would have become bitter at what was done to you."

Nathan squeezed her hand. "I would willingly suffer more, if you would not have to."

Salome's eyes held tears. "When you were beaten in Egypt, God gave grace for me to watch you suffer. I hung on to the thought that God was good. The bad makes us stronger. It makes me look to Him. And when I look to Him, I have peace."

Nathan studied her hand as it held his. He followed her finger up her arm. He did not like seeing her so tired. He felt helpless to do anything. He couldn't make her gain weight.

"Dwelling on the suffering only makes it hurt more. Remember His care, rather than dwelling on the times you couldn't see His care."

He swallowed. When had God shown that He cared? When she had to go without water until she almost died? When he had to give her water by drops because she was so weak that she didn't even know who he was? He had been frightened that he had lost her then. He hadn't been able to do anything.

When he looked into her face again, he swallowed. "That's my problem. I doubt His care."

Salome smiled. "Tell Him. I asked why too many times to count. But I found that it only made me swirl in a sand storm. When I stopped asking why, I realized His care goes deeper than the things that I can see. He cares enough about me to make me His."

Nathan squeezed her arm where his hand rested. "He gives us things, then tears them from our hands when we love them."

Salome rubbed his arm. "Adlai told me about Job. He loved God. Job lost everything but his life. Job asked God why. Do you know God's answer?"

Nathan shook his head. He didn't want to think of losing Salome.

"God asked Job if he knew how He hung the earth in space, how the water stayed in the sky to come down as rain...things too great for any of us to understand."

Nathan waited, but when Salome didn't offer further information, he asked, "So...God didn't answer Job?"

Salome nodded. "I thought so, too, at first. But as I thought about it, I realized that God can do what He wants. He's God. That gives me great peace."

How could anyone have peace when wrong happens? "Why?"

Salome stroked his beard. When she spoke, her voice trembled, "God is good. He won't do anything that is not good. So this must be good. I don't have to understand it. But I can accept it."

Nathan nodded. "Doubts are strong."

"But God is good."

Zipporah walked to where the animals were kept. She needed more kindling for her cook fire. The people used the animal dung as fuel. She had let her fire burn too long that morning as she waited for Moses to return to eat his first meal. It had used all her fuel.

The afternoon's heat still beat down, although the sun was starting to fall in the sky. Normally she worked close to her mother and Keshet, whenever she could. She could ignore the stares and comments from the women when her mother was close. But now they were still resting from the heat of the day. She wanted to be ready in case Moses came home early for the evening meal. She grunted. When would he come home early? The people consumed his time like the sand drank water. She shifted her basket. She must stop thinking of the people's demands. They only made her angry.

When she heard whispering, she glanced behind her.

Miriam was among those who followed.

She stopped at their next words.

"How can you feel safe, living close to her?"

She recognized Miriam's voice. "I watch her and my things."

Zipporah's cheeks burned and she pulled her hood farther over her face. Why had she come to live among this people? She saw nothing of Moses ,and the people did not want her here. Zipporah picked up her unfilled basket and hurried to her tent. She did not have enough fuel for her fire, but she had enough fuel bubbling inside her to ignite a fire of a different kind.

That night, Zipporah curled against Moses before he dropped off to sleep. "Was Miriam always bossy?"

Moses muttered, almost asleep, "She likes to be in charge."

"She came into your tent without a greeting."

"She means no harm."

Zipporah rubbed Moses's back. "I feel watched, like she's waiting to catch me doing something wrong."

Moses hugged her under the sheepskin. "I'll speak to her."

Zipporah knew Miriam would not change. How could she protect her boys? The Midianites did not live in tents. They built rock fortresses with dry mortar. Sheepskins covered the doorway, blocking the hot air from entering during the day. They would also keep people from slipping inside without her knowledge. Moses was too busy. Would her brother build the house? She could have Gershom help gather the rocks.

Zipporah squinted to see the outline of Moses's face in the darkness. Was he sleeping? His breathing wasn't heavy yet. She never could really talk with him. His mind seemed on the people, not really hearing what she was saying. "Moses."

Moses shifted.

"Even if we don't stay long at a place, may Hobab build a dwelling place like my people's?"

Moses mumbled. "Fine."

Zipporah settled against him until she heard his deep breathing. She would have something that felt more like home, and she would feel better protected from Miriam and from these people who thought that they must watch her.

Moses paused before Miriam's tent. He knew that she'd be awake early, and he wouldn't have time later in the day after judging. He hoped that this would take little time, but with Miriam, he could never know. Miriam did not take correction well. She only heard what she wanted. He took a deep breath. "Shalom."

"Be at peace, Moses. What brings such a busy leader to my humble tent?"

Moses smiled. "You."

"I'm glad that you haven't forgotten your only sister with your family demanding so much of your time."

"My family doesn't demand my time. They deserve my time. Though, I can't spend enough with them."

"You're never at your campsite. You should not take your task so seriously. Share it with Aaron. You need to control your family."

"What do you mean?"

"Well, they are not our people. They don't value what we value. They need help to live like us."

Moses sighed. "My wife is a descendant of Abraham. Treat her like family."

"Keturah's blood taints her. They are thieves and slave traders."

"They are a peace-loving people. Be kind. Accept her ways. Crowds make her nervous."

Miriam shrugged. "Because she feels guilty?"

"Miriam." Moses waited until she looked at him.

Miriam dropped her eyes, "I only wish to help. What harm can

I do?"

Moses mumbled as he left, "If you only knew." Had anything been accomplished by talking with Miriam? He felt like a rag whipped by the wind after being in her presence. He also knew that she would not leave Zipporah alone. How could he rule this people, when his own sister caused dissension behind his back?

Naima placed her hand on Zipporah's shoulder. They had gone into the desert to look for herbs and their baskets were almost full. "Your father says we will depart soon."

Their time together had gone too fast. Zipporah could feel her breathing quicken. How would she manage without her mother? "When?"

"This coming Sabbath. Hobab will stay. You must make friends."

Zipporah nodded, swallowing the lump that rose in her throat. "Moses is so busy. He leaves early and comes to bed exhausted. I never see him. It's so different here."

Naima squeezed her. "Moses is a great man. You must be strong, so he can do his work."

Zipporah's voice broke. She worked to feed Moses and clean his clothes, but did he even notice or care? "Am I any use to him?"

Naima picked some stems that would make a tea. "Your presence gives him a feeling that all is well. Think what his meals were like without the chatter of Gershom and Eliezer....That would be a lonely meal."

Zipporah laughed. "At least a quiet meal."

They were quiet as they walked, looking by boulders where the herbs could find pockets of water to grow quickly. "How should I deal with Miriam? She watches me, always looking for something to accuse me of."

Naima looked back at the campsite. "Miriam needs something to do. Correcting others gives her a sense of control. Just be yourself. Be kind."

Zipporah clenched her teeth. "Kindness is hard."

"But necessary."

Gershom came running toward them. "Look what I found! A lizard for Aunt Miriam."

Naima looked at Zipporah. "Why would she want a lizard?"

Gershom held the lizard to Naima's face. "She looks for something."

Zipporah gasped. "You mean she comes inside our tent to look?"

Gershom nodded. "When you leave for water or animal dung."

Zipporah looked at Naima with raised eyebrows.

Naima petted the lizard with one finger. "Kindness, Zipporah."

Gershom held the lizard against his chest. "I'll put it in that basket in the corner of the tent. She always looks there first."

Zipporah bit her lip. That basket held her treasures from home. How dare that woman!

Gershom stroked the lizard on its stomach. It relaxed and did not move.

Zipporah finally smiled. "What an excellent idea! Find more lizards to keep it company."

Her mother said behind her. "Kindness, Zipporah."

But Zipporah did not want to hear.

The mid-morning air was split by shrieking.

Gershom covered his mouth, but did not smother his laughter.

Miriam searched the dark interior as she hissed. "What have you done to me?"

Gershom caught the two lizards in the basket. He held them to her face. "Which one would you like?"

Miriam held her hand over her neck. Her heart beat in her throat. "How dare you laugh at me!"

Zipporah stepped through the doorway. "How dare you search my things!"

Miriam adjusted her clothing.

Zipporah stepped toward her. "You accuse me of stealing; then you come into my home and rummage through my things!" Grabbing the basket that once held her treasures, she threw the remaining lizards at Miriam. "Get out!"

Miriam screeched as she ran from the tent.

Zipporah spat, "You are not welcome at our campfire again." She breathed heavily.

Gershom stood beside her as they watched her leave.

Zipporah squeezed his shoulder. "You did well. We just might be free of her. Didn't she look funny when she jumped?"

Gershom laughed. "Was that the kindness Grandmother told us to show?"

Zipporah stroked his hair from his forehead. "No. But it was fun, was it not? Tell me if she comes back.... Stealing her things, indeed! Wait till your father hears about this."

Miriam had waited until after the heat of the day to wash her garments. She sat under the shade of a tree, at the water's side. She was still fuming over her visit to Moses's tent that morning. Every time she thought of it, her heart beat faster. She could still feel the lizard as it darted up her arm when she had opened the basket's lid. She wiped her arm again, still unable to forget its feet against her skin. Her washing was forgotten. She must find some way to control that woman. She planned her words.

This was the group of women who listened to her and respected what she said. "That Cushite woman, doesn't she wash her garments?"

One woman glanced around the water at the other groups of women washing. "I never see her washing."

Another wiped her arm across her forehead. "Maybe she has so many garments that she doesn't need to wash so often."

Another woman whose basket held only a few pieces of clothes said, "Wouldn't that be something?"

Others joined in the discussion, imagining that they had seen chests of clothes brought into Moses's tent when she arrived.

Miriam smiled inwardly. They were easily led. "Well, she is a Cushite after all." Miriam paused to look around the circle of women. "You do know what they do?"

Several women shook their heads.

Danya, Korah's wife, spoke. "Don't they raid caravans?"

"And steal people to sell as slaves." Miriam looked from one to another as they stopped washing to look at her. The alarm on their faces told her she had made her point. Sensing the time was right, she said, "So why did Moses bring her into our camp? Shouldn't he be protecting us from such people?"

She paused to allow them to think. Then added, "I've looked at her things. She doesn't keep much where one can see. In fact, I've yet to find where she hides her riches."

Danya shook her head. "Have you seen her clothes? They're nothing but skins. Wouldn't she wear better, if she had them?"

Miriam continued to lead the women. "She makes us think she's poor, so she can better steal from us."

"Miriam, aren't they your family? Surely she's not like that. What is she like?"

Miriam had been waiting for this opportunity. "I offered to help with a meal. She threw lizards at me and sent me away."

"She didn't."

"She even told me that I wasn't welcome at her campfire."

"Well, we must beware of our things then. She doesn't hide behind deception; she shows herself boldly."

Miriam paused. "Indeed. We must beware. I shall miss eating at Moses's campfire with my own family."

Another asked, "Would Moses allow such behavior?"

Miriam sighed. "He hasn't gotten control of her yet. What hope does he have with a nation?"

As she wrung out her cloak, she remembered a judgment Moses had given to a family in their tribe. Moses's judgment had been harsh. They had stolen someone's sheep. But Miriam had enjoyed the meat that they shared with her. It was only a sheep. The shepherd had others.

She scrubbed at a soiled spot on her tunic with some sand before rinsing it again. If Moses would allow Aaron to judge, she could manipulate Aaron by appealing to his compassion.

If Zipporah weren't here, Miriam knew that she could control Moses better. He required wearing down. He seemed different now that Zipporah had come; more determined, more focused on the people, harder to control. She smiled, but not because the stain had lightened on her clothes. She had found her solution. "Why doesn't Moses's wife make something decent for Moses to wear? Joshua looks better than Moses. Moses still wears those shepherd's skins. A leader should wear something suitable."

Another whispered, "There she is now." They stopped talking and watched with eyes that looked for wrongdoing.

Zipporah filled a vessel and left.

When she left, they continued. "Did you see her son? He runs like a sheep unable to find his way home. He watches the soldiers train. Doesn't she watch him?"

Another woman paused in wringing out water from her cloak to wipe a strand of hair out of her face. She watched the men practicing on the other side of the water. "All the boys watch the soldiers. It attracts them like flies to honey."

Danya asked, "How will Moses lead a people when he can't even contain his family?"

Miriam nodded. "Should he lead at his age?"

"How old is he, Miriam?"

Miriam emphasized her answer. "Eighty-one. But he must control his family. Leading all these people keeps him from taking care of his family. Do you know who should lead us?" Miriam could sense Danya's desire for her husband, Korah, to be leader.

Danya responded, "We need someone else."

Miriam smiled. "Aaron has no family. His wife died. His boys are grown. He could easily lead us. He almost does. Doesn't he perform the sacrifices?"

Nods of agreement circled the women.

No one asked what the Lord thought. No one cared. But their laundry was clean, so they returned to their tents.

Moses and Zipporah finished eating a quiet meal, for once without interruption. The sun had long since set. The fire cloud shone brightly in the dark sky studded with stars. The boys had fallen asleep, waiting for Moses to come home. Zipporah leaned against Moses. "I do not wish to burden you."

Moses moved his vessel to make room for her. He held her. "Zipporah, you don't burden me. Your concerns are my concerns." As she hesitated, he prompted, "What is it?"

"My father leaves tomorrow."

Moses nodded. "We come close to our Land."

"I'm afraid of your people."

He looked at her face. His voice rose. "Do they threaten you?"

Zipporah shook her head. "Nothing like that. It's disapproval...distrust, dislike. I wish to return to my people, but I want to be with you."

Moses squeezed her tighter. "I miss the hillsides of your father's lands. Sometimes, I recall even their smells. In Egypt, I'd walk to the pastures just to see the lambs frolic. It reminded me of you. When you weren't here, I longed for your presence." He cupped her face in his hand. "Zipporah, I need you. If the Lord called me to lead this people, then He will enable you to live with them."

Zipporah sighed. "It's hard. Did my father tell of giving our land to my sister? I've nowhere to go. I have no home."

Moses rubbed her back. "Jethro mentioned his gift to your sister. I give it with blessing. We will have a new home, given by the Lord. He will make sure you are settled with His people."

Zipporah swallowed. "His people hold me at arm's length and look with judgment on everything I do."

"Even Carmel?"

"No, not Carmel. But I walk among your people and only wish to be friends and to try to help them. They act like they don't even want me to touch them." Zipporah moved away from him. "Can this people live peacefully with another people, when they can't even live with each other?"

Moses shook his head. "The Lord must unite this people. But first, they must look to Him. You must, too. You will find He is enough."

CHAPTER 9

Moses walked with Adlai from the tent of meeting. The sun had long since set. The fire cloud brightened the night sky. The day had been long. Even without judging, the people seemed to have many needs that required his leading. Some things were practical, like proper sanitation with so many people. But so much of it was how to treat each other. If they knew God, they would treat each other better.

"In Egypt, how did you teach your classes truth?"

Adlai shrugged. "The Hebrews I taught were educated and already knew how to read. I taught them our history, just as you do."

Moses wondered how much listening week after week helped. If they heard, wouldn't their problems be less? "Is there a better way to tell what the Lord expects of them? Hearing doesn't penetrate their hearts."

"They don't listen with their hearts. It takes willing ears to do what they hear."

Moses smelled food. Many people were finishing their evening meals. The smell of flatbread and smoke lingered in the air. He had forgotten to eat all day. His insides rumbled. "How do you make hearts listen?"

Adlai laughed. "And forget about eating?" He shook his head. "Are you God?"

Moses nodded to Nathan who had finished his meal and was watching his children play around his tent. "I tell of things that they don't see."

Adlai allowed some children to run by him. "You compete with what they do see. You can't make their hearts listen. Nor does God...look at Pharaoh."

Moses looked at the fire cloud. "Yes, I remember Pharaoh's stubbornness. Every time I told of another plague, I'd hold my breath, hoping that he would help his people. If I could have..."

Adlai put on his hood for the chillness of the night. "God gives us choices. Sometimes we don't choose...the best."

Moses studied the cloud. "You do well to remind me that I can't choose for each person. God holds all these things in His hands."

Adlai squeezed Moses's shoulder. "The men are hungry to know the written word. That encourages me. With the elders judging minor disputes, do you have more time?"

Moses resumed walking. "I have time to record our journey."

Adlai nodded. "The testimony of His faithfulness." They had almost reached Adlai's campsite. He hesitated. "How about more time with your family?"

Moses shifted from thinking about the people to his family. "I had hoped by not judging that I'd get home earlier. I don't see my boys awake." He shrugged. "I miss too many meals. What can I do?"

Adlai looked at his tent. "Carmel feels things that I don't. The people torment Zipporah."

"How?"

Adlai swallowed. "They don't like her different ways. She doesn't complain, but Carmel finds her crying."

Moses sighed. "If I can't change their hearts to hear God's Words, how can I make their hearts love?"

Zipporah returned after washing. She had started early in the morning, after feeding the boys. The sun hadn't warmed the water, her hands were cold and chapped and the skins wouldn't dry before they needed their cloaks for the cool nights. She had washed them and returned them to her basket. Now her basket full of wet sheep skins was heavy and burdensome as she carried it to her tent. Having watched other women wring out their linen clothing with ease, she knew theirs would dry quickly. She looked at her sopping pile of skins. They required days to dry. She tried not to wash them too often, for they took too long to dry, even with the hot afternoons. To her the sodden skins were just another reminder of the distinction between her and this people.

She swallowed a sob before it escaped. She missed her mother. Naima had made washing a time for support. Blinking back tears, she spread the skins in the sunshine around her tent. She sucked up a breath to prevent another outburst. She must stay busy so she would not miss home.

Gershom burst into their campsite. "Ima, may I watch the army practice?"

"Do not go too close."

"Thank you." He spun around and left.

The word had flowed smoothly from his lips as if he had been born to this people: "Ima." Would she ever feel a part of this people? She bent for another soggy sheepskin and longed for her home, letting the silent tears wet her cheeks.

After hanging the skins to dry, she went to the basket where she always placed her ring from Moses. Where was it? She wiped her eyes and looked again. She shook the basket upside down.

She sat on her heels, thinking. The boys had been with her. They would not have bothered it. Where could it have gone?

She recalled other times, when she had returned from gathering fuel or getting water, that skins were rearranged or herbs moved. She did not have much, but she knew where she put things. Had she put her ring there? Was she losing her mind?

Would Miriam take it? Miriam was controlling, but would she steal? Zipporah shook her head. She couldn't understand. Family helped. At home, she depended upon her sisters when sickness came, during lambing, when the rains brought the herbs she needed to gather. They worked together. She didn't even resent her sister who now lived in her house with her flocks. Her family needed the land. But would Miriam steal from her own family? The idea did not leave. What had she ever done to cause Miriam's hatred?

She lit a candle from the fire embers and searched the ground under the basket. The ring had to be there.

Eliezer came to her side and patted her arm. "What's matt'r?"

Zipporah put him on her lap. "Mama lost her most treasured possession."

"Your ring?"

Zipporah nodded. "Can you help me look?"

With a nod, he crawled in the dirt, looking.

Zipporah searched the darkened interior. She retraced her steps to the water's edge where she had cleaned the skins. She searched the entire day.

Moses returned late that night. He hugged her. He studied her face. "What's wrong, my Desert Flower?"

Zipporah could not hold back the tears. "I washed today. When I returned, my ring was gone. I've searched the house, the water's edge, the skins. It's gone."

Moses rubbed her back. "It's just a wooden ring. I couldn't even give you a gold one."

"But it was from you." Zipporah hugged him tighter. "It reminds me of happier times."

"Happier times?"

"When I could see you every night. When I knew that you would lie beside me until the sun's rays rose over the mountain. When I spoke to you, and you listened..."

"I don't listen to you?"

Zipporah hesitated.

"Tell me."

Zipporah responded. "When you are home, you are here in body, but your heart is somewhere else. Your mind thinks on other problems. My problems are not yours. You hear, but they do not touch your heart."

Moses nodded.

"I stopped sharing my thoughts because you do not hear with your heart. I hold them tight within me."

Moses took her face in his hands. "My precious Flower, who grows stronger by the trials that I send her, I'm sorry."

Zipporah pulled back from his touch. "You must complete your mission."

"I need you, in order to do it."

"It's late. You must eat."

"I'll help you look."

Zipporah's voice broke and she bit her lip. "I've searched all day for it. It's gone. Don't waste your time." She stirred up the embers to warm his meal.

Moses came from behind her and turned her around in his arms. "I'll help you look. You value the ring. I value you. I'll search."

Zipporah clung to Moses, her tears finally falling. "It's gone."

As the sun sank in the horizon, Aaron joined Elizur from the tribe of Reuben and Nethanel from the tribe of Issachar outside the tent of meeting. "How was judging?"

Nethanel shook his head. "The people are needy."

Elizur adjusted his head covering as the sun shone in his eyes and the evening chill began to fall over the campsite. "I just came to watch. The lines were long! They seemed to grow as the day got hotter." He turned to Aaron. "How'd you get out of judging? I'd think that you'd be the first to be chosen."

Aaron shrugged. He had wondered the same thing. As more decisions were made, he felt more removed from them. First the dedication of Joshua, now he wasn't even involved in judging. Moses never had enough time to be at his own campsite, yet he wouldn't give any of the work to him. Did Moses think that he couldn't do it? Or did he just want all the leadership for himself? "I wasn't chosen."

Elizur slowed his steps as he looked at Aaron. "Can't Moses share his leadership with you?"

Aaron didn't want to discuss his thoughts right now. He had wondered all day why Moses had not allowed him to judge. He clenched his lips as he thought about Moses "allowing" him to judge. He was the elder brother, not Moses.

Elizur touched Aaron's shoulder. "I wish that you were judging, rather than Moses."

Aaron studied Elizur's face. He worked to hide his anger. "Why's that?"

Elizur returned his look. "You understand the people's needs. You give grace for wrongs and don't expect perfection. The people are weary of sand, heat, and travel. They need a break. You would remember that."

Aaron nodded, but did not speak. He did feel more for the people than Moses. He saw their pain first-hand. As a doctor, he helped to heal their ailments and wounds.

Nethanel tightened the belt of his cloak. He put his hands in his pockets and picked up their pace. "I thought that the day would never end. On a break, I looked at the sun. I had only judged for part of the morning! And this is only the first day! How can I sift through all their yelling to find who caused what?"

Elizur laughed. "Don't take it so seriously. They're like children, following a crowd. You have to be in charge, or you'll have fights, even in your lines."

Nethanel grunted. "I did. I was listening to one argument, when behind me three other men were yelling. No wonder Moses was exhausted. I'm more tired listening to arguments, than I would be if I had made bricks all day."

Laughing, they separated to go to their own tents.

Aaron continued to his campsite, but his laughter soon stopped. Why didn't he judge? Was Moses too jealous of his leadership role to allow Aaron to share any of his glory? He didn't like his thoughts, but he didn't stop them. As Aaron walked through camp, he listened. He found those whom Moses had judged. He asked how they felt about Moses's judgment.

They were right in their own eyes. Not one felt he deserved his punishment. "Moses expected me to pay back seven times what that ox was worth."

Instead of admonishing them that justice was done, Aaron listened over their fires and shook his head. "Seven times is a lot of money." He had decided he would create a following. He would be ready, when the time was right. His little brother would not take his position from him.

Days blended into days. The people followed the cloud when it moved, and camped when it stopped. The routine gave them stability. They had stayed in one place long enough for Zipporah to have a house built.

After the rest during the hottest part of the day, Carmel stopped at Zipporah's house. "Shalom." She stepped into the darkened shelter. "Come with us to do laundry."

Zipporah looked at her pile of skins. "It's too late for my skins to dry in the sun."

Carmel shifted her basket on her hip. "I'd never thought about the time it took to dry those heavy skins. Next time, we'll start earlier."

Gershom lifted her basket. "I'll help you carry the basket, Ima. Can we go?"

Zipporah hesitated. Maybe she could just do a few of the things that wouldn't be needed tonight. She would like to spend time with Carmel. She felt like she needed someone besides the jabbering of little boys.

Carmel encouraged her, "Come, tell us about the Land we're going to."

Zipporah sighed. She reached for her soap made of sheep fat and herbs. "Come Eliezer."

The others had already gathered by the water by the time they arrived.

Zipporah washed on the outside of their circle.

"What does Nathan think he'll do in the new Land?" Dinah asked. "Ellis worries about providing for us once the Lord does not give us everything, every day."

"When will He stop?" Hannah asked.

Dinah looked over the water. "Someday, won't we be like other people? We won't live in a tent, getting our meal from heaven. Don't you wish for lush greenery? Or is Egypt the only land that's green?"

Carmel spread a tunic on the sand. "You speak of the green of Egypt, but you forget we left Egypt destroyed. Egypt was barren."

Hannah asked, "What will the new Land be like?"

Pelia held her clothing against her as she stared over the water. "I dream of going behind a boulder without someone else with me."

They laughed.

Carmel added. "We're all weary of staying in pairs for safety."

Reut shook her head. "Michael learns leather-working and training horses. You should see him on the horse he bought. He flies as if he were a god conquering the ground. Maybe I speak too boldly of his dreams..."

"Who else but you can get that man to say anything?" Hannah chided. "How do his visits go?"

Reut looked over the water. "As if the desert does not exist."

Pelia countered. "It's easy to see the sky when your nose is in the clouds. Michael visits you every evening. I've seen you watching him from the shadows as he stretches his neck around your abba to see you. He is your champion. Me, I argue with my brother who hates rules, seeks adventure, and wants more than just food and water. What am I to do with that?"

Hannah answered. "Come to my tent, where you can hide in the shadows with me while Amos stretches his neck to see you."

"No!" Salome and Dinah said simultaneously. They all looked at Pelia who blushed crimson and lowered her eyes.

Hannah laughed. "Have I betrayed your secret, Pelia? Your teasing of Reut makes me wonder how much of the desert sand you see these days."

"Have we missed some news?" Dinah looked at Pelia.

Hannah looked at Pelia's nod before continuing. "Pelia brought Magal over to get his wound sewn up. Amos put fifteen stitches in his arm.

"The horse's tail almost wasn't long enough. Pelia nursed him at our tent. But," she looked at Pelia. "She noticed only Amos, who sewed up the wounds."

"Amos stitches wounds?" Salome's eyebrows raised.

Pelia shrugged. "His stitching is better than mine."

They laughed.

Carmel explained to Zipporah, "Pelia has reason not to know how to sew. Her mother wasn't there to help teach her. She lived with her older brother in the pastures of Goshen where he kept his sheep."

Pelia sighed. "It healed my heart after losing my abba and ima. Nothing but green grass, blue sky, and the soft fleece of a lamb against my face."

"But now," Hannah's eyes twinkled. "Her stitching improves by watching over Amos's shoulder."

Pelia laughed. "I don't know about improving my sewing, but Amos is patient with me."

"You're good for Amos. He's spoken to your brother about *ketubah*?" Hannah persisted.

Pelia put her dried blanket in her basket. "Esmail knows only sheep. He would not even know that I was married, until I forgot to help with lambing."

Zipporah spoke for the first time. "What about you, Hannah? No one for you?"

Everyone looked down at their laundry and became silent.

Zipporah looked from one to another. "What have I said? What's wrong?"

Carmel leaned forward and whispered. "The man who seeks her, must prove himself."

"How?"

"Her father has spoken of one who has requested her. But he wishes for Hannah without wanting the Lord. Hakeen demands that he must give God control, or he will only hurt her."

Zipporah nodded. Could she hurt Moses by not allowing God control? Did the Lord take anything, unless He took it all?

CHAPTER 10

As Moses hiked the mountain of Sinai where they had moved from Rephidim, he looked over the campsite spread before him. The people were as innumerable as the sands of the desert. He couldn't count the tents, much less all the people. No one could meet all the needs of so vast a multitude, yet the Lord provided. Moses saw an eagle soaring. He shaded his eyes from the sun and watched it circle, floating on the air without moving its wings. His heart felt like that, like an invisible hand supported and sustained him, as he walked away from the people's needs and closer to the cloud and God.

Zipporah's presence helped relieve the weight of all these people, too. Just knowing that she was at home, creating a haven he could come home to at night gave him added strength to fight the battles of the day.

He continued to watch the eagle...so free. His heart overflowing with praise, he cried out, "O God, You have carried us here so that we can obey You."

The Lord spoke, "Tell the sons of Israel, 'You have seen what I did to the Egyptians. How I carried you from Egypt as if on eagles' wings. I brought you to Myself. If you will obey and keep My covenant, you will be My people.'"

Moses returned from the mountain invigorated, ready to encourage the people. He assembled the elders and told them the words of the Lord.

And all the people responded. "All that the Lord says, we will do."

When Moses presented the people's commitment to the Lord, God instructed, "Consecrate the people to Me. Tell them to wash themselves and their garments today and tomorrow. On the third day, I will come to this Mount before the people. Put boundaries around the mountain so that the people don't get too close, for if they touch the mountain, they will die. When the ram's horn is sounded, assemble them at the base of the mountain."

The people wondered what the Lord's visit would bring. Would they be safe? Could anyone be even prepared?

Zipporah had washed clothes all day yesterday. Today, she had cleaned their house of all the sand and bathed the boys. She was weary, not so much from the work, although it was much, but from her thoughts. When Zipporah had been startled by Miriam standing in the doorway, she had thought to be kind.

Miriam's first words had removed that desire. "You don't plan on making yourself presentable to the Lord, do you?"

Zipporah brushed the hair from her face. "Didn't you hear Moses?"

Miriam nodded. "That is for God's people. You don't belong to Him. You could never wash clean enough for His presence."

Zipporah was glad that she held the basket of heavy skins. She was angry enough to throw something right now. She deliberately placed the basket on the floor. "I will obey the words of my husband, regardless of whether or not I'm acceptable before your God."

"Don't think that you can please God." Miriam turned and left.

Could Miriam be right? Did God only want Miriam's people? Could she ever be pleasing to this God?

Miriam's words repeated in her mind, "You could never wash yourself clean enough for His presence." Did God not want her? One of His people had just told her that she could never be accepted. How could washing all these things make her acceptable to God?

If she could speak to Moses about it, she would feel better, but he did not return home the first night.

Why had she come here? Was she not even acceptable in Moses's sight?

When Moses entered their tent late in the evening of the second day, Zipporah wanted his assurance. Her thoughts had told her all day that she was not a part of this people and would not be acceptable to the God that Moses worshipped. She grabbed Moses's cloak and pulled him toward her. She raised her head to kiss him.

Moses took her hands in his and firmly removed them from

his chest. "Zipporah, I'm consecrated to the Lord's service. He gave instructions not to be with a woman. I must obey Him, both for your protection and for the protection of His people."

She had waited two days to speak to him. Not only did his God did not want her, but Moses did not want her either. His rejection stung. "Your people always come first. How will what you do with me tonight affect the Lord's people?"

Moses stepped away from her. "If I'm dishonest with the Lord, how can I live honestly with you? Tonight, I must focus on the Lord, as I have promised to do."

"He gets all your time, energy, and strength. I should have stayed with my family and missed you where I could not see you, instead of missing you where I can see you."

"Zipporah, if my heart were divided, would you want it? If I only followed God half-heartedly, could you trust me?" Moses looked at her with such intensity, that Zipporah turned away. When she did, Moses slipped out of the tent.

Zipporah waited all night for his return.

He did not come back.

She wished that she understood, but she did not. Her heart was given totally to Moses. But even that was not good enough.

The day began, unlike any other. Miriam heard the trumpet sound for the people to gather in front of the tent of meeting. She returned her empty basket beside her tent flap with a sigh. She had no time to gather manna, or even start her fire. She pushed her way to the front of the gathering, where Moses waited for God's' arrival. Out of habit, she looked for the cloud that they always followed. It had disappeared! Its absence was unsettling. She looked anxiously for Moses. How would they reach the Promised Land without it?

Before Moses could raise his staff to quiet the people, the ground trembled beneath her, rocking her as if she were on a boat. She grabbed Aaron, who stood beside her. She could hear the animals, outside of camp, panicking. They neighed, bellowed, bleated, and brayed.

Lightning flashed through the sky, striking the top of the mountain. A ring of fire flared up where the lightning struck. The fire grew, falling off the edge of the mountain like a waterfall, taking boulders, dirt and ash with it. It rolled down the mountain, gathering speed, collecting more rocks and dirt, burying everything in its path. The falling mountain reached the bottom, but did not stop. It covered their campsite.

It rained: not water, but ash, rock, and dust fell from the darkened sky. Pieces fell in the lake they used for drinking, sizzling from its heat. Ash dusted the water with its fine powder.

A hissing, greater than the blowing of seventy trumpets, came from deep within the mountain, as if air was trapped inside trying to escape.

Then the mountaintop was gone. In its place a fire glow remained.

A smoking, black, ominous cloud rose about it.

Miriam felt the flame's heat against her face as it shot far into the sky. Its white fire burned her eyes. She fell down on the ground, throwing her arms over her head to shield it from the raining rocks. She fell to her knees, holding her breath in silent worship.

Time stopped.

God had come.

Would she be consumed?

She had seen the glory of this God. It could not be contained.

But this...this showed the power of this God. She felt the ground tremble, as if it could not support this God Who flattened a mountain peak with a single step.

How could she stand before this God?

She raised her head, opening her clenched hands. They brushed against her cloak, leaving ash streaks. Rubbing at them only made them streak more.

Had anyone seen her fall to her knees in fear? Looking around at the others about her, she rose to her feet.

Others rose around her. Their faces streaked with soot. Their eyes reflected her own fear.

How could anyone be worthy of this God?

Her words spoken to Zipporah came back to her. How could Miriam have thought that she would be worthy?

She looked back at her campsite for a place to hide. Her tent lay covered by the mountains' dirt! She gasped. If she had stayed in her tent, she would have been killed. Her life had been spared by standing here with Moses.

She looked again to the mountaintop. The smoke was too thick to see it.

Then the Lord spoke, "Moses, come to Me."

She trembled. Would she see her brother again? She looked around her. Would anyone keep him from meeting his death? No one stopped him.

She watched as Moses walked up the smoking, thundering, rumbling, shaking mountain. She followed his form until he became a speck on the hill.

Who was worthy to go before God's presence and live?

Moses looked at the top, where once a peak pointed to the heavens. Now only a crater remained with a raised edge, glowing with heat. He had learned obedience in the desert when God had spoken through the burning bush. He had witnessed God's deliverance in the plagues sent upon Egypt. Now he would obey again. The desert morning's coolness had left when the fire had come. He loosened his cloak's belt. Ashes, rocks, and dust still fell. He covered his head with his hood and began to pick his way up the mountain. Slides, where rocks and boulders had fallen, left rutted pathways that kept his feet from slipping. He held his staff to secure his footing.

When Moses reached the top of the mountain, he could see no peak. The mountain top was gone. A crater, with a rim several rods high, remained, like God had stepped on the mountain, and it could not hold His power and so had sunk. Throwing off his hood, he knelt near the rim of the crater, bowing his face to the charred ground.

Moses overflowed with praise. "You, O God, are all power. One step upon Your creation, and it crushes. It folds before Your presence in worship. What man can stand before You and live? We are a people of uncleanness. All our righteousness is as dung. Yet You draw us to Yourself and want us to know You."

The Lord interrupted. "Return to the people. Remind the people not to reach beyond the boundaries. I want no one killed for touching the mountain. Remind the priests that they will be given no special treatment. Afterwards, return to Me, along with your brother, Aaron."

Moses returned to the people. The purity of the mountaintop, burned clean from the fire, contrasted sharply with the ashes, dirt, and rocks that still settled below the mountain. As Moses descended the mountain, the sin of the people seemed to settle on his back, weighing him down. He could barely place one foot in front of another. When he looked below him at the people, he realized he had only come half-way down the mountain. Is this what God felt when He entered the tent of meeting to speak with him?

Obedience was what God required. Descending the mountain was harder than going up to God. Why couldn't he just stay up at the top with God? He could worship. He could sing. He could praise God. Moses sighed. God had commanded him to return to the people. He was their leader. He must lead, even if no one followed. He forced his feet to take the remaining steps.

He looked into the ash-streaked faces.

They looked relieved, as if they had feared God would kill him.

Did they really think that God would strike him? He almost laughed. He had not been afraid, going before God. He had wanted to be with God. He had felt safety, peace, purity. Moses smiled. He raised his staff. "Stay off the mountain. The Lord is holy. Do not touch it."

He turned to the Levites congregated by the tent of meetings' doorway. "All the priests must stay off the mountain. The Lord has given specific instructions for you." Then he looked around. "Where is Aaron?"

From the Levite tribe, Aaron made his way to the front of the congregation.

Moses motioned. "Aaron, follow me."

Aaron looked at the mountaintop, then at Moses.

Moses nodded, retracing his steps. The path was easier this time. He thought only once to glance at Aaron.

Aaron was pale. His eyes wide.

Moses stopped to tap his staff on the ground. "God is good. Do not fear."

They began again. This time Moses did not even remember to look back at Aaron again. He could not wait to reach God.

When they reached the crater, he fell once again on his knees and bowed his face to the ground.

God began. His voice, thundering down the mountainside to where the people stood, demanded attention. "I am the Lord your God, Who brought you out of the land of Egypt, out of slavery.

"You shall have no other gods before Me.

"You shall not make an idol. You shall not worship them; for I am a jealous God.

"You shall not take My name in vain.

"Remember the Sabbath, and keep it holy.

"Honor your father and your mother.

"You shall not murder.

"You shall not commit adultery.

"You shall not steal.

"You shall not bear false witness against your neighbor.

"You shall not covet anything that belongs to your neighbor."

Moses listened. This was what God's people needed. This would show them His Way. The people would know God, and they would be His people.

At the bottom of the mountain, the people had backed away from the mountain.

As Moses and Aaron descended, no one came forward to hear what Moses would tell them.

The elders shouted to Moses even before they passed the rope. "You speak to us. We will listen. But do not allow us to hear the voice of the Lord, or we will die."

Moses shook his head. Instead of seeing God's power and yearning to know this God, the people wanted to get away from Him. How would they learn to know Him, if they always stayed away? He raised his hands. "The Lord desires you to fear Him, so that you will not sin."

Aaron returned from the mountain along with Moses. He had seen God's holiness. He had heard His voice. Yet he walked down the mountain, not with worship, but with troubled thoughts.

Moses had specifically told the priests to stay away, as if they were not presentable. He had spoken to Aaron, as if he were a child. Who did Moses think he was?

In Egypt, hadn't he spoken for Moses? Hadn't he faced Pharaoh along with Moses and reported to the people? The people had sought him out for healing when their daughters were sick. They had brought their sons to him when close to death. He had shown them the Lord. He had interceded for the people.

After leaving Egypt, Moses had taken control. The people came to Moses for their disputes. They asked Moses for water. The people looked to Moses as their god. His younger brother had stolen the respect of the people.

When Jethro visited, Aaron had expected to counsel with them as they discussed the wonders of the Lord in Egypt and in the desert. He was included because he always ate with Moses. But when Jethro had suggested appointing judges, Moses turned to him, as an afterthought, asking him to find the men.

Aaron spit out ashes that had fallen into his mouth. They stuck to his tongue like chalk on a finished brick. He shook his head. He would spit out Moses if he could.

He remembered the men who were judged so uncompromisingly by Moses. Aaron had listened to them, empathizing with their dissatisfaction. They would remember. They would follow him.

He had waited for the right time. It was coming soon.

When God again called Moses to meet him on the mountain, Zipporah had watched with her heart in her throat. She stared at him until the ash, dust, and black cloud swallowed him. Why had the people told Moses to go talk with the Lord alone? Could he still live? Would he return? What would she do, if he didn't?

The hemp rope kept the people from touching the mountain. How would they find out if Moses was all right?

She was the last to turn away from the mountain when Moses was no longer visible. She returned to their house. The boulders had rolled and bounced around the house. Some of the walls leaned. Ash coated everything. She pushed her hair from her face and sighed deeply. Keeping her hands busy, even though her mind stayed with Moses at the top of the mountain, she shoveled out their house from under the dirt. Would it be easier to just make another house and forget all her belongings? She wished Moses was here.

As she worked, she watched for Moses's return. The dark cloud hovered over the mountaintop. It would be a miracle for Moses to come back alive, but she needed one. She found Gershom's cloak buried in the pile of ashes. She shook it.

The cloak had not dried completely from the other day when she had washed it. Now ashes stuck to it. The smell of fire, not from their cook smoke, but of destruction, hung in the air, keeping her insides in turmoil.

The next day, although she tried to keep busy, she could not stop looking to the top of the mountain. She found Eliezer's clothes and piled them by their bedding. Everything must be washed. She glanced at the pool. A thin layer of ash had fallen on it. Even with the people getting water, the ash continued to thicken and float on the top. She had made flatbread that morning for the boys...the manna was still spread over the desert each morning, on top of the ashes. She could not eat. Her insides pinched and knotted like the jumbled mass of a coarsely spun thread. She wiped her face; then looked at her cloak. The ashes had probably streaked her face with soot.

She saw a fragment of the basket she always kept her treasures in. Kneeling, she dug like a dog making a hole for his bone. If Moses were gone, where would she go? She had no home. This people did not want her. Her tears were falling steadily now. She did not try to stop them.

Someone grabbed her shoulder.

She ignored it and continued digging, as if getting her basket back would bring Moses back too.

"Zipporah!"

Zipporah turned, her eyes widened. She squealed. She clutched Moses's cloak and sobbed. "You didn't die. Your God didn't kill you."

He held her, rubbing her back.

She couldn't stop the tears. Her insides flopped in circles. "When you didn't return, I thought..." She stepped out of his embrace and wiped her eyes with her sleeve. He offered his cloak. She took his face between her hands. She didn't want to ask, but she must know, "You will stay here?"

Moses shook his head. "No, Zipporah."

"You're returning to the mountain?"

Moses nodded.

"You'll come back?"

Moses drew her to himself. "We need the Lord's Words to bring peace to our hearts. I must hear what the Lord tells me."

She leaned her head on his chest. "Why can't someone else listen to what He says? Why must it always be you?"

He laughed. "Maybe I listen better?"

She did not laugh. She held her tears back by a thread. "When the mountain shook and spewed smoke and fire, I was so afraid for you. What would I do without you?"

"Zipporah, I'll return."

"Can time stop? The sun stands still while you are gone. I watch through all the dust and smoke, flying through the air. I wait, but you do not return."

"Being there with the Lord, Zipporah...I can't explain it. Time stands still there, too. Time is not important. The past does not exist, the now, nor what will take place. It's all one.

"Night doesn't come; for the light is ever present. I don't grow tired. I could stand before Him forever. I feel my littleness in His presence, for He is a great God. His presence surrounds me, upholds me. Does that make sense?"

Zipporah shook her head. How could he not know he had been gone two whole days? How could God's presence make time unimportant?

Moses continued as if she understood. "Not only time, but distance. Distance is swallowed like a cloud. I see far and near as if it's all one. Is that how He sees?

"Time is nothing. Distance is close. And things lose their feeling of heaviness. I could carry a boulder if I had to. Its force would not weigh me down. His presence makes even burdens lighter."

Zipporah looked into his eyes. She wished her own life weren't so weary. Could her burdens be lifted by this God?

Moses's face reflected a light not his own. His eyes shone with energy that spoke of power and worship. "God gives me a glimpse of what He sees and makes me worship. I can do nothing else."

Zipporah stroked his beard. "I see the smoke and fire. I feel the tremor. It makes me so afraid! Too afraid to worship. How can you worship? How can you be so peaceful?" She stopped.

He was looking at the mountain. He didn't hear her. It happened often.

She sighed.

He worshiped; she panicked.

He focused on the mountain; she lived in the valley.

She rested her head on his chest. She would treasure this bit of time. Her worship was directed toward something more tangible than a fire that smoked without fuel. She wished Moses would stay and make her time disappear...instead of going and making each day last forever. She sighed. It could not be.

Zipporah watched as Moses returned to the top of the mountain. She saw the people turn once again from watching him to digging their belongings out of the ash from the mountain.

At the top, Moses read the commandments as the Lord wrote them out on stones with His Finger.

The Lord gave each commandment and its penalty for disobedience. The Lord's commandments left no questions. He told how, what, when, and where to sacrifice. He described the Tabernacle, the priests' garments, and the tools for worship.

He told how to treat slaves, servants, and strangers.

Moses lived with God. He marveled at His wisdom. This was the answer for His people. Every problem that had been brought to him to judge was mentioned here. God had a clear answer for everything.

The people had lived under others' rules for years. Most of these rules weren't based on right and wrong, but on the whims of a selfish ruler. They had lost their standard, their ability to accept responsibility, and to problem solve. They were told what to do and when. Now, God provided structure, boundaries, rules, and stability; not out of cruelty and desire for power, but out of love, for their protection, for their good. He was setting them apart from any other nation on earth. They would be His own people, if only they would listen and obey.

Moses saw the holiness of this God, but he also felt God's love, uniting His people with Himself. He was calling them by name.

CHAPTER 11

Moses had been gone over fourteen days. Initially the people worried over his absence. Could he survive in the presence of God? Would he return to lead them to their Land? They put their questions aside and went to dig their belongings out of the rubbish. With every salvaged vessel and treasured find, the people rebuilt their campsite. As the days passed and the smoke and ashes sifted from the sky, they forgot Moses and his God and turned to Aaron for leadership.

Aaron breathed deeply of the power that was his alone. His thoughts were as far from the Lord as were the hearts of the people he led.

Aaron was in his tent mentally counting the men loyal to him. He had blown out his candle. The smoke still lingered in the air. A shadow darkened his doorway; then materialized inside his tent. Aaron stood. "What do you want?"

The man laughed, without mirth. "To help you be the leader that you should be."

Aaron peered at the silhouetted figure. Should he relight his candle? "How do you know what I want?"

"Would anyone want his little brother telling him what to do in front of an entire people? Everyone heard Moses say, 'Stay off the mountain, especially you, priests.'" He laughed wickedly. "Doesn't he show you any respect, Aaron?"

Aaron licked his lips. "What do you want?"

"I want my respect back, just like you."

Aaron felt uneasy with this man. He recognized the voice, but he could not remember why. "What did Moses do to you?"

"If you're respected, I will be, too."

Aaron swallowed. Could he trust this man? "What will you do?"

The moon's rays outlined the man's silhouette as he crossed his arms. "I'll give you respect."

Aaron did not like his cockiness. But he liked his idea. He would get his respect. "What will I have to do?"

The man sat in the dark and unfolded his scheme to Aaron.

Moses had not returned for several weeks. As Shelumiel left the tent of meeting after judging all day, he met Elizur, also on his way home from a day of judging. Though Moses hadn't felt Elizur should be a judge, Aaron had recently appointed him anyway. After all, Moses hadn't returned from the mountain. Someone had to take charge.

Shelumiel asked, "How's judging?"

Elizur shrugged. "The people need a new leader."

Shelumiel glanced over the tents at the cloud of fire. "We have not lost our leader, but the judging becomes more difficult the longer Moses stays away. Without his presence, a sense of holiness has left the people."

"It's Moses's fault that the people do wrong. Moses strutted through camp as if he was god."

Shelumiel stopped walking. "Moses knows the Lord. He executed judgment without causing dissension. Remember your judgment last week? The people repaid what they stole, but with moldy manna stuck on it. They obeyed the letter of the Law, but their hearts were not changed."

Elizur laughed.

Shelumiel did not. "Your judging creates havoc. You stir up anger and disrespect against the rules."

Elizur kicked a weed as they walked toward their campsites. "Aaron cares more for the people than Moses."

Shelumiel shook his head. "When Aaron sympathizes with those who have done wrong, he makes the laws unimportant. The people don't look to the Law but to Aaron who excuses the action. That kind of leadership encourages wrongdoing. The victim pays twice."

"This weighty responsibility of judging often keeps me awake at night, wondering if my decisions were just."

Elizur chuckled. "You take the Law too seriously. Find humor and you'll sleep."

Shelumiel wiped his brow. "The people don't think their grievances are funny. God's holiness is not to be taken lightly."

Elizur juggled a rock from hand to hand. "This task weighs too heavily upon you. Ask Aaron to find someone else to judge for you."

"Perhaps you should, until you look at things as the Lord sees them."

Elizur laughed. "And ruin my entertainment? I see God just fine. I'm not the one that can't sleep at night."

"Yes, but will you wake up?"

The days had moved to weeks and still Moses had not come. Zipporah gazed out the window toward the top of the mountain. Hobab, her brother, had helped to reconstruct their house after the mountain had fallen on it. She made sure that she had a window where she could see Moses return. Was he still alive?

She was so engrossed in watching the mountain that she didn't hear someone behind her until a voice spoke by her ear, "Prepare yourself."

Zipporah jumped and put her hand on her heart.

Miriam stood behind her. She hissed through taunting lips, "Moses will not return. You cannot stay with my people."

Where was Eliezer? Zipporah spotted him, standing safely at a distance from them. She breathed a sigh of relief. "Moses will not leave his duty undone. He will return. I won't move until the fire directs me."

Miriam stepped toward her, forcing her against the wall. "Moses is dead. How could a person live this long without food and water? If he lives, he is a spirit. He will be like a god. You'll be of no use to him. Leave now." Her breath was hot in Zipporah's face.

Zipporah felt the heat rush through her body. "The Lord keeps Moses alive. Didn't you see water come from the rock when Moses hit it? Don't you collect manna from the desert floor every day? The Lord will care for His leader until his duty is done." She stepped forward, pushing Miriam backwards. "We need Moses. He is not dead. He will return." She continued backing Miriam toward the fire pit.

Miriam tripped.

Zipporah grabbed her before she stumbled into the burning embers and pulled her toward herself until their faces were one palm apart.

Miriam trembled, looking back at the flames.

Zipporah stepped back, continuing to hold her.

When Miriam regained her balance, Zipporah let her go.

Miriam breathed deeply.

Zipporah pointed to the doorway. "I believe you were leaving my husband's house."

Miriam stumbled over the rocks around the fire in her haste to depart. When she reached the doorway, instead of leaving, she turned to Zipporah. "I've warned you! When Moses doesn't return, you will be chased from this campsite like the stray dog that you are. You will take nothing with you. You will not be the leader's wife. You will be the dog that he kept out of pity."

When Miriam left, Zipporah watched the sheep skin move back and forth across the doorway. Finally, it stilled. She leaned against the stone wall, eyes closed, holding her heart.

Eliezer tugged on her tunic. "Ima, what's wrong?"

Zipporah breathed deeply. "The Lord, my God, has become more real to me than ever before. His protection is ever before me and I will thank Him. If only I could always remember the words that flew from my mouth when I spoke to Miriam. Moses lives, and so does my God."

The mountain still smoked; the black cloud hovered. Ashes and dust continued to float to the ground, coating the tents.

But the people lost their sense of awe. Their focus turned inward once again.

Aaron felt this change. He listened to the people and sympathized.

The leaders gathered for another day of judging.

Nahshon looked at the top of the mountain. "Moses demands too much. We must relax the rules. The people need a break."

Shelumiel objected, "Without rules, we have chaos."

Elizur shook his head. "Isn't living in this desert enough suffering?"

"The people suffered more in Egypt," Shelumiel countered. "They now have freedom."

"Not with Moses oppressing us with all these rules."

Shelumiel shook his head. "Rules are for our protection. The Lord Himself has given them. He directs us because He has chosen us to be His own people. Aren't we different from other nations?"

Nahshon sighed. "We are gullible, following anyone. We need

a new leader."

Elizur turned to Aaron. "How long must we wait?"

Aaron was tired of waiting, too. Moses had been gone thirty days. Aaron sensed the unrest of the people. They chafed against the rules, the waiting, the unknown. He could lead them to the Land.

Elizur nodded to Aaron. "Make us a god that will lead us to our Land."

Aaron gulped. He expected to take leadership, but not to make an idol. He had never owned idols, even in Egypt. The Lord would not be pleased. He looked to the top of the mountain. Just the cloud lingered.

The people needed something to see.

What harm would a symbol be? Of all the idols of Egypt, the bull was not a god, but a representative of Pharaoh's authority. The people would not be worshiping an idol, if he made a bull. They would be remembering the higher authority that the bull represented. Wouldn't the people remember the Lord better with a visual image? Aaron drew his lips in a line of determination. "Bring me your gold. I will make you a figure to remember."

Throughout the day, families and individuals brought their gold. At first, Aaron thought that a small cow would be enough, but as the day passed and the pile of gold grew, he envisioned a bull larger than life. He could even sit on it and show the people how Pharaoh used to ride through his countryside as their king.

Aaron approached Bezalel's camp. "Shalom." He pointed to the silver plate. "Your hands don't stay idle for long. Eh?"

Bezalel moved his tool away from the flame to cool. "I wish to do things of beauty. But not like in Egypt. Their idols directed people away from the Lord. I want to point people to God."

Aaron nodded, glancing around at Bezalel's tools. "You were the best silversmith in Egypt. People of high stations requested your work. They were always pleased." Aaron coughed nervously and looked away from the tent. "May I request, as Moses's spokesperson..." His words trailed off. He cleared his throat and started again, "I have gold, enough to make a life-size bull, just to give the people a reminder of authority."

Bezalel stared at Aaron.

Aaron could feel his face turn red. He raised his voice. "It wouldn't be to worship, only to represent my authority, so the people know that I'm in charge." He coughed. "At least until Moses returns."

Bezalel turned the silver plate so that the words faced Aaron.

Aaron read them, "You shall have no other gods before Me." Aaron swallowed and did not meet Bezalel's eyes. He strode from Bezalel's campsite, sweating. Who did Bezalel think he was, correcting him?

If Bezalel was going to be stubborn, how was he to get the cow made? He needed that cow to show the people that he was in charge.

His quick stride slowed as he considered another idea. Bezalel's son, Seth, had apprenticed under him. He could make the cow. By his service, Seth would demonstrate his loyalty to Aaron and shame his father in the process. Aaron smiled. This plan was better.

Aaron found Seth with other men, watching the women wash clothes. The men no longer trained as soldiers. The man, who came in the dark, had suggested cancelling training. The people needed a break. Idleness bred discontent. Conditions were ripe for a new leader. Aaron smiled at Seth. "Your father recommends you for a job. Would you help?"

Seth thrust his shoulders back and sat straighter.

"Could you make a life-sized bull of gold?"

Seth looked over the water to where the girls were washing. He grinned. His eyes gleamed. "I could do that." He looked back at Aaron. "You said, life-size? You have enough gold, or do you want gold plating?"

"I'll show you."

Seth strutted back with Aaron to his tent. He saw the piles of gold. His eyes widened in surprise. "You truly do desire a life-sized bull! I assumed my father declined the job because it belittled his talent, but...did my father tell you 'no'?"

"He looked busy. I didn't want to burden him. I heard of your work, how your skill excelled many in your field."

Seth flexed his fingers. "I've done nothing but cart my tools over the desert these past five moon cycles." He sifted through the piles of gold. "This is quality gold." He stood and nodded toward Aaron. "I'll do it."

Aaron prophesied, "Seth, your workmanship will outlive the memories of anything done in Egypt."

Seth began immediately. The gold's quality amazed him. The people had taken Egypt's riches when they left. The dross had already been removed. The fire softened the gold, making it easy to pour into molds.

His hands were no longer idle. Seth worked with zeal, reminding him of Egypt, during the time the Lord had shown Himself to the people. Egyptians had competed against this God by making more and more of their own gods. He had been busy then.

Why did the Lord's people never request an image of the Lord? He had never considered that before. The question gnawed at him. Why had his father declined? Would Aaron ask him to do something the Lord would not approve of?

Seth burnt his finger on the hot prongs. He dipped it into his water vessel to cool the burning. He must stop questioning and concentrate. He would make something the world would remember.

Several times Seth had to run back to his tent for another tool. It would be more convenient to work at his tent, but he received more attention at Aaron's campsite. People came to talk with Aaron. They stayed to admire Seth's work. He basked in the attention.

"What are you doing, Seth?"

Seth glanced up from adjusting the fire's heat. "Tamara. Do you seek to watch talent at work?"

She giggled and hovered nearby as he worked. She stoked the fire or added fuel, as needed. Then she sat and watched.

"Why do you watch?"

Tamara put more fuel on the fire. "You're doing something valuable."

The days passed, but Seth's doubts continued. As Seth studied the mold that he was forming, he asked, "What does your abba say about this project?"

Tamara wrapped her arms around her legs as she sat. "My abba is too busy to know what I do. Besides, I sit here all day and don't have time to tell him."

Seth pursued. "Your ima doesn't ask?"

"I tell her that I'm with you. She is reassured."

Seth nodded. Hearing that reassured him. Aaron would not allow him to displease the Lord.

He remembered grabbing Tamara from the bitter water as others pushed her down. He had held her dripping body close to his. She would soon be a beautiful woman with her dark, flashing eyes and long, silky hair. She loved action, yet sat and watched him. He enjoyed her company.

Several mornings later, Tamara arrived, offering flat bread to Seth. "How long did you work last night?"

He grabbed a flat bread from the stack. "Until my eyes couldn't stay open and the light of dawn lifted the darkness from the night's shadows."

"You didn't rest?" Tamara sighed. "I missed too much. How far did you get?"

"Close your eyes." He took her hand and led her over to the blanketed image. He positioned her right in front of its head. "Close your eyes. Ready?"

Tamara bounced on her toes. "I can't wait!"

He threw the blanket to the ground; then placed his hands on her shoulders. "Open them."

Its horns reached to the sky, carried by the magnificent head, raised proud and conquering. Its eyes glowed in the early sun's rays. It stood, ready to charge at them. Its muscles bulged. Its gold portrayed a strength and glory that not even a living animal would possess.

Tamara said nothing.

"What is it?" Seth turned from looking at the bull to her face. "What's wrong?"

"Seth, you've made a masterpiece. I had to remind myself that he wasn't charging me; that I was safe in front of his horns."

Seth gazed into her eyes. Her deep brown eyes danced with excitement.

She swung her arms around his neck and squeezed. "All the people will know of your skill." She hung on his neck for a moment, before she danced around the bull, examining every angle of the animal. "You have made him come alive."

"Here, let me help you up." He boosted her on its back.

Tamara squealed with delight. "I can feel its muscles ripple as it charges."

Seth glowed with her praise. He picked up the blanket and polished the statue by her leg.

"Help me stand up on its back."

He held her hand as she stood.

"Bow to me, I am your princess of authority and power."

He lowered his head.

At just that moment, Tamara slipped and squealed as she fell.

Seth caught her.

She lay in his arms. "You've saved me twice, Seth. I will stay close by you so I know that I will be always safe."

"And I will always be ready to catch you."

Seth's smile faded. Aaron would be pleased. But the Lord's Words entered his mind, "Thou shalt have no other gods before Me." Would this please the Lord?

CHAPTER 12

M aessai walked through camp toward Aaron's tent. It was daylight, but he wasn't afraid of judgment. He was confident Aaron would actually welcome him. When Maessai had planted the idea of an idol, telling some of the judges to suggest it to Aaron, he had been surprised at how quickly Aaron accepted the idea. His plans were moving along nicely. He called out a cheerful greeting as he reached Aaron's tent.

Aaron put his arm around Maessai's shoulders. He felt uneasy for a moment, wondering why Maessai reminded him of something unpleasant in his past. He shook his head. He couldn't remember. It probably wasn't important. "Come see. I don't like that the bull looks exactly like the Egyptian god..."

Maessai walked beside him. "Don't worry. The people have forgotten all about Egypt."

Aaron hesitated to uncover it. "I don't seek to be worshiped like Pharaoh, only recognized as their leader."

Maessai consoled him. "You are their leader. This only reminds them. Uncover it. Let me see it."

Aaron slid the blanket off the broad back.

Maessai worked to contain his surprise. "Your people are rich to be able to provide such gold." He circled the monument, touching the solid gold statue. "No ordinary, unveiling ceremony is good enough for this masterpiece." He chose his words with care, watching Aaron's face across the bull's back. "Nothing short of a festival would do it justice." He studied Aaron's reception of the idea.

Aaron smiled.

A man seeking power will stop at nothing once he ignores his conscience. Maessai directed Aaron's thoughts away from the laws. He continued, sharing his ideas as if he had just thought of them. "A special feast with plenty of meat would appeal to everyone. They would recognize your authority. Aren't they tired of manna?"

Aaron considered. "Those who are hesitant to partake of the festivities might reconsider if there was a chance to have some meat." He looked Maessai in the eye. "I could pay for the slaughtered animals with the extra gold."

Maessai turned his head to hide his surprise. "You have extra gold?"

"Plenty."

Maessai restrained his excitement. His words were measured as if he were merely making the necessary calculations "How much more do you have?"

"I'll show you."

Maessai fingered the piles of gold. He had used his time away from camp wisely. He had sought merchants, none of course coming out of Egypt, to barter for wine. His bartering power had increased when he promised Israelite girls in exchange for wine. "I could use this gold to help persuade the people."

Aaron eyed Maessai.

Maessai held his gaze. He could feel Aaron testing him. Aaron was not in charge here, he was. And he would stay in charge until he got what he wanted.

Aaron dropped his eyes and found a linen sack. "If this is not enough..."

Maessai looked at the remaining gold. "It won't be. I'll need more."

Aaron swallowed. "I'll need some for purchasing the meat..."

Maessai shrugged. "Tell the people they must give for the sacrifice. You are in charge."

Aaron retrieved several more sacks.

Maessai helped to fill them.

Maessai left the campsite with all of the gold. Aaron was easily exploited. All he had to say was "respect" and "control," and Aaron agreed. It had been too easy.

He had spread contempt for Moses's authority. Finding people disgruntled with Moses's punishments and control made the atmosphere ripe for what he had in mind.

Men follow anything when they are idle, discontent, and lacking a purpose.

When Aaron informed the camp of the need for more gold for the festival, he had avoided those who might oppose the idea. Now, with the meat as a gift, he could perhaps convince them of the rightness of his actions. He could show them that he only desired the good of the people.

He first gave Nathan a leg of beef. "Shalom. Here's to help in the festivities tomorrow."

Nathan looked at the meat, without touching it. "Festivities?"

Aaron smiled. "The shepherds have donated the meat for the sacrificing tomorrow."

Nathan shook his head. "After seeing the mountain smoke and having Moses gone for so long, shouldn't we be fasting instead of feasting?"

Aaron nudged the meat closer to Nathan's hand. "The people grow weary of manna, don't you?"

"But shouldn't we be seeking the Lord for His direction?"

Aaron looked back at the cart that held more meat. He had many to convince. He could not spend too much time with each one. "Doesn't the Lord give us meat as well as manna?"

Nathan followed Aaron's glance. "The shepherds gave all this meat without payment?"

Aaron smiled. "All are ready to feast unto the Lord. I trust you will be a part of it." He pushed the meat again at Nathan.

Nathan looked over the meat in the cart and accepted it. "I was going to pray at the bottom of the mountain tomorrow. I could pray after we eat, instead of before."

Aaron nodded. "Then you will be able to focus more clearly on the Lord's Words." He continued through the tents distributing the meat.

Aaron paused before turning to Adlai's tent. He selected the biggest cut of meat to offer him. "Shalom. I've brought you something to help with the festival tomorrow."

Adlai looked up from his scrolls. "You've been busy trying to fill your brother's sandals. Yes?"

The meat was not even acknowledged as he placed it beside Adlai. Just the implication that he was less than Moses incited Aaron. He masked his anger, choosing his words. "It's a role that I take with great seriousness."

"Moses will have much to share when he returns. Think what all the Lord is telling him that will help our people."

Aaron weighed his words, watching Adlai for their acceptance. "Moses has been gone a long time. The people have forgotten him. They look for someone to follow."

Adlai's look penetrated him. "You don't think that Moses has died, do you? He hasn't completed his mission. God will lead us to the Land."

Did Adlai know his plans? Aaron shook his head. He must unite the people under his leadership. He had other people that he must speak with today. Why waste time trying to determine whether or not these particular leaders would agree to follow him? He turned away, stating, "When the sun rises and chases away the darkness, the people will offer sacrifices of praise for the Lord's leader. May His people be ready."

Before the sun shone over the mountain, Aaron prepared the altar in the center of camp. He slaughtered a cow, laying its parts on the altar. He called the people to bless it. Before he lit it with incense, he directed the bull to be wheeled in front of the altar.

The sun's rays peeked over the smoking mountain and sparkled off the bull's back. The gold blinded his eyes. He could see nothing but the sun's reflected glare.

The people gasped and bowed before the gleaming image.

Maessai stood in the back of the congregation. "It's a sign from God. We are blessed." His words were echoed throughout the crowd.

The people crowded close to see this great sign. "We have been delivered from all of Egypt's hardship."

Aaron felt the praise of the people. Why had he doubted their favor and their acceptance? He studied the people before him. They were enthusiastic, unlike when they came before Moses to hear the Words of the Lord. Sometimes, when his brother spoke, they seemed to sleep on their feet. Now, they were excited. They listened to his words. They appreciated the gift of meat that he had given. They needed this change. He raised his arms and said, "Let the feasting begin."

Aaron watched as the people rose from the ground and began feasting and celebrating. His longing for the people's respect was satisfied.

But his thirst for control had been awakened. Can that desire be satisfied? When someone has some, doesn't he want more?

How much control was enough?

Once, the people were occupied, Aaron returned to his tent. Phinehas met him there. "Shalom, Grandfather."

"You look troubled."

Phinehas wore his sword. "Remember the man who abducted Adlai's daughter and Hannah?"

Aaron's insides churned. He did not want to hear the rest. That was why the man looked familiar. Why hadn't he remembered him?

Phinehas continued, "Maessai stirs up the people against you."

Aaron sighed. Why had he trusted Maessai? He reviewed the plans that Maessai had told him. He was to encourage judges and people to grumble about Moses's judgments. If he did this, Maessai had said that people would turn from Moses's leadership and look to Aaron.

Aaron had pardoned some of those whom Moses had judged rather harshly. Others had expected him to look the other way when they committed the same offense. He had. He had felt the power of leadership. He could choose to pardon someone. He could determine their future.

But Maessai was stirring people against him? Aaron's voice broke, "Against me?"

"If he questions Moses's Law, doesn't he undermine your authority?"

Aaron frowned. "Moses's Law is harsh. The people needed a break from the strictness. No one could live under the Law."

Phinehas smiled. "God shows His justice and His love by giving us His Law."

Aaron's brows furrowed. "Why are you defending the Law?"

Phinehas took a sip from the dipper at the tent's door. "You told me to battle my arrogance, that my pride is an affront to the just and holy God. I remember His glory. I see His holiness." Phinehas pointed to the top of Mount Sinai. "That mountain smokes and simmers, the air rains ashes, reminding me of Who He is. I see His justice. His holiness. His power. He alone deserves respect, praise, and honor. His justice demands that we change." He pointed to the bottom of the mountain where the rope boundary kept the people from crossing. "I'm beginning to see that it's because of His love, He keeps us on this side of the rope. Maybe someday I'll be with Moses. I want to change enough so that I can be in God's presence. Do you think I can?"

Aaron fell back against his cushions as Phinehas finished speaking. What had he done? How could he lead the people to the holiness of God? He hadn't been a better leader than Moses. He had led the people away from God, away from being acceptable in His sight. What could he do now? He covered his face with his hands and moaned.

Phinehas grabbed Aaron's hand and pulled it away from his face. "What have I said? I thought you'd be pleased. I'm willing to let Him change me."

Aaron could not speak for a long time. He looked into Phinehas's face. He felt the weight of what he had done smothering him. The praise of the people echoed in his mind from this morning. He had accepted it, as if he deserved it. He had forgotten God's praise. How had he started down this path of jealously and hate toward Moses? Because he wanted Moses's power. But Moses did not have the power, God did. Aaron had competed with God for His respect. He could never win. Aaron squeezed Phinehas's shoulder and mumbled, "You speak truth. When you want control, you will stop at nothing to get it. It soon masters you."

Phinehas asked again, "What should we do with Maessai?"

Aaron shook his head. How could he stop it now? "Nothing."

Phinehas suggested, "Do you want me to approach him? I will."

"He has control."

Phinehas paced. "What do you mean, he has control?"

Aaron covered his face with his hands. "Leave me." He could hear Phinehas pacing for several minutes before leaving the tent.

When Aaron lifted his head, he was alone with his thoughts. He did not like where his thoughts led him. Noticing a crate full of wine just inside his tent, he reached for a bottle.

Maessai must have given it. He had thought of everything.

Aaron balanced the bottle in his hand. How long had it been since he'd something besides water? He opened the lid and gulped. He would forget about what he had done for a little while. What harm could one day bring?

The meat's smell as it cooked slowly over the embers had spread through camp all morning. Wine had been distributed to all. Michael sat with Adlai and his family as they ate their noon meal.

Tamara reached for more meat. "I've missed meat."

Carmel nodded. "The quail was good, but it only came for a month. This makes me crave Egypt's food."

Adlai nodded. "True, but is that good? Should we be thinking about the glory of Egypt?"

Reut gasped. Her face lost all color.

Michael followed her gaze and saw Maessai passing in front of their tent. "Adlai." Michael nodded toward Maessai.

Adlai's eyes widened.

Michael stood. "I'll be back."

As Michael came within hearing of Aaron's campsite, he heard laughter.

A group of men lounged around Aaron's cook fire.

Maessai approached Aaron, squatting beside him. "You've found my gift?"

Aaron spoke. His voice slurred and deliberate. "Yes. And what a gift it was!"

The other men raised their vessels in salute to Maessai.

Michael had seen enough. He accepted the Law as the boundaries for their people. But when the boundaries were ignored by the leader...what could the people do?

He would protect Reut, even if it meant defying the leadership that ignored the Law. Michael backed away, never telling Aaron of the respect he had lost.

As Michael walked to Nathan's tent, he slowed his steps, calming his insides. He could fight a foe outside the camp, but this danger lay within. How could he fight that?

Nathan welcomed him, smiling. "What brings you to our meal?"

Michael could not speak.

Nathan stopped smiling. "What is it?"

"Maessai walks through camp."

"You spoke with Aaron?"

"Aaron's in no condition to help." Michael hesitated at Nathan's puzzled look. "Aaron's drunk by gifts from Maessai."

Nathan nodded. "I'll tell Hakeen. We should stay together. If Maessai walks boldly, danger is close."

Michael shifted. "Should we meet at Adlai's tent?"

Nathan stood to leave. "Bring them here. Maessai doesn't know us. I wish that I'd fasted instead of feasted. No meat is worth the wrong that this has brought."

Michael retraced his steps to inform Adlai.

Adlai nodded. "There's safety in being together. The situation's ripe for chaos."

As they prepared to leave, Carmel looked around the tent. "Where's Tamara? When did anyone see her last?" Her eyes met Adlai's.

Adlai took Carmel's hand. "I'll look for her after I settle you and Reut at Nathan's."

As they reached Nathan's tent, Hakeen's family arrived.

Adlai hugged Carmel before leaving. "I'll find her."

Carmel's widened eyes betrayed her fear.

Amos grabbed Adlai's shoulder. "I'll search with you."

Adlai nodded, swallowing. Could he trust God again for his family's protection against evil?

Phinehas walked away from Aaron's tent. Maessai must be stopped. But how? A sword fight was not the answer, nor would he win if he provoked one. Maessai's influence had escalated into a mob-like control. The people would not listen to reason. Even his grandfather had resigned himself to his evil. What could one man do to stop it?

He reached the center of camp where the golden bull still stood. The sun had risen, and the shine of the morning was gone from the image. But what drew his attention was the lawlessness of the people. The sacrifices had long since been finished. The feasting had begun. Cartloads of wine were given to all. Water was forgotten, and so was God.

They drank. Inhibitions were less when drink flowed freely.

Women played tambourines.

Men watched in pleasure.

The unaccustomed wine brought movements that should be reserved for a husband alone.

Today was a day of feasting and this was allowed.

As the women danced, they threw off head coverings, shed cloaks, removed sandals. Their hair fell down their backs.

Some men did not find enough pleasure in watching, but drew women into their tents. Their actions were unnoticed by others too busy with their own pleasure.

They had no boundaries. They had no rules. And no God would tell them what to do.

Phinehas had once enjoyed feasting with high Egyptian officials. Their entertainment brought similar scenes.

As he saw what the maidens offered under the drink's influence, Hannah's image came to mind. She pleased God. These women shamed her image. He could not enjoy it, but walked away.

Hakeen's words came. "I will know when you know the Lord, and don't just know about Him."

Now, he understood the difference.

Pelia loitered over cleaning the vessel from their feast. She had eaten in the darkened corner, while Magal ate with his friends. If she had thought it safe, she would have walked out into the wilderness where Esmail was, and spent her time with the flocks, but she was afraid to walk alone. The people had become increasingly raucous. She feared even to leave her own tent now. Would the God Who showed Himself in a burning cloud share His glory with a golden cow? She did not think so. But Aaron was their leader.

Magal lounged with his friends, drinking. "Pelia!"

She wrinkled her nose at their unwashed bodies and spilled wine. She waited his request.

Magal smiled. So did his friends.

Why did he look at her like that? She looked from him to his friends. "Magal, what do you want?" She felt their lust and backed toward the tent's flap.

Magal laughed. He pointed to one of his friends. "She'd be good for you."

She could feel heat rise to her face. She hid her face in her hands. "What are you thinking, Magal?"

Magal demanded, "Come here, Pelia." He reached for her wrist.

Pelia ran from the tent, without thought of any destination.

He stumbled behind her, shouting at her to come back.

Where could she go? She hurried toward the altar. That's where God was worshiped. She could find protection there.

When she reached the camp, she saw Aaron stumble into the dancing and fall.

Someone kicked him. Another pushed him out of the way.

If no one respected their leader, how could she hope for someone to help her? What she saw sickened her. No one who remembered the glory of the Lord could act like this. She turned from the sight.

A man grabbed her.

She pounded on him. How could she have run from one danger

into the hands of another? "Let me go!"

The man would not. He held her tighter.

The noise of the people drowned out her screaming. No one helped. Had she escaped Magal to be caught by another? She fought harder.

One voice penetrated through all the noise. "Pelia. Stop!"

She looked at her captor's face. Her fist stopped in mid-air. "Amos."

He would protect her.

She buried her head in his chest. How could Magal have done that to her?

Maessai watched the sacrificing and the feasting. He nodded here and there to judges, supporters, facilitators of his plan. He did not crave positions of leadership, but he did enjoy controlling things from behind the scenes. Manipulating his older brothers, when he was younger, had helped hone his skills. He planned, then made his brothers carry out his plans. Then when punishment came, Maessai was cleared. Now, Aaron held the leadership. Moses's absence came to his advantage. The people were ripe for change. They would follow anyone. But when judgment fell, if it even would, he would not be accountable.

As Maessai surveyed the scene by the altar, everything was going as planned. He moved among the dancing women, searching for the one. He signaled men along the sidelines when he selected a girl. The man would enter the dance; lead the girl from camp to an awaiting wagon to be sold.

Maessai was not drunk, nor had he taken anything to drink. He was consumed with finding the girl who had escaped him, not once, but twice. Today, he would have her. He had walked by her tent earlier, but then was not the time. Later, she was no longer there. He must find her. When the time was ripe, he would have her. He watched for her.

Among the dancers, he noticed her sister. Maessai watched for the right moment. She swayed with the music, swirled around the cow, and danced with total abandonment. Her cloak lay beneath her feet.

He eased through the crowd, grabbed her arm and drew her against his body.

She would tell where her sister went, and she would make a

good slave.

Tamara looked into the face of the man who held her. She remembered him. She struggled to break free, for she knew what this man could do. But she couldn't win against his strength. She must think. His hand dug into her wrist and held her back firmly against his body. She stopped struggling. When she did, he relaxed his hold. Her ima rubbed her abba's arms when he was tense. She slid her fingertips up and down his arms. She calmed her breathing. She could think. If she could not escape his strength, then she must outwit him. She leaned against him.

He hissed in her ear. "Where's your sister?"

The music played behind her. She still felt its movement inside of her. She stood on tip-toe, pretending to whisper into his ear. She brought his head close to hers. Tamara stretched to reach his ear. She clamped down on it.

His cursing could not be heard over the music, and he did not let her go.

Nor did she. She held on until his ear lobe fell into her mouth. She spit it in his face.

He sputtered.

She squirmed free, dodging dancers and musicians, escaping to her family's tent. No one was there. She couldn't stay here. Did he know where she lived? Would he follow her? Where should she go? She grabbed a cloak. As she left, she took a candlestick. If he caught her again, she could hit him with it. Darting through the tent flap, she ran to the only other place that she could think her family went, Nathan's tent.

She arrived breathless and panting. She looked around the group of people.

Her mother looked over her disheveled hair and sandal-less feet. "Tamara, where have you been?"

Tamara hung her head. "The music compelled me. I had wings like a bird." She locked her eyes on Reut. "That man grabbed me. He asked for you."

Reut glanced at the tent flap, turning pale. "Did he follow you?"

Tamara's brows drew closer. She looked around the circle of faces. Had she led him to her sister? She shook her head. She hoped that she hadn't. "No."

Now that she was safe, her insides began to settle. Her heart slowed. Her breathing became normal. She felt his touch again and shivered. She wiped her mouth, smelling his taste again. Taking the dipper by the doorway, she filled her mouth, spitting through the tent's opening. Nothing could remove the stench of that man from her mouth. She shivered as she wiped her wrist and fixed her tunic.

Tamara looked at the circle of faces.

Was anyone safe?

CHAPTER 13

Time on the mountain had been as nothing. The light continued to shine. The quietness had been calming. Moses sat by the stone tablet and watched as the Lord wrote His Words with His Finger. These rules would make His people truly His. All would know that God was just and righteous.

Moses shifted as the Lord paused in His writing.

His Finger stopped.

Moses sat back, waiting for the Lord to continue.

Instead, the Lord spoke, His voice trembled, "Go. Your people sin. They worship a golden cow. They profess deliverance from Egypt by its power. Let Me destroy them, and I will make a great nation from you."

Moses laid his face against the Words freshly inscribed on the stone tablet. Hadn't he just left the people? They had committed themselves to follow the Lord and had prepared for His coming. How could they already have forgotten God, and sinned so greatly? Their fickleness stabbed him to the heart. He didn't want a new people to lead. These were his people. Hadn't he joined them in their suffering in Egypt? Hadn't he left all to follow God's call, risking his own life to bring them to freedom? Hadn't he pointed them to see God? Why couldn't they know Him?

"O Lord, if You consume Your people, won't Egypt and all the other nations in the world who watched You free Your people turn with contempt against You? You promised to make of Abraham a great nation—as many as the stars in the heavens. These people are Your promised ones."

The silence of the Lord was a terrible thing.

Moses looked at the stone tablets. The Law was not finished.

The Lord had stopped in the middle of a command. Would He ever finish? What help would this people have if God did not help them?

Moses must make atonement for the people. Their only hope was in God's mercy. He grabbed the two tablets and ran down the mountain.

When Moses reached the roped area of the mountain, Joshua stood waiting for him. "It sounds like war in the camp."

Moses ran faster. "It's not war, but singing."

Zipporah still watched for Moses. Their rock house stood on the outskirts of the campsite, facing the mountain. She could see the black cloud as it lingered on the top of the mountain. Hearing the music and loud shouting, she had hidden inside her dwelling, praying that Moses was still alive.

She had not been given meat, but she could smell it lingering in the air from nearby cook fires. Her insides rumbled at the smell. Gershom had asked to see the sacrifices and festivities. But...

Cartloads of wine had entered the campsite. Wine loosened tongues.

She did not wish to hear their comments about her and her sons. She kept her sons inside their dwelling.

The afternoon's rays were slipping beyond the horizon. Another day was passing without Moses's return.

Gershom tugged on her tunic. "Ima, what's the music for?"

She shook her head, but remained focused out the window. She wadded a rag in her hands, tightening her grasp on it. Again, she shook her head and sighed. Today, he would not return.... She was weary of staying inside their dwelling, but she feared leaving. How could she continue to hope for his return, when the days melted into one another without any sign?

A few minutes later, Gershom tried again. "Ima, couldn't I just see what everyone is doing?"

Still focused out the window, she spoke harshly, frustrated that Moses did not return. "Don't ask me again." Looking into Gershom's face, she noticed his disappointment. She gentled her voice and stroked his hair from his forehead, "The people do not please the Lord. You will be hurt. They hurt the Lord."

"Then they will hurt Abba," Gershom added.

"Yes." She placed her hands on his shoulders. "Why don't you show your letters to Eliezer? Use the beads to form them. Would that help?"

Gershom nodded and scampered to teach Eliezer.

Was that movement far on the mountain? Her heart beat faster. "Moses lives! He's alive." She didn't realize she had spoken out loud, until she felt Gershom straining to see by her side. She wouldn't be cast out of camp. She would be protected by his presence.

She moved to the doorway.

Moses joined Joshua, who had waited, worshipping at the base of the mountain. They both were running. Was he running from his God?

His stride, instead of calm and sure, was short, rough, choppy. One arm held tablets of stone at his side. His other arm was tense, with his hand clenched tight.

As he grew near, she could see his face. His eyebrows were drawn in a straight line across his forehead.

She stepped back, afraid.

Gershom hugged her waist. "Did the Lord send him off the mountain?"

"We'll know soon."

Moses did not stop at the house, but ran past them.

She strained to hear anything besides the music and the people.

Several long minutes later, a crash followed, then silence. The music stopped.

Zipporah backed towards the door frame, straining to hear.

Gershom squeezed her. "What is it, Ima?"

Eliezer pressed against her side.

She rubbed their backs, shaking her head. What had the people done now?

Joshua and Moses ran into the midst of the people. Moses stopped running, his breath coming in ragged gulps.

The people did not even know he was there. Their dancing brought heat to his face. He looked at the people and moaned. His body shook, his shoulders hunched.

Where were the people who had promised obedience to the Lord's commands? Were these the same people who had consecrated themselves to God?

He stalked toward the altar.

In the wake of his steps, a silence followed as people became aware of his presence.

Moses reached the altar. He threw off discarded head veils and cloaks that were draped on it.

He saw the bull by the altar, standing to receive the sweet smoke of sacrifice. He stared. He slumped, bowing his head. His whole body shook. Moses's hands trembled, his vision clouded. He could no longer hear the din of the people, only the pounding of his heart in his ears.

He wanted to destroy this idol, this image that kept people from seeing God, this thing that stood between God and His people. He raised his arms over his head and brought the stone tablets down on the back of the bull.

The crash caught the people's attention.

Tambourines stilled.

Singing silenced.

The people stopped.

No one spoke.

Moses stared at the shattered pieces of the only hope for His people.

These people had broken the Lord's commands in more ways than the stone had shattered into pieces.

Moses raised his head and wiped his face with the sleeve of his cloak, searching each face.

No one looked him in the eye. They stared at their feet, grabbing garments to cover themselves. Men backed away from Moses.

Moses focused on Seth, who seemed to fidget more than others. "Do you have a hammer?"

"Yes, Moses. I'll get it." Seth ran to retrieve it.

Moses smote the bull's head. He beat it over and over again. Chunks broke off. But he didn't allow the pieces to remain. He pounded like a man gone mad. He pulverized the gold into fine dust, scraping it into a cloak.

After gathering the fine gold dust, Moses stalked to their water pool and dumped it.

Turning, he commanded. His lips twitched as he struggled to form the word. "Drink."

The people had followed him to the water's edge. But now they backed away from him.

Moses swallowed. He looked at the people. "Drink, all of you."

Seth bowed at the water's edge and drank.

Others followed.

No one said a word.

After watching the people drink from the gold water, Moses strode through the camp. Empty wine vessels lay scattered around tents. Spills stained and stank clothes and tents. The whole place reeked. As his breathing calmed, his heart steadied. He walked back to the altar meant for worshiping God. He stood before it, head bowed. How could the people have forsaken God so soon? He walked around the altar...and found Aaron lying beside it.

Aaron sat up, pulling his cloak around him and tightening his belt. He stood up, bracing himself against the altar. He did not meet Moses's glance.

Moses stood before him. "What did this people do to you, that you led them into such wickedness?"

Aaron held his head. "Don't be angry. You know this people. They wanted something they could see. They brought me their gold. I simply threw it into the fire and out came this bull."

Moses shook his head. "You allowed them to get out of control. Even their enemies mock them."

Moses walked to the edge of the mountain. He looked toward the top. Wasn't it just a few days ago that he had sanctified the people? In so short of time, they had come to this?

Just having the Law would not make this people turn to God, ready to be His people. What could be done?

God would have killed them all, had Moses not petitioned for His mercy. But God's justice must also be met.

Their sin was great.

Turning, he faced the people. "Whoever is for the Lord, come to me!"

No one moved.

The air crackled with tension.

Phinehas stepped forward and nodded to Moses.

Moses met his eyes, studying him, then returned his nod and smiled. Something good had happened while he was on the mountain: Phinehas had acknowledged God.

Other Levities gathered behind Phinehas.

No one else moved. But all waited.

Moses faced the Levite men. God was holy. He was jealous of the glory that belonged to only to Him.

The people must acknowledge this God as supreme. They must value His Words as important enough to follow Him, even when they couldn't see Him. They must recognize His demand for their obedience.

Moses couldn't allow this sin to remain. The Lord was making them into His people, set apart unto Him.

"Kill your brother, friend, neighbor."

The people cringed in shame, trembling in the face of judgment. But still they were blind to the holiness of God. They didn't bow before Him, nor cry out in repentance or regret. They were not ready to enter the Promised Land.

The Lord would make them ready.

Phinehas had sought to meet the God Who owned him. He had found that God was holy. When man, even a good man, resisted God's laws, he was worthy of death.

Even if they had not openly shaken their fists at God, in their hearts, they had ignored God's command. Had He not just told them to have no other gods before Him? The entire camp had followed Aaron in the sacrificing to the golden image. God would not be ignored. As Phinehas drew his sword to obey Moses's words, he knew that he stood for right. He would execute justice for the Lord Who had called him to Himself. Phinehas's sword flashed in the light of many fires that night as he searched tents. Men covered their nakedness, begging for mercy. Phinehas, remembering God's jealousy, allowed no mercy.

Phinehas had watched the feasting turn to drunkenness, dancing to fornication.

He knew those who grumbled against God's authority.

They would not stir up rebellion again.

These men had followed a leader.

Phinehas searched for that one.

He could not find him.

Phinehas killed not in hate and anger, but in justice and obedience. He reported to Moses. "We have killed three thousand men."

Moses admonished the Levities, "Dedicate yourselves to the Lord. He will bless you."

Moses did not enter his house for a long time that night. Zipporah trembled in the darkness, waiting, keeping the embers burning.

Did he still burn with anger?

When he entered, all she could say was, "You are home."

"Zipporah." He drew her to him.

She melted against him, feeling his vulnerability.

"While I learn of God's desires, the people break His heart. I ran with fear for my people. The Lord was angry with them for their sin. They should have prepared for the Lord's Words."

Zipporah listened as he shared his heart.

"They built an altar not for the Lord, but for a cow—like in Egypt. The Lord freed them from their bondage to those gods.

"They danced on the altar meant for God alone. They adorned themselves with gold and silver and nothing else.

"When they saw me, they covered their nakedness. Their shame was great. Why can't they feel shame without my presence? Why don't they see the Lord in their midst?"

Moses collapsed on his pallet. He held his head in his hands and sobbed.

Zipporah sat beside him and leaned her head on his arm. "You have spent forty days with your God. You see a world that the rest of us can never imagine. How can you see God and not be changed? We remain in the valley and see only ourselves. We don't know that change is possible, or that we even want change.

"Moses, I see the Lord through you. And I want to know Him."

Moses shook his head. "I'm not a god. I want you to see the Lord yourself."

Zipporah slipped her hand into his. "I see your God, slowly as a toddler must take one small step at a time. I reach to Him and put my hand in His. I ask for His help in little things. He hears my request and helps me. I trust Him with bigger things."

Moses hugged her, resting his chin on her hair. "Zipporah, you are learning to know the Lord as He wants to be known. You give me hope."

A spark from the embers allowed her to see him in the darkened room. Zipporah rested her head on his chest. She would not be cast out. Her God would protect her.

And Moses was back.

CHAPTER 14

Aaron plunged his head and arms into the water. The morning rays of the sun blinded his eyes and made his head pound. Having his sons and grandsons killing their own people had sobered him more quickly than the water. He lingered long at the water's edge. He didn't want to enter the campsite, where women mourned their loss. How could things have fallen apart so quickly?

Moses squatted beside him at the water's edge. "What were you thinking?"

Aaron shook his head. "In Egypt, we were a team, you and I. We prayed together. I helped lead. But here in the desert, the people saw only you. I was no longer needed...The people complained about your judgments. I sympathized, encouraged, and gained my own following."

Moses started to speak, but shut his mouth.

"When you were gone, the people came to me. I pardoned sin, instead of punishing it. I allowed freedom without holiness. I became the revered leader that you are."

Moses sighed. "Do you want the people to stone you when they have no water? The Lord has built toughness in me, allowing me to see the people's needs without forgetting their hard hearts. You sympathize too much with their suffering to execute the punishment needed. That's why I wouldn't allow you to judge the people."

Aaron dropped his head into his hands. "No one would be dead, if I had led like you. What can I do?"

Moses squeezed his shoulder. "Repent. Seek God. The Lord does not want you to be like me. You show them the God Who cares. You mediate between the people and their God. But you cannot forget His holiness."

Aaron moaned. How could he remove the suffering that he had caused? How could he look into the faces of those whose fathers had been slain...and those who were missing their kidnapped daughters?

Moses assembled the people in the morning. "You have committed a great sin. I will plead for you before the Lord. In His mercy, He may forgive."

The people listened. They saw their iniquity, but not through the eyes of the Lord. Heads of families, sons of mothers, husbands were lost to them forever. Young girls had vanished, never to be found. The people mourned.

Moses returned to the Lord's presence at the top of the mountain. He could not forget the days of perfect peace while listening to God's Words as He wrote on the tablets. The Words came to his mind. Moses hung his head. He felt the people's shame. How could he face God with their iniquity? How could this people be His without His mercy? "If You cannot forgive these people, blot me from Your book, rather than destroying them."

The Lord responded, "Whoever sinned will be held accountable. I will blot them out of My book. Now go. Lead the people."

Moses returned to the people. His steps were deliberate as he picked his way to where the people had gathered. He raised his staff above his head to quiet them, "The Lord will no longer lead you by His presence, lest He consume you, for your sin is great, and you are an obstinate people." He spoke to the people about God, but they did not know Him.

Later as Moses walked with Zipporah around the water pool, he discussed his thoughts with her. "How can I impress upon the people the righteous jealousy of God? He longs for His people to know Him."

Zipporah held his hand. "They must seek Him for themselves."

Moses skipped a stone across the water. "The Lord told me to move His presence outside the camp for the safety of the people. If I construct a tent, so I can communicate with Him, the people will be safe. But they won't be close to His presence to know Him."

Zipporah squeezed his hand. "They know where to find God. They don't want to know Him. He shows them who they are, and they don't like it. Until they want to be changed, they won't seek Him. Until they seek Him, it's better that He stay outside the camp for their safety."

She paused in walking to place her hand on his beard. "You desire all to see God as you do. But you cannot make them. They must choose."

Moses had asked Amos to make a tent so he could meet with the Lord outside camp. The people would know the Lord was close, but the distance would protect them from His wrath.

The completed tent became His sanctuary.

Moses kissed Zipporah before leaving for the tent again.

Zipporah held him. "Must you go so often? I fear for your life every time the cloud covers you."

"He speaks to me face to face, as a friend."

"Don't you fear His sudden anger?"

"He doesn't punish without cause. I don't fear His wrath. I fear disappointing Him. It's like what you do for me. You love me and seek to please me. I do not like too many herbs in my flatbread, but just enough to enhance the flavor. I like my flatbread a little bit undercooked so it is soft and chewy, not hard and crunchy. You make it just the way I like it, not because you fear my wrath, but because you desire to please me out of love. See the difference?"

At her nod, he squeezed her. "I want to know the Lord."

Zipporah smoothed his cloak around his neck. "Your love compels you to seek Him. My fear keeps me from His fire and judgment, but doesn't transform my thoughts to be like His. I don't know how to get where you are, Moses. I feel like I have lost you to another."

Moses took her face in his hands. "Zipporah, you haven't lost me. Without Him, I wouldn't be the man you love. He has made me who I am. Trusting Him has given me the peace that you seek, the confidence to do the impossible. If He commands it, He will enable it.

"Remember the staff turned to a snake? The danger was not the snake. The danger was in disobeying and not grabbing the tail. Do you see the difference?"

She nodded.

"My trust was built in the desert where the sand and winds turned my eyes to Him alone. He brings harshness into your life to push you to Him. When those trials come, there is nothing for you to do but trust. That is when you find that He is enough."

Zipporah said, "Faith is hard."

"Not when you know Who your faith rests on." Moses kissed her on her head and breathed deeply. "It's hard when we look at what we must obey. It is easy when we look to Him Who called us. Maybe it's not faith when we are close to Him, because He asks only what is good. Abraham was willing to sacrifice his only son to the Lord because he knew He was good."

Zipporah interrupted, "Would you?"

Moses laughed. "He did not kill his son, the Lord spared him. Faith stretches us to see Him more clearly. The task is insignificant. So does that make it less faith? I don't know. But I do know that I must go meet Him. Shalom, my love. I won't be gone long."

"Be at peace, my only love. Your time with Your God is as nothing for you but an eternity for me."

Moses entered the tent ready to hear the voice of the Lord. He was not disappointed.

Moses asked the Lord, "Let me find favor always in Your sight. Let me know Your ways, that I may know You."

The Lord responded. "My presence shall go with you."

"If Your presence doesn't go with us, do not lead us any farther. You distinguish us from all the other people upon the face of the earth."

"I will give what you ask. I will lead you. For you have found favor, and I have known you by name."

Moses hesitated. Should he ask? Without asking he would never know the answer.

The Lord encouraged. "What do you want?"

Moses bowed before the Lord. He had seen a glimpse of God's glory in the desert. He had watched the Finger of His God write on the tablets of stone, but it was not enough. How could he know God? How could he understand this God Who was so holy and above all, yet sought his companionship? "I want to see Your Glory."

"You don't know what you ask. My Glory is too much for you."

Moses's shoulders sagged. He wanted this more than taking another breath.

The Lord caught his attention again. "But I can do this."

Moses raised his face expectantly. He hoped in His answer.

"I will make all My goodness pass before you. You can't see My face, for no man can see My face and live."

As Moses walked home from the tent of meeting, he felt the people watching him from their tents. They were not ready to worship. By staying in camp, they felt safe—out of the reach of a God Who demanded total allegiance. By focusing on what they had lost, the people were blind to the God Who gave. They resented Him for taking life, instead of seeing the God Who spared their lives. They demanded fulfillment of their wants, without recognizing the God Who provided all their needs.

They avoided God, for their shame was great. But they would not approach the tent to be changed.

Moses felt their distance. He knew their restraint. He was torn by their separation from their God. How could he show them the God Who longed for His people to talk with Him?

Early the next morning, the Lord called Moses to the mountain.

Moses walked away from the people, away from the duties of camp life. He entered the silence of the desert. The Lord had promised to show him His Glory.

An eagle cried as it soared over his head.

He paused to watch. He tapped his staff lightly on the sand. His legs trembled with excitement. A burst of laughter escaped his lips. He turned back to the mountain and walked faster.

When Moses reached the pinnacle of the mountain, the Lord spoke, "I will show you the rock where you should stand. I will protect you in the cleft of the rock and cover you with My Hand. I will pass by. When I take My hand away from the cleft's opening, you will see My back, for You cannot see My face."

Moses pressed his lips together to keep from smiling, and then he laughed out loud. His request would be granted. He would glimpse his Friend. His heart soared. He spun in a circle. He could see the campsite far below. He looked again to the top of the mount. He was meeting his God.

He arrived at the designated rock and waited. Quietness settled over him like a cloak of peace. His heart calmed from the walk, and he breathed deeply. As he waited, he was drawn by His Presence to step inside a rock split by a powerful force. He looked out. He could only see what was in front of him.

The cloud enveloped the mountain. Darkness covered him like a blanket, creating the feeling that he was somewhere away from the world that he knew. This darkness was not like the plague, covering Egypt for three days. Fear and terror had prevailed then. This darkness protected Moses, giving him security.

Peering into the mist, he saw nothing.

Touching the cold stone that he was wedged within, he gained equilibrium. He heard his own heart pound. His body felt weightless. He waited.

He could feel the Holiness of his God.

What had he asked? Could he breathe of this goodness and live?

He had watched God write with His Finger. The air had felt holy then. But now, it felt like an absence of even this world's air. As if the fallen creation had been purged. He couldn't find words to describe how he felt. It even smelled of holiness. He tingled all over, as if his body was almost suffocated, yet at the same time made vibrantly alive. Moses held his breath. His throat thickened, and he tried to swallow. Protect me, O Great God, for my body is weak. My soul knows its wickedness. My heart longs for only You.

He closed his eyes and felt peace. The fog passed the opening. He dared to open his eyes. The Lord's Hand removed the protection of His mercy.

And there was the back of God.

Moses would have fallen in obeisance if he had not been wedged so tightly in the cleft of the rock. His breath caught in his throat. Even if there were words to express what he saw, he could not have spoken. Holy was the only word that came to his mind. How could he not be consumed by this Holy God Who was the very essence of goodness, glory, and life?

The Lord moved away.

Moses was alone. His legs buckled. He stepped outward, faltering, falling on the rock where he had waited to see the Lord. He trembled. He worshiped. He didn't know how many hours he spent in this manner before regaining the strength that seeing God's back had demanded of him.

Time was not.

Life would never be the same.

The sun was setting over the horizon when Moses stood. He didn't want to leave the mountain. Must he return to the people?

His duty pushed him to descend. Isn't that what he had told Zipporah—that he obeyed because of his love for God? Obedience was hard this time.

He stopped to drink at the water. He lingered over his drink. He pushed himself to return to the campsite.

When Moses entered the house, Zipporah stopped shaping the flatbread. "You are well? Your face glows of light."

"I've seen the Lord's back."

"It is what you asked?"

Moses nodded.

Zipporah waited until he looked at her. "Gershom disobeys me. He doesn't collect the manna."

Moses's ecstasy at seeing God crashed to the ground. Why had he returned? How easy it would be to walk up the mountain and never return!

He was eighty-one years old; let a young man bear the load. He shook his head, trying to clear it of such thoughts.

Love required obedience. He must complete his mission. Now he must serve God by leading a people who knew Him not.

Gershom waited by his side.

Moses placed his hand on his son's shoulder. Then he lifted it again and looked at his hand. It felt unclean. He tapped it on Gershom. He was still part of this life.

Gershom pled with his eyes. "Abba, don't you have some man job? Collecting manna is..." he whispered, "woman's work."

Normally, Moses would have found humor in Gershom's desire to be a man. Today, he only saw how far his family was from knowing the Lord. He squeezed Gershom's shoulder. "Whatever your ima gives you to do, do it cheerfully with a grateful heart. By obeying your ima, you show me you're ready for man's work and for the Lord's work. Your disobedience tells me you're not ready. How can you hear the Lord's still small voice, Whom you cannot see, when you cannot obey the voice of your ima, whom you can see?"

"But how do you hear God?"

Moses sat.

Gershom settled at his feet.

Moses hugged him closer to his lap. "When you want to hear the Lord, nothing can stop you from being quiet and still in His presence. Oftentimes, He speaks when you are doing what you should. He whispers, prompting your heart."

Gershom wiggled, trying not to look at Moses's face.

"Look at me, son." Moses waited for his attention. "The Lord whispers to those who want to hear, not to those too busy to listen. Now for your correction..."

Gershom shifted in his seat.

Moses squeezed his shoulder. "You will collect manna and bring water fourteen days. After that, I will seek the Lord for a service worthy of the man that you are becoming."

Gershom's face reflected the anticipation of great things. "Thank you. I will prove worthy."

"But," Moses hastened to add, "even then, you will continue to bring water and gather manna."

Gershom bowed his head. "Yes, Abba. As you wish."

Moses saw his disappointment. "What I wish, Gershom, is for you to know the Lord. You must obey, before He shows the next step. Obedience comes before He gives you a mission."

"Yes, Abba." Gershom rose, and grabbed the water vessel by the entrance, and ran to do his father's bidding.

Zipporah settled by Moses's feet. "What was it like to see the Lord? Were you afraid?"

Moses held her hand. "It was like waiting for my father's blessing. I knew that it would be too much for me, but I wanted it, ached for it, longed for it—like a passion that would consume me if I did not see Him."

Zipporah listened. "I wish that I could see as you, Moses."

"Search for Him only. When you do, everything else falls away.

CHAPTER 15

Moses had rested from his experience on the mountain. He had slept throughout the night and the next day. Now, he must return to the mountain for the Lord to finish the laws for the people. His own words to Gershom came back to him, "Obey." It was hard to obey, and meet the needs of the people, when he would rather sit at the feet of the Lord. He prepared to return to the Lord. He was ready to leave the people again, but were they ready for him to leave?

He bowed to Hakeen outside his tent. "Shalom. The Lord needs two stone tablets for the Law."

"When?"

"By the morning."

"I will make haste."

Moses turned to leave, but Hakeen called after him, "What was it like to be in His presence?"

Moses looked at the mountain. "Words cannot describe my desire to worship, the peace...my satisfaction. I have no wants. I care for nothing but His presence." He stopped and turned his gaze to Hakeen. "It's beyond words."

Hakeen suggested, "I could make the stones of gold to show everyone its value."

Moses shook his head. "The Lord requests stone. What His Hands have made is enough for His Finger to touch." Moses shrugged. "If it were gold, the brightness would keep the people from reading. The stone's commonness will allow them to see the words that will change their lives."

Hakeen bowed to Moses. "I wish my tools were worthy of the project entrusted to me."

Moses shook his head. "Your tools are what the Lord gave you. What He asks, He provides."

Before the sun lifted its rays from the horizon the following morning, Moses stood at the base of the mountain, looking toward the top. He could not wipe the smile from his face or still the stirring in his insides. He would soon be with God again.

Aaron shifted beside him.

Should he leave the people? What would happen while he was gone? Moses laid his arm on Aaron, hesitating to admonish him again, yet feeling that he must. "Remember, no man must approach the mountain. Aaron, don't sin again."

Aaron flinched.

Moses squeezed his arm, then began his climb. He quickened his steps. He wanted to leave this people. Their petty arguments wearied him. If they knew the Lord, they would not have these problems. Their trust would be in God. He would be enough.

He looked at the campsite, extending into the desert as far as he could see. These people did not know the Lord.

How could he show them Who God was? Moses was leading them, not just to their Land, but to their God. His glimpse of God was not just for him to hoard to himself, but to use to bring this people to see Him, too. The immensity of the mission fell on his shoulders like a load of sand. He began the ascent with added determination to fulfill the mission given to him.

The Lord descended in the cloud, covering the mountain's top, enfolding Moses.

"Lord God, compassionate and gracious, slow to anger, abounding in truth, forgiving iniquity, transgression and sin."

The Lord interrupted, "I will not leave the guilty unpunished. Their iniquity will remain on the children and on the grandchildren to the third and fourth generations."

Moses fell to his face and worshiped. "Lord, if I have found favor in Your Sight, stay in our midst, even though the people are obstinate. Pardon our sin. Take us as Your people."

"I will make you a covenant. I will perform miracles never seen before among the nations of the earth. The people will see My Hand working. Obey, carefully and completely. I will drive out the Amorites, Canaanites, Hittites, Perizzites, Hivites, and Jebusites before you. Make no promises with any of the inhabitants. They will ensnare you in their evil, and I won't bless you.

"I am a jealous God. Tear down their altars. Destroy their images. Have nothing to do with their practices, or they will invite you to eat of their sacrifices, and worship their gods."

Moses stayed with the Lord forty days and forty nights. He did not eat nor drink anything. He couldn't wait for the people to know Who the Lord is.

God wrote His Law for His people again on the tablets of stone.

As Moses returned to camp, the people turned away from him, as if they did not see him. He entered his house.

When Zipporah saw him, she stared, stepping back. She covered her face with her hands, yet continued to look at him through her fingers.

"What's wrong?" Moses grew concerned, recalling how others had avoided him.

"Your face shines like the heavens. You frighten me."

"Can the Lord contain His glory? It spills forth, flooding anything it touches. If I am His vessel, I should shine for Him."

She hesitantly touched his cheek. "Have you become part god?"

He placed his hand over hers.

She trembled.

He laughed, hugging her tightly. "The Lord allows me to stay in my body. Zipporah, you can know Him like I do."

Zipporah stepped away from his embrace. "No, Moses, your people won't let me be one with them." She leaned against him. "The glory of Your God keeps me from you, and your people keep me from belonging with them. I am caught between the two, never to feel at home."

Moses squeezed her. "It doesn't have to be so hard. The Lord will give you a home."

CHAPTER 16

A aron fidgeted at Moses's doorway, waiting for Moses.
Moses stepped outside his house. "Shalom, I didn't know you were waiting for me."

Aaron looked at his feet. "Be at peace. I didn't want to interrupt your meal."

"What's on your mind?"

"The people don't want to worship."

Moses had felt a difference in the people, ever since he had returned from the mountain with the Law. Were they finally seeing the holiness of God? "Why?"

Aaron finally looked at him. "You show the people their need."

Moses corrected, "The Law shows men their need."

Aaron straightened his belt and pulled his hood off. "They cannot look at your face. You radiate God's glory."

Moses shook his head in disbelief. "Can a man be in God's presence and not reflect His glory? What am I to do about that?"

Aaron shrugged. "The people worship you."

Moses paced. "That must not be!"

"They fear to stand before you."

"The people must see God as a Friend, wanting their presence. But also as their God, Who is holy."

Aaron placed his hand on Moses's shoulder. "The people tremble, but do not change. Do you want to chase them away from God?"

Moses raised his voice. "How should I teach them the Law?"

Aaron softened his voice. "If you wore a veil, the people may hear the words."

Moses nodded. "Then I will wear a veil."

On the next Sabbath, Moses looked over the assembly, wearing a veil. The shine of God shone through, but the people listened.

"The Lord requests anyone with a willing heart to give Him an offering: gold, silver, and bronze; material of blue, purple and scarlet; fine linen, goats' hair, rams' skins, and porpoise skins; acacia wood; oil for lighting; spices for anointing oil; incense, onyx stones, and gems. Those skilled in making the instruments for sacrifice are needed for His service."

After Moses dismissed the people, he heard snatches of conversations about what the people could bring. His heart was warmed by the spirit moving among the people.

The Lord would stir hearts to serve Him.

Reut retraced her steps to their tent after Moses's request for an offering. She overheard her ima and abba already searching their chests.

Carmel pointed to a pile of material that she had gathered on a cloak. "Adlai, would you mind if I gave these things?"

Adlai hugged her. "The Lord poured the wealth of Egypt into our hands. Give it all."

Carmel looked at the piles on the floor. "The Egyptians gave because they feared Him. We give because we love Him."

Reut fingered the amulet around her neck. It reminded her of Egypt's wealth, power, control. She rubbed the gold. Could she give this?

She stepped into the tent and helped her mother take bundles of material to the tent of meeting. She sorted their offerings onto designated piles. She gazed at the mounds of gold, silver, and precious gems.

Hannah stepped behind her and dropped her statues on the growing piles. The gold clanked and tinkled. "Shalom, Reut."

Reut glanced at the statues that Hannah had put on the piles.

Hannah whispered, "Even if the gold was made into a false god, couldn't the Lord still use it?"

Reut pointed to the pile. "Look at all the other statues. God must not be picky."

Hannah smiled. "The statues were gifts from Egyptians. I wanted to make sure that God would be pleased."

Reut shrugged. She fingered her necklace again.

The Lord had enough.

She did not need to give. Her heart pricked her as she thought of the gifts the Lord had given her. She ignored her heart and walked away.

Pelia wanted to give. The Lord provided for all their needs since coming to this desert. But what she had must help her in the new Land. When the seasons changed, bringing the rains, those extra goats' hair blankets would be needed to keep her warm. Did God expect her to give things that she needed herself?

Today was the first time since the day of feasting around the golden bull that she had returned to her own tent. She had been staying with Hannah. She walked to her tent without thinking.

Reaching it, she saw Magal. She looked around for his friends but only saw him.

Magal stood when she entered. "Pelia."

She avoided looking at him.

"During the feasting, I drank too much..."

She nodded but still did not look at him.

Magal's voice trembled. "Look at me."

She did not want to look. She wanted distance. Could she feel safe around Magal again? Would he give her away to any man who wanted a good time?

Magal's voice broke as he pled, "Pelia."

Magal commanded, never petitioned her. His entreaty broke her resolve.

She met his eyes.

He extended his hands toward her.

She ran to him.

He hugged her like the day they had lost their parents. "Pelia, I'm...the drink made me do it."

Pelia wiped her tears on his tunic. "I was so frightened."

Magal squeezed her tighter.

This was the old Magal, the one that she had know growing up, the one who had cared for her when their parents had died.

She pushed away from his chest and searched his face. "I want to give something. Do you have something that we could give?"

Magal dropped his arms and stepped back. His face became hard. "Moses said, 'only if you're willing to give.' I'm not willing to give this God anything."

Pelia didn't understand the quick change from his tenderness and almost an apology, to this hardness. What was he angry about? "But I want to..."

"I wouldn't give anything to this God. He killed my friends."

She bit back a response. How could he not want to give to God Who had provided everything they needed? Turning from Magal to hide her hurt, Pelia stirred the embers. Telling Magal that his friends were killed in judgment would only make him angrier.

She shuddered. That day of feasting had turned into a nightmare for her. After she ran into Amos, he had taken her to Nathan's tent for safety.

Later, when the Levities were executing God's judgment, Pelia had searched for Magal. When she found him with a woman, Pelia shook him, screaming for him to leave. In his stupor, he had put his arm around her and lain back on the pallet.

Magal's friends were killed.

He did not see his life as spared; only his friends' lives as taken.

Magal sat, sharpening his dagger and sword. His face remained hard.

Her thoughts moved from that day, to this Sabbath. She wanted to offer a sacrifice for God's protection, not just His provision. She blew into the embers, feeding little bits of dung into the flames. She moved from habit, trying to think what she could give. Her belongings were few. When others had received gifts from Egyptians, she had been helping Esmail with the sheep.

What could she offer that God needed? Her eyes fell on her pile of goats' skins. She smiled. She would ask Esmail if they could shear the flocks, so she could weave cloth. She could give a work of her hands.

Nathan lounged after the noon meal. "I wonder..." He tousled his son's hair.

Salome leaned against him. "What?"

"If the Lord is reassuring us of His love, because we sinned. Like when Jabin disobeys and repents." Nathan put Jabin on his lap. "He clings to me, seeking to make things right. He helps me with a task, and he is reassured of my love. That's what the Lord is doing with His people. We sinned. Now, He welcomes us back, not just to continue as before, but to serve Him."

Salome rubbed her hand over the baby growing inside her. "What do we have to give? We're like the little boy who borrows what belongs to his father to give it back to his father for a blessing."

Nathan nodded. "Maybe I can help build the Tabernacle."

Salome's hand stopped massaging the babe. She took Nathan's hand and laid it where the baby's foot still lay.

He pressed gently. The foot moved again.

Salome rested her hand on Nathan's.

"Do you feel the baby?" Etania wiggled closer to her mother. She put her hand on top of Salome's.

Jabin laid his hand on top of all of theirs.

Nathan put his other hand on top of all the hands. He thought about God's ownership of his family, especially since the coming of the child. He struggled daily to allow God control. Moses's words had assured him that his heart must give, not just his hands. He squeezed their hands gently. "We must give the Lord our child."

Etania's big eyes turned to Nathan. "Does God need our baby?"

Nathan laughed. "No. We'll raise him to serve Him."

Jabin puckered his mouth. His eyes filled with tears. "You won't give me away?"

Nathan ruffled Jabin's hair. "No son, but we'll train you to be His servant."

Etania leaned against Salome. "Don't we want to be free?"

Nathan nodded. He had found by doubting God, by trying to be the one in control, he had lost his freedom. His mind was bound by thoughts that swirled and circled in doubt and questions. He had lost his freedom. He must give Salome to God, too. No matter how much he loved her, God loved her more. He nodded again. "We were made to serve God. When we do that, we have freedom."

Salome asked, "Why do you help me? Do you feel like you are enslaved to me, Etania?"

Etania chewed her lip and shook her head.

Nathan squeezed her hand. "We serve God because we want to please Him."

Etania wrinkled her forehead. "But, Abba, does God need us?"

Salome squeezed Etania's shoulder. "God needs nothing. But we need Him. And we want to give Him what we value most, to show Him how much we value Him. You three are most precious."

"Why give?" Etania asked.

Nathan looked over his family. Without giving what he loved, could it be a sacrifice? He met Salome's gaze and smiled. "Because He wants our fellowship. Etania, your questions have made me want to give what I should to God." He leaned to kiss Salome.

Etania leaned against Salome. "He wants us to be His friend."

The sun was already high on the day after the Sabbath. Esmail motioned for his dog to circle a goat. The dog nipped its heel. It twisted and leaped toward Simon. Esmail smiled. This goat would not get away. "Grab its leg!"

Simon ducked as the goat leaped at him. Before clearing Simon's head, it kicked him.

Esmail laughed. "You all right? That one has done that to me before. Made me want to butcher him on the spot. If he wasn't such a good buck, I would."

"Good buck or no, I'd butcher him." Simon shook his head, rubbing it gingerly.

Esmail signaled his dog to circle the goat again. "Don't let him rest. He'll soon tire."

The next time the dog nipped him in the heels, Esmail caught his back leg.

Simon said, "You make it look easy."

"When you live with them, you know them." Esmail placed the goat in the temporary stanchion to shear it. "You're getting there. You enjoy sheep and goats, yes?"

Simon looked over the buck's head. "Especially holding this one."

Esmail chuckled. "Pelia wishes to spin goat's hair to give to her God."

"I've heard about that Tabernacle they are building. Why not the sheep?"

"The sun would burn their backs if we shear them now. We'll wait for the rains. The goats are hardier toward the sun's rays."

"Do you ever feel distant from our people, living away from camp?" Simon let the goat loose and waited for Esmail to point out the next goat they would catch.

Esmail studied Simon. "Are you growing weary of herding?"

"Not at all. I used to thrive with camp activity, but now it doesn't seem important."

Esmail smiled and nodded. "The sheep are getting under your skin. That is good."

"But I wish to know more about the God Who leads. I hear He gives laws to follow. I'd like to know what He says."

Esmail shuddered. "When that God kept water from my herd and caused my good ewes and lambs to die, I no longer was interested with what He wanted."

"My family suffered, but it was through that suffering that I got here. Does it sound wrong to thank this God for hardships?"

Esmail almost spit the word out. "Why?"

"Because otherwise I wouldn't be here doing this with you."

Esmail thought for a moment. "I'm glad you're here. But I'm not ready to thank God for His part in it."

Moses approached Bezalel at his tent. "Shalom."

Bezalel bowed and motioned for him to sit. "You honor my tent by coming."

Moses sat and fingered the gold plate that lay beside his cushion. He traced the engraved letters with his finger. You shall have no other gods before Me. Moses looked from the plate to Bezalel. "You made this?"

Bezalel nodded to the plate. "You gave those laws the day before you left. My fingers itched to do something for God. I made that."

Moses's fingers now tapped the plate. "You were asked to do the bull, weren't you?"

"Well, I was approached..."

Moses looked straight into Bezalel's eyes. "Aaron told me."

Bezalel hung his head as he remembered all the gods that he had made in Egypt. "Remember the glory in the desert? His glory glowed more than any gold fired by my hands. It burned a hole in my heart."

Bezalel's eyes teared. "I want my hands to be pure for the Lord. How do I make them so?"

Moses nodded. "The Lord wants you to make the instruments for His worship."

Bezalel's mouth fell open. He squeezed his eyes shut, then blinked. "The Lord asked for me? After I made all those idols in Egypt? Why, Moses? My hands are so unclean. I am not worthy of His work."

Moses looked again at the plate in his hands. He tapped the plate. "When He chose me for this mission, I asked the same thing." He looked into Bezalel's eyes. "You can never be good enough to please the Lord. He makes you pleasing. But you must be willing. Are you?"

"With all of my being."

"Then the Lord will be pleased with your work."

Moses placed the plate in Bezalel's hands. "The Lord trained you in Egypt to be the best. He requires service, not to appease a god who cannot see, hear or touch. You will please the God Who made your hands and gave you skills for His service. He will see your work and be pleased."

The people had brought their offerings to the tent of meeting. Moses and Aaron walked among the workmen, noting their progress. Moses stopped to watch Oholiab instruct another. He held the wood like a treasured friend. He caressed the smooth edge. Moses nodded to Oholiab as he spoke to Aaron, "How did you know he worked so well with wood?"

"In Egypt, he made a wooden leg for Amos."

Moses pointed to Oholiab teaching woodworking to another. "The Lord teaches the men skills so that they can provide for their families. Their hearts are dedicated. Their minds challenged. Their hands perform more than they've ever done."

Aaron nodded. "Bezalel's skill exceeds anything done in Egypt. The Lord's Spirit is upon him."

Bezalel approached Moses and Aaron. "A word, if I may?" He paused, waiting for their nod. "Tell the people, they've given enough."

Moses looked at the mounds of riches and nodded. "Yes. How does the work go?"

Bezalel walked to where Seth kneeled. "Here's the ark." The Ark of the Covenant would be placed in the Holy of Holies. It would contain the Words of the Lord, as well as the omer of manna that Moses had saved, reminding the people of God's provision.

Acacia wood, common in the desert, provided the framework. Pure gold covered it, both inside and out. Rings were welded to carry it. Two gold cherubs faced each other, covering the mercy seat with their outspread wings, pointing toward heaven.

The mercy seat was the top of the ark. The Lord's cloud would rest on it.

Whenever the priests offered the sin sacrifice, they would sprinkle the blood from the sacrifice on top of the mercy seat. By the Lord's acceptance, atonement was given. Mercy was shown.

Seth dusted the golden wing of one of the cherubs. "Fit for a king."

Bezalel corrected. "For the King. The Lord demands all knees to bow before Him."

Moses lightly touched the mercy seat. "The Lord will administer justice here."

Seth shook his head. "To think I worshiped a bull. This mercy seat is just one thing that will please Him."

Bezalel shook his head. "Things don't please Him. He wants us."

Moses lifted his hand off the mercy seat as if it contained God already. "He needs nothing, yet wants us."

Amos spread the fabric in front of him. He could not imagine losing a leg as something good, but as he stitched, he realized that his loss had prepared him for his task today. His hands were strong from stone carving, but able to sew the fine stitches needed for this work.

He stitched the priests' garments. The blue, purple, and scarlet material of fine twisted linen required strong hands to keep from slipping, especially after Bezalel hammered sheets of gold, cut into threads and woven into the material.

He considered Aaron. He patted his stump. Without Aaron's help, he wouldn't be alive. In Egypt, Aaron had saved his life by removing his leg that had been crushed by a statue falling on it. In Egypt, Aaron had pled with the king to relieve his people's physical suffering. Now as priest, he would plead with God to have mercy on their heart's suffering. Amos looked at the linen woven with gold. He was glad Aaron would wear something worthy of his service.

Pelia approached his campsite. "Shalom."

Amos laid aside the material. "Hannah has gone to look for herbs, but she'll return soon." As he spoke, he attached his wooden leg so that he could stand. "Would you wait? I could keep you company."

Pelia nodded. She sat beside him. She pointed to the fabric. "Is that the priest's garment?"

"Yes. Feel the material."

Pelia fingered the fabric. "It's soft, yet strong. The weave is thick with richness. How do you push the needle through the fabric?"

"Try it."

Pelia's ears turned red. "My stitches aren't small."

"I will help place the needle."

Pelia giggled. "When I was young, I spent more time in the fields with the goats than learning to cook and sew."

"I've seen your goats' blankets. They require skill."

"It's something I could give to God." Pelia had spun the sheared goat's hair, a skill learned by watching shepherd's wives and mothers when she was young. She scrubbed the hair many times, and then dried it. Taking each tuft of hair, she carded them for spinning into a continuous thread, gaging the thickness of the thread by her moving fingers. Once the threads were prepared, she wove them into thick blankets. "The gift will form the walls of the Tabernacle."

Amos held her hand to pull the gold-lined thread through the material.

Pelia blushed, but allowed Amos to continue to help her stitch. "You must have fingers that could milk a sheep."

Amos laughed. "And when would you milk a sheep?"

"After giving birth, if a ewe is too full of milk for the lamb to grab, Esmail milks so the lamb can latch on. I don't have strength to hold and squeeze." Pelia pointed to the fabric. "That's the strength you needed to pull a needle through this material."

Pelia retrieved her hand from his hold and stroked the material. "Can you imagine sleeping on this? You could only have good dreams."

Amos studied her. "What dreams could be bad from a head as beautiful as yours?"

Pelia blushed.

Had he overstepped his boundaries? She had no father to grant permission for marriage. He must speak with Esmail. He heard the story of how Esmail had threatened death to a bigger man. That was just over sheep. What would he do to him, when he asked for his sister in marriage?

She stood. "I should go. I'll speak with Hannah later. It wasn't urgent." She laughed. "What could be urgent in the desert where time stands still?" She turned to go.

"Pelia," Amos stood.

She faced him expectantly.

He reached for her hand. "Pelia." Amos watched her face with nervous anticipation. "I wish to speak to your brother Esmail. Would that be acceptable to you?"

Her eyes shone. "Then I could be sure never to have any bad dreams." She fled to her tent.

Amos stared after her fleeing figure. When her words registered, he broke into a smile.

Aaron returned to camp from Mount Sinai after sacrificing with seventy of the leaders. He paused to look over the Tabernacle. It stood apart from the people, but surrounded by his tribe, protecting the people from the holiness of God. He could see the fire-cloud, rising above the Holy of Holies, the inner sanctuary of the Tabernacle made for God's presence.

It had taken the people close to a year to complete the Tabernacle. They had not moved from Mount Sinai as they had worked to complete it. He sighed.

Moses stopped beside him. "What?"

Aaron motioned with his staff toward the Tabernacle. "The people were united during the construction of the Tabernacle. They are becoming His people."

Moses nodded. "God finds pleasure in us."

Aaron started walking again. "Why did God choose us as His people?"

Moses laughed. "It's not that we are a great nation, rather we're the smallest of any nation. Abraham pleased Him. And God chose to reward him."

Holding a branch, Aaron stepped over a boulder. "The people are learning His laws."

Moses smiled. "By learning His laws, we know His heart. They are learning to obey." He stepped around an area where the ground had fallen away. "When we obey, He is pleased. When we don't," he shrugged, "we are most miserable."

They continued down the mountain. Both lost in their thoughts.

Aaron interrupted the silence as they reached the Tabernacle. "In Egypt, I was afraid of Pharaoh and what he could do. Pharaoh's power looks so little now that I have seen what God can do."

Moses nodded. "My one fear is that I won't complete the mission He's given me."

Aaron studied his brother. "I can't even imagine that you wouldn't take us into the Land. Why are you afraid of that?"

"I'm afraid I will disappoint Him."

"Failing comes easy for me, but you?"

"Do you think that I'm less of a man than you?" Moses laughed. "Every day I must decide if I will obey His voice."

"Isn't it a habit?"

Moses shrugged, "It's a daily decision—no, a moment's decision, to put away what I think is best, and look to Him for what He wants. The closer I get to Him, the more I see myself unworthy of this task."

Aaron took a drink from the dipper at the doorway. "I know what you mean. When I think about how He has appointed me as the interceder for this people.... Why does He think us worthy?"

"Our worth comes from Who He is. By pleasing Him, we find contentment. I crave that satisfaction of making Him happy."

"You encourage me to know His Law, so that I will please Him. I must study the sacrifices."

Moses nodded. "This Sabbath, we must consecrate the finished Tabernacle to the Lord's good will."

Aaron nodded before entering the Tabernacle to study the scrolls.

The following Sabbath, Aaron wore his breastplate and turban. He stood with the other Levites inside the Tabernacle. They had washed ceremonially, wearing their finished tunics, girding on their sashes, covered by their robes.

Moses anointed the Levities and the Tabernacle with oil, consecrating all their efforts to the Lord.

Aaron sacrificed a bull for a sin offering, a ram for a burnt offering, and an unleavened cake for a wave offering. He followed the law's details. Then, he raised his hands over the people. "The Lord bless you and keep you. Oh, that you had such a heart in you, that you would fear the Lord, and keep all His commandments always, that it may be well with you and with your sons forever."

The Lord was pleased. He sent fire from heaven to consume the sacrifices.

Aaron fell on his face in worship. His satisfaction was complete.

Moses read the Law to the people. "The Lord did not set His love on you nor choose you because you were more in number than any people, for you were the fewest, but because the Lord loved you and kept the oath which He swore to your forefathers."

Aaron rose from his knees. Could the people be ready for the Land promised to them? What more could God desire?

CHAPTER 17

As the sun was setting, Aaron stood outside the judging tent. The leaders were finishing judging. The people had already been sent home.

Aaron stopped Elizur as he was leaving. "How's your daughter?"

"The burn heals after your treatment."

"Good. How was the judging today?"

Elizur shrugged. "Same. People fight."

"How soon do you judge the people after they dispute?"

Elizur shrugged. "Within one or two days."

Aaron nodded, watching Elizur. "The punishments are accepted?"

Elizur laughed. "No one wants to acknowledge wrong. Are we to celebrate?"

Nahshon joined them. "Elizur, why do people laugh whenever you pronounce judgment?"

Elizur looked around first, as if he could not understand why he needed to explain himself, before answering. "If the punishment is harsh, that is all they will remember. But if they have cause to remember the silliness of the dispute, then they will think longer before they do it again."

Aaron nodded. "So how do you help this remembering?"

"Varies. Today someone had sliced another's tent into strips. Instead of just replacing the tent, his family must share his tent with the family whose tent was destroyed, until he replaces the tent."

Nahshon asked, "Is that what caused all that laughter?"

"The man whose tent was destroyed said that he wouldn't live in the same tent with the offending man for so much as a day." Elizur paused. "I silenced his complaints when I offered his daughter to the offender for marriage."

Aaron prodded. "Do the people accept your judgment?"

Elizur defended. "They don't do it again. Isn't that the goal?"

Nahshon hid his smile in his beard. "His courts are always packed with people, not to be judged, but to listen."

Elizur shrugged. "I'm not trying to entertain."

Aaron laid his hand on Elizur's shoulder. "What are you trying to do?"

Elizur attempted meekness. "Don't we all want justice?"

Aaron asked. "Was your verdict be just?"

Elizur raised his eyebrows, acting innocent. "Just because I don't do it Moses's way, does not mean I'm not just.... What is justice anyway?"

Moses approached the tent of judging. "Shalom. A word with you, Elizur, if I may?"

Elizur had just stepped out of the judging tent, laughing. "Moses, what may I do for you?"

"Your judging has become a time for festivities."

"People should remember what they've done and not do it again. Isn't that what you wish?"

"My people must not only remember the Lord's Law but respect it. Your court has made the law frivolous. The Lord is holy. His judgment is righteous. People should be humiliated to see the Lord's holiness, not humbled by what another man has done to them. You have made the Lord's Law into a game."

Elizur held his chin high. His expression showed sternness. "My tribe does not wait many days to be judged. Look at the lines for the other tribes. They are longer than mine. Because of my judgments, people fear to transgress your Law."

"It's not my law, Elizur. It is the Lord's. His Law will not be taken lightly." Moses continued. "Your tribesmen request to be judged by someone outside your tribe, rather than by you. At first, I did not consent, but as more asked, I decided to investigate.

"I don't find humor in someone's sin. My heart breaks over the sins of my people. I wish for them to know the Lord better, not be humiliated by a verdict."

"You are misguided, Moses." Elizur corrected. "They are not your people. They are a free people.

"You cater to their wrong by allowing them to leave my court. I curbed wrong. How can justice be done, if you interfere?"

Moses shook his head. "Justice? By giving someone's daughter to another, when she wasn't the problem? Does one wrong make another right? You mock the Law. You don't see the holiness of God's Words when you judge. You know nothing of justice, if you know nothing of the Lord. You see only with your eyes and not with your heart. Elizur, you are released from your duty as judge. The elders will replace you with someone who knows the Lord and respects His word."

Elizur opened his mouth, then shut it slowly. Anger flashed from his dark eyes.

Moses looked to the top of the mountain. He always did when he wished for strength. His words had been harsh. But Elizur justified his own actions rather than acknowledging his flippant attitude toward God. Truth cuts deeply into what will destroy the soul. Moses extended his arms in a gesture of peace. "The Lord wants to use you."

Elizur brushed passed Moses, ignoring his outstretched arms.

Moses dropped his arms. The people hurt when they turned from the Friend of Abraham. Moses could point them to Him, but he could not make them obey.

After the evening meal, when the cloud turned to fire, Elizur whispered, concealed in the hidden darkness beyond the fire's glow. "Nahshon, my friend."

Nahshon stepped away from his fire into the dark shadows. "Be at peace. I heard what happened. I'm sorry. I'm most sorry that I will miss the sounds of laughter through the tent walls."

Elizur shrugged. "I'm too busy executing justice."

"What do you mean, 'executing justice'?"

Elizur chose his words carefully. "Moses thinks too highly of himself. He is threatened by anyone who challenges him. Yet he protects his wife, who is an exception to his own Law. Is he allowed, by the Law, to have a foreign wife? Justice must come to his house."

"Speak no more of this, Elizur. The Lord's power rests on Moses. Think of your own family."

Elizur barely looked at him as he turned away. "I thought you were my friend. I was wrong."

Nahshon caught his arm. "I am. But I fear God."

"We must have a new leader."

Nahshon squeezed Elizur's arm, his eyes widening. "I left slavery. I do not wish to return to another man's control."

Elizur brushed Nahshon's hand off his arm. "But you submit to the control of Moses?"

"He is the Lord's leader. I cannot fight against God."

Elizur nodded. "Then I will tell the people myself how Moses does not obey the Law."

Zipporah stirred the embers of the fire in the early morning. She wished for the privacy of her mountains. Too many people made her feel trapped. She missed the sheep and goats, the comfort of their familiar smell. She was glad for her rock fortress, thankful that her brother Hobab and his family had stayed. He had built the house, from rocks Gershom helped gather. The stone's coolness and the protection of the stone walls reminded Zipporah of home.

She left the safety of her dwelling with a basket to gather manna, conscious of others stirring. She kept her head down and hurried.

"Zipporah." Carmel hurried to catch her. "Mind if I join you?"

Zipporah enjoyed the solitude, but she waited. Carmel did not chatter.

"It's hard to get away in the morning without getting busy in the activities of camp." Carmel breathed deeply from hurrying. "I don't know how you do it with a little one underfoot and another so full of questions."

Zipporah smiled. "Yesterday, Gershom asked if he could give his lizard a house. I should have questioned what he meant. Now I have a lizard living with us inside my own house. Every time I see it, I think that a snake lives with me."

Carmel shook her head. "How do you stay ahead of that child?"

They drifted apart, gathering their daily bread.

Several women settled not far from Zipporah. "If the Lord is content with a tent for His worship, why must she have stone?"

"She thinks she's too special to live in a tent like everyone else."

"Why does Moses allow such a thing?"

"Moses doesn't rule his own house. She does what she wants."

They moved away as they gathered, but their words stayed in Zipporah's mind.

She brought her basket closer to her lap and looked toward the dawn.

Carmel laid a hand on her shoulder, startling her. "Zipporah, pay no attention to unkind words. If they would have thought to build a house like yours first, they would be singing its praises, not condemning its use. Your house gives you security. You have done well. I have vessels, reminding me of Egypt. Gives me a bit of comfort in the midst of all this sand and grit. It reminds me that this is not my home. We move to something better. Your house is like that, too. It gives you comfort that helps you deal with today. Enjoy it, but do not hold it too close."

Amos had sought Hakeen's advice about speaking to Esmail. Now he walked toward Esmail's flocks. In the distance, he saw the shepherd, preparing for the noon meal. The man was not talkative, but with a few words and a nod, directed Amos to join him in his meal of flatbread and stew. The lamb tasted good after days with just manna. They ate in silence, and when the meal was over, they relaxed under an acacia tree in the heat of the day.

Amos washed his face and arms before refilling his waterskin. The cool water was refreshing. He took a deep breath before speaking. "Your flocks do well on the desert's pasture."

"We find enough."

"Your contribution to the Lord's Tabernacle was admired by all."

"Pelia is skilled at weaving the goats' hair into fine cloth."

"I wish to speak to you about Pelia."

"Yes?"

Amos squirmed under the shepherd's scrutiny. "I wish to marry Pelia."

"Why?"

Amos had not prepared to answer that. If he had asked how he would provide for her, how she would complete him, or how the future would be brighter, he could have answered. His silence made the man chuckle. Amos looked up. He did not want to be made a fool, but he was willing if Esmail would grant permission. What did he want? He began again, "I would take care of Pelia, not only with all that I have, but with all my heart."

The man stood. "I believe..."

Amos's heart dropped when he saw his expression.

"I believe..." He stopped again, a curious twitch tugging the corner of his mouth down.

Amos could bear it no longer. "Tell me. What must I do to have your sister? I'd give you all that I have so that I may spend my life with her."

"I will take all that you have, if you wish to give it to me." The man again took his time in answering. "But I do not have a sister Pelia."

Had Pelia not told him this was where he would find her brother? His anger rose quickly. "You're not Esmail?"

"No, son. I only work for him. He will be here for the evening meal, if you wish to wait. Otherwise, it might be some distance to find him." The twinkle in his eye belied the fact that he would have stretched Amos's discomfort longer if he could help it. "Be at ease. Esmail will come. Then you may ask your question and give everything that you have to him," he added as he turned away.

Amos could feel the color rise on his face. He sat against the tree and breathed deeply. He would have to prepare himself all over again to speak to Esmail. The anticipation would sap him of all his strength.

Amos rubbed his hands down his tunic as he watched another shepherd approach the campfire. The sun was just sinking behind the mountain. He had waited all day, pacing, rehearsing his speech for Pelia's brother. He looked again at the man approaching. He looked as if he could slit someone's throat, if angered. Amos stood and took his waterskin to fill at the water side. He would continue to wait until the man had filled his belly. Perhaps his words would then be more readily received.

Esmail watched the boy closely throughout his meal, but said nothing.

When he finally finished his meal, Amos swallowed another gulp of water from his waterskin and began. He presented his case as he had earlier in the day. When he finished, he raised his head to look into Esmail's eyes. What he saw was unbelief. Amos started to panic. Would he not grant permission?

Instead of answering him, Esmail looked around the campsite. "How will you provide for my sister?"

"In Egypt, I apprenticed as a stone sculptor, but since the accident," Amos patted his leg, "I learned to sew canvas for the sails of Egypt's great ships. The skill has served me well. I keep busy mending the people's tents. The Lord's tent of meeting and much of the Tabernacle fell to my hands as well."

"And your father?"

"He is Hakeen, son of Zaccur, from the tribe of Judah. He has done service for Moses for the tablets of the Law."

Esmail nodded. "If Pelia is willing."

"She's willing. I could not ask without her encouragement."

Esmail chuckled, "I'll speak with her. Much has happened while I've been watching my sheep."

"Nothing that you would not approve. Nothing tarnishes her loveliness or purity."

Esmail's hand swept to his side where his scabbard lay. His eyes narrowed, and he said, almost too softly, "See that you don't. Or you'll answer to me."

Amos saw the intended gesture and remembered the story from Michael. "No need for that, sir. I promise."

"See that you keep that promise." Esmail lowered his voice as if talking to himself. "Is this the babbling of a nervous man or a guilty one?"

Did he expect an answer? Amos swallowed. "I may babble, but only because my heart is full of love for your sister."

Was that a smile that almost reached Esmail's eyes? Amos wiped his sweaty palms down his tunic.

Esmail extended his arm. "Pending my talk with Pelia, welcome to the family." He no longer hid the smile that showed through his beard.

Amos grabbed his hand in both of his and shook it. "Thank you."

Hakeen looked behind him. His tribe pushed around him. He could not see Amos at the back. Normally, his family would stand together during reading of the Law by Moses. Hannah had hurried toward the front. Had she forgotten Amos's need to stay away from crowds, so that he could keep his balance?

Hakeen was ready to discuss the mohar for Hannah ever since Phinehas had executed justice for the Lord after the golden bull, but Phinehas had not come. Had he been wise to require waiting? Had he prevented Phinehas from crushing his daughter's heart?

In his peripheral view, he studied Hannah. He sighed. Her interest at being at the front of the people was more than just seeing eighty-four-year-old Aaron dressed in his finest. She watched a younger Levi.

Hakeen had watched Phinehas during the construction of the Tabernacle. He had changed, helping in any menial capacity.

Phinehas had found the Lord, but in finding God, had he forgotten Hannah?

Moses read the Law to the people. The Levities performed the sacrifices. By seeking God's atonement through fulfilling the sacrifices, the sons of Aaron interceded for the people. God's holiness was shown. His requirements were fulfilled.

The Law gave part of the sacrifice to the priests, Aaron's family, to be eaten as payment for their service to God. Some of the meat was required to be eaten at the time of the sacrifice.

Aaron looked around the gathering. His four sons and grandsons stood attired for worship and service. He swallowed, wishing his wife were still alive to see them now. He felt proud that the Levites were chosen to carry the needs of the people before the holy God. He also felt humbled. The responsibility was great. He wiped his face with his tunic sleeve. He prayed that his sons were ready for the task.

Phinehas hung up his priestly garment. "The Law shows us how to please God."

Aaron nodded as he removed his own breastplate and turban. "It's a responsibility not to be taken lightly."

Aaron's second-born son, Abihu, put on his sandals. "It's just preparing animals for our dinner."

Phinehas shook his head. "It's presenting our needs before God."

Abihu rolled his eyes. "But then we get to eat the best cuts."

Eleazar, Aaron's third-born son, nodded. "The Lord leaves nothing for us to wonder about. He clearly states His requirements, and He blesses our obedience."

Aaron nodded toward Abihu and his first born, Nadab. "Prepare yourselves carefully so that you are ready to offer the sacrifices next Sabbath."

Ithamar, Aaron's fourth-born son, asked, "How do you know all the laws and procedures? I can't remember what to do next."

Eleazar looked to where the scrolls were kept in the tent. "We can study together."

Ithamar turned to Abihu. "Want to join us?"

Abihu shrugged. "It'll come with practice."

Ithamar shook his head. "I don't want to practice with God's worship."

"Nor should you." Aaron squeezed Abihu's shoulder. "Know the Lord's Words. They may save you from heartache."

Abihu shrugged as he sauntered toward the campsite. "Practice works for me. Who wants to waste time in study?"

Phinehas shook his head. "Are we headed for heartache?"

Aaron cleared his throat. "Looks like it."

When Aaron stepped out of the tent, he noticed a group of men surrounding Nadab. He stood at the back of the gathering.

Dathan spoke often with Korah, another Levite, about the inconsistencies of the Levite positions, especially when the people packed to move. He led the gathering now. "As the firstborn of Aaron, shouldn't you be given more duties in the temple than the other sons?"

Nadab shrugged. "We will take turns."

Another asked as his stomach growled, "How was the meat?"

Nods of assent could be seen.

"The smell of meat from the sacrifices made me hungry."

Nadab nodded. "The privilege of being a Levite, I guess. Sorry you missed the feast. It was great."

The men sighed. Some started mumbling.

Aaron cleared his throat. "We each have a part to play in the Lord's worship. Men, come with a heart ready to worship, not a stomach empty to be filled."

The men noticed him for the first time. They stopped grumbling, wandering away. Aaron and Nadab stood alone.

Nadab turned to Aaron. "I was just talking. Didn't mean any harm by it, Abba."

"The men are easily led to discontent. I've learned the hard way that sympathizing with grumblers makes you lack peace, too. Worship from your heart. But before it can come from the heart, it must be known in the head. Study the Law. Know it. Prepare for worship. The next time, you will lead the worship."

Nadab nodded. "I watched you today, Abba. I can lead next time."

Aaron shook his head. "Worship isn't my way or your way. It's God's way, or no worship takes place."

Nadab agreed halfheartedly and ambled back to his tent.

Aaron watched him. Heartache indeed.

After the sacrifices and the reading of the Law, Adlai left the assembly preoccupied.

"What is it?" Carmel asked as she walked with him.

"How can the people know the Law?"

Carmel reminded. "Men are reading it. Look at Michael. He struggled at first, but he searches to know the Friend of Abraham. Groups all over camp read the scrolls. These men see God through His Laws."

"The men move beyond reading of the law, to studying the Law. I don't have enough time to answer all their questions."

Carmel pulled her cloak's hood farther over her face as the sun shone brighter. "Could you delegate more teachers? Like what Moses did with the judging."

Adlai considered and nodded.

"Ask one of Aaron's sons to instruct," Carmel encouraged. "There's Abihu. Speak to him."

Adlai quickened his pace to walk with Abihu, Aaron's second born. "Shalom."

Abihu nodded to him. "Be at peace."

They walked for a few steps, before Adlai cleared his throat. "After reading the Law, men ask questions about it. Would you be willing to answer them?"

Abihu smiled. "I'd be honored. Do you choose the text or may I?"

Adlai did not like the gleam in his eyes, but he wanted the men asking questions to have answers. "You choose the text. What do you have in mind?"

Abihu rubbed his hands in apparent pleasure. "I have a few ideas."

Adlai's heart sank. What had he allowed? He returned to his tent, deep in thought.

Carmel laughed. "What problem are you solving now?"

Adlai hugged her, trying to smile. "Perhaps my concern for someone to teach the Law should have been secondary to finding someone who would treasure the Law."

"What do you mean?"

"I asked Abihu. But he seemed to find pleasure in it."

Carmel laughed. "Don't you?"

Adlai paused to explain. "I enjoy the Word because it is the Lord's Words."

"And..." Carmel prompted.

"I fear Abihu's intent is not to use the Lord's Law to teach the people about God."

"How else could he teach the Law?"

Adlai hesitated. "Can you use God's Words to intimidate and coerce the people?"

Carmel sobered. "Moses may be angry at what we've done, but he never beat us with God's Word. He cares for the Lord's Words and the Lord's people."

"That's what, I fear, is missing with Abihu. He doesn't love God or His people."

Abihu arrived early to teach the following morning, dressed in part of his worship attire for the Tabernacle. He thrust back his shoulders. "Is my class ready?"

Adlai coughed when he saw him. "Should you wear the tunic that was set aside for worship?"

"Shouldn't we worship when we hear God's Words?" Abihu stood taller. The worship tunic gave him authority over Adlai. "I'm a Levite. I know the Words of the Lord. Now if you will excuse me, I should instruct my class."

Abihu walked to the front of the group. He surveyed the men and smiled. He had selected the right laws. He rocked on his heels as he greeted them. "Shalom. I come as a spokesman of God, bringing His Words for your benefit." He cleared his throat. He had chosen laws on immoral relations. When the golden bull had been in the people's midst, he had watched fathers with daughters, mothers with sons. Now, as he read the laws, he gazed at one man who had broken that law. He waited until he blushed and looked down. He then moved to another law and another man.

As the morning progressed, Abihu noticed Moses enter and sit in the back. Abihu straightened his tunic and continued. With Moses's presence, he would show his knowledge of the Law. "Any questions?"

Silence greeted him.

"Does everyone understand the law so well that no one has questions?" His tone was condescending and sarcastic.

Moses coughed.

Several men turned and noticed him for the first time. They blushed anew.

Moses began. "Abihu, you have shown us your knowledge of the Law."

Abihu stood straighter.

"But these sins have been covered by the blood sacrifice of the Sabbath. These men should not be shamed by past sins. The Law is given to point men to look to the Lord—"

Abihu pursed his lips. "But the Law speaks of how we should treat each other."

"Yes. But we do not use the Law as a rod to beat people or to shove their noses into their past shortcomings."

Abihu smiled, quoting Moses's own words, "Will we look to God if we don't see our need?"

"Beating the people with the Law won't turn their hearts toward God; it will turn their heads away from any desire to know Him."

Abihu enjoyed a good argument. Again he quoted Moses, "Without the Law, won't we have chaos?"

"We need the Law as our standard. The Law shows man his need for God, not by force, but by His gentle voice convicting of wrong. Also, as a Levite, your job is to read the Law, not make sure the people obey it."

Abihu threw up his hands in a gesture of hopelessness. "Who makes them obey?"

"God gives rules for our safety. When we disobey, He executes judgment."

Abihu ran his finger under the neckline of his tunic. "Then why do you rule as supreme judge?"

Several of the men gasped.

Abihu gloated over his verbal blow.

Moses remained sitting, in spite of Abihu's challenge. "I do not judge. I listen to God's Words and act as His instrument."

"That's what I am doing." Abihu stood taller.

"Not when you disobey His Laws. Without obedience, His Words are not heard."

Abihu's voice rose in challenge. "How do I disobey?"

"Your tunic is only to be worn for sacrifice. You are wearing it now."

A few men stifled chuckles.

Abihu looked for those who laughed. His face grew hot. He stepped toward Moses.

Moses persisted, "Are you sacrificing?"

Abihu looked around the room of men. "I will next Sabbath."

Moses now stood. "When you disregard God's Words, you live outside His protection. Know the law and the Law Giver before you sacrifice this Sabbath, or His judgment will fall on you."

The next Sabbath, the sun glittered off the gems on the breastplate that Nadab wore. Each gem represented one of the twelve tribes. He breathed deeply of the incense. Sandalwood. It reminded him of his abba's room back in Egypt, where he kept all his herbs for making tinctures for healing. He watched the smoke rise and disappear before it reached the ceiling of the Tabernacle. The Tabernacle had space around the altar for all the work to be done. Earlier that morning, he had laid the wood on the altar, to be ready for the sacrifices. The animals were waiting. The time had come for him to perform the sacrifices. As he tried to recall last week's ceremonies, a pit grew in his stomach. He whispered to Abihu, "Do you remember what is next?"

Abihu nodded. "Follow me."

Nadab watched Abihu sacrifice the fellowship offerings and the drink offerings. They ate the meat that was allowed them. Nadab whispered to Abihu, "This meat's better than the manna from breakfast, isn't it?"

Abihu laughed as he took more of the meat. "Especially when we have all the people watching, but unable to have any. We can have wine, when everyone else has water. Here's to us and the sacrifices!" He drank, finishing the cupful that he held.

Nadab poured him more.

The wine was good. This was the first time since...since the golden bull sacrifice that Nadab had drunk wine. It slid down his throat smoothly. He drank more. The meat's roasted flavor filled the air. He could eat like a pharaoh. He shook his head. He must remember to follow what Abihu did.

Abihu took the common fire from the fellowship offerings to light the incense. He hurried the burning, without reverence.

Nadab watched. They were almost finished. He began to light the incense. Nadab concealed a slow smile. He knew the Law well enough to get along just fine.

But his confident smile was never expressed.

As Nadab and Abihu dressed to perform the sacrifices, Aaron and Phinehas also changed their tunics for the robes of the priest. "Will you be ready to lead the sacrifice soon?"

Phinehas wrinkled his brow. "I studied with Eleazar and Ithamar, but there is much to learn."

Aaron placed his hand on Phinehas's shoulder. "Study and you will be ready."

They stepped toward the altar inside the Tabernacle to watch the sacrifices performed.

They partook liberally of the wine and the meat.

Phinehas whispered, "Grandfather, they are abusing the sacrifice for gain!"

Aaron's tongue stuck to the roof of his mouth. His feet felt rooted to the ground. His heart willed his sons to follow the Lord's instructions, but he was unable to speak or act on their behalf. He watched helplessly, unable to turn away.

When Abihu approached the common fire to light the incense, Phinehas gasped. The fire was unclean, as the Law had told them. He looked at Aaron questioningly.

Aaron kept his eyes focused on his two sons.

He glanced at Phinehas out of the corner of his eye: his eyes were closed and his lips moved as in prayer.

Both sons lit the incense. Only one priest should light it.

Aaron's stomach dropped. He closed his eyes, praying for mercy.

Before they finished lighting the incense, fire fell from heaven. Brightness filled the Tabernacle.

His sons' yells would forever scream in his memory. Aaron smelled burned flesh. His insides rolled with nausea. He blinked to focus his light-burned eyes.

Phinehas squeezed Aaron's arm.

Aaron's two sons lay dead.

He had warned them to know the Law.

They had not taken it seriously.

His chest felt crushed as if a cartload of bricks had fallen on it. He struggled to breathe.

Silence reigned.

Aaron stepped toward his sons, but Moses, who had been watching the ceremony, blocked Aaron with his arm. "Those who come near God must treat Him as holy." He called, "Mishael and Elzaphan, come here."

The two men stood before Moses, glancing at the bodies behind them.

"Take your relatives outside the camp."

They hurried to obey.

When the bodies had been removed, Moses addressed Aaron and his remaining two sons, and grandson. "Do not grieve outwardly. The Lord's anointing oil is on you, so you can't leave the Lord's house or you will die. The people may mourn."

Aaron felt like he had just been punched. How could he worship when his sons were being buried outside the camp? The pit in his stomach grew as he watched Eleazar and Ithamar, his other sons, complete the worship service. Would they know what to do? Aaron's stomach churned with each act they performed. Could they concentrate?

Ithamar's hands shook as he lit the incense. Would he be able finish the offering?

Aaron wiped his forehead.

Moses remained at his side.

They ate the wave offering which was their due.

Moses searched for the goat of the sin offering. It had been burned. He turned to Eleazar and Ithamar. "Why didn't you eat the sin offering?"

Aaron stepped forward. "Could they feast after what they witnessed by the Lord's Hand today?"

Moses nodded but said nothing more.

Eleazar and Ithamar completed their duties.

Worship was finished.

Holiness cost.

Aaron left the Tabernacle with a heavy heart for what his family had learned and lost.

God expected His people to honor Him enough to know His Word.

Dinah could not stop thinking about what had happened at the Tabernacle. Was there no room for error? If she forgot, would the Lord smite her, too? This God was worse than the gods of Egypt. They may threaten evil, but they had no power to do it. This God demanded such holiness that death came to any who fell short.

Japhet sat drumming a stick on the rock by the fire.

Dinah smacked his hand when he grabbed for a manna wafer before she had kneaded it into flatbread.

He wailed.

She squeezed his hand. "You're not hurt. Stop feeling sorry for yourself."

Ellis watched the interchange. He turned her to face him. "What is the matter, my Love?"

Dinah sighed. A long silence. "Nothing."

"What makes you angry? The deaths?" He brought her face to look into his.

She sighed. "They were worshiping. God demands too much. What happens when we don't obey instantly or perfectly? Will we be dead, too?"

Ellis hugged her tightly. He didn't speak for some time. "The priests were to know the Law. That was their duty. When they sacrificed, they didn't know the Law. They hadn't studied."

"But they were trying to worship, Ellis. What happens when we try to obey, but fall short?"

"I asked Adlai. The Law explained clearly what they were to do. Only one priest was to light the incense and not from the common fire. They disrespected the Law. Moses confronted Abihu earlier in the week. He did not repent. Moses warned him of judgment if he did not know the Law before he performed the sacrifices. We can't choose what Law we obey. The Lord did what is right."

Dinah pulled away from Ellis. "But they're dead over a wrongly lit fire?"

"God's Word is important. Won't you consider more carefully what God tells us? If you told Japhet to stay inside the tent, and he wandered beyond the camp, wouldn't you discipline him for his safety?"

Dinah nodded.

"Safety is found by staying within His boundaries, not straying outside of them. God is holy. We don't even know what that is, Dinah. We think that we're good, until we see Him."

Dinah rested her head on his shoulder. "Obedience seemed so much easier when we had less freedom."

Ellis continued to hug her. "Freedom brings accountability."

The sun was setting over the desert, tinting it the color of blood, reminding Miriam of the sacrifices of the Sabbath. She shivered, but continued on her search to find Aaron. When she found him, he stood unmoving, looking at the gravesite of his two sons. She studied him a moment before speaking. His head was bowed in grief; his lips moved as in prayer.

She paused, not wishing to interrupt his grief. She placed her hand in the crook of his elbow. "I am sorry."

At first he did not respond, and she repeated them. "The sand swallows everyone. I am weary of it."

Aaron shook his head. "It's not the sand that wearies me, Miriam, but my lack of training that caused this..." He motioned to the graves.

Miriam squeezed his arm. "You did not kill your sons, Aaron. This God did."

Aaron shook his head. "God expects us to honor His laws. My sons didn't even know Him."

Miriam reached up to wipe Aaron's tears from his cheek. "I don't understand this God."

Aaron cupped her face in his hands, and looked into her eyes. "We'll never understand God." He wiped her tears, that she didn't even know she had shed. "I mourn my sons. But I mourn more that I didn't show them to care for God's Law."

Miriam grabbed his shoulders and shook him. "Why are these laws so important? It keeps us in this sand, day after day. It takes away our family, when they serve Him."

Aaron hugged his sister as she fell against him, crying. Aaron swallowed before trying to speak. When he did, his voice broke. "Because He is most important. Until we learn that, we will feel like the sand of this desert."

Unable to hide the bitterness in her voice, she questioned, "What are we supposed to feel like?"

Miriam felt Aaron raise his head as he stroked her back. "I need to look to the cloud."

She pulled away from his hug and studied his face. He was staring at the cloud. She could see the reflection in the wadi as it changed from cloud to fire. She shivered, seeing again the lightning striking her nephews. "What good is the cloud when our family is gone?"

Aaron's shoulders slumped. "I should have showed them how God is important."

"How much more could you show them? They were set apart as God's instruments for the people. They were given the Law and told to sacrifice—"

Aaron interrupted, "I knew they weren't ready to sacrifice..."

Miriam raised her voice, "How can we be ready to stand before this God?"

"They were proud, not willing to study...." His voice drifted off.

"Don't blame yourself. This God demands that we do everything perfectly. Who is perfect? I fear to worship next Sabbath, lest this God think my sandals are too sandy.

"No, Aaron, you didn't kill your sons." Were her words making an imprint? She shook her head. Not any more than her footprint in the sand.

He swallowed, speaking, but not to her. "I sent them to their graves, as if I had struck them."

Miriam grabbed his cloak front and pulled him toward her. She clenched her teeth, unable to veil her anger. "It was God's doing."

Aaron's voice softened, in sharp contrast to her own that grew harsher. "He wants us to look to Him and see that He deserves it all."

She turned from him, facing the flaming cloud. Its flames leaped out from the cloud, licking the sky, as if searching for another victim whose sandals did not meet His approval. She bowed her head. Did He deserve her all?

Phinehas was learning about this God. He remembered the glory in the desert. He could not meet the Lord's favor.

When he had studied about the sacrifices, especially the sin offering, he had seen God's holiness. How could man stand before such a God?

He had looked from his grandfather's ashen, mourning face to Moses's. Moses mourned his nephews, but he focused on worship. How could he see God so clearly that he worshiped first before he grieved?

Events of the past came to Phinehas's mind. When Moses was on the mountain watching God write His Words on stone, Aaron had allowed Maessai into the camp. When Moses was judging the people by the Law, Aaron had sympathized with the judged. The difference in their response lay in how they knew God.

Aaron had repented from his wrong. He even told Phinehas to

look to God, but Moses showed him God. Moses's God penetrated his heart; changing his entire being.

The difference was in how much of God had gotten a hold of the man.

Phinehas shouted his greeting at the door.

Zipporah came to the entryway. "You seek Moses? He stays at the Tabernacle until dark. You can find him there."

Phinehas nodded, but hesitated to leave.

Zipporah searched his face. "Was there something else?"

"Would Moses have time…" Phinehas looked at his feet. "Could I learn the Law from Moses?"

Zipporah's expression remained guarded. "Do you wish to know the Law out of fear of yesterday's happenings? I would seek your scribes or even your abba."

Phinehas raised his eyes to look into Zipporah's. "I wish to know the Law Giver."

She smiled and nodded. "There is no one better than Moses."

Phinehas smiled. "Then I have come to the right place."

"You may wait for him here, if you wish. He comes home exhausted. But in this request, he would find great delight."

Phinehas tousled the hair of Eliezer who had wiggled through the doorway. "I would not hinder his time with you and the boys?"

"We can all know the Law Giver better."

CHAPTER 18

The cloud had moved, the first time in over a year since they had camped at Mount Sinai. Korah and his sons, from the tribe of Levi, carried the Tabernacle's instruments: the ark, table, lamp stand, altars, and tools of sacrifice. Korah breathed heavily from the weight of the Ark of the Covenant. He led his sons toward where Eleazar, Aaron's son, pointed.

Why did he have to be a descendant of Kohath? He was a descendant of Levi's third son, so his priestly duties consisted of dragging all these sanctuary tools of worship across the desert. He looked behind him at the other descendants: the descendants of Levi's first-born son were the Gershonites. They cared for the coverings of the tent, the curtains and the ropes for hanging the curtains. The descendants of Levi's second-born son, the Merarites, moved and set up the Tabernacle's frames: its posts, bases and tent pegs. They used carts pulled by oxen.

But Korah and his sons could not even use carts. They must carry the poles on their shoulders. Korah shifted under the pole inserted into rings built into the ark.

He shifted under the weight of the ark. Its gold panels added a lot of great weight. He would be sore tonight from the journey.

They covered the sparkling gold when they traveled. Not to prevent his own blindness, but to protect its shine. Nothing was for his benefit.

Korah stumbled, tripping over a burrow from some desert rodent. He almost fell, but caught himself on his right knee with a sudden jerk. The ark shifted dangerously, almost touching the ground. He regained his footing. He couldn't see his knee from his stumble, but could feel the blood dripping down his leg. It made him itch. But there was nothing he could do about it.

They could not let the ark touch the ground, for it was holy.

He looked back at his son, Ebiasaph, holding the other end of the pole. His face was pale. "Are you at peace, abba?"

Korah nodded and stood on wobbly legs. He had almost touched the ark. What would have happened if he had? No one could touch it. Not even Moses. It was holy. He had seen enough of the fire of God to know that His Law was to be followed. He did not want to test this holy God.

Eleazar motioned for them to stop.

Korah's family arrived first and waited, holding the ark until the Tabernacle was erected. He shifted under his load as he watched how slowly the other Levites strung the curtains on poles and put them into their stands. "Hurry up! Can't you see we're waiting?"

Eleazar nodded. But there was no hurrying the process. All must be done in order.

Korah licked his lips. He watched the people hurry to the water with vessels. He could not even drink from the waterskin at his belt. Both his hands must brace the pole.

Ebiasaph consoled him. "They're going as fast as they can, Abba. We'll be finished shortly."

Korah shook his head. When the Tabernacle was set up, Korah and his sons could place the instruments where they belonged inside. Only then could they attend to their own needs.

Korah watched the tent slowly rise. No one appreciated his work, yet it must be done right. Korah sighed. He watched Moses walk toward the stream. The people parted for him, and he drank. Korah licked his dry lips again. If he could just be like Moses. The people would part at his presence. What respect he had! He set his chin forward as he watched. His bloody knee forgotten. His thirst forgotten. He wanted what Moses had.

Zipporah paused scrubbing her skins to watch her boys. They had grown so much this year. She had sewn new skins for their growing bodies. Eliezer now played with other children instead of staying close by her side. His weaning days were over.

Zipporah sighed. Hobab had asked Moses if he could return to his people. But Moses promised the Lord's blessing, if Hobab would stay and guide them through the land that he knew.

Hobab's concern was for their father's age. He was getting old.

Zipporah had told him, "Hobab, you can't leave. What will I do without you and your family?"

"You cling to the past. You want things to stay as they were when Moses did not lead this people."

Zipporah opened her mouth and then shut it. Her chin trembled and she swallowed hard.

He softened his voice. "You cling to what is no longer here. You imagine how great yesterday was. When you watched sheep, they were dirty, smelly, stupid animals."

She tried not to laugh. "I did complain about them, a little."

"No, Zipporah, you were ecstatic when Moses watched them for you." Hobab nodded as she did laugh. "You want Moses all to yourself. He is no longer just a shepherd of sheep; he is a leader of men. He has become a great man of God, but you want him to sit at your feet with sheep. He has moved on; you have not. You want everything to stay the same. You must let go of what is not yours."

She sighed as she remembered his words. Had Hobab been right? Did she hinder Moses's ministry? She didn't demand that he stay by her side. She missed talking with him. She scrubbed at the same spot on the skins.

"Why do you sigh?" Carmel touched her hand.

Zipporah jumped, startled. "Hobab wants to go home."

Carmel looked into her face. "Is it still home to you?"

Zipporah took a deep breath. "That's what Hobab told me. I want things the same. Maybe that's why I like the desert; nothing changes."

Carmel laughed. "What do you miss the most about home?"

Zipporah thought. "At first, I'd say the hills, the sheep and goats. But Hobab reminded me that I hated the sheep and was relieved when Moses watched them." She started scrubbing another skin. "I miss what the sheep represented."

"What was that?"

"That Moses would be home. That we would talk."

Carmel prodded. "You don't talk to Moses now?"

"I can't remember the last time that we ate a meal without interruptions. Phinehas comes in the evenings, seeking to learn all that he can from Moses."

"Does that interfere with your time with Moses?"

"He comes home faster. Phinehas soaks it up like water in sand."

Carmel rinsed the tunic she was washing. "You're a strong woman to leave your family and live with another people, especially when your husband is never at home."

Zipporah shook her head. "Not strong, just desperate."

"Why desperate?"

Zipporah looked over the water. "My father told me that my land was no longer mine."

Carmel gasped.

Zipporah faced Carmel. "If he hadn't, I would have returned a hundred times. My father knew that." She wiped a tear from her eye with the back of her hand. "I have no home."

"What is home?"

Zipporah wrung out the dripping cloak. "Home..."

Carmel helped her twist the cloak. "Would going back to your family be home anymore?"

Zipporah laughed without mirth. "When Moses went to Egypt, I couldn't leave my land and my family. It was all that I knew. Moses was gone over a year. I longed to hear whether or not he was still alive. I was willing to go anywhere to be with Moses. But when I came here, it didn't seem to matter to Moses. I'd almost rather live at home and not see him, than see him but not be able to talk with him."

Carmel helped drape the cloak over a basket. "Moses bears the weight of caring for these people. Every time someone is unhappy, they run to him to make it better." She scrubbed her clothes again. "I've heard whispers of what his family does to you behind his back."

Zipporah's lips trembled. "I expected help from his family. It's hard."

Carmel dropped her tunic and hugged Zipporah. "The desert teaches us all many hard lessons, doesn't it? Your home is here with Moses. Moses walks home, not like before with dread, but with a smile. I've seen the difference. Do not lose heart, Zipporah. Your presence makes a difference in Moses's life. Your home is with Moses. Do not believe the evil that says differently."

Zipporah hugged Moses when he entered their house. She noticed his furrowed brow. "Why the frown?"

Moses stared beyond her. His voice seemed far away. "I was rereading the Law today. I had never noticed that law before...maybe because we were concentrating on constructing the Tabernacle. But I read the law stating Aaron can no longer lead the worship."

"Why?"

Moses sighed. "God gave specific years for the priest to lead the worship, from twenty-five to fifty years."

Zipporah gasped. "How could we worship without him?"

"His sons share in the duties of sacrificing, but overseeing everything..." He shook his head. "Eleazar knows the Law. He would do fine, but..." Moses shook his head.

"What will Aaron do? Surely the Lord didn't mean him when He gave that Law?"

Moses wrapped his arms around Zipporah's waist. He rested his chin on her head. "I don't know what Aaron will do. He could still pray and intercede for the people. I can't count how many times he has sacrificed while I prayed, so the people would not be killed. I don't understand the holiness of God. I feel little in His presence. When I look to the Law, it is clear. When I look to the people who must obey the Law, I want to make the Law less than what it is. How do I see the holiness of God in the day-to-day living?"

Zipporah suggested, "His interceding in that leadership role is different than when he wears the priestly robes and sacrifices. He can still intercede for the people, but not during the worship in the Tabernacle, right?"

Moses shrugged. "I think so. It's hard to understand the mind of God. His Law is clear, until you add people."

Moses sighed. "Aaron already feels like I've taken over the leadership of the people."

Zipporah stepped back to study Moses's face. She stroked his beard. "He's jealous of you. This will make things worse."

Moses squeezed her tighter. "But the Lord makes no exceptions. His laws are for everyone. I wish that I didn't have to tell him."

"Shouldn't he know the Law? Couldn't you wait until he complies on his own?"

"I don't know all the Law. The people think that I'm God Who knows all the Law. When they bring the hard cases for me to judge, I must search the Lord's Words to find the answer and listen to God speak to know how to judge. I found this one after re-reading it several times.

"Remember his sons? Their disobedience brought instant death. Do you wish that for Aaron?"

Zipporah buried her head in Moses's cloak. "I don't understand this holiness of God."

Aaron finished serving the Passover to his family. Miriam was present, as was his grandson Phinehas, Aaron's two sons and their families, and the families of his two sons now missing. While eating the roasted lamb, Aaron remembered last year, the final night when the Lord's people still suffered under the bondage of slavery.

Miriam cleared her throat. "Did I tell you about Moses's youngest?"

Aaron shook his head. He tried to refocus after thinking about Egypt.

"He peed on the neighbor's coals, laughing as smoke rose and clouded his face."

Trying to keep a straight face, Aaron asked, "What did my dear sister do?"

"I dragged him to Zipporah.

"Zipporah wiped his blackened face with her tunic and asked me what I did to him!"

"I dropped his hand as if it had leprosy, wiping my hand of his dirt. 'Nothing but keep him from burning his very maleness off of his dirty body!'

"Zipporah stopped wiping his face. 'What has he done?'

"'Desecrate someone's cooking fire by peeing in it!'"

Aaron hid his smile behind his beard. "What did she do?"

"She laughed! I was never so shocked in all my life. 'You encourage this behavior?'

"She said, 'He's two years old, Miriam. Do you want him to run to the desert where a lion could eat him, when his urge comes? I was washing the bowl; he couldn't wait.'"

Miriam sputtered, still angry. "She doesn't train them. I expected a Hebrew response of remorse, not a Cushite response of mockery."

Aaron said, "Perhaps, you speak too harshly of Zipporah?"

"Indeed." Miriam gulped air to continue. "That Cushite refuses our customs."

She glared at Aaron. "Don't mock me, Aaron." She pounded her fist into the dirt beside her. "Another thing, why can't you perform the priestly duties in the temple? Who is Moses to tell you that you are finished worshiping at the temple?"

Aaron's smile disappeared. "What do you mean?"

"Didn't Moses tell you?"

"Tell me what?"

Miriam looked down. "Moses said...you would no longer sacrifice in the temple."

"What do you mean, I will no longer sacrifice?" Aaron's voice rose. "What are you talking about, Miriam?"

All the other family members stopped talking at Aaron's raised voice.

She glanced at his furrowed brow and cold eyes. "I overheard Moses tell Zipporah that you can't sacrifice anymore." She looked down but continued. "Who is Moses but your younger brother? Why should you no longer lead as priest, yet he keeps his leadership over all? Do you know what I think?"

She did not wait for his response. "Has the Lord spoken only through Moses?"

Moses entered. He looked from Aaron to Miriam.

Miriam shut her mouth.

When Moses finally spoke, his voice was low and controlled, "You two, come with me." He strode to the Tabernacle.

Miriam whispered to Aaron. "Have you ever seen Moses this angry? I was right in questioning his leadership. God will make you leader."

"Miriam..." Aaron walked behind Moses. Could he be finished serving at the Tabernacle? His anger was gone. He had allowed Miriam to rile him like when they were children. Then she would manipulate him to do what she wanted. Aaron shook his head. Why did he not learn?

Miriam followed Moses and Aaron into the tent of meeting. She had never entered. Now, she was one of the privileged few, and a woman. She stood taller.

As Miriam looked around, she had expected something more than clusters of cushions on the floor in various places in the huge tent. When the people came to be judged, shouldn't there be something more than cushions to indicate where the leaders of the various tribes held court? Shaking her head, she dismissed her disappointment. She licked her lips in anticipation of her appointment to leadership, trying to hide her satisfied smile.

The Lord's cloud descended over the tent. He called, "Aaron and Miriam, come to Me."

Moses remained where he stood.

Miriam raised her chin as she walked beside Aaron to the cloud.

"Hear My Words: If there is a prophet among you, I shall make Myself known to him in a vision, speaking in a dream."

Miriam grabbed Aaron's arm. "We'll both be prophets. We'll tell visions."

"With My servant Moses, I do not speak in a vision or a dream. With him, I speak mouth to mouth. He sees Me. Yet you speak against him? Why are you not afraid?"

The cloud turned to a flame, burning hotter.

Aaron fell before the flame, covering his head with his arm.

But Miriam stared at the flame. Her face burned.

The fire withdrew from the tent.

Miriam watched it leave. When would she be appointed as a leader? She blinked as her eyes adjusted to the darkness.

Aaron stood slowly. He looked older. He looked at Miriam, and drew a sharp breath. "Miriam, you're a leper!"

She looked at her hands. Could these white-skinned fingers be hers? She covered her face and felt holes where skin had been. She moaned. "What have I done?"

Aaron turned to Moses. "We've sinned! Do not let her be as dead, with flesh half eaten away."

Moses fell on his knees before the ark of the Tabernacle. "Oh God, heal her!"

The Lord spoke. "I will, but if her father spat in her face, would she not bear her shame for seven days? She will stay outside the camp for seven days. Afterward she may be received again."

The cloud did not move for seven days.

Miriam stayed alone outside the camp.

Moses returned from the tent of meeting after the Lord demonstrated his leadership to Aaron and Miriam.

Zipporah laid down the sheepskin that she was sewing. "What happened?"

Moses hugged her. "You don't doubt my leadership, do you?"

Zipporah laughed. "Would I be here if your God did not call you? Why?"

Moses rubbed her back. "You feel the people's tension so much more than I do."

"I try to ignore what others say." She shook her head.

"Living with this people has been hard for you. If I didn't have your support, I couldn't do what I do. When I finish for the day,

I come to a haven you've prepared."

Zipporah stepped away from him to heat his flatbread. "Your God has become my God. What is the pettiness of a group of women?"

"Even when they are led by my sister?"

Zipporah winced. "I expected more from family." She shrugged. "She gives what she gives."

Moses swallowed. "Miriam got leprosy."

"No!" Zipporah pulled away from his embrace. "She was fine the other day, when she..."

"When she corrected you about Eliezer—"

"How'd you hear about that?"

"Miriam questioned my authority. She has been punished with leprosy. The Lord healed her, but she will remain outside the camp until the seven days of separation is completed. You should have some relief from the trouble she causes."

"I only wish to be accepted by your people. When I'm told that the Lord cares for me, yet His people hold me at arm's length, as if I had leprosy...I struggle to believe.

"Would Miriam accept meals from me?"

Moses took her face in his hands and studied her earnest expression. "You are God's gift to me. That may go far to reach her. But even if it doesn't, you have done the right thing."

Zipporah hummed as she ground the manna of the morning. She would add her extra herbs and then cook them. She had easily volunteered when Moses looked so appreciative, but now anticipating Miriam's reception, she was not so willing. She reviewed the different times Miriam had spoken to her. None had been pleasant. What had she been thinking to volunteer?

She stopped humming. Humming made her feel braver, but not peaceful.

She packed her basket. They all ate the same thing. How could she make manna special? It was already sprinkled over the earth by the Hand of the Lord. How much more special could that be?

She slowed her steps. "Eliezer, don't dawdle."

Gershom kicked at a stone. He waited until it stopped rolling. "Why are we giving Aunt Miriam food?"

Zipporah took Eliezer's hand to help him walk faster. "She is unable to come close to others."

"Why?"

"She had an illness."

"Will we get it?"

She looked beyond the water's edge. The walk would be long. "The Lord will protect us."

Gershom walked with big strides to keep up with her. "Is this the kindness that Grandmother told us to show?"

Zipporah squeezed Eliezer's hand to encourage him to keep walking. "You remember that comment?"

Gershom took Zipporah's hand. "Aunt Miriam watches me like an eagle diving for a mouse. I don't like her."

"It is hard to be kind to unkind people. Sometimes they need our kindness the most."

Gershom wrinkled up his nose. "Why?"

Zipporah squeezed his hand. "They test others, to see if others love them."

Gershom squeezed her hand back. "She makes me want to hurt her."

Zipporah nodded. "I respond poorly, too. But what she needs is someone to love her."

Gershom took the basket from Zipporah. "So that's why we're giving her food?"

Zipporah breathed deeply. "Yes."

They had arrived at Miriam's campsite on the other side of the water. Because everything would have to be burned after the seven days, only a small tent and a fire ring were made. A vessel of water sat by the tent opening.

Miriam stood as they approached. "You came to gloat."

Gershom extended the basket. "We come to show kindness."

Miriam huffed. "Kindness. What's this?" She lifted the blanket and touched the flatbread. "There're warm." She looked first at Gershom, then at Zipporah. "What did you put in it?"

Zipporah held Eliezer's hand tighter. "Just herbs."

"Do you think that I'd be deceived by your kindness? You probably put in an herb to make me sick." She took the flatbread and threw it into the fire.

Gershom knelt to retrieve it as the flames licked it up.

Zipporah grabbed his shoulder. "No, Gershom!"

"But we waited to eat, until she had hers."

Miriam threw the basket at Zipporah.

Zipporah shielded Eliezer from the impact, grunting when it hit her.

Gershom turned to Miriam. "You may need kindness. But I won't give you any!" Gershom took Zipporah's hand and faced the campsite. "Come on, Ima. You have showed enough kindness today." He tried to stomp away.

Zipporah held him back. She struggled to keep the words of anger within her. She turned to Miriam, the holes from leprosy still raw on her face. Zipporah took a deep breath. She would try to do right. She swallowed. "Are you warm enough at night? Those linen blankets don't look thick enough. I could bring a sheepskin."

Miriam opened her mouth, then closed it. Her expression softened. "I was cold last night."

Zipporah nodded. "I will bring them." She retraced her steps to the campsite. She would give what she had and do what was right.

Nathan turned in his sleep, semi-hearing a groan beside him. He raised himself on one elbow and touched Salome's side. "You are well?"

Another groan answered him.

He was now fully awake. He could see her from the shine of the full moon through the tent's flap. "What is it Salome? Is it time for the baby?"

She turned to lay on her back and grabbed his hand, groaning again. She licked her lips. "Stay with me. Don't leave me."

Nathan sat up and looked into her face. The pain that he saw there brought him to panic. He didn't know anything about helping her. "Let me go for the midwife." He watched her face relax from the pain, but her hand kept squeezing his hand, though not as tightly.

She opened her eyes and smiled. "I wish I could be with you in the Promised Land."

Nathan held her hand in both of his. "But you will. You'll be there. You have to be."

Another pain came. Her face showed concentration. She held his hand as if she'd never let go.

He was on his knees now, kneeling before her. "Let me go for help."

Her face relaxed of its pain. She stroked his cheek. "You have led your family to see God. Now God is leading you to know Him as His." She sucked in some air as another spasm came.

He watched in helplessness. He held her hand and watched her suffer. He must do something.

"Nathan, we gave our children to God, but I didn't give you to Him."

Nathan watched her take a deep breath.

She seemed taxed by the exertion. Her strength was slipping away. "I treasure you, more than I should."

"What do you mean?"

She had a break in the pain. "In Egypt, when you were beaten, I could do nothing. I had to give you to God." Another contraction came, and she squeezed his hand tightly. When she could speak again, she continued, "I had to trust God to do what is right. You believe that He is good?"

Nathan swallowed. He knew where she was leading this conversation. He didn't want to say it.

"Answer me, Nathan. I need to know." Her voice rose even as it required more of her strength.

He sighed. "He is good."

"I had to give you into God's Hands to do what He wanted. That was the hardest thing that I ever had to do. But what I found was that His Hands were sufficient. He was good." She took another deep breath. "Help me sit."

Nathan was glad to have something to do. He braced her against the cushions until she was squatting.

She leaned against him. She was sweating, but shook like she was chilled. She was too pale. Why did she not have enough strength for this? She had done this before.

He wiped her forehead with the blanket before covering her with it. He studied her face as the moon shone through their tent flap. There seemed to be a pause in her pain. She hardly moved. Did she even breathe?

"Nathan, promise me..."

He breathed deeply, relieved that she still had strength. Nathan dreaded her words. He didn't want to promise something that he couldn't do. "Save your strength, Salome."

Salome licked her lips before speaking, "Promise me you'll seek God."

Nathan shuddered. That was the last thing he wanted to do.

"Please." Her hand reached for his.

"Don't leave me, Salome. I need you to help me know God."

She squeezed his hand, this time not in intense pain, but in release. "Nathan, I'll know Him. I'll know Him without pain. His ways are best."

He did not hear the infant that Salome had delivered. He could only feel his heart stop beating for the wife of his youth, for the love of his life, for the reason he went to the Promised Land. He could only remember the promise that she wanted him to keep—to know God. What had he promised to do?

CHAPTER 19

M oses went up the mountain to spend time with God before another day began. When he had reached his favorite spot, he turned and looked over the campsites. The people spread out over the sand like the ripples of the waves of the sea. They were approaching their Land, and he could feel the excitement stirring the people. What would the Lord require of them before they would be ready?

He turned his attention to the cloud that rose above the Tabernacle. It seemed to reside above the Holy of Holies. Not that anything could contain God. Still, it was reassuring to know that the Lord's presence was with them.

The voice of the Lord came to Moses. "Count all the men twenty years and older who are able to go to war. Each tribe will have its own standard and camp under it. Don't number the sons of Levi. They camp around the Tabernacle to remind the people not to come too close to the holy place."

Moses nodded. Numbering the people would be like counting the sand. He smiled. Just like the Lord had promised Abraham. His descendants would be like the sand of the desert. God kept His Word.

When he reached the bottom of the mountain, he greeted Joshua and gave the Lord's instructions to him.

Joshua nodded and sent the word to all the tribal leaders to carry out the command.

Each tribe recorded their tally of fighting men, by family, by clan. All the people were numbered except the tribe of Levi, for they were exempt from the duties of war.

Once the census was completed, Moses requested twelve leaders, one from every tribe. As they stood before him, he consecrated them to the Lord, then he instructed them on their mission. "Go to the Negev, then into the hill country. Spy out the Land. Who lives there? Where are their strongholds? How are the cities fortified? Report back to me all that you find."

Moses could feel the people's excitement as they watched the spies head to the Land of Promise. Could their journey be almost over?

Forty days would answer.

Reut walked beside Hannah. The group of women that she washed her clothes with had grouped together as they followed the cloud. Reut did not have to carry anything, but she needed to get away from Tamara's chatter. She looked to the east. "I want to see the green of the countryside from the top of that mountain. Don't you?"

Dinah turned to Etania as she struggled to carry a blanket. "Here, let me put that in your cart. Why don't you play with the boys?"

Etania sighed but gave up the blanket. She ran to where Jabin and Japhet played beside their cart.

Dinah turned to Carmel. "That blanket was Salome's."

Carmel shook her head. "Children hold their grief until those around them finish grieving."

Dinah drank from her waterskin. "Nathan hasn't even named the baby."

Carmel glanced back at Nathan driving the cart behind them. "It's not uncommon to wait to name a child."

"He never comes to see him. Thankfully, I'm able to feed him enough, even though Japhet is about weaned."

Hannah asked, "Does Phinehas or Aaron have anything that would help Nathan?"

Carmel shrugged. "What can help someone grieve?"

Pelia joined them. She had a spring to her step and a sparkle to her eye. "I can't wait to get to the Promised Land."

Hannah smiled. "Amos seems happy." She watched Pelia's face turn red. "He paced the tent like a caged lion. Abba nearly sent him to sleep in the desert until he got an answer from Esmail. Amos couldn't even sew straight."

Pelia laughed. "Yes, Esmail did enjoy causing Amos grief, didn't he?"

After a pause, Carmel asked, "What kind of report do you think the men will bring?"

Zipporah spoke. "Merchants, passing through our land, described the Land we're going to. Sheep grow fat and cows give rich, abundant milk. They were always anxious to return to their land, where the water flowed freely and the land gave abundantly.

The other women stopped walking to listen.

Carmel prompted. "What did they grow there?"

Zipporah stared off into the mountains. "My brother traded for good wine. The cheese could not be compared, and the honey..." She paused as she licked her lips. "The honey was light, clear, and delicate, from fig and almond blossoms." Zipporah stopped. A flush crept across her cheeks.

Reut's eyes glistened. "Tell us more."

"The merchants brought dried grapes, figs, pomegranates, dates. As a small girl, I wished to go there. If a land produced all those things, it must be where the gods live."

Tamara asked. "Why didn't you go and see the land?"

"The land was not for my people. We grow strong in the desert. If we left, neighboring tribes would take our water. Then we'd never get the land back."

Carmel drank from a vessel. "You must be glad to have your brother here."

Zipporah looked toward the horizon. "Especially as we get closer to the Land. He knows this Land well. He traveled much for my father to bring back what we could not grow or make."

Reut sighed. "I cannot wait to be settled in the Land. Aren't you tired of sand and brown? Everything is brown: the mountains, the ground, the tents, even my skin looks brown from the sand. Don't you long for greens, blues, flowers, and beauty?"

Tamara grabbed Jabin and tickled him under the chin. She smiled at his laughter. "We've only been in the desert a little over a year. You hurry to reach the Land, because you wish for a wedding."

Reut's voice took on a whining tone and she slowed her pace. "Michael waits until he is in the country with a means of providing for me."

Tamara spun Jabin in circles. "Desert time waits for no one. You can't hurry the trip nor make it any less brown. But maybe you can persuade Michael that brown is fine for a wedding."

"I want a wedding with flowers. Can I get that here?"

Tamara put down Jabin and picked up Japhet and started spinning in circles with him. "Do flowers make you more married? Don't you only see Michael anyway?"

Reut shrugged "You're right."

"If it makes you feel any better," Tamara slowed down. "I'm tired of sand, too. But I don't let it rub me the wrong way." She laughed. "It just rips off my skin." She put Japhet down and watched the horizon. She pointed. "What's that dust?"

Dinah shaded her eyes to look. "The men are returning!"

They watched as the dust cloud grew closer.

Dinah squinted. "What are they carrying?"

Hannah added, "It looks like a big tree."

Pelia jumped. "Those are grapes!"

The women hurried to the front of the people to hear the men's report.

News traveled fast. A crowd rushed toward Moses as he met the returning men before they approached the people.

The people gathered to hear the report.

Shaphat, one of the spies, looked over the people. "The Land flows with milk and honey. These grapes were sweet, plentiful, and large." He grabbed a bunch off the vine and tossed it to the crowd.

The people scrambled to catch them.

Someone yelled. "What about the cities and the people?"

Caleb stepped forward. "God has given them to us. He will give us the victory!"

Gaddiel pushed Caleb aside. "The people live in fortified cities, like we've never seen. The hill country swarm with giants. The northern lands have chariots and horses unequaled even in Egypt."

As the people's enthusiasm shrank before Gaddiel's words, Caleb encouraged them. "The Lord has promised us the Land. Let's claim it."

But the other spies shouted over his words, "The people are too strong for us. We're like grasshoppers to them. They will annihilate us and take our wives and children as loot."

Joshua interrupted the men. "Listen to what Caleb has to say."

But the people pushed him to the back. They wanted more information about the enemy people. "How are we to deal with giants?"

Korah stepped forward. "We must negotiate with these people. We could never conquer giants."

Dathan stood beside him. "We could be their servants. We would leave this desert and enjoy the fruits of the Land."

Joshua shouted. "Remember the Lord's deliverance from the bondage of Egypt. He did not deliver us so that we could become servants again. He gave freedom so we could be His. He has promised us the Land. He is the Lord our God. He broke the bars of your yoke and made you walk free. Let's go in the name of our God, trusting His promise, and take the Land."

But the people had surrounded the spies. "We can't win without chariots and horses."

Elizur shouted from the back of the group, "If we had a new leader, we would not need to wait on a cloud nor an old man to tell us what to do."

Several added their agreement, looking for whoever had spoken.

Elizur continued. "Moses does not even follow the Law himself. Look at the wife he has." He had gained the attention of some. "All we need is a new leader."

Moses turned from their grumbling and walked up the nearby mountain.

The people did not even notice.

The Lord's cloud descended. "How long will this people spurn Me? They do not believe Me. I will smite them and make you a greater nation."

Moses fell on his knees before the Lord. "The entire world knows of Your Name, and Your promise given to these people. If You slay this people, won't the nations say, 'The Lord could not bring them to the Land that He promised'? Let Your power be great, Your anger slow, Your loving kindness abundant, Your forgiveness ever reaching to all. Pardon this people for their unbelief as You have before."

The cloud shone brighter.

Moses crawled back from His light. Could a people be so stiff-necked that they thought they could snub God? How could God forgive them of such sin?

"I will pardon them, but all the earth will be filled with My Glory. These people have seen My Glory and My signs from Egypt, yet test Me all these times. They will not see the Land."

Moses's heart dropped. God's forgiveness spared the people. He would not destroy them. But not to see the Land? The people's disappointment would be great.

"Caleb possesses a different spirit. He follows Me fully. He will enter the Land. His descendants shall possess it. Joshua, too, will enter. But the rest will die in this wilderness. All the numbered men, twenty years and older, will not enter the Land. Their children, whom the people said would become prey, will possess the Land.

"For every day the spies searched the Land will be a year that these people will wander in this desert. I have spoken."

Moses stayed on his knees before the Lord. Tears gathered in his eyes. They spilled down his cheeks. What would this news do to the people? Their disappointment would be great. He mourned for the cause: they did not know the Lord. God wanted to be their God. They still did not recognize Him as the source of all they needed. They did not know Him.

Moses walked down from the mountain with a heavy heart. He saw the spies waiting in the shade of the tent with the people. How could he tell the people the Lord's judgment?

Before when the people were foolish, the consequence was immediate. This time, their unbelief brought a long term effect—forty years. Moses was suddenly tired of his mission. Could he lead these people another forty years? Could he not rest with his family? He looked over the crowd.

Shammua renewed his efforts to inform the people. "The people are giants. I was like a child to them. We cannot take their land."

Before he finished speaking, he groaned, holding his midsection. "Help me." He stumbled forward, falling.

Magal caught him and helped him to the ground. He felt his heart. "He is dead."

A wave of panic rippled through the people. "If we don't enter the Land, where can we go?"

Shaphat, another spy, said, "If we return to Egypt, we'd find green pastures." He fell.

The people stared at the dropped men.

The other spies backed away from the parting crowd. Before the eight other spies with the evil report could escape, they died.

Moses closed his eyes. He must direct them to their God, Whose Words are final. He shifted his rod in his hand. "The Lord pardoned your disbelief." He paused and licked his lips. How should he tell the people? When would they look to the Lord?

The people fidgeted, wanting reassurance, hope.

"But He will not lead you into the Promised Land. He will lead you forty years in this desert until the numbered men have died. He will lead those who did not murmur into the Promised

Land."

Moses watched their expressions change from expectation to hopelessness. Moses closed his eyes to keep from seeing the despair in their eyes.

Magal caught his good friend, Shammua, before he hit the ground. He had laid him on the ground and felt for his heart. It had stopped. Magal wanted to scream in denial. How could any God kill a man who had served Him? Shammua had risked his life to scout out land. And for what reward? Death, because some God didn't like his report about what he had seen with his own eyes?

Magal's grief turned to rage.

He seethed as he listened to Moses tell how they would not enter the Land!

No. God would not dictate what he would do.

Shammua's death would not be forgotten, nor would it be for naught. Magal would honor his friend's service. Shammua's death would inspire the people to victory. They would enter the Land.

Before the people could return to their tents, Magal shouted, "Will you allow these brave men to die in vain? They risked their lives so that we could enter the Land. And we do not go? What have we trained for? To cower in our tents because some people are giants? We are strong. We are many. We can win. I go to the hill country to fight tomorrow. Who will go with me?"

The people listened. Their shouts of assent resounded over the desert sand.

Magal watched as their despair turned to hope. It gave him a sense of power. He could take this people to victory. He pointed to the shore. "Meet by the water when the sun rises. We will conquer these people!"

The people dispersed excited. They would not spend forty years in this brown, sandy death. They prepared for battle. Excitement filled the tents that had just held mourning. Victory filled their minds over tomorrow's battle.

Moses approached Magal's tent. "Shalom."

Magal lounged on the cushions, ignoring him. He sipped from his vessel.

Moses squatted beside him, uninvited. He remained silent.

Magal shifted on his cushion and finally acknowledged Moses's presence. "We can win."

Moses remained quiet.

"I cannot die in this desert when the Land waits for us."

Moses stared at the top of the distant mountain.

Magal grew angrier with his silence. "What do you want?"

Moses took a drink from a vessel that wasn't offered him. "A leader is responsible for his people. If you take this people to fight without God, you will lead them to their death. Is that what you want?"

Magal glared at Moses. "You are not the only one who can lead. If we follow you, we will end up dead, too!"

Moses emptied the vessel's contents, and left.

When Moses declared judgment on their unbelief, Pelia's heart sank. She had left as soon as Moses said they would remain in the desert. How could she endure forty more years in this desert? When Magal encouraged the men to battle, she was tempted by his words, but as Moses confronted Magal, she feared for her brother.

Pelia served Magal his meal.

He ate in silence.

"Magal."

He did not look up.

"Should you fight against the Amalekites? Remember when we fought them before? We only won as long as Moses's arms were raised."

"Do you really believe that, Pelia? A man stands on a mountain with his hands in the air and the army wins? We won, because we were better than they. And we will win tomorrow, because we can."

"The Lord won't be with you."

"Was He with my friends who were killed after the golden bull feast? And today, all the men who risked their lives to spy out the Land were killed by this God."

"Even Shammua?"

"He was the first to die." Magal swallowed. He drank from his vessel and attacked his meal.

Shammua and Magal had been friends since boyhood. "I'm

sorry. I hadn't heard." Pelia fell silent. If Magal would not listen to Moses, would he listen to her? She bit her lip, trying to find the right words to persuade him.

Magal jammed more meat in his mouth as if by eating he could bring his friend back to life.

"I'm sorry, Magal. But the Lord—"

Magal looked up for the first time. His eyes held hate. "Do not speak to me again of this God! He takes all I value and gives me nothing."

Pelia bit on her lip, trying to stop the tears from forming.

"Tomorrow we fight. Tomorrow we will win." He gulped down the rest of his drink, wiped his mouth on the back of his hand, and pushed himself from the pallet.

Pelia touched his arm. "Magal, you do not fight the Amalekites, but the Lord. You cannot win."

He flung her hand off his arm and walked away.

The night was short. Moses met the people gathered before the sun rose.

They were arrayed for battle, grabbing a few flakes of manna, their food for the day.

Moses shouted over their commotion. "Peace will not meet you on this battlefront. The Lord's presence is not with you. Do not go. You will fall by the sword."

They shook their swords at Moses. "We sinned, but now we've changed our minds. We'll take the Land that the Lord has promised."

They marched to the ridge of the hill country.

They did not look back.

They did not have the Ark of the Covenant, their leader, or the presence of the Lord.

They did not know what they missed.

CHAPTER 20

After the soldiers left, the camp quieted. Women, whose husbands were fighting, watched the hills for their return. Men, who stayed behind, wondered if they should have fought. Even the children sensed the need to remain quiet.

Women congregated around the tent used for judging. No judging would take place today. The spies' bodies had been laid inside.

Miriam fanned herself with a cloth. Heat would attack the bodies quickly. "We must prepare their bodies for burial." She turned to several women. "Bring water to bathe for their final dressing."

The women nodded, lifting vessels to retrieve water.

Miriam surveyed the room.

Zipporah entered, lighting incense at each body, covering the smell of death. She laid a comforting hand on the shoulder of one mourner, who hugged her.

Miriam watched her mouth open. These were not her people. What right did she have to be here? Miriam strode toward her.

Before Miriam reached Zipporah, Moses slipped inside, and whispered something to her.

She left.

Miriam approached Moses. "Moses, I'm glad you came. Zipporah doesn't belong here while we grieve.

"Did she steal that incense from the Tabernacle?"

Moses opened his mouth to speak, then shut it again. After shaking his head, he finally spoke. "Didn't the leprosy teach you anything about how the Lord sees my wife? She's not a stray dog. I did not send her away from here. Others needed her help.

"She asked my permission to share her father's incense with these hurting women who've lost loved ones. She brings healing to their hearts, rather than hatred over the color of their skin."

Zipporah entered the tent of meeting to comfort those recently widowed. She understood feeling alone. How could she remove the hole that death had brought to these hurting women? She carried a smoldering stick. Lighting first one incense candle, then another, she smelled deeply of its smoke. The smell reminded her of her father, worshiping God. She placed a candle by each body.

When she came to one body, she was surprised to see Pelia.

Pelia wiped her eyes with her hand. "Magal's childhood friend."

Zipporah offered her a cloth.

"Magal left this morning with the soldiers." She shook her head, and hiccupped. "I thought if I helped here, I wouldn't worry about Magal. But it only makes me certain that he will be killed."

Zipporah patted Pelia's hands.

Zipporah was startled when Moses touched her arm.

"Hakeen requested help for the wounded soldiers."

Zipporah turned to Pelia. "Want to help?"

Pelia nodded. "You will watch with me for my brother?"

Zipporah squeezed her hand. "I won't leave you alone."

When they reached Hakeen's tent, Hannah helped them clean wounds and tend soldiers.

Hakeen lifted one soldier to give him a drink. "How does the battle go?"

The soldier shook his head. "It's lost. Never had a chance."

Zipporah met Pelia's eyes across the tent.

Hakeen stopped tilting the dipper. "Will the army come home?"

The soldier groaned. "The Lord was not with us. We alone escaped with our lives."

As the soldiers came to Hakeen's tent for care, Pelia watched for Magal. Her hopes fell.

She went for water to clean more wounds. Squinting into the distance for any returning stragglers, she watched the sun color the water crimson as it set behind the mountains. She shivered.

She was startled when Amos squeezed her shoulder.

He stood behind her, watching the sunset. "Pelia, we'll search in the morning."

Her voice took on a flat tone. "He's not coming home. I knew he would not return. I begged him not to go. He had no need for God." Pelia grabbed Amos's cloak and shook him. "Why did he go?"

Amos put his arms around her and held her close. "You're tired. Don't stay at your tent tonight. Stay with Hannah. Tomorrow will be better."

The sun would shine again tomorrow. But would she see its light through her tears?

How can anyone scoff at God, yet breathe the air that He gives?

Early the next morning, Moses gathered the people. How could he place the Law in their hearts so that they lived the Lord's love without thinking, served Him with their being, and wanted Him more than anything?

He read the Law. "But the person who despises the Law shall be completely cut off."

Eleazar offered sin offerings for the people.

Aaron retired as the Law stated.

The people mourned, not only for the men lost during the plague and the battle, but for their own loss. They would remain in the desert. They must depend totally on the Lord for the next forty years.

The congregation fell into a routine.

They no longer anticipated the Promised Land. They had been given a glimpse, tasted its fruit, but would not enter.

Unbelief had a heavy cost.

Ellis dumped a load of firewood by their fire. "It's nice to have wood, rather than animal dung for burning."

Dinah nodded as she formed the flatbread. "I don't know what would have happened if we hadn't taken Nathan's baby. I enjoy his children here, but they need to see their father. Is Nathan healing?"

Ellis shrugged. "At first I thought he was just grieving, but now... He's angry and bitter. I've tried to talk with him..."

"He's had weeks. Ask him to come for dinner. He's lost weight."

At the tent's opening, Ellis called. "Nathan!"

As his eyes grew accustomed to the dim, he searched the room. It held nothing but disorder: cloaks left where they had been taken off, pallets still on the floor from the night's rest.

Ellis found Nathan slouched in the corner, as he had every other evening that he had stayed with him since Salome's death. He shook him and pulled him to a sitting position.

Ellis went to the doorway for water. The vessels were dry. He took several and ran to the water pool to fill them.

Once Ellis brought the dipper to Nathan's lips; he wet his lips but shook his head. Ellis pushed the food that Dinah had sent in front of Nathan.

Nathan picked at the food, but did not eat. Every movement was labored.

"Drink the broth." Ellis sat with him. He stirred the dead ashes and started a new flame.

The silence hung between them.

Ellis had spent many evenings with him in silence, grieving with him. There was no need to speak.

Nathan swallowed, licked his lips, attempted to speak, but gave up. His shoulders shook.

Ellis grabbed him. His tears blended with Nathan's. "I hurt for you, my friend. Tell me how I can help you be the man the Lord wants."

Nathan swallowed. "I don't want to be His man. I don't trust Him."

Ellis gripped his shoulders tighter. "You told me in Egypt He was worth trusting. You told me, when I had doubts, to look to the Lord, to see His hand holding me through the pain."

Nathan broke away from his grip and walked to the darkest corner of the tent.

"The Evil One wants you to doubt." Ellis followed him, standing behind him. He squeezed his shoulder. "You have grieved. And that was fine. But now, you no longer mourn Salome's loss. You pity yourself."

"Salome helped me to see God. How can I live without her?"

Ellis smiled, sadly. "My abba was taken from me when I was small. I watched him die under the cruelty of Egypt's rulers. I needed him. God took him away, so that I would know Him. I don't like it, but that seems to be His way."

Nathan did not speak for a long time.

Ellis waited.

Nathan's shoulders slumped. He attempted a smile. "The Evil One will not get the victory.

Ellis nodded. "May the Lord be known."

Nathan took a moment before speaking. His voice was husky. He cleared his throat and wiped his face on his tunic. "He will be, indeed."

Nathan stretched as he woke for the new day. He had grieved, and now he must live. He had eaten with Ellis and his family for several days before bringing his own children home to be with him. Of course the baby still stayed with Dinah. Last night had been the first night he had kept the children. He had actually slept through the night. Perhaps having Jabin snuggle against him in his sleep had helped.

He had told Ellis that he was ready for his children to stay with him throughout the day. How hard could it be?

Ellis and Dinah continued to keep the baby, which he had better name soon.

Etania grabbed a vessel for carrying water. "I can't make flat-bread without water and manna."

Jabin rubbed his eyes with his fists. "Where did Ima go?"

Etania shook her head at Jabin. "Don't bother Abba. We must get water."

Nathan squeezed Jabin's shoulders. "She's where no pain can reach her."

"Why does Japhet still have his ima?"

Nathan swallowed. How had Salome answered questions all day long? No wonder she was tired. "Japhet's ima has things to do here."

"Didn't Ima?"

Nathan stared at the tent flap for a long time before answering. "I thought so, but I don't make the rules..." He shook his head. "Let's get water. Can you carry this one for me, Jabin?"

At the waters' edge, Nathan partially filled Jabin's container.

Etania carried another. "Should you make Jabin carry so much, Abba?"

Nathan tapped Jabin's shoulder. "You can do it. Can't you, big man?"

Jabin grunted but nodded.

Nathan turned to Etania. "It keeps him busy and let's my

thoughts rest."

Etania doubted. "Do your thoughts rest?"

Nathan smiled at Etania. "Not while you ask me questions."

Etania bit her lip and kept quiet for a time.

Nathan looked at her. "Is it hard not to speak?"

Etania nodded. "But your mind needs a rest."

Nathan waited, allowing Jabin to reach them. "I think it's rested enough. What do you want to ask?"

Etania shifted her water vessel. "Will Ima be gone forever?"

"Forever is a long time." Nathan swallowed. "When God takes us to be with Him, we'll be together again."

Etania hesitated.

Nathan nodded. "Go on, ask."

"Will we ever have another ima?"

Nathan shifted the vessels on his shoulders. "Who puts these thoughts into your head?"

Etania pushed back her shoulders. "My head comes up with them all by myself."

Nathan shook his head. "You are a girl, growing to be a woman. Do you ever think about being an ima someday?"

"All the time."

Nathan sighed. He had avoided her question. "You'll make a good one. You help your brother like Ima would want."

"Dinah says that I have a sensitive heart. What does that mean?"

Nathan placed the vessels inside the tent's door. "It means you can feel others' pain."

"Is that a good thing? I don't like feeling pain."

"When you feel others' pain, you can help them know they are not alone."

Etania took a sip of the water. "Does God feel our pain?"

"That's why we're free now. He saw us struggling under slavery and took it from us."

"But didn't we have more pain when Ima died?" Etania reached for the basket to carry the manna.

Nathan stared into the vessel of water.

Jabin tapped his hand. "Does your mind need another rest, Abba?"

Nathan shook his head and squeezed Jabin's hand. "God gives pain so that we will look to Him, so we can see Him better."

Etania stood taller. "Does that mean that I see Him better, because I feel more pain?"

"Ready to go for manna?" Nathan walked out the tent's door. "Etania, are you looking to Him?"

"Yes."

"Then you will see Him better."

Jabin put his hand inside his father's as they went for manna. "Do you see Him better?"

Nathan paused. "Only when I look to Him."

Etania took his other hand. "What happens if you don't look to Him when you suffer?"

Nathan squeezed her hand. "Your heart gets hard and ugly."

Etania swung her basket. "If I look to God, will I glow like Moses?"

"Moses sees God face to face. His glow comes from God." Nathan studied Etania's face. "The closer you know our Friend, the more others will see Him by looking at you."

Nathan looked at the desert sand covered with manna. They had completed one task for the day.

The rising sun over the manna showed another task to be completed. How could he get through another day without Salome?

How could he show his children the Friend of Abraham, when the hole in his heart allowed all feelings to fall into it and be lost?

Nathan watched the cloud all day, as if it were his very life. When doubts came, he stopped everything and looked. It was a moment by moment choice. He would know his God. And His peace came.

Even without a battle, the sick and wounded still came to Hannah. Sometimes Phinehas worked beside her, treating hard or dangerous cases. Children burned from tripping in the cook fires. Men hurt by army drills, snake bites, and other hazards of desert life. The crowded conditions brought danger of sickness due to uncleanliness. The Law gave guidelines, but they had to be obeyed if they were to provide protection.

Hannah returned from the hillside, after searching for herbs. She slipped into her tent and placed her basket by the doorway. When her eyes adjusted to the darkness, she gasped.

A man lay sprawled on her pallet.

Her face flushed, for his tunic didn't conceal the wound between his legs. She grabbed her water vessel by the tent flap and hurried to him. "How did it happen?" She began washing the wound.

The man winced and sucked in a breath before answering, "My ox kicked me."

Hannah could hear someone outside her tent.

"Hori. Are you in there?" The woman did not wait for an answer, but barged into Hannah's tent. She gasped when she saw the gaping wound.

Hannah turned to the woman, "Would you ask Phinehas for the salve that cleanses and heals? Your husband needs something stronger than what I have."

The woman looked at the leg then at Hannah. "I won't leave you here with my husband."

Hannah felt her face burn as she stood. "Perhaps you can clean the wound and stop the bleeding before I return?"

The woman spit out a response. "I can do that." Her lips shut tightly.

"I'll hurry."

The woman glared at her. "I'm sure you will."

Hannah hurried. Her cheeks burned at the woman's insinuation. She had only wished to help the man quickly. Usually her abba or Amos were present. Today, she had not noticed their absence.

She hurried, finding Phinehas explaining the Law to Michael. She breathed deeply, catching her breath. "Phinehas."

Phinehas looked up from his reading. His eyes brightened when he saw her.

"A man was kicked by his ox. The wound's very large and dirty. I don't have enough herbs."

Phinehas grabbed his herbs. As he hurried beside Hannah, he asked, "Why didn't you send someone for me?"

She picked up her pace.

"Your cheeks are flushed. You're upset. Why?" Phinehas grabbed her arm and turned her to look at him.

"Abba and Amos weren't in the tent. The man came. I thought only of helping. The wound is high on his leg, where the tender part meets the trunk. His wife sent me away. I..."

"She didn't trust you with her husband." Phinehas finished. "Nor would I trust any man with you alone, Hannah. You can't imagine the evil of people."

"I should know, for they tell me often."

Phinehas commanded, "Who does?"

She shook her head.

"What do they say?"

"It's nothing."

Phinehas lifted her chin to make her look at him. "Tell me."

"I'm too old to marry. That the only way I'll have a husband is to use theirs." She lowered her face despite his finger resting on her chin. Her eyes filled with tears.

She could feel him tense. She looked up.

Phinehas's expression was hard. His lips pressed together. "What they say is not true. I'll speak to your father. I study to be worthy of you. I didn't realize what the waiting was doing to you. Your abba and I will make arrangements. Would that be something you'd want?"

She nodded. "With all my heart."

Another Sabbath had come.

Moses ate of his left-over flatbread.

Shelumiel arrived at his campfire with a group of men. "Shalom."

Moses gestured for them to sit. He looked to the man they brought. "Do I know you?"

The man they had brought looked away and did not answer.

Shelumiel glanced around uneasily, wetting his lips. "He judged for his tribe."

Moses nodded. "I remember now. Your position was given to another. You come today, because?"

Shelumiel looked to his companions. "Elizur gathered wood today."

Moses studied Elizur's masked expression. "Is gathering wood necessary on the Sabbath, when you have all the days before to acquire it? The Lord gives time for all that He requires. You disobey out of defiance, not ignorance of the Law."

Elizur glared at Moses.

Moses did not look away. "Instead of becoming soft and pliable by knowing the Lord, you are hardened by the very Law that you ignore. But you do not just ignore the Law, you ignore the Law Giver. He has called you to know Him and you have refused. You have trampled Him."

Elizur pursed his lips. "Where was your God when we were slaves for over 400 years? Why should I acknowledge Him when He ignored us?"

"He never ignores us. He only waits for us to seek Him."

Elizur interrupted, his voice raised in anger. "I called to your God for water. He led us three days without it. My baby died. My wife mourned her loss and your God killed her by fire. You say she murmured against your God. I'm supposed to want to know this God?"

Moses sighed deeply. "Elizur, the Lord calls you to Himself. Instead of seeking Him, you blame Him." Moses cleared his throat and drank from a vessel before him. "I will seek the Lord's penalty. We will execute it, when the sun rises over the mountain for another day."

The men rose to leave.

Moses squeezed Shelumiel's shoulder. "You did right. You upheld the Law. The Lord is pleased."

Shelumiel worked to swallow. "Then why do I feel like I betrayed my best friend?"

"Your best friend needs to know the Lord. By enforcing the Law, you show Elizur his need for God. Be at peace. When you please the Lord, He will make all things right."

The morning dawned, promising another day. Moses watched from the mountainside as the women gathered their daily meals of manna before the sun turned it to mist.

When he heard the trumpet blast, summoning the people to the Tabernacle for a special meeting, Moses walked down the mountain.

The people had already gathered when he reached the bottom. Rumors had circulated like fire through the group. Pending doom hung over the congregation as they waited Moses's words.

Elizur came to stand beside him.

Moses raised his rod over his head to quiet the people. "Keep the Sabbath. Elizur gathered wood on the Sabbath, against the Lord's holy Law."

Many in the crowd remembered this man, Elizur, as judge. They had attended his courts to be entertained.

"Elizur knew the Law, but he did not acknowledge the Lord as his authority. He did not respect the Lord. His penalty is death by stoning."

A hush fell over the congregation. The penalty seemed harsh for the crime.

Moses and Elizur walked side-by-side to the wilderness beyond the camp. Moses leaned heavily on his rod. He had to focus on each step that led him toward the judgment scene. His heart was heavy over the sin. Elizur showed no repentance. No acknowledgment of God's control. No sign of even seeing God.

What could Moses have done to prevent this? He shook his head. He could not make the people obey.

The people followed.

Elizur stood before the people. He gazed not at his feet in repentance but at the people, daring them to kill him. He crossed his arms, taunting them with his lips curled in a humorless smile.

Outside the camp there were many stones to serve the purpose. Children gathered them, while the adults received further instructions from Moses.

Moses licked his lips and leaned on his rod. "The Sabbath was given for our good. Remember Egypt, when you had no rest? You worked seven days without fail. You faltered. The Lord wants you to rest, to focus on Him, to remember His commandments."

When the piles of stones were made, Moses looked to the people. "Let us fulfill what the Lord has commanded." He picked up a palm sized stone and threw the first stone.

The men followed.

Women hid their children's faces from the scene, but watched themselves.

As the stones started, Elizur taunted them. "Is that your best throw?" As he was hit, he bowed under the pain. He stopped jeering. He groaned. He fell to his knees, covering his head with his arms.

The stone pile was almost gone. Elizur bowed his head. He would not again dishonor the Lord's Law.

Moses threw the final stone, then turned to the people. "Remember the Sabbath. Keep it holy."

The people returned to their tents quietly.

The day was only half spent, but Moses did not go to the tent of the Tabernacle.

Moses sat like a stone, staring out of unseeing eyes. He was weary of this people who did not obey, who squabbled over little things, who looked to each other for their standard of right and wrong.

Another life was taken because he did not believe the Lord meant what He said.

Zipporah dished a meal of flatbread and stew from meat that had been shared with them by a shepherd. She placed it before Moses. "Eat, Moses. Your spirit is low. Your body needs meat."

Gershom settled beside Moses. He leaned against Moses's chest. "Abba, how can I remember all the Lord's laws?"

Moses hugged his son on his lap and tried to smile. "Gershom, how do you remember all the practice moves of the soldiers?"

"I watch...study...learn...practice. Then I feel like I was made to do them."

Moses nodded. "So it is with the Lord's laws. If you love God with everything that is inside of you, you will watch His face. You will study His Law. You will practice His will until it becomes your life."

"Aren't you afraid you might forget something in His Law?"

Moses tapped Gershom's leg. "He doesn't give His Law to make us fall. His Law protects us and shows us what is good. What happens when you fight Ima over a rule?"

Gershom thought a moment. "I get hurt."

"Rules are meant for your safety. What happens when you obey those rules?"

"Ima smiles on me."

Moses looked in the direction of the mountains. "Same with the Lord. Live to see His smile."

"You make it sound so easy. But I get busy and forget to listen and then I'm not even doing what I should."

"That's why the Sabbath is so important—to remember Him, to keep your focus."

Shelumiel walked to his tent after the stoning. He could have been the one stoned today. He had laughed with Elizur at his judgments. He had resented Moses's authority.

During the golden bull feasting, he had enjoyed unrestrained lawlessness. His face grew hot at the memories. Afterward, when the Levities ripped through the campsite, he had hidden, ashamed of his disregard for the Law.

His own guilt almost hindered him from bringing Elizur to judgment. Who was he to pass judgment on his friend? Did he have any right to enforce the Law?

When Moses threw that first stone, he had watched Moses. He always thought Moses enjoyed ruling over the people, telling them their wrongs. But what he had seen today was pain. Moses's face reflected the pain that a father would show for his own son. Moses had done what was right, not because he enjoyed it, but because it was right.

Shelumiel knew that he also had done right.

Shelumiel did not want his life ending like Elizur's. Today was his warning. He would learn the Law. He would live the Law so the Lord would find nothing wrong.

After settling the Tabernacle's most holy instruments, Korah had finally settled his own campsite. Traveling with the Ark of the Covenant on his shoulders was hot, heavy, loathsome work.

Remembering Aaron's sons, his own uncles, burned while sacrificing kept him from lowering the ark as he carried it. Fear was a good motivator, but it gave no satisfaction.

When they reached camp, he was told where he could pitch his tent—by the Tabernacle. Camping by the Tabernacle with all its sacrifices drew flies as thick as a cloak. They covered his tent. They tormented him while he ate and slept.

After finally settling his own family, he hiked to a plateau away from any flies. He lingered by the moon's light, watching the glow over the distant cities. The cool air did nothing for the turmoil stirring inside him. Licking his lips, he could taste freedom from these oppressive rules.

Returning to his tent, Danya, his wife, waited. "Where were you?"

Korah massaged his shoulders where the pole had rubbed. "I loathe these tasks."

"Moses does what he pleases. Do you see him carrying the ark on his shoulders? He's a Levite!"

Korah responded with a laugh. "Do you think that he could?"

"His age does not hinder him from putting you under bondage." She paused. "What about Shelumiel?"

"What about him?"

She put her hands on her hips as if the conclusion was obvious. "He delivered his best friend to death. See the spy system that Moses has? Friends turn in friends."

Korah nodded. "What should I do? Kill him?"

"You are better than that. Think of something that will make you leader. Then you can do what you want."

Korah nodded. What would it be like to be in charge?

CHAPTER 21

E smail saw Hakeen and Amos approach. "Shalom."
Hakeen looked over Esmail's flock. "Be at peace...though I sense you cannot help but be at peace out here. We've come to settle Pelia's mohar." Mohar, the dowry, compensated the bride's family for their loss of a worker. She would work with the groom's family.

Esmail squatted beside his dog. "Sheep are her life. Can she live without them?"

Amos interrupted. "She puts aside her childhood to become a woman, accepting my occupation."

Esmail shook his head, still seeking to understand his sister having grown up. Where had the years gone? "I'll miss her."

"When there is need, Pelia can help you."

Esmail stared toward the mountains. "Your offer is generous."

Amos added. "We also add these to the mohar." He handed Esmail a bag of gems, acquired the last day in Egypt from those who wished to appease God.

Esmail opened the bag and sifted the gems with his fingers. "A more than generous offer, if my heart could let her go."

Amos quickly reminded. "But you've already consented."

Esmail laughed. "Never fear. I cannot make Pelia do what she does not wish to do. She wishes to wed you." He shut his hand over the gems and returned them to the bag. He closed the bag and extended it to Amos.

Amos refused it. "Keep it as a token of my promise."

Esmail placed the bag in the pocket of his cloak. "The mohar is satisfied, although my heart is left with a hole."

Esmail stared at the distant hills. After their parents' death, Magal was the brother that he could not tame. Magal's loss seemed far away. Now Pelia was leaving.

Hakeen extended his hand in acceptance. "You lose not a sister, but gain a family."

"Family is something that I've not had for a long time. It will be treasured." Esmail shifted his eyes from the hills to the sheep. "I'll provide mutton for the feast."

Amos looked over the sheep. "You will make it for the festivities?"

Esmail laughed. Was there a way not to go? He shook his head. "Pelia would have something to say if I did not appear."

Amos considered Pelia's gift for the *mattan*, the groom's love gift to his bride. He didn't know what women liked. Without his mother, he felt the loss more.

When Phinehas had made arrangements with his abba for Hannah, Amos couldn't have been happier for his sister. When Phinehas had given Hannah a ring, Hannah's countenance had glowed for days. Amos caught her gazing at the ring with such a look of love that he knew that he could do no better for Pelia. "May I see your ring?"

Hannah extended her hand.

Amos laughed. He had admired Bezalel's work since the building of the Tabernacle. "Can you take it off? Or is it stuck?"

She laughed but hesitantly removed it from her finger.

He studied it. The band was gold, intertwined with small stones of blue and green. The wings of an angel were engraved on it. The inside band read, "Know the Lord." Amos laughed. His Father's condition for Phinehas would mark his journey to knowing Him.

Amos handed the ring to Hannah with a nod. "Why the angels' wings?"

Hannah slipped it on, touching it once there. She blushed. "Phinehas calls me his 'angel of mercy' who saved him from destruction."

"He's right. You did." Amos was quiet for a moment. "Does Pelia speak of anything that she treasures?"

Hannah considered. Her eyes sparkled as she blurted out, "Sheep. She tells of the lamb's antics in the spring, the shearing and spinning into soft blankets. Sheep, Amos. Engrave a lamb on the ring!"

Amos nodded. "Your idea will speak to her heart."

"You have not seen her since the betrothal started. But you

wait until after this week of separation, she prepares herself for you. This separation is hard, no?"

Amos nodded. "It's worse than waiting for my stump to heal."

Hannah laughed. "Yes. Time indeed stopped then."

Amos had stopped listening. His thoughts rested on Pelia's ring. He could hardly wait.

After the stoning of Elizur, Korah mulled. Speaking to the judges, he voiced his thoughts. "Moses has too much power. Look at Elizur. He was stoned. For what? Picking up sticks on the wrong day! Do you think you're better than Elizur? Can you remember and obey all these regulations? Should we wait until we forget a law? It'll be too late."

Murmurs of agreement spread through the group.

From the crowd, Dathan spoke, "Moses holds our lives in his hands. He has become like Pharaoh, killing when he wants. We must crush his power."

Abiram shouted from the back of the group, "Moses is but a shepherd from Midian. He brought in a foreigner as his wife. Yet we cannot go to nearby lands to find a wife. Does he think he's more holy than us?"

The group nodded their approval.

Korah proclaimed, "What are we waiting for? Let's go deal with Moses now."

The crowd followed Korah to the Tabernacle. "Moses! Come out."

Moses stepped out of the Tabernacle.

Korah shook his fist at Moses. "Moses, you've gone too far. The congregation is holy. Isn't the Lord in our midst? You exalt yourself over us."

Moses fell on his face.

Korah took a step back. How could he fight the man while he lay on the ground?

Moses spoke from the ground, "Tomorrow morning, we will all meet here. The Lord will show Who He is. He will show who is holy. He will choose His leader."

Korah looked around at the men's faces.

They waited for him.

Korah nodded with determination. "Tomorrow, it is."

When the sun rose over the desert and the manna had disappeared into the mist, the people assembled in front of the Tabernacle.

Moses had not walked up the mountain to watch the people, as was his custom before the sun rose. He was weary of their sin. He was frustrated with their stiff-necked stubbornness.

Zipporah pushed a flatbread closer to his hand. "The people tire you."

Moses shook his head. "People want the appearance of the Lord's holiness, but do not want their lives changed."

Zipporah patted his hand. "Isn't that why the Tabernacle stands apart from the people? So the glory of the Lord won't shine too much on their activities?"

Moses grunted. "As if God's glory could be contained."

Zipporah sipped from the dipper. "Without His glow in their hearts, can they see their own darkness?"

Moses slouched against the cushions, not finishing his flatbread.

Korah shouted outside their doorway. "Moses, come, prove to us your leadership."

Zipporah began putting on his sandals. "Couldn't they wait until you've eaten?"

Moses sighed. He tied his belt around his cloak. "They wish to be rid of me as soon as possible."

Zipporah adjusted his cloak around his neck. "Don't they learn?"

"Like sheep, they must learn the same things over and over again."

Zipporah clutched his cloak, drawing him to her. "They may stone you."

He kissed her. "I'm under God's protection."

Zipporah held on to him. "Let Him shine His own light."

Moses held her face between his hands. "I must stand between their darkness and God's light and show them Who He is." He wiped a tear from her cheek.

Zipporah nodded and handed him his staff.

Moses stepped outside his doorway to face the crowd gathered. He raised his staff for quietness. "Take censers. Put fire in them. Lay incense in them. The Lord will choose who is holy, tomorrow."

Moses studied the faces before him. He saw their stubbornness, their greed, their arrogance. His anger grew. "You've gone too far, sons of Levi. Isn't it enough that God separates you from the rest of the congregation to mediate between man and God? You stir the people, not against me, but against the Lord."

Moses searched the crowd. "Where are Dathan and Abiram?"

They did not step forward, but answered from the crowd. "Isn't it enough that you show us our Land, then tell us we will die in this wilderness? Must you lord it over us? Do you want to kill us like you did Elizur? Nay, we will not come to you."

Moses's muscles quivered. His body flushed hot. He breathed deeply. "May the Lord reject your offerings!"

He spoke to the crowd. "Have I ever taken anything from you, or brought harm on any of you?"

He looked at Korah. "Tomorrow, present all the leaders before the Lord here."

Moses turned from them and entered the Tabernacle. Must he defend his leadership again?

Ebiasaph, Korah's grown and married son, heard of Korah's complaints. He approached him by his campsite. "Abba, shalom."

Korah was filling his firepan with incense, preparing for the morrow. "Be at peace."

"Are you at peace, my abba?"

Korah looked at his son. "Why wouldn't I be?"

Ebiasaph chose his words carefully. "You challenge Moses's authority."

Korah's hands balled into fists. "Don't you weary of carrying the ark every time we move?"

Ebiasaph shrugged, tossed a twig into the embers and watched it burn. "It is our service to God. He ruled it. It pleases Him."

Korah shook his head. "You will amount to nothing if you follow all the rules and try to please everyone."

"I do not try to please everyone. I please my God. If that is all I do, I have done well."

Korah filled his firepan with incense. "You know when you please God?"

"I have peace."

Korah turned his back on his son, dismissing him.

Ebiasaph did not leave. He watched his abba finish the task.

"When you question God's leader, be prepared to lose it all."

Korah's hands shook so much that he dropped the firepan, spilling the incense. He looked at the spilled grains. He spit at his son. "You warn me?" He stooped to gather the incense again. "God does not even know you exist."

Ebiasaph softened his tone, "He favors those who seek Him. Are you seeking His favor?"

Korah stood before Ebiasaph. His neck muscles bulged, his face grew red. "You question me? Am I judged by my own son?"

Ebiasaph stepped back. "Abba, consider your actions before tomorrow."

Korah slammed his firepan against the ground and stalked away.

The next morning, Korah again interrupted Moses's morning meal. Moses rose, without finishing his flatbread, and walked past the two hundred and fifty leaders to the tent of meeting.

The crowd had increased since the previous day. More were eager to have new leaders and better judgments.

Moses lingered in the tent of meeting. How could he make these people see God?

The Lord's glory descended on the tent.

Moses removed his sandals and bowed before Him.

The Lord spoke, "Move away from this people before I consume them."

Moses fell on his face. "When one man sins, will you judge the entire congregation?"

"Stand away from Korah, Dathan, and Abiram."

Moses walked to the Levite section of the campsite. The Levites' tents stood apart from the people to better serve the Tabernacle and the Lord.

Moses turned to the Levites who had tents pitched close to Korah, Dathan, and Abiram. "Separate your things from theirs."

Ebiasaph stood beside Moses.

Moses nodded toward him. "You carry the Ark of the Covenant?"

Ebiasaph nodded.

Moses remembered him. He served with devotion and love for God. "Stand apart."

Ebiasaph's eyes reflected concern. "I do not fight my God."

Moses rested his hand on the young man's shoulder. "You do well."

The crowd thronged around Moses, quieted by his request, but eagerly watching to see whom God would choose to lead them.

Moses stopped in front of the tents of Korah, Dathan, and Abiram.

Levities around them pulled up their tent stakes, and moved their belongings.

Moses clenched and unclenched his fists, waiting. He stared at the cloud, hovering over the Tabernacle. He closed his eyes to focus on the peace that only God could give him.

One woman whispered, "He's as angry as when he returned from the Mount with the commandments."

Another asked, "What did they do?" They quieted, backing away from the tents and Moses.

Korah stood outside his tent with his arm around Danya, his wife. He held his toddler. His sons and daughters, still living in his tent, hovered around him. He stood tall, expecting merit. He smiled.

Danya held her chin up, meeting Moses's look.

Likewise, Abiram and Dathan stood, waiting with their families by their tent's doors.

Moses looked to the cloud that stayed on the outside of camp. "If these men die from normal cause, then the Lord has not sent me."

Korah's smile faded. He glanced at the crowd, now standing far from him. He stood alone, with his family. He looked at Moses, uncertain as he listened.

Moses's gaze remained on the cloud. He could not understand God's holiness. How could any man stand before God's presence?

He swallowed, and looked at Korah and his followers. His next words would not change their hearts. How could a people defy their very Creator? God's judgment must come. "If the Lord opens the ground and swallows these men alive, then you will know that they have spurned the Lord."

The ground rumbled, growled, and vibrated.

People pushed and shoved in their panic to get away from Korah and the others' tents.

The earth split open.

For a moment in time, there was silence. As if the Lord had suspended time and space.

Then Korah, Abiram, and Dathan and their families dropped

into the earth.

Their screaming replaced the silence as they fell into a bottomless abyss.

Moses did not know when the screaming stopped. The sound played over in his mind. He blinked and shook his head.

They had denied their Creator.

God had renounced them.

The earth shut its mouth. The hole was no more.

They were gone. Nothing remained.

In the silence that followed, Moses looked at the people. For once, they did not grumble or complain. Their faces held shock, disbelief, and fear.

When he lifted his head to look at the cloud, fire broke from it and fell, consuming all two hundred and fifty men, holding firepans. The blaze flared until nothing remained.

Would their rebellion never end? Moses was still trying to catch his breath from the ground closing up. And now he watched the smoke drift toward the sky. As the smoke lifted, he called. "Eleazar!"

Eleazar stepped forward, trembling. "Here I am, Moses, your servant."

"Scatter the ashes over the desert, but retrieve the censers, for they are holy. They presented them to God. Plate the altar with them, reminding the sons of Israel that I am God's appointed leader."

He shook his head. What a high price they had paid for their pride.

Zipporah removed Moses's cloak when he entered their house. It smelled of smoke, burnt flesh, and judgment. She hung it outside the door on a peg on the wall. "Sit. I'll make you tea."

When she made the drink, she sat before him. "Is it hard to be part of this world, yet live with your thoughts in another?"

He held his drink in both hands. "I long for the presence of God, but am torn by the needs of this people."

Zipporah stroked his beard. "How can I know this God that pulls at your heart and makes you long for His presence?"

He put his vessel down and held her face in his hands. His eyes held tears. "My sweet Desert Flower, hold nothing back, for He is your Master and Lord. Give Him the respect, honor, and care that you show me.

"He will be your Friend, Comforter, Provider, Protector. He will be your family."

At the last words, Zipporah gasped. Her darkened skin and different ways made living with this people hard. Their hateful remarks pierced her, no matter how many times she tried to ignore them. If God could truly be her family, if He could accept her as family, then this God was worthy of her heart.

The next day began as all the others, with the sun rising over the manna-covered ground. Moses looked beyond the white covered sand to the hills and thanked God for His faithfulness. He was wooing Zipporah to Himself. Moses lifted his voice in a song of praise to God. With joy in his heart and a spring to his eighty-four-year-old step, he approached the tent of meeting.

Why were the congregation gathered before its entrance? Shouts of anger arose above the stillness of the morning.

The brightness of the rising sun and the prayers of praise faded.

The Lord commanded him. "Get away from these people. Let Me consume them."

What had they done now?

The people chanted. "You killed the Lord's people."

Moses stopped beside Aaron, touching his arm. "Hurry, Aaron! Make atonement for the people before the wrath of the Lord falls!"

The mob pushed forward. They shouted against Moses and God. "Will you kill us here in this wilderness! We won't wait forty years. We won't follow you another step! We'll enter the Land without you." They picked up stones to throw.

The plague began, sweeping through the mob as they spewed their threats. It moved swiftly, like a consuming fire, taking any in its path.

Aaron fought through the crowds to bring fire from the altar. He raised his firepan toward heaven, between the dead and the living, interceding for the people before their God.

The fire rose into the air.

The cloud of the Lord lifted from the Tabernacle and covered the smoke. He stopped the plague.

But not before 14,700 died.

The people mourned.

Moses heard the mourning of the people. It was not like when they suffered from Pharaoh's hand in Egypt. Their own stubbornness caused this weeping. Moses shook his head. They must acknowledge God before He could truly make them His people. They had far to go.

The Lord told Moses, "Get a rod from each of the twelve tribes. Engrave their name on each rod. Write Aaron's name on the rod for Levi. Place them in front of the testimony in the tent of meeting. I will choose My leader. You will know by the rod that sprouts. Aaron's rod will remind these rebels of your authority. This should end their dispute over authority and against you."

The following morning, Moses took each rod before the people, as they waited outside the tent of meeting. He withheld Aaron's rod.

Each man examined his own rod. None showed growth.

Then Moses removed Aaron's rod. It had sprouted, budded, blossomed, and produced mature almonds.

As the men saw the difference, they cried, "How can we stand before this God and live?"

CHAPTER 22

The betrothal for Amos and Pelia had not been the customary year duration. But Hakeen and Esmail both approved the timing. Ketubah stated the mohar, the rights of the bride, and the promises of the groom. The bride and groom had fulfilled their week of separation.

The final part of the wedding was the festivities.

Amos fidgeted, adjusting his belt, as he waited in his tent.

Hannah touched his arm. "You are handsome, Amos. If you look at your reflection again in that silver platter, I will throw it across the tent."

Hakeen entered. "The wedding guests are here to escort you."

Amos swallowed and glanced again at the tray.

Hannah pulled him to the tent flap. "You are ready. Go."

His throat constricted and he swallowed. "I thank you for bringing Pelia into my life."

"We have the Lord to bless for what He has done," Hannah corrected. "We can only escort you, if you do the walking!"

Their guests escorted Amos to Pelia's tent.

Amos whispered to Hannah, "Will Esmail be there?"

Hannah laughed. Tradition did not allow them to inform the bride when the groom would appear, but they had told Esmail. "He would only leave his sheep for Pelia. He'll be there."

When Amos arrived, he wiped his palms on his tunic and spoke his practiced words to Esmail, "Before all gathered, grant me Pelia, your sister, to be my wife."

Esmail nodded and stepped aside as Pelia entered the tent doorway.

She was dressed like a queen, her dark hair braided with precious stones. Her long tunic, sewn during their week of absence, did not conceal her beauty. Somewhere desert flowers had been found that were draped around her neck. Amos removed Pelia's veil, to confirm that the bride was truly his beloved, a custom started after Jacob married Leah when he thought he was marrying Rachel.

Amos whispered. "You are my rare and precious jewel."

Pelia's cheeks colored at his praise. "And you are my king whom I will serve."

The wedding party escorted Amos and Pelia to Hakeen's tent. There they would wait for Esmail to present Pelia to Amos.

Esmail turned to Pelia. "I don't know where the time went. You were little and now you are..."

"A woman?" Pelia laughed. "Esmail, you are too preoccupied with your sheep. You see life as shearing, lambing, and changing pastures. You must know more of life."

"I am fine."

"But are you happy, Esmail?"

Esmail shrugged. "Happiness comes with a healthy flock."

"Is that enough? Don't you yearn for the hole in your heart to be filled?"

"Since when has my little sister grown wise enough to be my instructor?"

"Esmail, I've found the Lord to be a Friend that fills my heart and allows me to enjoy even the struggles of life."

"Amos colors your view, and you see green pastures when there are none. I wish for your happiness, so I won't spoil it by telling you differently today."

"Amos makes me happy, but the Lord gives me peace."

Esmail glanced down the pathway at Amos, who stood waiting. He said with husky voice, "It is time, my little sister."

Pelia glanced up to see tears in Esmail's eyes. She kissed him on the cheek. "I couldn't ask for a better brother to raise me. I only wish Magal could still be here."

"He would already be partaking of your wedding wine."

Pelia gave Esmail a hug. "Yes, our little family has shrunk."

"But you and Amos will bring little ones to my knees, so that I will see you again as when you were a little girl, begging to sleep with the lambs." Esmail wiped his eyes. "The groom waits. You must walk to your new master."

Esmail walked Pelia to Amos.

Pelia gave Esmail another kiss on the cheek, before standing beside Amos. She circled Amos seven times, symbolizing the new family circle.

Aaron blessed them. "May the union of this couple reveal the blessing of our God." He held the cup of wine, blessing their future together. Amos and Pelia answered together, "Amen."

Aaron gave the cup to Amos. He held it for Pelia to drink; then he drank, sealing the blessing upon them. He passed the cup to Hakeen.

Amos pulled from his tunic's pocket the ring. "With this ring, you are consecrated to me in accordance with the laws of Moses and Israel, signifying my commitment to you." He looked into her face as he placed the ring on her finger.

Her face shone.

Aaron pronounced the benediction. "Blessed is the Lord for the food given for our needs. Blessed is the Lord for bringing us from the land of Egypt, for making His covenant with us. Blessed is the Lord for this couple who has been brought together to allow His commandment to be fruitful and multiply to be completed in them. Blessings be on the family they have become."

Amos and Pelia responded in unison, "Amen."

After the ceremony, the guests escorted Amos and Pelia to a special tent where they could spend time alone.

Amos hugged Pelia.

Pelia threw her arms around Amos.

Her sudden unexpected movement caused Amos to lose his balance. They both toppled to the floor. "I'm sorry. I'm crushing you." She sat on his lap, her veil off, her dress in disarray. She wiggled into a better position.

Amos did not let her go. "Don't be sorry, my lamb. You're light as a bird, and flighty as well. Sit still and let me look at you." He turned her face with his finger so that her face was against his. "You have brought me dreams of happiness and pleasure."

Pelia blushed at the intensity in his eyes. She took his hand off her face to hold it tight. Her eyes filled with tears.

"What's wrong?"

"My tears wash the sorrows of the past away. My ima and abba would have loved you."

"And I, them." Amos took back his hand and held her face. He leaned forward and kissed her.

The kiss was their first, and it was sweet.

Pelia reminded, "We have guests."

They arose from their tumble, brushing themselves off.

Their entrance into the main tent signaled the start of feasting and dancing that would last for seven days.

The sorrows of the past had drawn Pelia to seek the Lord. Her service to Him would be directed toward Amos and his work. She was at peace.

Adlai found Michael out with his horses. "Shalom."

Michael looked up from making a halter. "Be at peace."

Adlai studied the mare with her week-old foal beside her. "The rainy season brought pastures in time."

Michael finished the last knot. "The Lord's timing is best." He approached the mare with his hand outstretched.

She smelled it, sniffing loudly.

Michael turned his hand to rub her nose and between her eyes. Adlai had given him the horse, after seeing his care of other horses. "Your gift was generous. She birthed a fine one with good breeding."

Adlai patted the neck of the mare. "I couldn't care for a horse and teach reading."

Michael brought the halter close to her nose, so she could smell it. "Your sacrifice has made me rich."

"Richness is in the eyes of the beholder." Adlai laughed. "I did not see caring for another horse, especially with a birth impending, as a good thing."

Michael brought the halter over her ears and under her chin. He patted her neck. "The rains came at a good time. She gives plenty of milk. The young one grows quickly."

Michael watched the foal nuzzle and drink. The silence made room for deep thoughts. "How does teaching the reading go?"

Adlai nodded. "Much like the pasture that grows rich on the rains. Those who thirst to know God find Him."

"How do you make the Words of God a part of you?"

Adlai glanced toward the grazing herd. "How do you train your horses?"

"Practice. But how do I practice with the Lord's Words?"

Adlai looked at the mountains. "Give the Lord time to make what you know in your head become part of your heart. Think about it throughout the day."

"Other things press on my mind then."

Adlai watched Michael. "Like Reut?"

Michael laughed. "All the time."

"She waits for you to assign the mohar."

Michael slapped the mare, startling her so that she jumped. He placed his hand on her back to calm her. His voice broke. "But I'll never enter the Promised Land."

"Are you going to live in misery, because something bad may happen tomorrow?"

Michael spoke harshly. "God keeps His Word."

"But you may live thirty-nine more years." Adlai patted the horse on her neck. "I cannot protect my family. Does that make me live in fear? Once, yes. But I have learned to obey one step at a time. I depend upon Him today."

"But I might die, leaving Reut without a provider."

"If I worry, I don't obey today's commands. He tells me, 'Trust Me.' He does not light my life, only my next step. If I don't take that step, I won't see the path."

Michael thought for a moment. "Knowing only a little bit of the Lord is too much for me. How can I hope to grasp more of Him?"

"You hold to the little bit that He shows, and He shows you more. Your hands and heart can only hold so much, right?" Adlai turned to leave.

"Adlai."

"Yes?"

"When may we determine the mohar?"

"Now you're talking, my son. We'll make plans."

"Is Reut willing?"

"It can't be soon enough for her."

Michael laughed. Then sobered. "Adlai, how does she adjust to her fear?"

"I still hear her in the night, screaming from her nightmares."

Michael probed, "How can I help?"

"She must learn as I am learning...that the Lord truly owns her and will not let her go."

CHAPTER 23

The cloud moved and the people moved with it. They reached Kadesh. There was no water.

The people's habit was to complain. They did not think back on the Lord's past provisions. They only sought water for their throats now.

The people met at Moses's tent. "Why did you take us from Egypt to let us die in this land of sand without water? Where is the grain, figs, or pomegranates that you promised?" Anger spilled from their mouths, showing what they held in their hearts.

Aaron and Moses brushed passed the people, entering the tent of meeting to approach the Lord.

Together they fell on their faces. "Meet the needs of Your people, O Lord."

The Lord spoke. "Take your rod. Speak to the rock on the mount before the people. I will give them water."

Moses and Aaron stood before the rock. Moses held his rod. Looking over the congregation, he saw anger and need. He licked his own dry lips. How this people wearied him! His authority was constantly attacked, rubbing at him like sand. "Shall we bring water from this rock?"

Someone pushed through the crowd toward him.

As the figure came closer, Moses realized it was Zipporah. Why was she coming with this unruly mob?

She stood before him in front of the people. She bowed her head, then looked into his eyes.

Moses licked his lips and softened his voice. "What is it, Zipporah?"

"Miriam calls for you."

The crowds pressed around her, shoving her. "Give us water. Get this foreigner away from us."

Moses stepped toward her. If this crowd would stone him, what would they do to her?

One man shoved her. "Get her out of here. She doesn't belong with us."

"Give us water."

Men pushed Zipporah to the ground, then trampled her.

She struggled to rise.

As Moses pushed toward Zipporah, the crowd kicked her. Using his rod, Moses made an opening in the crowd. "Grab my hand."

Her face already showed bruises where she had been kicked. She winced as she stood.

Moses stepped back, holding her with his arm. Making sure she could stand, he turned to the crowds. Were these people just animals, kicking and stomping on his wife, because she was a different color? How long had he been with them, and they had not changed? They acted like they had the first time they were without water. Hadn't they been teaching God's Law to these rebels every day? Yet their hearts did not change. Moses could just picture a stubborn donkey. He would destroy such a beast, if it refused to be taught. He could feel the heat rush to his face. His arms trembled as he held his rod tightly in his clenched hand. These people were not worth the sand in his sandals. "You rebels! All you seek is full mouths." Raising his rod with both hands, he struck the rock.

Lightning fell from heaven, splitting the rock from top to bottom. Water gushed from its core.

Moses shook. His rage had suddenly left him, and an emptiness took its place. God had given the people water, yes, but he had not obeyed God's Words. He looked at the rod in his hands. He wanted to throw it. But it was not the cause of his disobedience. He looked around at the people, waiting for judgment. They had made him angry. But he had struck the rock. He had disobeyed God's Words. He felt ashamed, undone. He didn't want to look at the cloud of the Lord. He would sense God's disappointment, His disapproval. His legs shook. He used his rod to steady his feet.

The people were already pushing forward to drink, oblivious of his struggle.

Zipporah stood there, waiting for him.

He studied her from head to toe. His hands still shook, not from rage, but from spent energy. His knees trembled. He brushed her bruised cheek. "You are well?"

Zipporah winced, but nodded. Sandal marks on her clothes showed where bruises would emerge later.

"Why did you come?"

"Miriam is dying."

Moses nodded. Even the death of his sister did not touch him like disobeying the Lord. He felt numb. He still felt unsure. He searched the crowd for Aaron as he guided Zipporah away.

Aaron's eyes met his, and he nodded. They pushed against the crowds toward Miriam's tent.

Aaron and Moses did not speak.

As they walked away from the crowds, Moses's trembling settled, and a heavy grief covered him. He felt sick. He had not spoken to the rock. His anger had so consumed him that he had struck the rock. He had lost sight of the Lord's Words, seeing only the whining, selfish, cruel people and their mistreatment of Zipporah. He mourned his separation from the Lord.

Before reaching Miriam's tent, Moses stopped. Turning to Aaron and Zipporah, he said, "I must speak to the Lord."

Aaron studied his brother. "I will take Zipporah safely to Miriam."

Moses nodded. "I'll come when I finish."

Moses entered his tent, and fell on his face. "Lord, forgive me. I allowed circumstances to influence my actions. I have sinned. Cut this blackness from my heart. You are holy. I disrespected Your Name by disobeying Your Word."

The Lord responded, "Because you did not treat My Words as holy in front of the people, you will not bring them into the Land."

Moses could not speak. He could offer excuses: Zipporah being abused, the people querulous; but all that was insignificant compared to his disregard for God's Words, especially in front of the people. He had feared only one thing, and that was not completing the mission God had given him. Now, he would not. He had disappointed his God. His heart broke. He wept. He did not rise from his knees for a long time. When he did, he proclaimed to the Lord, "You did that which was just. Your Name will be praised."

Zipporah met Gershom at Miriam's tent. "Thank you, my son."

Gershom nodded. "I waited with her, but she didn't speak."

Zipporah hesitated to enter. "You did well to come for me."

Aaron squeezed Gershom's shoulder before entering.

Zipporah stayed just inside the tent's opening. She had watched the water flow from the rock but did not drink. Now, she licked her dry, cracked lips wishing for just a swallow of water.

Something had happened at the rock with Moses. Zipporah could see it in his face when he struck the rock. She was torn between returning to Moses and staying here. Was she even wanted here?

Miriam lay unmoving, her eyes closed. She was weakened from traveling without water.

Aaron knelt by her side. "Moses is coming soon."

Miriam nodded with effort. "The people always call him away."

Aaron patted Miriam's arm. "You have influenced the women toward the Lord."

Miriam grabbed his arm. "No. I influence. But not for the Lord. I've caused division. I was jealous of Zipporah."

Zipporah gasped. "Why?"

Miriam sighed. "With your position, I could have influenced so many. I told all who would listen how you turned us away from our Land."

Aaron brushed her hair from her forehead. "Miriam, save your strength."

"For what, Aaron? To die in my guilt? Is Moses's son here?"

Gershom stood from squatting at the door beside Zipporah. "Yes."

Miriam pointed. "Lift the vessel of oil in the corner."

Gershom did as he was told. "Ima's ring!"

Zipporah gasped, covering her mouth. She wanted to spill out angry words, but she breathed deeply and listened.

Aaron looked at her. "Why do you have it, Miriam?"

"It held great strength over her. It would bring me power."

Gershom gave it to Zipporah. "I knew she took it!"

Miriam picked at her blanket. "Where's Moses?"

Moses stepped inside the tent. He led Zipporah and Gershom to Miriam's side. "I am here, Miriam."

Aaron prodded further. "Tell us, Miriam, about this ring."

Moses looked at the ring in Zipporah's hand. "What do you know about the ring, Miriam?"

Miriam squeezed her blanket. "Zipporah controlled you with it. She held it always. I wanted her power."

Moses shook his head. "Miriam, I made that for her mattan. It reminded her of my love when I was not home."

Miriam grabbed Moses's arm. "It wasn't the first thing that I stole. I rearranged things in your house, so she would leave."

Zipporah bit her lip to keep from speaking. She had not been losing her mind.

Moses clasped Zipporah's hand. "Why?"

"She took my baby brother from me. You obeyed me, growing up. When she came, you didn't listen to me."

Moses looked at Aaron. "I didn't even have time to listen to Zipporah."

Miriam lay still for a time. She tried to swallow. Her breathing slowed. "I repent."

Zipporah could not clear the lump in her dry throat. She could not even form tears. She had wished for family. Miriam had kept that from happening. Was it too late?

The silence lengthened. Zipporah held Miriam's hand. "I forgive you."

Miriam sighed. Her eyes fluttered open to rest on Zipporah's face. "You know the God of Moses? I could tell."

Before Zipporah could speak, Miriam turned to Aaron. "Will my sin be covered by the sacrifices?"

Aaron's eyes met Moses's. He shook his head.

Moses coughed, unable to clear his dry throat. "Miriam, the Lord seeks your heart. The sacrifice shows a heart that willingly obeys."

Miriam's voice was edged with panic. "You put the blood on the altar, but what does it mean?" Her voice was growing weaker. "How can a sacrifice pay for my wrong?"

Moses responded. "I don't understand a woman, but that doesn't mean I cannot love her."

Miriam laughed. "So I don't have to understand it all?"

Zipporah squeezed her hand gently. "Understanding a great God Who made us? We never will. I accept His Ways and find peace."

Miriam asked, "My wrong is covered by the burnt sacrifice?"

Moses nodded. "If you seek Him."

Miriam repeated, "Accept His Ways and find peace." She closed her eyes and remained quiet a long time. A smile formed on her hardened features. "If I seek Him."

They waited.

Aaron felt her wrist and nodded to Moses.

The people mourned for Miriam many days.

CHAPTER 24

J oshua and Caleb approached the king of Edom on behalf of Moses and the Israelites.

They had left the desert of Sinai and had entered inhabited land. The Edomites were descendants of Esau (the brother of Jacob, the father of the twelve tribes of Israel). Their land was promised to them by God, so the Israelites would not fight them. But the King's Highway, as it was called, allowed merchants and travelers to pass through their lands without harm. It enabled travelers to voyage to Egypt with speed. Joshua stood before the king. "You heard your brother Israel faced suffering under the Egyptians' rule. But the Lord heard our cry and delivered us out of their hands. Now we are camped at Kadesh, a town on the edge of your territory. Permit us to pass through your land. We will not walk through any field or vineyard. We won't drink any water from any well. We will stay only on the King's Highway until we pass through your territory."

The king of Edom answered, "You shall not pass through my land. If you do, I will set my army against you."

Joshua bowed lower. "Please, we will stay on the highway. If any of our people drink of your water, we will pay the price. Only allow us passage."

"Be gone from my presence. I will watch to ensure that you leave."

Joshua and Caleb were escorted from the king's presence. The army guarded the highway, preventing the Israelites from using it. So the Israelites turned from his land and went to Mount Hor.

When the cloud had settled at Mount Hor, the people camped. Aaron motioned for Moses, and Eleazar. "Hike with me. The Lord calls me to come to Him."

Moses nodded, putting the scrolls in the Tabernacle.

Aaron leaned on his staff. "Did you ever think that our lives would be changed so, Moses? You have gone from a slave's son to a pharaoh's son to a leader of God's people. And I have gone from a slave's son to a doctor to a priest of the Most High God."

Moses paused in his ascent. He looked over the campsite. "We have seen the Lord work. He delivered, sustained, and called us by name. He has made us a people."

Eleazar asked, "What words would you share with me, Abba?"

Aaron did not speak for a moment, as he, too, studied the campsite. He squeezed Eleazar's shoulder. "You would think at the end of your life you would have so much to say. But what more is there, than to obey God?

"I led these people to the boundaries of the Land, yet I can't enter because I didn't help Moses obey at the waters of Meribah."

They returned to silence as they continued their hike, until they reached the summit.

Aaron removed his cloak and gave it to Eleazar. He embraced Moses. Keeping his hands on Moses's shoulders, he looked into his eyes. "You have shown me God."

Moses responded. "I couldn't have done much, without you by my side. You will be with God sooner than I."

Aaron laughed. "You live with Him. You lead as only one who knows Him could."

Aaron hugged Eleazar. "You, my son, will intercede for the people, because the holiness of God cannot look on the people's sin. Stay faithful. Obey. The price of disobedience is great and far-reaching. The Lord will be faithful."

The three men watched over the campsite and said no more. The sun spread its golden rays across the lands covered with a people as many in number as the sand.

The life of Aaron was a hundred and twenty-three years, and he died.

Moses and Eleazar buried Aaron on the top of Mount Hor.

The Israelites moved from Mount Hor to skirt its borders.

The king of Arad had watched this vast people enter his land of Negev. He foresaw his pastures, waterways, and cattle being diminished by their numbers. He would hold to his possessions by taking the initiative. He attacked them, taking captives, among whom were Ellis and Nathan.

In a stone cistern, Ellis groaned beside Nathan. "What makes our captors so wicked?"

Nathan licked his cracked, bleeding lips. "God plants in every heart a thirst for Him. We are made for Him. When people forsake God, He turns His back on them."

Ellis shifted against the stone wall. "Did you see their celebration when they brought us into the city?" He braced himself to speak again. "The women danced before the men, but they molested us instead! How can they do that?"

Nathan leaned his head against the wall. "Without God, we have no goodness, no standard of what is right. When we make our own ways, we think them good."

Ellis breathed shallowly from the pain of his cracked ribs. "If this is good, we are a corrupt people."

Nathan tried to stretch out his legs, but there was only enough room to push them against the wall. "We are indeed."

"If this represents the Land that we enter, we will need the Lord's mercy to shield us from this evil...and His Arm to execute judgment."

They sat in silence. The darkness never left the hole where they suffered.

Ellis felt for Nathan's arm in the darkness. "Nathan." Ellis heard Nathan's raspy breathing from the dampness. "I am ready to meet my God, because of you."

Nathan clasped Ellis's arm. "And you have reminded me to look to Him."

Returning from the king of Arad's attack and the battle that ensued, Joshua returned to drink outside their campsite. The water refreshed his dry mouth, but did nothing for his inner turmoil. He wiped his lips with the back of his hand, looking to the north where the city lay. The Israelites had been on the defensive throughout the entire battle. They had not been ready when the king attacked them.

Why hadn't he assigned more sentries, especially being so close to their city? The people had paid for his unpreparedness. The king of Arad hadn't only killed his men. They had killed women and children and taken captives.

Joshua faced his campsite. The wail of mourning split the calmness of the evening. It also pierced his heart.

He looked to the cloud of the Lord. He took a deep breath, and squared his shoulders. "I vow that, if the Lord will deliver this people into my hand, I will utterly destroy their cities." He entered the camp to prepare the soldiers to return and do battle with the king of Arad again. But this time, they would be prepared. And this time, the Lord would deliver them into his hands.

Joshua led the counter-attack, storming the king's palace. He rescued those captives that were still alive, and burned the city. He killed the king of Arad. He fulfilled his promise to the Lord. The Lord blessed.

CHAPTER 25

The people followed the cloud around the land of Edom. When the cloud stopped, they once again set up camp. They were in the foothills, which helped to shade them from the burning heat. The boulders and stony ground made level campsites a challenge. The people heard their soldiers' report of treasures from the king of Arad's palace. They were determined to have some of it for their own.

They gathered around the Tabernacle to wait for Moses. When at last he appeared, they mobbed him. "We're doomed to die in this wilderness."

"We have no food, except this manna."

"We hate this miserable food. And we have no water."

"The people that we fight had wine, and we want some of it."

"We're the ones who sacrificed our lives to destroy their cities. We demand wine."

Some took their pounded manna flour and threw it at Moses.

Moses wiped his face of the coarse flour. He took a deep breath, but did not answer. Could the people complain one time too many for God? How could a people who had watched God provide miracle after miracle to keep them alive in the desert, scorn His very gifts? He missed Aaron by his side, interceding with God for the people as Moses listened to their complaints. Aaron, at least, cared. Moses was having trouble caring about the calamity that would surely come as a result of these people's open rebellion. He leaned on his staff and waited.

The people finished speaking, ready to challenge any answer he would give.

Moses gave no answer. But he knew the Lord would.

The earth trembled and shook.

The people began to panic, looking to Moses for reassurance. They sensed a terrible calamity from his God.

Moses closed his eyes. The shaking was like thunder from a distant storm. The thundering of the earth changed to a buzzing that surrounded him. He opened his eyes.

Serpents poured over the hillsides, awakened by the earth's movement. They flowed over the boulders like the water the people craved. They did not creep over the ground, but flew through the air and bit those who complained.

The people screamed, covering their faces as they ran to hide. But there was no escape.

The snakes slid under baskets, into tents, and under clothes, wherever man could go. They struck with only the buzzing warning, too late to hide.

The victims moaned. "The bite burns like the prongs of a silversmith." No poultice soothed the burning.

The people ran to Phinehas to seek a healing potion. "What can be done?" They cried.

Phinehas listened to the description. "It's from the red saw-scaled viper. I saw only one victim in Egypt. He arrived in time to die." He shook his head. "The Egyptians knew of nothing. Death always came."

The day continued. So did the victims. Those bitten early in the day began bleeding from their mouth and nose. Bruising and tenderness followed. The burning never stopped. Once vomiting started, death was soon at hand.

The people cried to Moses, "We have sinned. We spoke evil against you and the Lord. Take away these serpents."

Moses prayed to God.

The Lord answered, "Raise a brass serpent on a cross. Anyone bitten who looks at it will live."

Moses found Seth in his tent. "Make a brass image of the serpent in haste. We will display it in camp." Moses turned to leave.

"Moses."

Moses turned back.

"The last image I made was a golden bull. I learned the hard way that the Lord does not want an image that others will worship."

Moses nodded, a smile creasing his face. "You wonder about an image?"

Seth nodded.

"You do well to remember. God gives the Law as a boundary to protect us, not as a restriction to bind us. We obey even when we don't understand. The people will not worship the serpent.

They will look to the serpent and find healing. We do not worship it. We will remove it from the banner after the burning and the bites are forgotten."

Seth smiled. "Then I will obey." He stood to begin the mold and form the creature.

How could a serpent's image save the people?

Those who looked at the serpent were healed.

The Lord removed the snakes from the camp.

The King of Moab watched as this people who came from Egypt approached his land. He remembered the destruction of Egypt close to thirty-seven years ago. He'd heard more recently of Sihon, King of the Amorites. Sihon had refused to allow them to pass on the King's Highway through his land, but attempted to fight them. This people, who were nothing but slaves in Egypt, had conquered the Amorites, taking their lands and villages. They had marched onto Bashan and Og, lands beside Moab. They fought, leaving no remnant, and occupied their land.

Who were these people that came from Egypt and covered the earth? Would they destroy everything in their path?

Balak, King of Moab, called a counsel of all the kings in the surrounding areas. When they arrived, Balak cried, "This people from Egypt, who cover the surface of the land, are living within a stone's throw from me. They will destroy us, as the ox eats the grass of the field."

None could offer any counsel.

A servant bowed low before the king. "I have heard of a prophet, Balaam, son of Beor. Whomever he blesses is blessed and whomever he curses is cursed."

The king waited to hear no more. "Send for him. He must curse this people for they are too mighty for me to fight."

Balaam watched the cloud of dust with interest as it approached his dwelling. What kind of caravan would be coming to see him? Whoever it was must be wealthy. Their saddlebags bulged, and their horses were of the finest breeding. He watched them dismount, trying to look as if he entertained their kind of visitors every day.

But when they bowed low before him, he was filled with misgivings. What could they want from him?

"We bear gifts from our king." They opened their saddlebags and showed him their gold, silver, and gems.

Balaam reached into the bags, handling the precious stones. He tried to keep his voice calm and distant as he asked, "What is it you want?" He allowed the gold to slip through his fingers. Some of the purest gold he had ever seen.

They bowed low again, eager to please. "Most noble sir, please look on us with favor, for we need your wisdom. There's a nation from Egypt, as vast as the sands of the sea, camped near us. Our king begs you to come and curse these people, for otherwise we will all perish. We know that whoever you curse will be cursed. Whoever you bless will be blessed."

Balaam held a fistful of gold. He could live well with this. He wouldn't have to depend on blessing the poor who could give nothing. However, he didn't want to look too eager. He was silent for several minutes while the men waited, clearly in suspense but unsure what else to say to plead their cause.

"Spend the night. I'll ask the Lord and let you know in the morning."

He fell asleep, dreaming of the riches that could be his. But during the night, the Lord came to Balaam. "Who are these men?"

"Messengers from Balak, king of Moab. He wants me to curse the people who came out of Egypt."

"Do not go with them. You shall not curse this people, for they are Mine. They will be blessed."

In the morning, Balaam told the leaders, with what he hoped was an air of regal authority. "Return to your land. The Lord said not to go with you."

He was filled with a sense of power when the men bowed to him and departed. But as Balaam watched them leave, he could think only of how the gold felt as it trickled through his fingers. Could he obey the Lord, yet still have the gold?

Many days later, Balaam saw the group returning, only this time with even more governors and dignitaries. He remembered the gold that he had touched, but could not have. In fact, the memory had always been in his mind. He could not forget it.

He met them in his stable.

These men, dressed in fine garments, fell on their faces before Balaam on the soiled stable floor. "Please come. We returned to our king, and our king would not accept your answer. Our people are doomed, if you do not come. Curse this people for us. The king will honor you, giving you whatever you desire, only help us."

Balaam studied their saddle bags, bulging with treasures. He rubbed his hands together, already feeling the silver and gold.

But he remembered the Words of the Lord. What could he do about that? He couldn't curse or bless without the power of the Lord upon him. His hands dropped to his side. "Though Balak give me his entire palace full of silver and gold, I can't speak against the command of the Lord." Was there a way to have the gold anyway? "Stay the night. I will hear the Lord's Words."

During the night, the Lord again awakened Balaam. "Return with the men in the morning. Only speak My Words."

Balaam dreamed of all the promised riches. He would no longer be treated as a mere prophet. He would not have to depend upon others anymore. He could ask for anything he wanted. He could live like a king.

The cloud brought the people to the hill country around the Land that the Lord had given them. The priests had finished the evening sacrifices, so Moses left the Tabernacle to return home. He met Hobab, also returning to his tent. "Shalom."

Hobab nodded. "Be at peace."

"I must speak with you." Moses led him to his tent.

Zipporah had already arrived. She saw her brother and placed the vessel of water on the coals to make some tea.

Moses cleared his throat and looked at both of them. "The people that lived around the land of your father, Jethro, tell me about them."

Zipporah's face grew ashen. "Moses, the Midianites are wicked. We descended from Abraham by Ketaruh, as they did, but we remained loyal to the Lord."

Moses turned to Hobab.

Hobab nodded. "They live in cities, where they have forgotten the One Who provides for them. They worship *Chemosh*, god of destruction, sacrificing their own people, even children. Fathers offer their daughters in worship to the temple priests. Men use them in their worship. Most girls do not last long.

"The people abuse their slaves, raiding neighboring countries to replenish their supply. When they conquer a nation, they are ruthless in their destruction, ruining even the land used to grow food."

"What about the Moabites?" Moses asked.

Hobab shook his head. "The Moabites descend from Lot and his daughters. They have not changed from their conception. They are a people of lust, immorality, and incest." Lot's daughters, after their escape from Sodom's destruction, made Lot drunk, so they could lie with him to continue their descendants.

Moses swallowed and looked to the north. "We approach their lands. I must prepare the people."

Entering the hill country, Michael could almost see the Land. His excitement could be compared to the day Reut and he were wed. He, a former slave, and she, a daughter of a scribe of high means. The desert had helped to equalize all men.

Now, as he and Reut returned from the sacrifices of the Sabbath, Michael pointed to the hills. "Would you look at that?"

Reut squinted to see the slight difference between the sand's color and the brown of the vegetation that grew on its border. She followed his finger as he pointed farther up on the hills where the brown fuzzy hue changed to grey-green. She gazed further to see green. She sighed. "Green."

"Do you know what this means, Reut?" Michael grabbed her around the waist. He did not wait for her answer. "The Lord has brought us through the desert. Our horses will grow on the fatness of His Land."

Resting her head on his shoulder, Reut gazed with him. "No more sand in my clothes. No more grit in my manna. No more living in tents. I will be able to rise from a bed in the morning, instead of a pallet on the ground. I will..."

"We will be home." Michael said with finality. "Free and home." He breathed deeply. "Can you smell it?"

Reut sniffed several times. "You can smell something besides sand?"

Michael laughed and hugged her. "I smell freedom."

"But you're already free."

"We had freedom from Egypt and the bondage of its gods, but

we were under the Lord's schedule. We rose, gathered manna, hauled water, ate, and moved on. We lived between two worlds. Released from one but waiting for the other. Know what I mean?"

Reut nodded. "Remember how you wished not to marry, because you didn't want to leave me without a husband?"

Michael nodded, laughing. "Think of the joy we would have missed." Their four girls roamed the desert on their horses, in spite of Reut's fears, and probably because of Michael's love for the wild.

"Life wouldn't be so...full." Reut stroked his beard. "I miss Abba."

Michael nodded. "He wished that all would read God's Law. He worked hard to make it happen. He didn't want them just to know it in their heads, he wanted them to feel it in their hearts." He squeezed her tighter.

He had started from their wedding day to tell her daily, "You are mine and the Lord's. No one can take you from our hands."

Over time, her nightmares had stopped, her memories had faded, but Michael could not convince her that Maessai was no longer to be feared.

Amos rubbed his belly, leaning on the cushion. "That was good."

Pelia gathered the dishes and stacked them by the tent's doorway. "It's nice to have something different to eat."

She relaxed by his side, looking at the distant hills. "This country is green. The sand is finally washed from my clothes and hair. I changed my bath water four times!"

Amos laughed. "Esmail's dream of twin lambs and fat flocks are in sight."

Pelia smiled. "Will we always call them Esmail's sheep, even though he no longer watches them?"

"It seems wrong to call them anyone else's, even though he's gone. Our boys do well with sheep, but none were as protective as Esmail." Amos looked over the hillsides. "If these lands are a taste of the Promised Land, it was worth all the sand in our eyes."

Pelia leaned against him. "I cannot wait to have a stone house."

Amos teased, "You don't appreciate the tent that I provide?"

"Your honorable trade has kept two of our sons busy supplying shelters for our people in this wilderness."

"They have done well."

Pelia watched Amos's face, "What will happen to the people of this land? Won't some seek revenge?"

Amos squeezed her leg. "We asked to pass through in peace on their highway. We were only asking what merchants and others request. Instead, they came for battle. The Lord blessed us. We move toward our Land."

The sun was setting; the evening coolness was settling over the land. Seth stood with Tamara looking over the water at the mountains they would soon enter.

Tamara shivered.

Seth put his arm around her. "Cold?"

Tamara shook her head. "Not cold, just remembering the waters of MarMara. My heart still gets tight, as if I can't breathe."

"And how you spit in my face when I rescued you?"

Tamara laughed. "I don't like crowds around water."

Seth nodded. "We'll soon have our very own well."

Tamara leaned against his shoulder. "Our boys make beautiful things, just like your abba."

"I miss him."

Tamara nodded. "He seemed to feel the heartbeat of God. Our girls loved to hear him pray."

Seth studied Tamara's face as the light from the sun was fading. "They have that zest for life like their ima."

Tamara shook her head. "Those three are too much like me. How did my ima stand all my chatter?"

Seth laughed. They walked hand in hand back to their tent. What would the new Land bring?

Balaam rode his donkey to King Balak's palace. The king was afraid. Fear made a man willing to pay a lot in hopes of relief. Balaam had dozed as he rode, contemplating the riches that he would request from the king. It would not do to ask too little. Instead of depending upon meager gifts from poor widows, he could live in comfort for the rest of his life.

His dreams were interrupted when his donkey stopped in the middle of the path.

Two servants behind him reined in their donkeys with loud exclamations, almost trampling him. One of their donkeys nipped his.

But his little donkey remained still, quivering.

Balaam never beat his donkey. But after several kicks to her side without obedience, he did.

Her haunches trembled and her muscles twitched, but she did not move.

Again he beat her.

The donkey stepped back, running into the donkey behind her. When she could not back up any further, she bolted off the path into a field.

The servants snickered behind Balaam.

Balaam could feel his face flush as he led the donkey back to the trail. He lifted his head. He would not be scorned by mere servants.

They continued.

Balaam thought of the riches that he would soon possess. No one would dare to scorn him them. Besides he would own the finest horse. He led his donkey through a valley. Cliffs rose on both sides of the trail.

Suddenly the donkey stopped again. She quivered, her sides heaving, but refused to move.

Balaam kicked and prodded. Finally, he struck her.

She backed into those behind him.

Their horses nipped her flanks, attempting to push her forward. Instead, she ran into the wall.

Balaam lashed at her in anger.

The servants of Balak taunted, "Ride our horses. Your beast grows weary."

Balaam bit back a nasty reply. "No, she has been with me since I learned to ride, and she will carry me now."

They passed through the tunnel of cliffs and approached the sunshine and open pastures.

Again the donkey stopped.

Balaam did not hesitate to beat her with a stick.

She lay down in the road.

The laughter behind him could no longer be hidden behind good manners.

Balaam beat her again and again. No stubborn donkey would disgrace him before high officials and dignitaries. He threw off his cloak and pushed up the sleeves of his tunic. He swung his stick over and over. He had never been so humiliated. Why did the stupid beast not obey? He could no longer hear the laughter, but concentrated on moving his stubborn beast.

The donkey's haunches quivered and flinched, but she would not move.

A voice broke through his fury. "What have I done to you that you have beaten me three times?"

He paused, holding the stick in mid-air. Who had spoken? He glanced behind him, only to hear the laughter again. He looked down at the donkey. Could she have spoken? He shook his head.

But the question came again, "What have I done to you that you have struck me three times?"

He wiped his brow and took a sip from his waterskin. He lowered his head and whispered close to the donkey's head. "You mock me. They laugh at my horsemanship. If I had a sword, I'd kill you."

"Have I ever done this to you before?"

He looked behind him again. The men had not heard the voice. He shook his head. It was his donkey speaking. He lowered his voice. "No."

"Then look for a reason." With that the donkey shut her mouth.

A bright light on the path before him drew his attention.

The angel of the Lord stood, holding a sword.

Balaam fell to his knees, bowing to the ground.

The angel towered over him. "Why do you beat your donkey? Your donkey hindered me from killing you these three times. If she had not turned aside, you would be dead."

Balaam looked at the donkey, then back at the sword. "I've sinned. I didn't see that you stood in the way. If the journey displeases you, I'll turn back."

"Go. But be sure to speak only what I tell you."

Relieved that his life was spared, but even more that he still had a chance at the money, Balaam continued. He felt humiliated, especially since the other men had not seen the angel. What would the king's messengers think of him now? Whatever they thought, they kept their silence, obeying their king's request to bring him to deliver their nation from this people at their doorstep. He briefly thought about this people, known only by their God. Obviously, He protected them even when they didn't know they needed it.

But Balaam thought most about the treasures in his dreams. Just as he had reached for them, they had vanished before his eyes. Yet his desire for them, only made him thirst for them more.

King Balak received word that Balaam was coming. He met him outside the city. "Didn't I request your presence? Won't I give you anything that you want? Why must I send two dispatches for your help?"

"I'm here now, aren't I?" Balaam responded. "But I must speak only the Lord's Words."

Balak took him up to a high mountain where they worshipped *Baal*. From there they could see out across the countryside for many days' journey.

Balaam regarded the campsite of this people from Egypt. He understood Balak's fear now. He spoke in low tones, as if he were afraid of inciting this army to fight, "They are like the sand of the desert, reaching beyond my sight."

Balak's voice shook, "We must sacrifice."

After Balak sacrificed to Baal, Balaam commanded his servants. "Build seven altars for me. Prepare seven bulls and seven rams." Balaam offered a bull and a ram on each altar.

He walked away from the altars to hear the Lord's Words.

God commanded Balaam. "Return to Balak. Speak My Words."

Balaam went back to Balak, moved by a power outside of himself. Out of his mouth words flowed, and he knew they were of God. "This people is a special people. The favor of God rests upon them. They will be separate from all nations. They are as vast as the dust of the desert."

Balak tore the cloak off his body. He stood nose to nose with Balaam. "What have you done? I bring you to curse these people and you bless them?"

Balaam stepped back. "I speak the Lord's Words."

Balak wiped his forehead and looked at the high officials and the dignitaries who stood with them. "Come with me to another place. You will see a smaller portion of their hosts. Then maybe you won't be so intimidated and will curse them for me there."

Balaam mounted his donkey and followed the king. Again they built seven altars and offered a bull and a ram on each altar. "Stand here," Balaam commanded Balak. "I will meet with the Lord over there."

When he returned from hearing the Lord, the leaders asked. "What has the Lord said?"

Balaam began. "God is not a man that He should change what He says. What He says, He will do. I am commanded to bless. When He has blessed, can man revoke it?

"The Lord God is Israel's God. He delivered them from Egypt. His Name is known throughout the world for His wonders. The people are called by His name. They rise like a lioness to devour her prey."

Balak grabbed Balaam by the front of his cloak. "Did I not tell you to curse these people? What have you done?"

Balaam took the kings' hands off his cloak and stepped away from him. "And didn't I tell you, that I must speak what the Lord tells me?"

"Please, I beg of you. Come to another place. Perhaps this place would be agreeable with your God to curse these people for me."

So they went to another mountain. They performed the same sacrifice with seven oxen and seven rams. Balaam had no need to request the Lord's desire. Balaam saw Israel, camping tribe by tribe. The Spirit of the Lord came upon him. "Israel's dwellings stretch beyond what eye can see, like a garden beside a river, like cedars beside the waters. Water will flow and his seed will grow. His king will rise beyond those around him and his kingdom shall be exalted. His horns will be like the wild ox, destroying his enemies. Blessed is everyone who blesses you. Cursed is everyone who curses you."

Balak shook. He clenched his hands restraining himself from grabbing Balaam again. "I have called you to curse my enemies, but you have blessed them three times. I could honor you greatly, but this Lord has prevented it."

Balaam did not falter. "Didn't I tell you, O King of Moab, that though you gave me a house of silver and gold, I could not change the blessing of the Lord on His people?" Balaam directed the king to his horse. He looked longingly at the saddlebags filled with gold, meant for his payment. "I must obey the Lord's Words, but perhaps I could advise you about what you can do to this people."

Balak mounted his horse. "Come with me and share your plans. I fear the blessings you've already given. I fear this people who cover my lands. I fear my future. Tell me what I can do against this people and their God."

The king of Moab took Balaam to his palace. He feasted with the elders of Moab and Midian. He ate the choice meats of oxen and sheep, meat sacrificed to the gods of Baal on the altars where he had blessed Israel. The slow-cooked meat fell off the bone and melted in his mouth.

He drank the wine that flowed from a good harvest.

He tasted of the fresh fruit from their orchards.

He saw the riches of this powerful king. The man had much to lose if Israel were not destroyed.

How could he destroy a people that the Lord owned?

When the wine had run full and his body was satiated, his eyes roamed the room for the entertainment to come.

King Balak had his choice of women from the slave traders that scoured the countryside. The wine, combined with the women's entertainment, let Balaam derive a plan for Israel that would not go wrong.

Just as he must obey the Lord to be blessed of Him, so it was for this nation the Lord owned. But if he could make them disobey their Lord, to run from their Protector, they would be easily destroyed.

What would lure a man away from his God? He knew the answer. He rubbed his hands in anticipation of the gold that he would be his. He had security for life. Balaam laughed out loud.

But Balaam didn't realize that his plan would sever him from the Lord's protection as well.

CHAPTER 26

The Moabite husbands agreed to the king's decree that all must give their wives to protect their lands. They sent their women to stand before the king. These women were perfect for the plan Balaam had devised. They did not have the hard look of the prostitutes from the temples. They looked submissive, willing to obey their husbands and procure safety for them all.

The Moabite husbands gave their wives to protect their lands.

Balaam sat beside the king as the women filed before them. He smiled and nodded at King Balak. This plan would work.

Balak leaned over his throne. "Several years ago, a man provided slaves, Israelite girls, for some of my top officials. He will escort these women to the enemy camp. And he will be sure to return with more Hebrew slaves for us." Balak stood, ending the conversation.

Balaam hesitated. More people involved in the planning meant sharing the spoils.

They walked to the palace stairs to watch the caravan leave for the Israelite camp.

The army escorted the caravan, containing meat, wine, women, and other carefully planned items for the Israelite's demise.

Balak turned to Balaam. "Your plan gives me hope."

Balaam clenched his hand into a fist. He could feel the gold. His plan would work. He smiled and nodded.

As the caravan traveled, the army settled into a relaxed march. Their leader did not wear the armor of a soldier, although he wore his dagger at his side. He rode his horse beside his sergeant. He studied the women as they settled for the ride. "I've never carried such cargo for war before."

The women's nervous, high-pitched laughter rose above their conversation.

The sergeant laughed. "They're as restless as cattle moving toward slaughter."

The general took another glance at one of the wagons. "Let's hope not to slaughter. If this plan doesn't work, we'll all be slaughtered."

The sergeant rode on to check the front.

The general drew his horse up beside the wagon that caught his eye.

While other women sat restless, Cozbi, the daughter of Zur, stood posed and confident. Her dress fit her well; the gathered waist revealed her form.

The general looked her over.

She met his gaze, looking directly into his eyes.

He nodded. "How does your father fare?"

Cozbi smiled. "He leads our people well." She flipped her hair behind her shoulders and tilted her head toward the general. "Just as you lead this army towards a successful mission."

"Your presence will ensure its success."

Cozbi laughed. "I know." She enjoyed catching him off-guard. "I will feast with their leader for the safety of our own."

The general eyed her as if he already owned her. "Then we cannot help but be safe."

She turned from him, as if dismissing him.

The general continued on his mount. With women like Cozbi, no man could resist this plan.

The morning started like all others. Reut met Tamara to gather manna.

Tamara paused to look over the ground. "Do you ever tire of seeing that? Manna spread over the sand, like diamonds to be gathered."

Reut grunted. "You make any job sound like a celebration."

"What's more important than food to a hungry man? What more could we need than what the Lord has prepared for us?"

Reut shook her head, but kept gathering manna. There was one thing she needed that she thought of often. But would God give it?

After serving Michael the first meal of the day, Reut worried as she did every day, about the Lord's promise to kill all men twenty and over before they entered their Land. They were getting close to that Land. She did not hear when Michael spoke.

Michael rose to leave. "I won't be doing army drills today; I plan to pray with Seth, and Phinehas, seeking God's direction for this Land and for our families."

Reut nodded, without listening.

Michael bent to kiss her. "It's hard to leave you every morning." He squeezed her, waiting until she looked at him. "Remember, you are mine and the Lord's."

She smiled. He had started telling her those words when they were first married. Every day he reminded her, without fail. At first it was to convince her, then to reassure her, but now it was a statement of truth.

He kissed her again and turned to go. At the tent's door, he turned back. "I love you without fail."

"And I love you," Reut answered as she watched him walk away.

Zimri, son of Salu, leader among the Simeonites, led the army drills. When he noticed a dust cloud approaching, he glanced toward the tent of meeting, where Moses and Joshua were. He squared his shoulders and watched the caravan arrive. Joshua had delegated him to prepare the men. He could handle a battle if that was what was demanded.

Zimri, with several leaders, advanced toward the caravan. "I don't see an army. What is it?"

Zimri's sergeant squinted. "Wagons full of women."

A man approached from the wagons, bowing. "Your people have come far. We bring meat and wine to welcome you."

Zimri had prepared for war, not feasting. The request seemed acceptable. The men needed a break. He wiped his lips with the back of his hand. When was the last time he had drunk wine? Shouldn't we be hospitable?

Movement behind the man caught Zimri's attention. A woman of unsurpassed beauty sauntered toward him.

When his gaze met hers, she winked and smiled.

What boldness! What beauty! Zimri sheathed his sword and welcomed them into the camp.

If he had known what lay ahead, perhaps he would have sharpened his sword and renewed his mind on the Law of his God. But he did not know, nor did he ask.

He allowed the feasting to begin. The meat melted in his mouth. He savored the taste. He sipped their gift of wine. It slipped down his throat in ecstasy. When he finished, the Midianite women, who had served them, entertained them. Cozbi hovered around him, encouraging him to drink more. Her singing, laughter, and movements enticed him, where his thoughts had no right to be.

Their welcome was complete. The partying had lasted all night. But the damage had only begun.

Balaam knew that the Lord still held a portion of their hearts, in spite of their night's activities. He had arranged the worship of Baal to be brought with the caravan. Baal worship did not have family-friendly rituals. Worshipers must emulate the sacred prostitution of their gods and goddesses to complete their worship. The Midianite women would assist the Israelite men in this process.

The women gave themselves for the safety of their country. They worshiped eagerly. After all, their husbands had blessed their sacrifice, and their king commanded their obedience. Now they danced, disrobed, and worshiped the Baal they depended upon to save them from this people who numbered like the sand.

They drew the Israelite men into their worship, casting their wiles like a net around them, entangling them like so many flies in a spider's web.

Moses had spent the day at the Tabernacle, recording the judgments, rereading the Law, studying the laws that the Lord wanted for His people. The Law would protect them from wrong. The people would need boundaries when they entered the land.

His tent was on the outskirts of the campsite, close to the Tabernacle. He returned home.

Zipporah helped Moses remove his cloak. "Can you not rest?"

Moses settled by the fire to eat. "I sense an urgency to make sure the Law is complete, and the history is written for the Lord's people." Moses listened. "The people are loud tonight."

Zipporah placed a bowl of warmed stew before him on the pallet. "They have been loud for several days. I have kept to myself."

"The stew is good." Moses ate, concentrating on the morsels before him. After eating, he fell asleep.

Zipporah covered him with a sheepskin and took off his sandals. The noise increased, but Moses slept through the night. In the morning, he arose early and left for the Tabernacle, before the men resumed their feasting.

Many wives heard the feasting, waiting for their husbands to return to their tents. Many men did not come. If they did, they brought a foreign woman. Had they not prayed for fertility? And hadn't Baal promised to grant it to them?

Tamara and Reut waited together for their husbands. As Reut heard the laughter and music, doubts took hold of her mind and distrust grabbed her heart. "I can't wait any longer. I must look for Michael."

Tamara asked, "Reut, should you leave? You are safe here."

"Am I safe with my mind asking me questions that my heart cannot answer?"

"Trust Michael, until you know more."

Reut shook her head. "I feel a heaviness that I can't explain."

Tamara grabbed her arm. "Sometimes, it is not for you to know the reasons. Leave it be."

Reut pulled her arm away. "I must know."

Reut stalked away. She slowed as she approached the dancing. Torches provided ample light to see the women. Could this even compare to the sin during the feast of the golden bull? She peered into darkened tents. What she saw killed any thought of good. If her husband stayed in this evil environment, he could not be...could he love her and do this?

She turned her head, blushing for them. When she did, she caught sight of a man she thought was dead, a man that her thoughts could not let go, who had abducted her almost thirty-eight years ago. She stared, unbelief, terror, and foreboding controlling her heart.

He grabbed her waist.

She tensed, unable to move.

He whispered in her ear, "You came to find me, didn't you? Your husband is busy with another. Now you can be mine as you should have been."

His words struck her heart like a dagger. She was too numb to struggle or scream. Could she believe this man? Where was Michael?

Maessai led her to the outskirts of camp where the Moabite army waited.

Other Israelite women and girls huddled together, guarded by the wagons.

Maessai bound and gagged Reut.

She was too numb to struggle.

The man who had tormented her dreams for years, had stolen her again.

She was now his. But this time, she did not care. She thought about Michael and what he had done to her. She wished to die.

Moses rose in the morning, with a heaviness upon his spirit. He did not meet the Lord on the mountainside as was his custom. Instead he walked through camp. The people had been louder the last few days when he had gone from the tent of meeting to his own house. He hadn't thought anything about it until now. What he saw caused his anger to grow. Wine vessels lay scattered around campsites. Where had they come from? Cloaks and garments lay where they had been shed along pathways. Evidence of rich food, lingering smells. What had happened in camp?

He approached the center of camp. What he saw made him stop and stare. A larger-than-life statue of Baal had been erected, its arms extended to welcome the sacrifices offered. A hole in its belly allowed the human sacrifices placed in his arms to roll into the flames. Moses's insides tightened. He turned quickly from the sight, hoping the picture of children offered to this god would also leave his thoughts. How could the people have turned from God so quickly?

The Lord spoke to him. "Execute all the leaders of the people."

Moses sounded the trumpet, calling the judges. "Slay the men who worshiped Baal."

The Midianite women fled to their wagons. They had done what they came to do. They would return now to their own land.

And with them Reut.

A plague broke out, bringing death to the men.

Phinehas unsheathed his sword, and obeyed Moses's command. He searched for Zimri, the leader who had allowed this feasting. Finding him, Phinehas stabbed him and Cozbi through with one thrust, then covered their nakedness.

As soon as this was done, the Lord stopped the plague.

Twenty-four thousand men were dead.

No curse of Balaam could have wreaked the destruction brought on by the Midianite women in the midst of Israel's camp.

Michael returned home in the morning.

Reut was gone.

He ran to Tamara's tent. "Where's Reut?"

Tamara crossed her arms and shook her head. "Where's Seth?"

Michael's forehead creased, "Seth went to speak to Moses."

Tamara pursed her lips. "Where was he?"

Michael shook his head, trying to be calm. "Seth, Phinehas, and I spent the last days and nights asking the Lord for wisdom as we approach the Promised Land. But where is Reut?"

Tamara uncrossed her arms. "She went to find you."

"When?"

"The first day of feasting, in the midst of the dancing, the noise...."

Michael's sense of concern heightened. "Where is she?"

CHAPTER 27

The camp was still mourning the loss of its men and its innocence, when Moses gathered the people, and prepared the army to retaliate.

Michael listened as Moses told the people the Lord's Words. "Take vengeance on the Midianites for their deception." Michael clenched his hands into tight fists. He would take vengeance. Vengeance was commanded by the Lord, and Michael would willingly obey Him. Moses continued. "Remember what these people have done to you and your families. Remember the depravity that the worship of Baal caused in your midst. Remember the thousands who died because of your sin.

"Spare no man.

"The Lord will give you the victory."

Michael fought with a passion that consumed him. Seth, beside him, cautioned him. "Slow down and think, or you'll be killed."

Seth entered another Midianite house to clear it before burning it.

Michael followed Seth. "The hardest part is not knowing where Reut is. Or if she is even alive."

Seth motioned with his sword to a dark corner. "She lives."

Reut sat, bound and gagged, her eyes large against her pale face.

Michael ran to her, untying her hands and feet, and removing the gag from her bruised and swollen mouth. "You are not hurt?"

She murmured, "He's alive."

"Who's alive?"

Her voice broke. "Maessai. He said you were with another."

Michael looked at her. "With another? Reut, what are you talking about?"

Reut no longer looked into Michael's eyes. "The music, the dancing, the women. I looked for you. He told me you were with another."

He spoke through the lump in his throat. "And you believed him?"

"I didn't know where you were."

Michael swallowed, regaining his control. "You couldn't trust me?"

Reut's eyes looked beyond him. She gasped and turned ashen. Michael turned around.

Maessai had stepped into the room, stabbing Seth in the back. Seth fell.

Maessai withdrew his sword, looking toward the corner.

Michael stepped away from Reut, drawing his sword.

Maessai looked from Reut to Michael. "I have come for my own."

Michael wiped his sweaty palm on his tunic before adjusting his sword. "You own her not. The Lord does, and He gave her to me."

The room was small with a table and bench in the center. Maessai shoved them toward Michael. The bench fell, clattering on the stone floor. The table scraped the floor, echoing in the bare room.

They approached each other with drawn swords.

Michael swallowed. How could she doubt him?

Maessai lunged.

Michael reflected it, stepping back.

Maessai advanced, pushing Michael against the overturned bench.

Michael's feet were off balance. He raised his arm.

Maessai struck down, slicing his arm.

Michael circled to avoid the bench. He held his sword at waist level and stabbed. He drew blood.

Maessai's eyes widened. "You'll pay for that."

Michael timed his next thrust. "Not any more than you for your lies."

Maessai laughed, his breathing becoming labored as they both circled for a better angle.

"Lies?" Maessai backed Michael against the wall.

Michael slipped.

Maessai raised his sword to crush Michael.

Michael lifted his in time to deflect it.

Pushing Maessai away from the wall with his sword, he repositioned.

The clank of swords echoed against the walls.

Michael had not slept since Reut's abduction, searching first the Israelite campsite, then every Midianite house. He breathed deeply to catch his breath.

Maessai smiled. He looked fresh.

His smile incited Michael to renew his strength. This man had tormented Reut's dreams for years.

He pushed Maessai backward toward the door.

Maessai tripped over Seth's body and fell.

Michael thrust his sword into Maessai.

Maessai's face showed surprise as the blood flowed out of him. "She was mine. I paid for her."

He looked at the ceiling. His eyes looked blank.

Breathing heavily, Michael stood over Maessai, awaiting his death. After wiping his sword on Maessai's cloak, he sheathed it. Still he watched.

Reut spoke, standing right behind him. "It is over."

Michael looked at Reut then back at Maessai. Her trust could be torn away with one simple question, one doubt awakened by an enemy. "Is it?"

She stood without moving. Her eyes widened, her pale face pleading.

He faced her. He couldn't ignore her helplessness. He extended his arms.

She stepped into them and sobbed.

Michael hugged her.

Black smoke billowed around them before they moved.

Michael thought of his Lord. How His heart must break over their lack of trust. The people had again wounded His heart.

Michael swallowed the lump in his throat. His heart didn't feel so good, either.

Joshua and the army had killed King Balak and his governors. They had killed Balaam, son of Beor. They had burned the city. Now they were returning to their people.

From outside the camp, Moses and Eleazar watched the soldiers approach. Moses squinted, asking, "Who are they bringing with them, Eleazar?"

"They return with cattle, flocks, goods...and women and children captives."

Moses paced. "Do they wish for the Lord's judgment to fall on them again? Why are they bringing the woman? Aren't they the ones who caused the sons of Israel to sin?"

Moses walked out to the army. "Don't you remember their deception? Kill every woman who has known a man." Only married women wore a veil.

Joshua moved to enforce his command. The soldiers slew the women.

Joshua reported to Moses.

Moses looked at the children. He sighed. In the practice of war, no one was spared. If boys were kept, they would starve. Their economy could not support feeding extra. Those who escaped to the wilderness would die of exposure. Killing was the most humane. Moses commanded their death.

Moses turned from the girls, sighing. The girls would be slaves. They could not support the girls easily.

Eleazar looked at him. "You show great mercy."

Moses shook his head, then turned to Joshua. "Stay outside the camp for purification. Burn the spoils. What cannot be purified with fire, wash in water. Afterward, you may enter the camp."

When the purification of the booty was complete, they would divide it among the soldiers and the congregation. Some would be offered to the Lord.

Instead of rejoicing, their victory came at great cost.

The Lord was a jealous God and did not want another in His place. He would not let them forget. He was separating the people unto Himself. They would not be permitted to forget it.

Michael's arm became infected. His body grew hot.

Reut stayed by his side, although he did not waken. Where had he been during those days of feasting?

Tamara placed food beside Reut. "Reut, you must eat."

Reut shook her head. "What happened on those days?"

Tamara put her hand on Reut's arm. "It's not what you think, Reut. Trust your husband after all these years. He was praying with Seth for direction for their families."

Reut covered her face and wept.

Tamara hugged her before leaving the room.

Michael thrashed off the covers, yelling, "The Lord owns her!" He thrust as if he held his sword, cutting through the air. His arm fell still again. He cried in despair, "How can I make her know my faithfulness?" He had opened his wound again. He lost much blood.

Reut cringed, taking his hand. Her chin quivered. "Please, my love, come back to me. I know you're faithful."

After many days, the heat left him. He opened his eyes and looked at her.

Reut moved closer, pushing the hair from his face.

He licked his lips and reached for her hand. "You are the Lord's."

Reut gave him a sip of water.

He swallowed. "I still love you." He closed his eyes for the last time.

Moses looked over the people from the side of the mountain. The people had reached the border of their Land. They had conquered the countries all around their border. As Moses looked over the outskirts of their campsite, he sighed. He would no longer see the women gathering the manna. The Lord had stopped giving the manna. The Land would provide for them. The Land promised fruit and green pastures in plenty. It flowed with water, not stagnate from standing in pools, but flowing. Such lands tempted them to linger here and enjoy a life of ease, instead of continuing to the Land promised to them by the Lord. Moses sighed again. It would be harder to see Who provided for them and to stay focused on the Lord.

The Land awakened desires never yet satisfied in this younger generation's lifetime. Their fathers had tried to fulfill their wants apart from God with the golden bull, but only while Moses was gone. Their fathers had suffered the consequences. But this was a younger generation, wiser than their parents. Or so, they thought. Yet they had not felt the yoke of Pharaoh's bondage. Their wants had been squelched in the desert by the Lord's structure and regulations. But here in the land with other cultures, they could experience freedom, opportunity, life. Moses shook his head. He hoped they were ready, but feared for the lessons they would yet have to learn.

Eleazar had numbered the people. They were like the stars in the sky.

A trumpet called them to worship.

Moses made his way down the mountainside to the Tabernacle for the morning sacrifices.

When the sacrifices were finished, Moses stood before them. "Drive out the people of Canaan. Destroy their gods and their high places. If you do not, they will prick your eyes out and stab your sides."

Moses gave the scrolls of the Law to Eleazar. "Read the Law to the people.

"Impress His Words on your heart.

"Let them penetrate your soul.

"Teach them to your children.

"Love and fear the Lord.

"Cling to Him.

"He is your God.

"Be strong.

"Possess the Land."

Then Moses called Joshua to his side. He laid his hands on Joshua's shoulders, looking him in the eye. "Be strong. The Lord will be with you. You will lead the Lord's people to their Land. You represent the Lord to this people."

Moses stepped away from the people and entered the Tabernacle one final time. Joshua entered with him. The Lord appeared as a cloud. "When you are satisfied and prosperous in the Land, the people will break My covenant. When troubles come upon them, these words will not be forgotten."

The Lord assigned boundaries for every tribe.

As Moses returned to his tent, Gad, Reuben, and Manasseh's tribal leaders approached him. "There's so much pasture here suited for livestock. If we have found favor in your sight, allow us to possess this land."

Moses leaned on his staff. "Shall your brothers fight while you rest? Remember when your brothers discouraged the people not to enter the Land? They died, never entering. Now you encourage the next generation not to enter?"

"Allow us to build sheepfolds and fortified cities; then we will enter, armed before our brothers. We won't return home until Israel has possessed his inheritance."

Moses nodded. Just as he thought, they would have trouble entering the Land after seeing this rich land before them. "If you fight the Lord's enemies on the other side of Jordan, then you shall return to this land as your possession. If you don't, you will have sinned. Do what you have promised."

The sun was setting for another day. The evening lights would soon filter through their tent flap. Hannah pushed back the vessels from their meal as Phinehas stretched out on the cushions.

Hannah rubbed his back.

Phinehas made himself more comfortable. "I started on this journey because I wanted you."

"Yes?"

Phinehas said, "That's the only reason I left Egypt."

Hannah paused in her rubbing. "Did you have anything to stay for?"

"Well, no. But I wanted you. Remember when I raced to you during the crossing of the Reed Sea to make sure you were not afraid?"

Hannah laughed. "I watched, wondering why you drove your horses so fast."

Phinehas defended himself. "I was concerned about you."

Hannah smiled. "Of course."

Phinehas turned over on his back. He brushed her hair from her ear. "Your curls drew me."

"Just my curls?"

"Just like the time I carried you when you pretended to trip, getting water."

Hannah huffed. "I wasn't pretending. I couldn't walk for weeks."

He twirled her hair around his finger. "Your curls were around your face again then."

"Did you think that I pretended to fall? Your memory is faulty."

"Then when I fought Maessai. Do you make your curls fall around your face intentionally, so I can see them?"

"Of course, that's the first thing I think of when someone is trying to steal me."

Phinehas nodded. "I knew it. It was also you who asked to marry me."

Hannah huffed again. "You asked why I was upset."

Phinehas sighed, wrapping her hair around another finger. "I guess that I would have married you anyway."

"You guess!"

Phinehas laughed. "Your father might have made me. He did want grandchildren."

Hannah laughed. "Yes, and he got them."

Phinehas unwrapped her hair and held the curls in his palm. He focused on her face. "You brought me to know the Lord."

Hannah's eyes pooled with tears as the subject turned serious. "You have defended the Lord's justice time and time again...with the golden bull, at Korah's rebellion, the plague with the snakes, when the Midianites came to our campsite...

"Other men fight in battles against strangers. You fight against wrong among your own people. That takes great courage."

Phinehas sighed. "God gives strength."

Hannah swallowed the lump in her throat. "What will the passing be like when we meet God? Abba left in his sleep."

Phinehas hugged her to his side. "His ending was peaceful."

She snuggled closer to him. "But he wasn't alone. He really knew God."

Phinehas stared at the roof of the tent. "God will lead us by the hand."

Hannah wiped at the tears spilling down her cheeks. "Are you afraid?"

"He is right there. No courage is needed."

The silence took over their thoughts.

A trumpet sounded.

Hannah sighed. "It's time for the evening sacrifices." Her tears were coming fast now. She could hardly speak. "So many of our friends have died. They won't enter the Land. I feel so alone."

Phinehas squeezed her. It was not his turn to serve tonight in the Tabernacle. "You're not alone, my angel of mercy. He's with you. He takes away all fear."

Hannah grabbed his hand. They didn't make it to the evening sacrifices. She wept for the many who would not enter the Land.

Phinehas was a Levite, not numbered with the men who must die. The Lord had given Phinehas the courage to stand for truth in a nation learning to know His Name. Together, Hannah and Phinehas must stand for Him in the new Land that He had promised.

After the evening sacrifices, Moses returned to his tent. He removed his cloak and hung it on a peg by the door. He glanced at Zipporah who lay weakly upon cushions. He knelt beside her.

Zipporah spoke without opening her eyes. "What's the matter?"

Moses took hold of her hand. "You can tell without opening your eyes?"

Zipporah tried to smile. "I can feel your unspoken sigh."

Moses wiped her hair from her forehead. "I have failed."

"Because you aren't leading the people into the Land?"

Moses nodded.

"You can't hold their hands forever. God knows what to do."

Moses half-heartedly smiled. He squeezed her hand. "Yes, He does."

"You must let go."

Moses nodded.

"And you're not a failure. One wrong, and you aren't allowed to enter the Land." Zipporah shook her head. "You were protecting me. I don't understand the holiness of God. These people have stumbled their entire way, yet they will go in..."

"I'm the leader. He holds me at a higher level."

Zipporah shook her head. "I'm ready to go on."

Moses squeezed her again. "Yes, I am, too."

Moses was one hundred and twenty years old. He fell on his face before the Lord. "You have shown me Your greatness. Who can perform the mighty acts that You do? Please, let me enter and see this good country."

The Lord responded, "Silence. Speak no more of this matter to Me. Go to the top of Pisgah. Look to the north, south, east and west. I will let you see it all. But you will not cross Jordan."

Moses entered his tent.

Zipporah was waiting. "It is time?"

Moses took her face in his hands. "I must go to the mountain of Abarim, Mount Nebo. The Lord will show me the Land He has promised."

Zipporah nodded. "As it should be. Long ago, my ima told me that you were great, that your faith was in the Most High God. You've led the people from Egypt, through the wilderness, to their Land. You've shown the mighty power and great terror of the God you serve. You've shown me this God Who cares for His people. He is worthy, providing daily for His people. I will meet you in the land of your God."

He hugged her until he could feel her breath no more. Her days had been long. Her life a struggle. "My sweet Desert Flower, you'll no more be without a people. You'll be home at last." Moses laid her on their pallet, covering her face with a sheet.

The Lord was gracious. He would not suffer her to continue on this side without Moses's presence.

Moses hiked Mount Nebo to the top of Pisgah. He saw the Land of Promise, its green pastures, its land rich from water flowing, its orchards heavy with fruit. He feasted his eyes on what could have been. His eyes glistened with tears and he swallowed the lump in his throat. His mission was finished.

He had brought the people out of Egypt. That had been a triumphal departure. The people had recognized their God Who delivered them. They had seen God's power.

Moses turned around to look over the people. God had prepared them to enter their own Land. Moses sighed. In that time of travel and waiting, God had provided for them. Those miracles were not any less spectacular than the plagues sent on Egypt. Yet they also showed the steadfastness of His presence, revealing His character; the kind of character He wanted them to have.

Now God would lead the next generation into the Land He had promised. What would that story reveal about God?

Would Moses rather have the great, powerful climax of deliverance or the steady faithfulness of the routine? He laughed.

God had prepared him for both. He had seen God's glory. He had known God face to face. His God was faithful, steadfast, a rock that he could lean on, a shelter where he could hide. God was enough.

Moses wiped his eyes with his cloak and nodded. Yes, God was enough.

Moses would not return from the mountain.

The Lord buried Moses's body, taking His faithful servant home.

Now at last, the Lord's name was not only known throughout the world, but His people were being called by His name.

THANK YOU

If you have enjoyed *I Have Called You by Name,* please help me spread the word. Post a review (how you liked it and why).

What is a reviewer?

Someone who reads my book and tells others what they thought of it.

What must you do?

1. Read the book.
2. Write four sentences about the book.

    a. The What sentence: summarizes the book.

    b. The Why sentence: tells what the book did for you, why others should read it, why you chose to read it. Example: you wanted to visualize the journey of the Israelites.

    c. The How sentence: tells how well you liked the book.

3. Post your review here:

    www.amazon.com

    www.goodreads.com

    www.sonyacontreras.com

Please allow me to use your review for marketing. Include a note in your message giving me permission.

Thank you.

SUMMARY REMARKS

I desire to weave the biblical account with archaeological and historical records to tell the story of the Hebrew journey through the desert.

Moses and Aaron maintained vitality until their death in their hundreds. Moses's children were young, as seen by Zipporah circumcising them. They aged differently than we do today.

Dr. Gerald E. Aardsma's research in Biblical Chronology changed the date of the Exodus to synchronize biblical and secular chronologies of Egypt. His research is explained in his book, *The Exodus Happened 2450 B.C.*

The Israelite route to the Promised Land remains to be completed. By tracing archeological finds, Aardsma proposed a route to Mount Sinai. He applies several tests for consideration of "Mount Sinai." The Mount Sinai, that he suggests, shows a large number of people camping at its base. Archeology supports two encampments at the base of the Mount. The first encampment can be explained by the presence of Moses's in-laws, the Midianties, who constructed stone houses of dry mortar (also shown by archeology) rather than the second encampment of tents by the Israelites.

The Israelites should have been carrying a mixture of their own pottery and Egyptian pottery. That is found in archeology.

Two strats within the "main settlement" can be explained, from the Biblical record, by a severe earthquake. (Both strats are from the same time period, same people.) Further explanations can be found at www.BiblicalChronologist.org.

Yam Suph from the Hebrew Bible/Old Testament has been translated Red Sea. More recently, a better translation of Sea of Reeds or Sea of Seaweed has been suggested. The location for Israel's crossing substantiated by archaeological records lies not in the modern day Red Sea area but at Lake Bardawil, close to the

Mediterranean Sea. This Lake Bardawil, walled in by mountains, trapped the Israelites with no escape. Aardsma gives depth calculations, substantiating the number of people crossing in the given amount of time.

Ebiasaph, son of Korah, was not killed with Korah, according to I Chronicles 6:33-38. I surmised that he was an adult at this time, and so not judged with Korah's family. He was his descendant known for singing and musical talents in worship in the temple. Many psalms were written by him.

When the census was done, the Levites were not counted. So when the all the counted men died, because of their response to the spies report, the Levites did not die. This explains why Eleazar continues as a leader for worship in the book of Joshua. (Phinehas also appears in Joshua.)

The Bible is not clear when the sacrifices started and when the Law was enforced. Perhaps, Aaron was permitted to continue sacrificing while they journeyed through the desert. Eleazar seems to continue an active role in Joshua, but maybe not in the actual Tabernacle sacrifice. He would have been over eighty years old.

According to the current standard of capitalization, God's pronouns, (i.e. Who, His, He) and His body parts (i.e. hand, finger) should not be capitalized. When those words have referred to little gods, I honor that standard. But for the sake of respect for God, as well as clarity in the text, I have chosen to capitalize them regardless of the standard. I trust the reader was not overwhelmed by the grammatical "mistake" of this choice.

The Bible tells the story in Exodus 15-20, 31-40, Numbers 1-4, 8-34, and Deuteronomy 1-11, 29-34. I also brought in Psalms 90, and 91, which were written by Moses. Read it for yourself.

I pray that you not only enjoyed the book, but saw God better through it. Let me know at www.sonyacontreras.com.

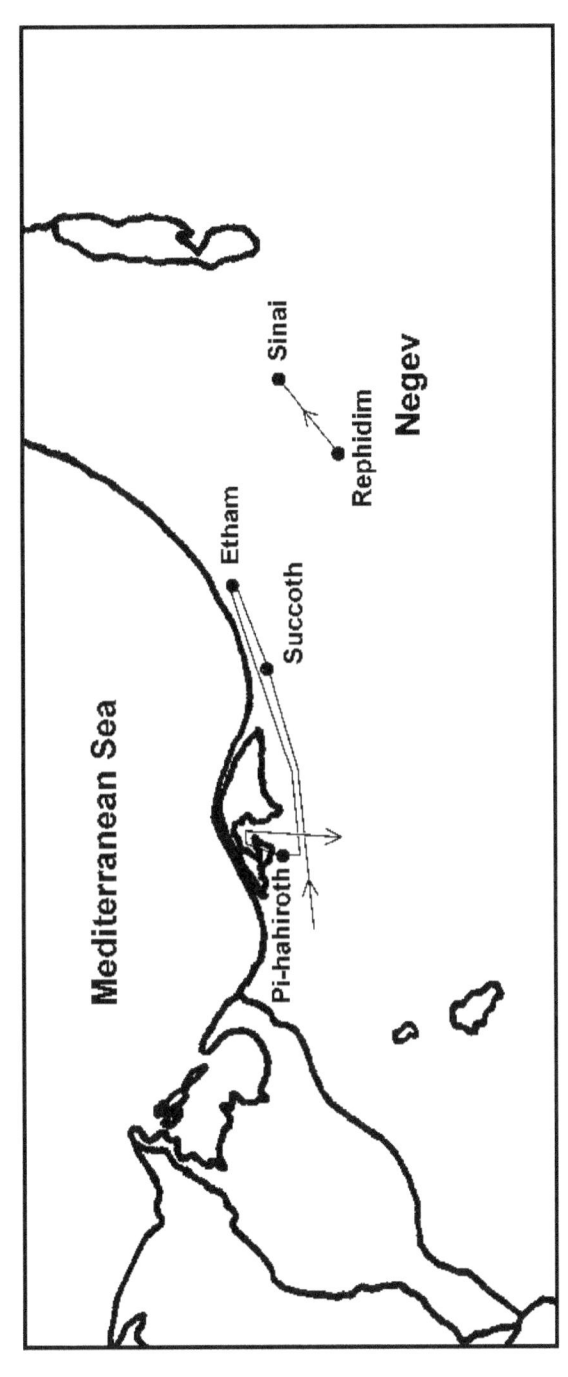

Map of the North Sinai peninsula showing the route of the Exodus which the archaeological data imply From Aardsma, Volume 6 Number 3 of *The Biblical Chronologist*. Reprinted with permission

ACKNOWLEDGEMENTS

The New American Standard Bible by Zondervan Publishers was used when the Bible was directly quoted. Scripture used in Chapter 3 is from Exodus 15. The Ten Commandments in Chapter 10 can be found in Exodus 20:1–17. The blessing of Aaron in Chapter 18 is from Numbers 6:24–27. Several portions of psalms, written by Moses, are also included: Psalms 90, 91, and 113–118. The plot follows Exodus 15–20, 31–40, Numbers 1-4, 8–34, and Deuteronomy 1–11, 29–34.

To interpret the archeological data, I trust Dr. Gerald E. Aardsma's conclusions. He researches from a conservative Christian perspective, assumes historical integrity of the Bible, and shows that the sacred and secular dates harmonize without difficulty when the date of the Exodus is right.

No book comes together without others. My husband's prayer group faithfully upheld me through the book's many revisions. Thank you, men.

My younger boys waited quietly, as I finished a thought before I could read to them. I thank you, James, Joshua, and Jeremiah.

My boys listened as I developed plot ideas, considered character flaws, and wondered about life during ancient times. Thank you, Josiah, Jonathan, Jonas, Jacob, James, Joshua, and Jeremiah.

Technology overwhelms me. If it were not for my son Joey John fixing formatting problems, this book would never look presentable. Thank you, Joey John.

To my editors, who saw all my mistakes and helped me correct them. Rachel Contreras evaluated the content, sharpening the message. Titania Porter gently, but firmly, corrected errors that hindered flow and reader enjoyment. "Thank you" is not adequate.

The Holy Spirit is the Comforter, but if there was anyone who could be personified as the comforter, it would be my best friend and husband, Joey. He came beside me when I doubted whether I could write a book. He read the book in its roughest form and said, "It is good." He supplied the funds for all the steps. He rejoiced with me when the chosen cover designer consented. He prayed me through the printing process. He celebrated its completion, assuring me that the sales would come. He reminded me of my purpose—for God and God alone. The words "thank you" are not enough.

GLOSSARY

Abba   Hebrew, endearing form of father

Baal   means "lord," god of storms and fertility in Canaan, lived in the underworld during dry summers, returned in autumn to revive the land; supplanted El as leader of gods; called on during battle to intervene in man's activities

Chemosh Midianite, god of destruction

Cubit   form of ancient measurement, length from middle finger tip to elbow bottom

Daughter of Lot   after Lot escaped Sodom with just his two daughters, the two daughters planned incest with Lot to continue the line See Genesis 19

Ephah   ancient measurement for dry measure, equal to about five gallons

Ima   Hebrew, for mother

Ketubah Hebrew, marriage contract

Lot   nephew of Abraham

Marmar Hebrew, bitter

Massah and Meribah   where the Lord's people quarreled and tested Him by asking, "Is the Lord here?" yet the Lord gave water

Mattan   in a Hebrew wedding, groom's love gift to his bride

Menat   amulet worn to secure divine protection and fertility

Mohar Hebrew, the bride's price, the dowry, compensated the bride's family for their loss of a worker. She would work with the groom's family

N'heyda desert's version of chamomile; has yellow flowers, sticky, small green leaves on thin twigs; good for colds, calming nerves, cleaning kidneys, eliminating kidney stones

Omer ancient measurement equal to one-tenth of an ephah or about six and a half pints

Shalom Hebrew, greeting for meeting and leaving, means "in peace"

Taberah Hebrew place named where women were consumed by flame for grumbling; the fire of the Lord burned among them

Taurt Egyptian goddess protecting pregnancies and infants, symbolized in a hippopotamus with human breasts, hind legs of a lioness and tail of crocodile

Wadi stream beds in desert catching flood waters when it rains

BIBLIOGRAPHY

Aardsma, Gerald. 2000. *The Bamah of Moses at Mount Sinai. Biblical Chronologist*, May/June Volume 6, Number 3: 1–10.

—. 2000. *Report on the Excursion to Mt. Yeroham Part I. The Biblical Chronologist*, September/October Volume 6, Number 5: 1–14.

—. 2000. *Report on the Excursion to Mt Yeroham Part II. The Biblical Chronologist*, November/December Volume 6, Number 6: 1–10.

—. 2001. *Report on The Excursion to Mt. Yeroham Part III. The Biblical Chronologist*, January/February Volume 6, Number 1: 1–16.

—. 1996. *The Route of the Exodus. The Biblical Chronologist*, January/February Volume 2, Number 1: 1-10.

Aarsdma, Gerald. 2000. *Yeroham: The True Mount Sinai. The Biblical Chronologist*, July/August Volume 6, Number 4: 1–18.

n.d. *Ahlan w Sahlan: Welcome to St. Katherine and the Sinai.* Accessed 2015. http://www.awayaway-sinai.net/main/about_away_away.html.

n.d. "Arnon River." *Bible History Online.* Accessed 2015. http://www.bible-history.com/geography/ancient-israel/arnon-river.html.

n.d. *Bible History Online. Cushite Woman: Ethiopian Woman.* Accessed 2015. http://www.bible-history.com/isbe/C/CUSHITE+WOMAN%3B+ETHIOPIAN+WOMAN/.

Burton, Judd H. 2014. *Chemosh Lord of the Moabites. about education.* December 15. 2014 http://ancienthistory.about.com/od/cgodsandgoddesses/a/chemosh.htm.

n.d. *Emotional and Psychological Trauma.* Accessed 2015. http://www.helpguide.org/emotional_and_psychological_trauma.html.

n.d. *Fauna.* Accessed 2015. http://www.thesinai.com/en/info.

n.d. *Flora.* Accessed 2015. http://www.thesinai.com/er_the_star_of_assalah.

Harrison, Jeffrey J. 1998. *The Search for the Real Mt. Sinai (Video Review).* Accessed 2015. http://www.totheends.com/sinairev.html.

n.d. *Headcovering Customs of the Ancient World. Bible Researcher.* Accessed 2015. http://www.bible-researcher.com/headcoverings3.html.

n.d. *Hebrew Names for Girls/Boys.* Accessed 2015. http://www.judaism.about.com.

Houston, *Drusilla Dunjee and John Bruno Hare.* 2004. "Sacred Texts." *Wonderful Ethiopians of the Ancient Cushite Empire.* Accessed 2015. http://www.sacred-texts.com/afr/we/index.htm.

n.d. *How the Torah Was Taught and Transmitted. Being Jewish.* Accessed 2015. http://www.beingjewish.com/mesorah/1_moses_to_joshua.html.

n.d. *How To Tell If Someone Is Drunk? In the Know Zone.* Accessed 2015. http://www.intheknowzone.com/substance-abuse-topics/alcohol/drunk-or-not.html.

Kaulins, Andis. n.d. *Midianites. Lexiline: History of Civilization.* Accessed 2015. http://www.lexiline.com/lexiline/midianites.htm.

n.d. *Oases Wadis Canyons.* Accessed 2015. http://www.thesinai.com/er.

n.d. *Origin Sinai.* Accessed 2015. http://www.the sinai.com.

Pratt, John R and Ronald P. Millett . n.d. *What Fiery Serpent Symbolized Christ? John Pratt.* Accessed 2015. http://www.johnpratt.com/items/docs/lds/meridian/2000/serpent.html.

Rudd, Steve. n.d. *Water from a Rock: Christ, the Rock of our Salvation.* Accessed 2015. http:::/www.bible.ca/archeology-exodus-kadesh.

n.d. *Ruth the Moabites.* Accessed 2015. http://www.antonbosch.org/Articles/English%202008/Ruth%20the%20Moabitess.html.

n.d. *Sacred Text. Arabia and Her Ancient Races.* Accessed 2015. http://www.sacred-texts.com/afr/we/we11.htm.

Shanks, Hershel. 1999. *Ancient Israel*. Washington DC: Biblical Archaeology Society.

n.d. *Sinai Peninsula Map*. Accessed 2015. http://www.egypttourinfo.com/sinai-peninsula-map.html.

n.d. *Sinai Plants: Medicinal Plants of Sinai*. Accessed 2015. https://sinaisafari-wordpress.com/tag/sinai-plants.

n.d. *The Biblical Covenant*. Accessed 2015. http://www.angelfire.com/sc3/we_dig_montana/Covenant.html.

n.d. *The Marvelous Arabian Civilization*. *Sacred Text*. Accessed 2015. http://www.sacred-texts.com/afr/we/we12.htm.

n.d. *The Sealing of a Covenant*. *Learn the Bible*. Accessed 2015. http://www.learnthebible.org/the-sealing-of-a-covenant.html.

n.d. *The Shivah Call: Comforting the Mourner*. *Being Jewish*. Accessed 2015. http://www.beingjewish.com/cycle/nichum.html.

Unger, Merrill F. *Unger's Bible Dictionary*. Chicago, Moody Press, 1966, pp. 729-730. n.d. *Midianites*. *The Mystica*. Accessed 2015. http://www.themystica.com/mystica/articles/m/midianites.html.

Wagner, Jordan Lee. 1988. *Daily Blessings: Eating Meals*. Accessed April 16, 2014. http://www.home.comcastnet/-judaism/siddur/transliterations.

—. 1998, 2000, 2001, 2002. *Daily Blessings: Eating Snack*. Accessed April 16, 2014. http://www.home.comcast.net/-judaism/siddur/transliterations.daily-blessings-eating-snacks.

2001. *What about God's Cruelty against the Midianites? Christian Think Tank*. May 1. Accessed 2015. http://christianthinktank.com/midian.html.

n.d. *What Is the Book of Jasher/Jashar and Should It Be in the Bible? Got Questions?* Accessed 2015. http://www.gotquestions.org/book-of-Jasher.html.

Wikipedia. n.d. *Yam Suph*. Accessed October 2, 2014. http://en.wikipedia.org/wiki/Yam_Suph.

THERE'S MORE

The series *Tell of My Kingdom's Glory* began with Book One, *I Have Called You By Name* where God brought all to see Him. The Israelites escaped Pharaoh's control and left Egypt's gods.

The series continues with Book Two, *I Have Called You by Name*.

The final book in the series is *I Am with You.* The Israelites enter the Land, eat its fruit, and want to rest. But first, they must destroy the inhabitants. They find the land's people know nothing of God, nor of His goodness. The Israelites must finish the battles before they can arrive at His rest.

The Time: 2408-2403
The Place: The Promised Land
Entering the Land is more than just possession.
I Am with You
takes Israel into their Promised Land.
Hear God's directions.
Follow His instructions.
Perform God's judgment.
Know God's goodness.
Feel His peace.
I Am with You reassures His people
of His presence with them
when they obey.
Read it to rest in Him.

KNOW HIM

God has paid the way for man to enter His presence. Not through our works, but only through what God has done for us.

We could never satisfy a holy God's requirements. We fall short of what God wants. So His Son died, a substitute for us. His holiness can now be satisfied. Our judgment can be removed.

Please do not hesitate to accept His Work in your life. Tell Him you fall short of His holiness. Recognize He paid for your sin. Ask Him to remove your sin. His requirements are satisfied. Thank Him. Seek to serve Him.

Knowing about Jesus is not knowing Him.

Know Him and be His.

ABOUT THE AUTHOR

Growing up with five sisters, Sonya Contreras asked God many questions, even when she did not like His answers. Graduating from Cedarville University and Institute for Creation Research with a Master's Degree in Science Education did not stop her questions. Marrying her best friend and homeschooling their eight sons, she found that dreams do come true, in spite of unanswered questions. Trusting God, Who knows all answers, she shares thoughts about questions that matter, each week at www.sonyacontreras.com.